"You're nice. And funny. And interesting..."

"And handsome," Trex said. "Don't forget I'm devastatingly handsome."

"And arrogant."

"*I'm* arrogant? I haven't even asked you on a date yet, and you're breaking up with me." He smiled.

He was beautiful and sweet and... *No. No, Darby. Knock it off.* "We weren't together to break up. I do like you, but I'm not ready for a relationship of any kind, and I won't be for a long time. And, by the time I am, I can promise you won't be interested."

"What about just a friendship?" he asked.

I sighed. His small grin was adorable, and it was chipping away at my resolve. Had I not been pregnant, I would have jumped all over this... and him. "I don't feel that's possible."

"Because you like me."

My head and my heart were at war, fighting over what I should do and what I wanted. It didn't matter, though. Even if I gave in to my feelings, one of two things would happen: Trex would change, because in my experience, that's what men did when they got what they wanted, or I would fall for him and in four to six months, my growing belly would send him running, leaving both of us—or maybe just me—heartbroken.

Praise for *FROM HERE TO YOU*

"This love story is raw, brilliant, and gives women hope in the impossible. Nothing is more precious than that."
    —Audrey Carlan, #1 *New York Times* bestselling author

"Jamie McGuire is masterful at emotional romance! *From Here to You* is both heartbreaking and hopeful, raw and sexy!"
    —Lauren Blakely, #1 *New York Times* bestselling author

"Heartfelt emotions, serious social concerns and exceptional character development result in a touching modern romance...a sure winner."
                                        —*Library Journal*

"A fantastic read...Highly recommend to all readers who like a sweet romance with their suspense!"
                                        —The Genre Minx

from here to

you

JAMIE McGUIRE

FOREVER

New York Boston

Copyright © 2018 by Jamie McGuire, LLC
Cover design and illustration by Elizabeth Turner Stokes
Cover copyright © 2019 by Hachette Book Group, Inc.

Forever
Hachette Book Group
1290 Avenue of the Americas, New York, NY 10104
forever-romance.com
twitter.com/foreverromance

First Mass Market Edition: August 2019

Forever is an imprint of Grand Central Publishing. The Forever name and logo are trademarks of Hachette Book Group, Inc.

The publisher is not responsible for websites (or their content) that are not owned by the publisher.

The Hachette Speakers Bureau provides a wide range of authors for speaking events. To find out more, go to www.hachettespeakersbureau.com or call (866) 376-6591.

ISBN: 978-1-5387-3001-0 (trade paperback), 978-1-5387-3004-1 (ebook), 978-1-5387-3003-4 (mass market)

Printed in the United States of America

OPM

10 9 8 7 6 5 4 3 2 1

*For Mama Dawn and her
pumpkin, Kelsey*

chapter one

Darby

The cold porcelain of the toilet felt like ice against my bare backside as I sat hunched over the white, billowing taffeta and tulle of my wedding dress. The faucet was running, nearly drowning out the sound of my soon-to-be sister-in-law and maid of honor, Stacy, pounding on the door. I pinched each end of the white stick between my fingers, watching as the second pink line darkened before my eyes.

The back restroom of the First Free Will Baptist Church in Fort Hood, Texas, could barely fit the toilet and sink, but suddenly there were two people inside the tiny room, and the walls were moving in closer by the second.

"Darby?" Stacy called again. "You're not getting sick, are you? Shawn won't wanna have to deal with throw-up on his wedding night."

"For better or worse, remember?" my bridesmaid Carly said. I didn't have to see her to know she was annoyed with Stacy.

My sister-in-law was a female version of her brother. Blunt, snarky, and generally grumpy, and that was before she was comfortable enough to show the extent of her cruelty.

I closed my eyes, holding the stick to my chest. Mascara thickened the tears puddled high on my cheeks. Shawn and I had met almost exactly a year before, just a few months after he'd been stationed at Fort Hood. Remembering the way I felt when he walked into Legend's Pub was what had helped me forget how bad the fighting could get, the times he'd pushed me to the floor, shoved me against a wall, choked me, or slapped my face, to that almost-quiet moment in the church. Shawn had gotten so good at groveling, I'd agreed to marry him after the last desperate apology and promise to change. I clasped the pregnancy test tighter. I couldn't afford bad decisions anymore. They no longer affected just me.

My right hand gripped the stick as I picked my cell phone off the sink counter and tapped the display with trembling fingers. Mama picked up after one ring. She'd moved to Baton Rouge just after I turned eighteen, exactly two years after the accident. I was the only person she disliked more than Shawn.

"I knew it. I knew you'd call. What? Do you need money?" she asked.

"Mama," I chuckled nervously. "Have I ever asked you for anything?"

She sighed. "Frank's family is visiting, and I've got things to do. If you don't need anything, why'd you call?"

"The um, the wedding is in a few minutes. I wish you were here." The only sound on the other end of the line was her breathing, and I imagined the lines around her lips from smoking since she was fifteen deepening as she refused to speak. I held the back of my hand that held the pregnancy test against my forehead. "How is Frank?"

"He's still off work. His back, you know. He moved in last month. Why?"

"Oh," I said, thinking about her two-bedroom apartment and how crowded it would be.

"And Johnny, too."

"Johnny. His . . . son? Isn't he thirtysomething?"

"Yep, got a divorce." She blew into the phone, and I remembered sitting deep in my chair as a child, avoiding the low-lying haze of cigarette smoke always present when Mama was home. That was no place to raise a baby. She was right. The phone call was a waste of time.

"That's great. I'm happy for you, Mama."

"Yep."

"I should probably, um..."

"Yes. Go."

I pressed End, and stood, placing the stick on the counter next to my phone. The faucet squeaked when I turned the knob. The cold water felt so good running over my fingers, freeing, as if I weren't stuck in the tiny bathroom trying to figure out how to leave with Shawn's baby growing inside of me. I thought about my options, and as grateful as I was to have them, the thought of walking into a clinic was too much. So was being tethered to Shawn for the rest of my life, the bond of a child more secure than any wedding ceremony.

The suds slid off my skin and down the drain. The reflection in the mirror caught my attention, and I froze. Most days I didn't recognize myself, but the fear and hopelessness had made a home in my eyes. My tears had pulled black lines down my cheeks. Honey-blond waves had escaped from my bun, poking out from beneath my veil and framing my mess of a face, the same one that had won Miss East Texas just four years before. I wasn't sure I remembered how to smile like that anymore. That girl was gone.

In less than twenty minutes, Shawn would be standing at the end of the center aisle, waiting for me to promise in front of his family and half the base that I would love and obey. No one would know about the child I was carrying, and even if they did, they had no clue that the added stress would only make Shawn's already short temper even more frightening.

I reached for a paper towel and used it to wipe away the bright red lipstick from my lips.

"Darbs?" A softer knock sounded. "It's Carly. Can I come in?"

I swiped the stick off the sink and opened the door, letting Carly slide through. She quickly shut the door behind her before Stacy could squeeze her way in. "It's just so small in here, sweetie. So sorry," she said to Stacy while closing the door in her face. The lock popped into place when Carly pressed the button in the center of the knob, and she leaned her back against the door. Between my dress, me, the toilet, and the sink, I wasn't sure how Carly could fit inside, but like all things—she made it work.

"Jesus, she is obnoxious," Carly hissed. "Her bratty kids are in the other room stuffing chocolate in their mouths in full view of their worthless father. How much did you pay for the flower girl dress and that kid's tux? They're covered in chocolate. Are you sure you want to attach yourself to that for life?" When I didn't answer, she blanched. "Oh, God. You don't."

"I called Mama."

"Oh, shit," she said, clearly not worried about swearing in a church. Her sweet, Southern drawl barely made it a cuss word. "To tell her you're backing out? Is she coming to get you?"

I shook my head and stared at myself in the mirror. "No one's coming to get me." My voice sounded as broken as I felt.

Carly fussed with my hair. "Listen, if you want to do this, we'll fix your face and you'll look beautiful." Recognition flickered in her eyes. "Darby...stop me if I'm out of line, but, honey, my car is right outside the side door. I'll grab your things when no one is looking, and I'll take you wherever you want."

Carly didn't say anything she didn't mean. She was a stunning blond Southern belle with glistening green eyes, a tan year-round, enough bleach on her hair to do ten loads of laundry, and shimmery everything. She'd been married to her husband, First Lieutenant J. D. Bowman, for eight years, and they had two beautiful blond little girls. J.D. was a good man and a strong officer in the army, but Carly ran their house, and no wife at Fort Hood was more respected. She made a killing selling makeup, and her parties were more like women's empowerment retreats. She'd tried talking me out of marrying Shawn as soon as she'd found out we were engaged. She'd also hosted our engagement party.

"I don't know. Everyone's waiting."

"No one would wonder why, Darby. We all know what happens at your house. You can walk away from this guilt-free."

Stacy began pounding on the door again, my entire body jerking in reaction.

Carly licked her handkerchief and wiped the skin beneath my eyes. "If this is what you want, I'll go get you some of my lipstick, because you need a little color. If it's not, I'm going to get my keys, and I'll be waiting for you outside."

"What about your kids? What about J.D.?"

She smirked. "He's a smart man. He'll figure it out." Her smile faded. "Darby, this moment is important—too important for you to be thinking about anyone else but yourself. What do *you* want?"

Carly hadn't seen the white stick I was holding behind my back. She had no idea that the decision I made would be for the baby I was carrying. I simply didn't care that much about myself to do something so embarrassing and outrageous.

Carly nodded and excused herself. Her voice carried

through the door as she coolly made an excuse to leave the Sunday School room the three of us were using to get ready in. I counted to fifty and then opened the door, smiling at Stacy.

"There you are," she said, her chestnut, frizzy waves already falling from her makeshift bun. "Carly's outside. She has her whole stash of lip stuff out there. She wants you to come pick a color so she doesn't have to bring it all in."

"Oh, that sounds nice. Would you mind making sure Allie and Jonah are ready? Did Allie's dress fit?"

"I just checked on them. I got most of the chocolate out. I swear Brian is dumb as a box of rocks. They're in the groomsmen's room with Shawn and Brian. Her dress is a little big in the arms, but she's really excited about her flower basket. And before you ask, yes, Jonah knows to walk slower this time."

I opened the door and peeked down the hall. The ceremony was about to start, the pianist was playing Pachelbel at my previous request—Canon in D. Shawn's family and all our mutual friends were in the sanctuary, and the side door was less than ten feet away.

"No one will see you. If you're going to pick something out from Carly, go now. We only have a few minutes," Stacy said. She had the same commanding tone as Shawn. Nothing was ever a request.

"I'll be right back," I said, stepping out. My heart was pounding, my hands sweating. Even though freedom was just outside the door, I'd never been so terrified in my life. The stick was slipping out of my sweaty hand, but I clenched my fingers, refusing to leave it behind. Shawn didn't need more reason to come after me.

"Darby!" Stacy called, sounding angry.

I froze.

She handed me the brown wristlet she'd bought me the previous Christmas. "You might want this. I'm sure Carly will want to be paid."

"Thank you," I said, taking the wristlet by the leather loop and turning on my heels. The side door slammed shut behind Stacy as she went back inside. I could breathe again.

As promised, Carly was sitting in her Lexus, her company name, Lipstick & Jesus by Carly, and her phone number in bright pink vinyl letters on the back window. I sat in the passenger seat, my wedding dress spilling over the console onto her side.

She grabbed my hand. "Where do you wanna go?"

"Anywhere but here."

"The bus station?"

I looked at the wristlet on my lap and nodded. "I have two hundred dollars. Think that's enough?"

"Don't you worry about that." Carly patted my hand and then used that hand to pull the gear into reverse. We backed away from the church, and we pulled out into the street.

I turned up the radio, trying to drown out the sound of the many voices warning me of the consequences that would come with leaving Shawn. He'd warned me dozens of times what would happen to me if I left him. Sometimes, by the look in his eyes, I was sure he didn't even want me, he just couldn't stand the thought of me with someone else. More nights than I could count, I'd lie awake to listen for sounds of an impending attack.

Carly turned down the volume and then grabbed my hand and squeezed. "You're doing the right thing. It's only going to get better from here."

"I know," I said, looking out the window.

"Do you need anything from the house?"

I thought about it, knowing that any minute, Shawn

would realize I wasn't there, and he would go straight to the house to catch me packing. I shivered at the thought of getting caught in a whirlwind of his rage and embarrassment.

"No," I said. "I can't chance it."

"Maybe I can figure out how to get in the house and grab some of your things. I could send them to you. Anything you can think of offhand?"

I sighed. "Photo albums. The picture of my dad and me on the nightstand. But Shawn'll probably burn it all."

"Oh, Darby. I'm so sorry."

One side of my mouth curled up. "Don't be. This is a good day."

Carly shook her head, her hair moving with it. "I knew it. I knew that son of a bitch was…I'm going to talk to J.D. when I get back. Maybe if Shawn gets in trouble that will slow him down. We'll all hope he doesn't look for you, but…"

"He'll come after me. All it'll take is a favor."

"You mean Shawn's brother."

I nodded. "Derek does something with computers for the government. He can't tell us exactly what he does—not that we'd understand, anyway—but he's mentioned meeting Edward Snowden before the whistle-blower thing. It's probably just a matter of time." I sighed.

"Then we need to get you far enough away he can't find you. Any ideas? Wait. Don't tell me. I don't want to know. Maybe try to call me when you get settled in? Stay off the grid and all that. Lord, I wouldn't even know how to do that. Cash, I guess?"

"I left my cell phone in the bathroom. And I don't know your number. Even if you tell me, I'm afraid I won't remember after I get where I'm going."

"No problem." At the next stoplight, she fished a black

Sharpie from her purse and opened her Bible, writing her number on the title page.

"Carly, I can't take your Bible."

"You'll need it. I'll send you what I can retrieve when it calms down around here," she said around the cap in her mouth. "I have a feeling Shawn'll be watching me for a while."

"I don't envy you," I said.

The light turned, and Carly pressed on the gas. She winked. "Don't you worry about me. I've got that little boy handled. He don't scare me."

The seat belt dug into my chest as Carly pressed on the brakes to keep from missing our turn and pulled into the Greyhound bus station. She fished into her purse, and then she tucked a thick stack of bills into mine. "I'm not sure how much is there. At least six hundred. It's the cash left over from my last party. Should get you a one-way ticket a few states away, meals, and a change of clothes."

I shook my head. "This is too much."

"You need it more than I do. I just want you to be safe. Besides, it's exactly a month away from Independence Day." She lifted her chin, a proud grin softening her features. "You'll be celebrating extra this year." She grabbed my hand, placed the palm of her other hand on the Bible, and closed her eyes. "Dear Lord, we pray for a safe trip for Darby. Watch her and keep her. We pray the next journey of her life is smooth, that she finds happiness, and continues to live her life in a way that honors you. In the name of our precious Jesus...amen."

"Amen. Thank you."

"Don't thank me. Thank Jesus. He's the one who's going to get you through this. He will, Darby. Believe it."

I hugged Carly over the mounds of white tulle and taffeta, wiping my cheeks the moment we pulled away.

"Okay, enough of that," Carly said, clearing her throat. "This is the rest of your life. It's a happy moment. I love you. Safe travels."

"Thank you. So much," I said, before pulling on the handle and stepping out. I slipped the pregnancy test into my wristlet, held the Bible to my chest, and took stock of my surroundings. No one, coming or going, tried not to stare. I focused on pushing through the glass doors and finding what I was looking for on the board above the ticket counters. The goal was to get away, far and fast. Texas and Louisiana were out. So was Oklahoma. *Kansas, maybe?* I cringed. Kansas didn't sound like a destination for an adventure. The station with the cheapest fare, farthest away from Fort Hood, and leaving within half an hour, was Colorado Springs, Colorado. I just hoped there were still seats available.

The gray-haired man behind the counter wasn't impressed with my attire. "Where to?"

"Are there any seats left for Colorado Springs?"

His fingers clicked on the keyboard in front of him. "One."

"I'll take it!" I said.

He noticed my dress. "It's economy."

"That's perfect."

He tilted his head back, looking at the computer monitor through the bottom of his bifocals. "Checking any bags?"

"No."

"One-oh-one eighty-two and your driver's license."

"A hundred and one dollars?"

He gazed at me over his glasses. "And eighty-two cents."

I counted out the cash and placed it on the counter, along with my license. The man behind the counter took it, and my heart began to thump against my chest again. I held my breath while the ticket printed, and exhaled only when he handed it to me, along with my ID.

"Next!" the man said, and I turned, looking for the bay number that matched my ticket. My dress swished as I walked to an empty seat in the corner. Just before I sat down, a woman with a thick Hispanic accent came over the speaker system and called for us to board.

The priority ticket holders lined up first. One by one, they walked out to the bus and climbed the steps. The urge to glance over my shoulder and watch the entrance was impossible to ignore. I imagined Shawn running through the doors, not calling my name in desperation, but yelling for me like a stern stepfather, making a scene. My knee bounced up and down, the used Steve Madden heels I'd bought from the thrift store digging into the back of my heel. The priority ticket holders were clearly in no hurry, so I wasn't sure why they'd paid extra to board first.

The announcer called for general boarding, and I stood, trying not to push my way to the front. I wondered if Shawn was at the house or calling to harass my friends on my whereabouts. He was smart. He would come to the bus station, and I had to be on the bus to Colorado Springs when he did.

I followed the tiny, hunched-over grandmother in front of me, helping her to climb the steps. Lifting her leg seemed to take hours, and pulling up to the next step felt like years. Finally, she was at the top, and then so was I. Those sitting in seats stopped settling in to gawk at me in the white, puffy wedding dress, undoubtedly noticing my smudged mascara. If anyone came looking for a runaway bride, the people in the station would point them in my direction.

My dress hit every person sitting in the aisle seats between the first and eighteenth row, where I finally found an empty seat by the window. I sidestepped in and sat, clenching the Bible to my chest. "Please, God, please help me get out of here safely," I whispered.

Every car that pulled up to the station, and every man who stepped out, caused a panic deep within me. It could be any moment that Shawn would step out in his suit, surrounded by his brother-in-law, sister, and friends in an attempt to stop me.

The bus's engine was a steady rhythm of low humming and whirring, and I watched as the driver and a few station employees loaded the checked bags and discussed something that definitely wasn't important enough to keep us sitting there even a minute longer.

Finally, the driver nodded once and climbed up the stairs, sitting in his seat. He grabbed his radio, his voice squished together and monotone as he attempted a joke and told us where we were going and passenger safety procedures.

I imagined seeing Shawn through the large glass windows, pushing his way through the station, his eyes finally settling on me. "*Please, please, please,*" I whispered under my breath. My knee was bobbing again, a scream building in my chest.

Just before I could stand and beg for our departure, the driver closed the door and put the bus into gear, pulling away. As the bus slowed for traffic before driving into the road, I sat back against my seat and sighed loudly.

I had escaped.

chapter two

Trex

"Thanks, Stavros," I said, holding the cold pint he'd just placed in front of me at its base.

The salt from the napkin felt gritty against my palms, one more familiar thing about the mom-and-pop hotel I'd found earlier that year. It was my second visit to the Colorado Springs Hotel, and although I found the staff to be more curious than I'd like, the beds were comfortable, the sheets were clean, and despite its being at capacity with hotshot firefighters, I could still keep to myself.

"Never too early for a beer. It's been busy, so I haven't had a chance to tell you: Glad you're back, Trex," he said, turning to take another order. I had to watch his mouth move to hear him over the low hum of conversation in the hotel lobby. Years of too-close grenade blasts, explosives, and gunfire had made understanding someone speaking with any ambient noise difficult.

More than two dozen hotshot firefighters surrounded me, discussing everything from the fire line to beach homes in Mexico. It was a plus having them there, if only because it was refreshing not to be the only one drinking at noon. The excited chatter sounded more like a high school reunion than home base for the dozens of interagency crews preparing to fight the Queen's Canyon wildfire eating up thousands of acres just a few miles out-side of town.

"What keeps bringing you back to town?" Stavros said, sinking a glass into the soapy water in a basin behind the bar. He reminded me of any bartender you'd see in the movies. The vest, bow tie, and black pants were overdoing it for a wannabe Holiday Inn, if you asked me—but he didn't. He was asking me for an answer I couldn't give.

"Work," I said simply.

"What, the fire? Wouldn't peg you for an interagency guy."

I offered a half-hearted grin, unflustered. Stavros was about to believe the lie I was going to feed him, and we would both go on with our day. Maneuvering around the truth wasn't difficult for me. Having a strict Baptist preacher for a father had given me ample practice at half-truths and outright lies. Rule number one: Never give away all the information.

It wouldn't be a far leap for Stavros to believe I was one of the hotshots, the ground crew, the helitack crew, or the brass. My ex complained more than once I wasn't much for conversation, and she was right. Talking about who I was and where I'd been led to inevitable questions about what I'd seen, and no one—least of all me—wanted to hear about that.

"I just go where they tell me to," I said, taking a sip.

Stavros wasn't convinced. "No one tells you anything. You look like the boss to me."

"One of them," I said. Now, *that* was the truth, even if it was in the wrong context. My cell phone buzzed, and I ex-cused myself from the bar, tossing a ten-dollar bill on the counter.

The caller displayed on the screen as Unknown, already a clue that it was my new employer. I headed toward one of the corners of the lobby, one of the few spaces out of earshot of the growing crowd of firefighters.

"Trex," I said, holding my phone to my ear.

"Hello, Mr. Trexler. My name is Bianca Calderon. I'm General Tallis's administrative assistant, and I'll be helping you with accessing the property tomorrow. Is it a good time for you to talk?"

"Good to go," I said. Bianca worked with military. She was used to short, simple answers.

"I'll be waiting for you at the first gate at oh-five-hundred. We'll process you there, then you and I will pass through Gates Two and Three. From there, we'll enter the Complex. After a short tour, I'll show you to your headquarters, and then you'll meet with your new team at oh-six-hundred. With the general at oh-eight-hundred."

"My team," I repeated, trying not to sound surprised. "Everyone?"

"Yes, sir. Everyone from your unit."

"Great." I checked my watch. "See you at zero-five."

"Sleep well, Mr. Trexler."

"It's just Trex. See you then, Ms. Calderon."

"It's Bianca."

I pressed End, and slipped my cell into my back pocket, bringing my pint back to the seat I had occupied. I hadn't seen my unit all at once in five years, and it would be good to have the old gang back together, even if we were all in different stages of readjustment to civilian life.

Now my seat was filled with someone slightly larger than me. His dark hair was buzzed, his skin looked like a doodle pad. I slapped his shoulder. "You're in my chair."

The man looked up. His smile faded, and he stood—not because he was intimidated, but because I was the last person he'd expected to see there.

"What the hell are you doing here?" he asked.

"Calm down, Maddox," I said, taking his seat. "I'm not here for you."

The conversations around us quieted, and his crewmates turned toward the commotion, making an impressive wall between us and the rest of the lobby. I couldn't blame them. The last time Taylor and his twin brother, Tyler Maddox, saw me was in Estes Park when I was carrying a federal badge and investigating a fire on a college campus that might have involved their little brother. As far as I knew, the case was still open.

"Then why are you here?" he hissed, keeping his voice low.

"Got a new job."

"You just happened to find a job in Colorado?" he asked, dubious.

"As it happens, I did. Now fuck off, and let me enjoy my beer. I've got to turn in early. Tomorrow's my first day."

"Where?"

"Why do you care?"

Maddox puffed out a nervous laugh. "So, what? You left one shitty job for another?"

"No, this is a private gig. Pays way better. Now, seriously. Leave me the fuck alone."

Maddox chuckled, taking a swig before joining his buddies across the room. They were younger than me but had been in more precarious situations than they could count. I could respect running toward the fire.

Stavros sat another pint on the bar and nodded to the group of men behind me. Maddox had bought me a drink. I didn't want to like him, but I couldn't convince myself that he was a bad guy. I bowed my head in thanks and faced forward.

"What was that about?" Stavros asked.

"Nothing."

"I guess you two know each other?"

"His little brother might have gotten into some trouble."

"And you helped?"

"Nope," I said, moving on to the new pint.

"You're crankier than you were the last time you were here, and I didn't think that was possible."

"Am I?" I asked.

"I'm guessing the new job has something to do with the Cheyenne Mountain Complex."

"What's that?"

Stavros smirked. "The only secret that can be kept around here."

"Well, it sounds a whole helluva lot cooler than what I'm doing," I said, keeping my composure.

The last thing I needed was the hotel bartender spreading the rumor that I was working for a top-secret facility before my first day. Stavros looked disappointed, and fully convinced that he wasn't right.

"Are you here alone?" he asked.

"Just me."

"Brand-new start, huh?"

I'd started over a few times, but it never felt brand new. Leaving home for the Marines, moving on to the FBI, and now private security. Like plenty of veterans, I was trying to lead my life after being conditioned for years to follow. An honorable discharge after having my knee blown out by enemy fire was bad enough. A decade in the Corps, multiple deployments, countless missions, and one kidnapped ten-year-old kid with minimal combat training ended my military career.

I touched my knee, feeling the raised scars. "Who knows? Maybe this will be the one."

"Oh, so you've done this before."

I nodded. After my knee had healed as much as it could, I called up an old buddy who ran Deep Six Security. Driving bulletproof but air-conditioned vehicles seemed like promotion at first, but protecting dirty politicians, weapons contractors, and warlords—the paycheck never helped me forget, and then my left shoulder was burned by a flash grenade during a midnight raid. When I was accepted into Quantico, I thought I'd finally found my calling. As it turned out, two years at the FBI was enough to know it wasn't for me. My boss in Denver was decent compared to the asshole in San Diego, but my colleagues were analysts and paper pushers. Even the field agents wore ties and blazers to work. No one who wore a suit came to get dirty. Working there was a decision made in desperation that I'd corrected as quickly as I could.

"She must have really fucked you over," Stavros said. "I don't even see a twinkle of regret."

"Nope. I haven't met her yet."

"Oh. You're a believer in *the one*, huh?"

I smiled before taking a drink. I'd had a few girlfriends, but I'd never found anyone who could help me shake the feeling that there was something—someone—more. I'd met Laura just after basic. She could have been a textbook military wife. We lived together for a year, but we both figured out it wasn't love, and I was the best man when she married my best friend three years later. There were a handful of dates and many other women my little sister Hailey called *time killers*, but no matter how amazing, how beautiful, how fun…I knew it wasn't her. My girl was out there somewhere, and I could feel her just as I could Maddox and his buddies staring at the back of my head.

My cell phone buzzed in my back pocket, and I stood,

dropping a rolled five-dollar bill into the tip jar. "I was just thinking about you," I said, walking toward the elevators.

"Of course you were. All settled in?" Hailey asked.

I weaved between firefighters, all sipping on their half-price IPAs. "As settled in as I can be in a hotel room."

"They didn't get you a place?"

"Nope."

"You still haven't told me what you're doing in Colorado Springs."

"And I'm not going to."

Hailey sighed, and I laughed. We'd spent a lot of time talking around the truth. "I don't have much time. I'm on my lunch break. But I'm excited that you're only a three-hour drive from here. Are you coming home for Easter? Dad has his sermon ten months early."

I pressed the button for the elevator and waited. "Isn't it the same thing every year? What is there to prepare for? Other than maybe deciding which of the stories he's going to tell."

"Stop."

"Seriously, have you read the gospels? Was there one man, two men, a man and an angel, or one angel at the tomb? It's different in Matthew, Mark, Luke, and John. And this is what he calls the infallible word of God." The elevator door opened, and I stepped in, immediately feeling guilty. "I'm sorry, HayBells."

"Since when did you become such a pessimist?"

"Since my first deployment when I actually read the Bible. Listen, I'm going to be breaking in the new job next week. I'm working long hours getting the team trained, so I might not be around the next couple of weeks."

The elevator shuddered as it slowed to a stop. The doors slid open, and I stepped out, turned left, and—even though

I knew which way to go—checked the sign to make sure my room was to the left. Room 201 was at the end of the hall, and I stopped in front of the door, digging for my room key while holding my baby sister's voice to my ear with my shoulder.

Hailey prattled on about junior prom, and the new boy sniffing around, and her college applications. I couldn't blame her for her ignorance of what life was like for me in high school. The yelling, the rules, the nonexistent privacy. I was the prototype. They had learned from me how not to drive a child away. Dad had relaxed, Mom put her foot down more often. Hailey's childhood had been almost normal.

"Did you hear me?" she asked as the lock to my room clicked. I pressed the door open.

"I'm sorry, you said the mission trip. It's to Honduras this time, right?"

"It was Honduras last time, too. I think you should go. I'd feel safer with you there."

"Wish I could, Bells. I start a new job tomorrow. No time off for a while."

"It's just a week. You could take off for a week."

I fell on my back onto the hard, cold mattress, looking up at the beige ceiling. I hadn't bothered to turn on the light, the sun spraying a few rays through a gap in the blackout curtains.

"I miss you, kid."

I could hear her pouting through the phone, and it made me smile. She always thought the best of me. It was a full-time job pretending to be the guy she thought I was.

"I miss you, too, Scottie."

"Tell Mom and Dad I love them."

"I will. Good luck tomorrow."

When she hung up, the room felt empty, darker. Hailey

was a light of her own. She, my parents, and my childhood home in Goodland, Kansas, were just a few hours away. For some reason, it wasn't as comforting as it should have been. Hailey would turn eighteen in a few months. She could get in a car at any time and drive to see me. I'd love nothing more than to spend time with my baby sister, but keeping secrets was easier when they were all a plane ride away.

I glanced at my watch. Another seven hours to kill before lights out. I closed my eyes, aiming for a half-hour nap, hoping it was just long enough to recharge, and short enough to keep the nightmares away.

Someone knocked on the door, and my eyes popped open. "Hold on," I said, stumbling to the door. I opened it to see Taylor Maddox and a few of his friends standing there. I tensed, ready for a fight.

"We're heading out to lunch downtown. Wanna come?" Taylor asked.

Food was better than fighting faceless men with rifles that never seemed to run out of ammo the moment I fell asleep. "I'll get my shirt."

chapter three

Darby

The cement floor under the wooden table I'd been ushered to by the host was sticky, but the glass enclosure of the Mexican restaurant I'd chosen was protection from the god-forsaken wind and smoke from a fire not far outside of town. That the newspaper and salsa were free was an added bonus.

My wedding dress was hanging in a pawn shop just north of downtown Colorado Springs, and the four hundred dollars it garnered had helped pay for the slacks, button-down shirt, bra, cotton panties, and flats I was wearing. Taking half what I'd paid for the dress less than six months before was down-right painful. My thrift-store backpack held the navy-blue hoodie and a pair of heather-gray lounge pants I'd bought from there, but I'd needed something to interview in, and women's work clothes were 50 percent off. So I sold the dress, saved the engagement ring in case I might need emergency cash later, and tried not to think too much about it. Any opportunity for immediate cash was nothing to thumb my nose at.

My bouncing knee kept hitting the table, attracting the attention of some small children nearby. I couldn't help it. I felt at any moment, Shawn would pull up in his stupid pickup truck and drag me back to Texas by my hair. I was free, but still afraid, and that made me angry.

The waiter had left a pen with the check for me to sign a

later credit-card statement, unaware I would pay cash for the seven-dollar check for a large queso and the Dr Pepper I'd ordered for a late lunch. Next to the empty bowls, I used the ballpoint to doodle in the margins of newspaper articles and circle ads in the classifieds—everything from a law firm secretary to a second- or third-shift desk clerk at a hotel. In Fort Hood, I'd been a waitress, and then I was the girlfriend of a jealous, overprotective, overbearing boyfriend who didn't want to chance me working around people who might put crazy ideas in my head—or around other men who might look too long or make me think I was smarter, funnier, prettier than Shawn thought I was.

"That's pretty good," the waiter said, pausing for a second to notice my drawing. "What is it?"

"A palm tree…and a hula girl," I said, trying to look at the thick lines and details through his eyes. It was pretty good. Too bad no one needed a professional doodler.

"Are you having Bible study here?"

"Oh," I said, looking to Carly's Bible next to me. "No."

"Hawaii," he said with a nod. "Cool," he said, and then walked away.

I'd never been there. I'd never been anywhere. Traveling outside of Fort Hood was something I thought I'd do with Shawn. Now I was a twelve-hour drive away, alone. But, as I noted my hunkered-down posture, my hesitation to look anyone in the eye, I knew he was still with me, standing over me like the cowering, kicked puppy I'd turned into.

I pulled one of my gently used black Toms away from the sticky floor to shift on the seat, barely noticing the atrocious noise it was making. I had to keep reminding myself that no one but me knew where I was, but I still took four glances a minute at the parking lot to make sure there were no familiar vehicles pulling in.

"You're okay," I whispered as I flicked more detail into the hula girl's long, dark hair. She was smiling and carefree, something I hadn't done or felt in a very long time. On the bus, I'd thought that once I arrived at my destination, I'd magically be who I used to be—no nervousness, no worrying, no overwhelming feelings of dread. As each hour passed and I felt no different, that hope was replaced by something much darker. I didn't want Shawn to have control, and there I sat, more afraid of him than I'd ever been.

The Colorado Springs Hotel was just a few miles down the highway, just past Red Rock Canyon. I wondered if the hotel offered discounts on rooms to employees. That would be worth the twelve dollars an hour they offered. I stashed the Bible in my backpack, left two five-dollar bills on the table, and walked to the hostess stand, paper in hand and everything I owned hanging from my shoulders. I'd arrived in Colorado Springs at seven thirty in the morning. Between fishing through thrift stores in my dress, finding a pawn shop, and locating a store downtown that sold regular cotton panties and toiletries, I'd had a productive day, even if I couldn't get the smoke smell out of my nose.

"Excuse me," I said to the man standing behind the podium. "May I borrow your phone?"

He shook his head. "No phone."

"No phone?" I repeated. He was lying. Of course they had a phone, just not for customers. I sighed. I prayed they would allow an interview when I got there. By the time I arrived, it would be too close to dark to find somewhere else, and I'd have to spend a good chunk of what was left of my money for a room. At least it was a place to stay for the night.

I readjusted my backpack and pushed out the door, walking across the parking lot toward the road and turning south. The sun was hidden behind a thick, hazy curtain, looking more like a pink, glowing ball, and I wondered if the sky would get dark quicker than usual. The road was congested with rush hour traffic and people leaving the Garden of the Gods and Red Rock Canyon before sundown. The exhaust and smoke made the air burn my throat with every breath, so I picked up the pace, hoping to reach the hotel sooner than later. Cars slugged along beside me on one side, a makeshift shelter on the other. A man sat on the ground next to a shopping cart full of his only belongings. His face was dirty and worn, telling a story of struggle and failure. From my side of the tin walls that shielded him from the wind, his life looked like one big open wound, bleeding so much and for so long, he barely noticed anything was wrong anymore.

I stopped at his home and handed him a twenty-dollar bill, and while he stared at his hand in confusion, I walked away, wanting to make sure I had real walls, running water, and a bed for the night.

The Midland Expressway had no walkway, and at times, not much space between red cliff faces and the shoulder of the road. Two sliding glass doors swept open for me when I approached the hotel entrance, and I stepped into smells of cheap carpet freshener and fresh-brewed coffee as air-conditioning blasted me in the face. The lobby was decorated in beiges and fake plants, devoid of color or that homey feel most hotels failed at emulating. At the back wall was the lobby bar, where a sign next to the last stool read WELCOME FIREFIGHTERS! HALF-PRICE IPAS AND APPETIZERS!

A man stood behind the counter, wiping it down with a white rag. His dark hair was stiff, gelled into place, his thick, over-manicured eyebrows pulling together when he noticed me.

"Come on over, sunshine," he said, offering one of the stools. I could tell when men were flirting with me, and truth be told, most did. I had been used enough to know if that was the intention, and sometimes men wanted to be used. But the bartender's tone was nowhere on the seduction spectrum, instead sounding more like he was speaking to his little sister.

I crossed the lobby, passing a group of men ambling around, two couches and a single chair gathered together in front of a large flat-screen television. The bar was in the corner, adjacent to the entrance to the elevator bay, and on the opposite side of the room from the check-in counter.

"Checking in?" he asked. His cheap name tag read *Stavros*. Faint lines around his eyes deepened when he smiled, matching the three on his forehead. Maybe ten years older than me, Stavros had probably seen hundreds of pretty women pass through his bar, and I was just one of many. He was decent enough a man not to attempt to bed everyone.

I sat on the stool, peeking over at the empty check-in counter. "I'm hoping to talk to a manager."

"Oh?"

"I saw the ad in the paper for the job."

He smirked. "Oh, the job. He should be back any minute. Can I get you a drink?"

I shrugged one shoulder. "Just a water, please."

He nodded. "You do look parched."

I breathed out a laugh. "Do I look like anything else? I walked here. I'd be surprised if I wasn't a sweaty mess."

"Walked here?" he said, dropping ice into a glass with a scoop and then using the gun to fill the glass. "From where?"

"A Mexican restaurant down the road."

He frowned. "Sweet pea, that's not down the road. That's at least four miles from here. You must really want the job."

"I do. And I was going to get a room for the night. Maybe for a few nights."

"Did you just get into town?"

I nodded. "This morning."

He gestured to my backpack. "What's in the bag?"

"My stuff. All of it."

He stared at me, dubious. "You don't look like a vagrant."

"I'm not."

"Trust me, there are plenty of vagrants here from Texas."

"I'm not from..." There was no point. He knew where I was from the second I'd opened my mouth.

He stared at me for a moment. "Why did you come?"

"Just seeing the world, I guess."

He smirked again. "Don't lie. I can already tell you suck at it."

I squirmed in my seat, crossing my arms over my middle. "I don't really wanna..."

"You didn't kill him, did you?" he asked, not so much afraid as he was intrigued. "The guy."

I shook my head.

"I see. What's your name?"

"Darby...Cooke."

"Uh-huh," he said, unconvinced. "You think with a first name like Darby the fake last name is going to help?"

I sunk back in my seat.

"Cooke it is, then. Your secret is safe with me." Stavros's attention was drawn to the check-in counter. An older woman had appeared from the elevator bay, chewing on the last bite of her meal and rubbing her hands together. She was standing, the computer waist-high.

Stavros rolled his eyes. "That's Tilde."

"She seems nice," I said, watching her work on the computer. She wore blue eye shadow up to her penciled-in brows, and bright pink lipstick. She was as round as she was tall, and occasionally she smiled, even if it was toward no one in particular.

"Mostly. She works second shift, three to eleven, so by the time she's comfortable enough to show her cranky side, you'll be on nights. She'll be training you, and she's been working double shifts to cover, so she can be testy at times."

"If I get the job."

"You've got the job," he said.

"What makes you so sure?"

"Because I own this place."

"Oh," I said, watching him walk across the room. He and Tilde had a quiet conversation about me, and then he waved me over.

"Tilde will get you a room and your paperwork. Employees get rooms for twenty dollars a night, bumped up to half price if we're full, no housekeeping services. Can you start now?"

My eyebrows shot up toward my hairline, and I blinked. "Now? Sure. Absolutely."

"Good. Get your things. You're just down the hall from the desk." He looked at Tilde. "One hundred."

Tilde nodded, returning to the desk and clicking away.

"Then I come back down here? Is what I'm wearing okay?"

He waved me away. "You look gorgeous. Once you can get a white button-down and black slacks, that's the typical uniform."

Tilde approached us holding a white key card, and I looked to Stavros. "You have no idea how much I appreciate this. Thank you so much."

He nodded, heading back to the bar. "We're going to get slammed soon. We've got hotshots coming in from all over. Just...try to keep up."

When he turned his back, I looked to Tilde. "What's a hotshot?"

"Firefighters," she said, guiding me to the elevator bay.

"They're coming to control the fires outside of town. Just watch me and smile at the guests. You won't learn it all in one night."

I half expected her to press the elevator button, but she kept walking to the end of the hall, just past a door labeled STORAGE.

The number on the door read 100, and Tilde gestured for me to try the key card. A beep sounded and a muted green light flashed when I pressed the plastic to the black square above the handle. The latch released, and I smiled at Tilde.

"Thank you," I said, pushing the door open.

"Can you be back at the desk in half an hour?"

"Yes. I'll just freshen up and be down."

The door slammed behind me, and I peered into the dark room, the sunlight struggling to burn through the slit of the blackout curtains. I reached next to the door, flipping on the light, then reaching up to swing the silver door guard over. The vent came on when I pushed up on the light switch. The single sink was surrounded by two feet of counter space, and a matching off-white shower curtain hid a shower and tub. The large mirror was spotless. For a fleeting moment, I wished housekeeping services came with my discounted rent, but that would just be too good to be true.

The short hallway opened to a twelve-by-twenty room with nightstands on each side of the queen-sized bed. A television sat on top of a wooden dresser with six drawers. The other furniture consisted of a desk, a desk chair, an upholstered chair that was supposed to match the green-and-blue patterned carpet but didn't quite hit the mark, and an AC/heating unit beneath the window.

I opened the drawers, realizing that one side was an empty refrigerator, larger than typical for a hotel room. In the wall the main room shared with the bathroom was an inset area for the microwave and coffee maker, and a two-burner range with a vent above. *I can cook!* I fell back onto the bed. Comfy. I couldn't believe my luck. Our luck. *Thank you, God.*

I touched my abdomen, the center point between my hip bones—a guess. "We're going to be okay..." Was the baby a girl? A boy? My expression screwed into disgust at the name *it*. I wouldn't know for a long time, if at all until he or she was born. My baby was the size of a bean or something. Bean. Baby Bean Dixon. "We're going to be okay, Bean."

I said the words aloud, more for myself than anything. Thoughts of how I would support a baby, where we would live, costs of diapers and day care. I was thankful for the job more than for the paycheck. Keeping busy would help pre-occupy my mind, away from the overwhelming fear. I was a single mother. I smiled. At least I was free.

Unable to remove the grin from my face, I dug into my backpack and fished out my toothpaste, toothbrush, hair-brush, and deodorant. I rushed to the bathroom, placed the few toiletries I owned where I wanted them, and squeezed a dot of toothpaste on the brush. Scrub and spit. Scrub and spit. Rinse. The toothbrush clicked against the edge of the sink, and then I used the glass as a holder. Deodorant, a brush through my hair, then I grabbed my key card and wallet and rushed out the door, walking quickly down the hall.

The elevator opened, and I smacked into a tall man, bouncing backward.

"Oh, God! I'm so sorry!" I said before I'd even caught my balance.

He grabbed me before I fell, looking down on me with concern in his eyes. "Christ, are you okay?"

"Yes. Yes, I'm fine," I said, brushing off his T-shirt, as if I'd left dirt on him.

"You hit me pretty hard," he said.

"I'm so sorry. Are you hurt?"

He laughed once, and I looked at him then. He was a head and a half taller than me, and his heavily tattooed biceps filled his sleeves, the artwork spanning down to both wrists. He looked like someone's bodyguard, instantly making me feel intimidated.

"What are you running from?" he asked.

"Me? Nothing," I insisted, my tone a bit defensive.

He raised an eyebrow.

"Oh! You mean the..." I pointed my thumb behind me. "Just going to work." I gestured to Tilde at the front desk.

"Here? You work here?" he asked, pointing to the floor. "I haven't seen you around."

"First day," I said, hoping my smile wasn't as awkward as I felt. "I should probably..."

"Oh. Sure."

"Sorry again." I walked away before he could respond. Speaking to men besides Shawn wasn't something I'd done in a long time. Certainly not when Shawn was around. News traveled fast on the base, and few things set Shawn off faster than hearing another man was paying me any attention.

Tilde smirked when I arrived, twin chains hanging from the earpieces of her glasses dangling in unison. "You okay?"

"I am so, so sorry. I shouldn't have been walking that fast. I was just excited."

"Are you kidding? That was pure gold. Besides, you couldn't put a dent in that one." Tilde coughed once to clear her throat, the same short, crackly, smoker's cough my mom had.

"You know him?"

"He's one of the interagency guys." I blinked in confusion, and she continued. "The hotshots. The one with all the tattoos checked in today. Maddox. He has a twin, and I'm not sure which is which, but I am sure he'll have a girl in his room at least once while he's here. You'll start getting real good at reading people. Married couples. Married couples who come here but aren't married to each other. Those that come for work, the regulars, the frazzled parents with five kids. The young couples who have dogs for kids. The older couples who have dogs for kids. The truckers. The druggies. The college kids. The vagrants. You'll see them all."

I watched Maddox stroll across the lobby and sit at the bar. He joked with Stavros for a bit, then with his fellow hotshots.

"They'll start coming in droves any minute. We should train you on the basics."

Tilde was patient, showing me the computer system, how to check in and out, create keys, set up a wake-up call and a reservation, how to know if an outside call is coming in, or a guest is calling, how to patch a phone call through to a room.

The double glass doors swept open, and a small group of men walked inside carrying duffel bags and backpacks, chuckling and trading light punches and shoving. They were distracted by the man sitting at the bar, and approached him, knocking off his ball cap and taking turns trying to shove him off his stool.

"Why do boys do that?" I asked. "They're so mean to one another."

"Mean? No, precious, that's just how they show affection. Men in positions like theirs...and policemen, soldiers, you know the like. They're all that way."

I frowned. "Someone should tell them it's not affection."

The hotshots were thin, their cheekbones protruding, eyes sunken. They seemed happy enough, teasing each other and laughing, as if they were old high school buddies reunited after years of being apart.

Tilde spoke through her smile. "Here he comes."

"Maddox?" I said, mimicking her hushed tone.

"Taylor Maddox!" she said when he was close enough to hear. "So good to see you again. How's the family?"

"Dad's good. Brothers are good," Taylor said, looking down as he fished his wallet from his back pocket. He tossed his ID and a credit card, then turned his attention to his phone, tapping out a quick reply. When he put it away, he looked up, catching my gaze. "Oh."

"Good afternoon," I said.

"Is everything satisfactory with your room?" Tilde asked.

He ignored Tilde to reply to me. "We ran into each other in the hall."

"I remember," I said.

"So...your first day, huh? How's it going so far?"

"Fine," I said, letting him know with my answer and body language I wasn't interested.

He chuckled, seeming to take no offense. "I have a king. I'll need a double, Tilde. Two keys."

"One double left. You're lucky," Tilde said, clicking away on the computer. "I'll just need your credit card again."

Taylor flashed a perfect smile, glancing at me for half a second before handing me his card.

I passed it on to Tilde, who batted her eyes. Anything that man said would make her blush. Yes, he was attractive, and charming, and on the surface, at least, he was kind and humble. I wondered if I was suspicious of him because of the wall I'd had to build or if there was something familiar about him—and not in a good way. With her mouse, she selected a room, and then input Taylor's name and information. She programmed two card keys and handed them over. *Seems easy enough.*

"All set," Tilde said.

Taylor signed his receipt, and Tilde returned his credit card, then inserted the keys into a small envelope, reaching across the desk with it. "There you are. Welcome home. Again."

"Thanks, Tilde. I didn't catch your name."

Tilde answered for me. "Darby. We haven't gotten her a name tag yet."

"Huh. Never heard that before. Has to be a story."

"A very boring one," I said.

"I'd like to hear it sometime, anyway," he said, walking toward the elevator bay.

Tilde hummed. "Oh my. You've already found trouble."

"Nope," I said, shaking my head. "Not interested in dating. Definitely not his type at all. No firefighters, hotshots, law enforcement, soldiers…"

Tilde chuckled. "You're right. Those jobs all require certain personalities, don't they?"

The phone warbled, and Tilde grabbed it quickly, holding the receiver against her chin with her shoulder. "Front desk. How can I help you, Mr. Trexler? Oh. I'm so sorry about that. Yes, I'll have some sent up right away." Tilde pressed down on the hook with one finger. "Damn it." She released and dialed another number. She waited. She sighed. She rolled her eyes and hung up. "Darby, there should be a housekeeping cart somewhere down the far hall. Grab four bath towels, four hand towels, and four washrags, and take them to Scottie Trexler in two-oh-one."

I pointed across the lobby to the opposite wall. "The cart is down that hall?"

Tilde nodded.

The lobby was difficult to navigate, a maze of mostly starved, grungy men, and a few women. I rounded the corner to another hallway, the interior wall broken up by another twenty or so beige doors. Halfway down, a housekeeping cart sat unattended, full of glasses, towels, washcloths, soaps, and those little bottles of shampoo and conditioner. I helped myself to the towels and cloths and returned through the lobby.

The hotshots gathered around the bar parted like the Red Sea, pausing their conversations long enough for me to pass with arms full of bleached cotton. The elevator shuddered as it approached the second level, and then bounced, the doors opening to a quiet hallway. A large, diamond-shaped mirror hung straight across from where I stood. The woman in the reflection looked different than the tearful, trapped bride in the mirror of the tiny church in Fort Hood. There was hope in my eyes. Independence.

Room 201 was just fifteen feet from the elevators. I rapped my knuckles against the door. "Housekeeping," I said, unsure if that was the right thing to do or not.

"Just a sec!" a man yelled, and then a crash sounded from somewhere inside the room. "Shit! Hang on!"

The door swung open, and my eyes scrolled up over five feet of white terry cloth, chest, neck, and then a pair of baby-blue eyes. The man was breathing hard, holding open the door, holding his breath when his gaze caught mine. It took him a moment to form a single word. "Hi."

"Hi." I smiled. "Towels?" I said, holding them up.

"Uh…"

"I'm sorry, did you…?"

"Yeah! Yeah," he said, taking them off my hands. "Sorry about that. I tripped over the damn…Never mind. Thank you." He grinned. Not the kind of smile a predator like Shawn would flash, hoping to draw me in. "I'm Trex."

"Darby," I said. Just the sound of my name seemed to please him. He couldn't stop staring at me, and I couldn't look away.

"Oh. Damn it, I'm sorry." Trex dug into his pocket, producing a twenty-dollar bill, and placed it in my palm. "Thanks again."

I peered down at the worn paper in my hand. "That's really not necessary."

"I insist."

I handed him back the money, forcing myself to say the words that came to mind. "No, thank you."

I turned on my heels, leaving Trex standing in the doorway, smiling all the way to the elevator. Saying no to someone for the first time in a long time—maybe ever—gave me a feeling impossible to describe to someone who'd never been a doormat most of their life. It was terrifying and exhilarating at the same time. I didn't remember feeling so happy.

"Darby," Trex called from his room.

I froze, looking at him over my shoulder. I wondered how long it would take for the paralyzing fear at the sound of a man's voice saying my name to flush from my system.

"Would you like to grab dinner sometime?"

I couldn't erase the ridiculous grin from my face. "No thanks."

"What about lunch?"

"No thanks." My smile probably wasn't convincing, but I couldn't help it.

"Do you just love shooting me down, or am I really that detestable?"

"Yes," I said, dancing the second I was alone inside the elevator.

Confrontation and saying no weren't something I'd been capable of. Even if it led to a horrible death, I would rather go along with a stranger and listen to the alarms going off in my head, desperate for me to exercise self-preservation, than hurt his feelings. I was taught to be polite, comply, appease, ever since I could communicate. Hug that stranger, kiss that aunt, smile to everyone, even if my gut said they were trouble. It's the reason I found myself on the lap of a friend's father at midnight during a sleepover with his hands down my pants, and why my grandfather was confident in persuading me to rub him in places I didn't want to look at, much less touch.

Saying no was my new superpower, and I would use it every time I had the chance, from now on.

chapter four

Trex

I kept staring at the last place I saw her, as if she might reappear and laugh like she was playing a prank, but the elevator chimed, and I was sure she was on her way downstairs. I shook my head. She looked like a beauty queen without twenty layers of makeup, complete with a world peace–creating smile and stage-worthy saunter. I'd come across beautiful women before—even dated a few—but I didn't expect to see a woman like her working in a place like this. She should be married to George Clooney and fighting for human rights, running her own charity for clean water, and basically saving the world, not in a shithole hotel in Colorado Springs.

I closed the door, suddenly embarrassed over spending so much time staring down the hall.

My cell phone rang, and I put down the towels in the bathroom, jogging over to my nightstand. I tugged on the charger and toppled over, back-first onto the mattress. "Hey, Val."

"It's been months. You couldn't call?" Val asked. Her voice was comforting, even knowing she was hundreds of miles away. She'd always had my back, had tried for years to be my voice of reason every time I'd wanted to walk out while giving my boss the finger.

"I've been overseas, trying to stay busy," I said, picking at the lace of my boot. "Guess who I just had lunch with today?"

"Your dad?"

"Very funny. Taylor Maddox."

"Bullshit."

"Why would I lie?"

"How did that happen?"

I chuckled, surprised myself. "They're on the fire near here. I'm staying in the same hotel. I thought he was going to attack me when I first saw him, then he asked me to lunch."

She sighed. "Those Maddox boys. So...how was lunch?"

"Good. I think Taylor's in love with the waitress. He just met her today, by the way. We forgot to tip her and he was freaking out about it. He's taking money to her tonight."

"Aw, that's kind of sweet."

"Yeah, if she didn't hate him."

"So, you like it there, huh? In Colorado?"

"I think I do," I said.

"Well...I guess that's it, then."

"I'll miss you, Val. I really will. Take care."

"You, too. But...Scottie? Don't be a stranger. And if you need anything, just call."

"Thanks, Val."

Pressing End wasn't the closure I'd hoped for. Val wanted me to say more, but there wasn't more to say. One kiss one drunken night at the local pub wasn't enough to make me want to stay. She would likely be over it this time next month.

My phone made a muted thud when I tossed it to the mattress. I mulled over the next day, excited about seeing my old buddies again, nervous about doing the job to the satisfaction of General Tallis. He was known for being a hard-ass.

The rest of my team would be waiting on me at six a.m.

sharp at the Cheyenne Mountain Complex. Some of us hadn't seen one another in years. The Complex was at least a half hour away, and I had to get my credentials first. I lifted my arm to see the red digital numbers of my watch. Just a few minutes after seven. I had just enough time to grab dinner and a shower before attempting eight full hours of sleep. My first day at the Complex would be at least twelve hours long.

I pushed myself up, my muscles aching from my workout at Iron Mountain Gym, where I'd bought a membership the week before. After lunch, I'd lifted until my arms would barely work to drive back to the hotel. Earbuds in, exhausting every muscle, I had made my thoughts go numb; my one safe space away from the worry, guilt, and anxiety that flooded my daily thoughts. Especially after quitting my job and moving, I had a lot of ground to cover. Soldiers were damaged goods, and we all had to find a way to live with the nightmares that played in our minds whether we were awake or asleep.

Once again, I was in the elevator. *I should find a place of my own soon.* Up and down in that box was going to get old fast, and it reminded me too much of the Bureau.

A chime sounded before the doors opened and I stepped out into the hall. The lobby hadn't cleared much. Instead of standing in line to check in, the hotshots were standing around with clear plastic cups full of beer. Part of me hoped I'd run into the housekeeping chick again, but she was standing behind the check-in desk this time. Hotshot firefighters, inter-agency brass, and higher-ups from the Forestry Department surrounded the front desk. Tilde was checking them in, one room at a time, and training Darby while she did it. Darby didn't seem flustered, though, her eyes taking in everything, all with a smile on her face.

One hotshot had his elbows leaned on the counter, a goofy

smile on his face while he spoke to Darby. She was clearly uninterested, concentrating on her training. Something stirred in my chest, watching her ignore the guy two feet away trying to woo her. He wasn't bad looking, and most girls fell for the firefighter shtick. Darby couldn't have been less interested. I wondered why as I approached the front desk and heard the poor bastard practically crooning at her.

"Tilde," I said, cutting in front of the waiting hotshots. *Be smart, Trex.* "Where's a good place to eat around here?"

"There's a Mexican restaurant down the road," Darby said. "Their queso is fantastic. That's all I know, though."

"Walking distance?" I asked.

"Goodness, no," Tilde said. "It's at least four miles."

"I walked here from there." Darby shrugged, a grin on her face.

I smiled back at her. A small gesture, but a smile was more than the hotshot flirting with her had gotten. Something about drawing her attention made me crave it more. Just before I asked what time she got off work, Tilde handed me a tri-folded menu.

"Jimmy's. Tastes like home-cooked meals. Across the street and down. Can't miss it."

Darby leaned over, trying to read the menu. When she saw me watching her, she stood upright, looking caught. "Sorry," she said.

"Hungry?" I asked.

Darby shook her head quickly.

Tilde watched her for a moment, then frowned. "You just had queso for lunch? We're going to be here until eleven. You'll be starving."

"I had salsa, too. I'm fine," Darby said, trying to focus her attention on the next hotshot checking in.

Her accent was fucking adorable. "They'll probably

close before your shift's over. I could bring you both back something."

"You are just the sweetest," Tilde said. "Let me get you some money, honey."

"Get it later," I said, reaching over the counter for a pen. "What would you hardworking ladies like?" I'd wanted to write down their orders, but Darby took a step back as if I were grabbing for her. I moved more slowly, as if I were in the presence of a wild animal. Darby's ivory cheeks flushed when she saw what I was reaching for. I held the pen over the paper, waiting for her answer.

Darby scanned a key card, keeping her head down. She was so confident before, but now she acted like a kicked dog. "I'm good," she said.

I jotted down my number, handing the paper to Tilde. "You'll be starving by the time you get off work. I really don't mind. Just text me what you want."

I began to walk away, but Darby tugged on my shirt. "Trex! I . . ." She tucked loose strands of honey-blond behind her ear. "I don't get paid for two weeks. I can't pay you back today."

"So, pay me back when you can. It's just food."

Her full lips pressed together in a hard line. She was barely wearing any makeup, clothes too big even for her Southern-belle curves, and yet she was stunning. I looked down. She was still hanging on to my shirt.

"I'm so sorry," she said, crossing her arms across her waist. She peered around, waiting for someone to tell her she'd done something wrong.

"It's okay, Darby. Just relax." Her shoulders lowered from her earlobes to a normal position. This girl was wound tighter than the girdle of a Baptist minister's wife at an all-you-can-eat pancake breakfast. "It's all right."

She nodded.

"You going to text me?" I asked.

"I don't have a cell phone."

"Just have Tilde text me, then. If you get busy, don't worry about it. I'll just pick something for you."

I turned, feeling her watch me walk through the automatic doors. Even with the summer sun hovering over the horizon and veiled by the smoke from what the news channels called a thousand-acre fire, its hot breath blew in my face. I took in my surroundings, seeing the neon sign that read JIMMY'S exactly where Tilde said it would be.

My entire walk was spent thinking about the blonde behind the counter, matching her voice with the one that had been ingrained in my brain, even when I was awake. She had an unapologetic shape I didn't see on many women in California. I could curve my fingers around Darby's waist, but half the buttons on her Oxford shirt were working overtime to contain her double D cups, and her hips didn't look like a Ken doll, instead rolling out gentle into thighs I could hold on to. I tried to shake the image of me running my hands over her curves, feeling my dick press against the back of my pants even as I dodged traffic while crossing the highway to Jimmy's.

It didn't take a genius to figure out someone had hurt her in more ways than one. That thought alone made any sexual thoughts melt away with a wave of guilt. Hailey was a stunner, too, and I'd threatened more than one guy who ogled her and had lewd thoughts before even speaking to her. Darby seemed sweet and didn't need some douchebag fantasizing about her.

"Welcome," the host said when I pushed through the glass door. He peered behind me. "How many?"

"Just one," I said, following him to a booth. Jimmy's

was too bright for that time of night, and it reminded me more of a truck stop café than the grandma's-kitchen feel I'd imagined, but the food smelled amazing. "I'm going to need the server over quick. I'm bringing back food to some friends."

"I'll let Ginny know," he said, handing me a menu.

Ginny arrived just a few minutes later. At least they had good service. "I hear you're in a hurry," she said with a smile.

I glanced at the menu one last time. "I'll have a water, a number six, and two number twos to go, please."

The waitress giggled. "That was easy."

I nodded, handed her the menu, and she pranced to the kitchen. I sat back, interlacing my fingers and resting them on top of my hair. I'd just cut it again, but unless my head was freshly shaved, the guys were going to give me shit in the morning. In the Marines, I hadn't kept more than an inch of hair on my head or a few days of scruff on my face. Working for Deep Six Security, I'd grown a long, scraggly beard. A buzz cut and lumberjack beard weren't standard in the FBI, and with a boss who raged over the smallest things, it was better to blend in.

* * *

The restaurant wasn't close to capacity, just a few families, a booth occupied by two women celebrating a night away from their families, and a few guys at the bar pretending they were more invested in the game on the flat-screen than in locating a single woman. Being alone was something I'd had to adjust to after being on a team for most of my adult life. Sitting in a booth across from no one was an adjustment, too, but it was better to have no one in front of me than someone who wasn't her.

The women in the booth across from mine stole a few glances in my direction. They giggled and took another sip of their truck stop wine, their wedding bands glinting off the fluorescent lighting. I wasn't sure why married women were so attracted to me. Even my ex didn't show as much interest until after she married my best friend. Maybe I seemed like the guy who'd be a good time, and easy to walk away from. I frowned, not sure how I felt about that. My career had left me never married and childless at thirty-five. *Now I'm here, and she's right across the street, and I have to act like I haven't been looking for her my entire adult life.*

In just ten minutes, I had paid for the plastic bag in my hand full of boxed meals and was out the door. The highway would have been easier to cross if I'd walked a quarter mile down the road, but I took the direct route instead, dodging cars and semitrucks barreling along the road at sixty-five miles per hour plus. Being in the middle of a busy highway felt strangely comforting. Focusing on surviving instead of the memories in my head was the reason why I missed being an active Marine every second of the day.

As soon as the automatic doors opened, dozens of heads glanced in my direction, but no one really paid attention to me until I gave the bag in my hand to Darby. The men in the lobby seemed overly interested in everything she did, and it bugged me.

I took my boxed food off the top. Tilde smiled. Darby hesitated.

"They're both the same. Meatloaf and mashed potatoes and gravy. I hope that's okay. I didn't get a text."

"Sorry about that, we had a short rush of check-ins. The meatloaf is perfect. Best thing on the menu!" Tilde said, grabbing for the next box. She handed it to Darby and then took one for herself. She sniffed the steam wafting from the food once she opened the lid. "Oh my. I'm salivating." She opened the plasticware and dug in, closing her eyes.

"Did I mess up? You don't like meatloaf?" I asked.

"I do," Darby said, staring at the unopened box. "It's my favorite, actually. Thank you."

I was glad there was no longer a line to check in so I had more time to talk to her. "You don't owe me anything, Darby. It's just food."

"I appreciate it," she said, her gaze fixed on the Styrofoam lid.

I leaned in, and she moved back, embarrassed again by her instinct. I wanted to beat the ass of whoever ingrained that in her. She hated it, I could tell.

"I won't ever talk to you again if you don't want me to," I said, hoping she wouldn't take me up on the offer. "I just didn't want you to be hungry. It's not a ploy to obligate you to me in any way."

Tilde stopped eating to watch for Darby's reaction. Darby still didn't make eye contact with anything but the food box. I flicked open the lid, and slowly placed a package of plasticware beside it before walking away.

"Thank you." Darby's voice was barely audible over the noise in the lobby, but I heard it, and I smiled.

chapter five

Darby

As soon as Trex walked away, I ripped open the plasticware and dug into meat. I didn't care who was watching,
or who thought putting so much on my fork at a time before
stuffing it in my mouth was disgusting. Easing the growling
that had been rumbling in my stomach for the past three
hours was my primary concern.

As I chewed quickly and took another bite, I considered
Trex's behavior. He was kind and thoughtful, but I wasn't sure
Trex was pursuing me. Most men at least attempted to flirt
with me, even some women. I'd never admitted that aloud,
but anyone who thought I was bragging hadn't experienced a
forty-plus-year-old making sexual advances toward her at the
tender age of twelve. I certainly hadn't asked for it. But Trex
didn't look at me like a potential target. He simply acknowl-
edged the human in front of him, and that was refreshing.

"Dear Lord," Tilde said. "You're allowed a dinner break,
you know. Half an hour. If you were hungry…"

"I need to go to the grocery store. I have nothing in
my room."

"There's a larger fridge in your room. You'll have plenty
of space to put groceries. Well, more than the other rooms."

"I can only carry so many bags at a time," I said, covering
my mouth while I chewed.

"Take a cab. Or I can give you a ride for a while. I'm old as dirt, you know; no telling when they'll revoke my license."

I giggled with my mouth full.

"Take advantage of the continental breakfast we serve in the mornings. Stavros doesn't mind."

"Thank you," I said, just before I swallowed. I dove into the mashed potatoes and gravy, humming with delight.

Tilde took one bite to my three, watching me attack every morsel in the Styrofoam box. When I dabbed my mouth and sat up to heave a satiated sigh, Tilde's twin chains swooping down from her glasses shook with her head. "I'm not sure what to think, to be honest."

"You were right. Lunch wasn't enough to hold me over. I didn't realize I'd be working today, or I would have ordered more."

"Or you don't have enough money for food," Tilde said, dubious.

"I'm just on a budget," I said, taking her empty box, and mine, too. The hotshots at the bar stopped talking when I dumped the contents in my hands in the trash and then used Stavros's sink to wash my hands.

"Where are you from?" one of them asked. He sat on the stool in front of me, nursing the last half of a blond pint that matched the hair that poked out from his red ball cap, and his scraggly beard. His blue eyes watched me with curiosity more than malintent.

"South," I said.

He smiled, his teeth contrasting against his tanned skin. "What's your name?"

"That reminds me. We need to get you a name badge," Stavros said. "This is Darby. Darby . . . that's Zeke and Dalton. They're the Alpine hotshots out of Estes Park."

"Nice to meet you, Zeke. I'm sorry, but I have to get back to work."

Stavros called after me. "It's a shame you're rushing off. These boys have been dying to talk to you."

"Oh," I said, stopping. I returned, waiting for whatever was next.

"It's okay," Zeke said. "No one said anything that wasn't nice."

"Depends on what your definition is," I said, forgetting myself for a moment. I was annoyed that Stavros had put me on the spot to stay, and I tried not to glare at him. By the smirk on his face, I could see he was trying to embarrass the boys more than he was forcing me to be social.

"Rude, crude, or inappropriate," Zeke said.

I smiled, and all eight men sitting at the bar cheered as if I'd just made a touchdown, so loud the noise startled me.

"Sorry!" Zeke said, holding out his hands and chuckling.

"They were beginning to wonder if you smiled at all unless it was to greet or say good-bye to a guest," Stavros said, amused.

I thought back to my afternoon and evening, wondering if they were right. "I thought you said it was all nice."

"They were worried about you, that's all," Stavros said. "You'd think these guys were all your big brothers. They've been warning the others to be polite for hours."

I sucked a tiny gasp through my lips. That was the nicest thing anyone had done for me. "Oh," I said, my tone more appreciative this time.

"You let us know if anyone gives you problems. We'll set 'em straight," Zeke said.

Stavros popped the top off a bottle. "Your boss has just informed me it's last call, boys."

The hotshots groaned, but to my surprise, instead of

ordering another round, they all paid their checks and headed to their rooms. All except Zeke.

"How was your first day?" he asked, leaning his elbow against the bar.

"It was great," I said, nodding.

Stavros grinned. "She has to say that. I'm her boss."

"Well. You have sweet dreams, Miss Darby." Zeke tipped his ball cap and joined the others in the elevator bay.

"You're going to have to share that magic with me," Stavros said, wiping down the bar.

"What magic would that be?" I asked.

"Whatever makes people fall all over themselves to talk to you, for you to like them, and to protect you."

I turned to watch Zeke and his friends step into the elevator.

"That's not really a thing...with me. I mostly have to protect myself, and I'm not that good at it."

Several seconds passed before Stavros spoke again. "I don't know what you left, but you don't have to worry about that anymore. Especially now that they've practically adopted you."

"That's sweet," I said, watching the empty place where they stood.

"I hope you got a good look. Some of them are leaving at first light, and they don't always come back."

"That's...awful." I swallowed. None of them acted like it could be their last night on earth. I suspected if any of them let that thought cross their mind, they wouldn't do what they do. Shawn thought he was invincible, too. Untouchable. But these guys were nothing like Shawn. He would have never told another man not to speak about a woman—a stranger—in an inappropriate way. He would've joined in. I'd heard it.

I wondered if Shawn's enormous ego helped him to stop caring when Carly had returned to the church without me and told him I was gone, or if he'd resolved to find me and drag me back. The thought of Shawn looking for me made me shiver, and I tried to push it away as soon as it came.

"You okay, kiddo?" Stavros asked.

"Yes." I looked at my watch. "Looks like it's quittin' time for me."

Stavros nodded once. "Good work today. Once you're trained, I'm putting you on nights. Our day guy is covering nights, too. He should be here any minute."

"Everyone's working doubles, huh?"

"We do what we must. Your schedule is Sunday nights through Thursday. Friday and Saturdays off. Can you handle that?"

I nodded once. "Absolutely. That's more than fair. Um… Stavros? If this isn't okay, I'll just figure something out. But I was wondering…can I be paid in cash?"

Stavros arched a dark eyebrow, scanning me before speaking. "How much trouble are you in?"

A skinny kid walked through the sliding glass doors, straightening his tie, and Stavros's smile quickly morphed into a frown.

"You're late," Stavros called to him.

He glanced at his watch. "I'm right on time."

"For the hundredth time, Ander. If you're not—"

"…early I'm late. Yes, I know."

"So, you're late."

He smiled. His jet-black hair, gray eyes, and square chin probably charmed anyone else but Stavros. "I love you bunches, Stavros."

Stavros grumbled, watching Ander greet Tilde with a hug.

"Tilde doesn't seem to mind," I said.

"He can do no wrong in her eyes. Ander is her grandson. Her favorite grandson."

"Did she say that? Surely not."

"I just know."

"How?" I asked.

"Because I'm her other grandson. Ander is my little brother."

"Oh," I said, watching Stavros close the bar.

As I walked off, he called to me. "You say that a lot. *Oh.*"

"I'll show you how to close down your shift tomorrow," Tilde said, using her shirt to cover a deep cough.

"Sounds good, thank you. Good night," I said, waving.

Walking down the hall, I hugged my middle. Being in Stavros's hotel around his family wasn't home, but I felt more welcome there than anywhere. Making friends in school wasn't easy for me. I usually rubbed people wrong somehow. Stavros saying I had a magic way of making people like me was the nicest thing anyone had said to me in a long time, even if it wasn't true. I wasn't sure why the people here liked me so much, but never being able to please people before, no matter how hard I tried, I appreciated it more than they would ever know.

An involuntary yawn took over my body as I trudged down the hall, my feet feeling heavier with each step. Once I stepped inside my room, a shower seemed like too much effort, so I collapsed onto the bed. After the second bounce, I wondered if I should do that because of the baby.

I rolled over, staring at the ceiling. There were things to do, like make a doctor's appointment. I hated not knowing what was okay and not okay. Until I could figure out how to pay for a doctor, I'd have to find some books. I'd do that in the morning before my next shift, but then what? If I couldn't afford a doctor, how would I afford a baby? I had no insurance, no savings, and things like the cost of diapers, bottles, clothes, and medicine began to crowd my mind.

My eyes closed tight, pushing out the forming tears. A deep pain ached in my chest at the thought of giving Bean away to adoptive parents. I wasn't even sure what kind of mother I would be. Most days, I didn't recognize myself. I'd given so much of myself away to Shawn in just the year we were together that I wasn't sure what was left. I remembered that girl, but she was so far out of reach. I had to believe that this was God's plan. For me to be half beaten to death before I finally left, pregnant and alone, didn't sound much of a plan, but I didn't have to understand it. There was something else out there for me, and maybe it was in Colorado Springs.

If I could go back, I would change everything. Guilt set in as I regretted wishing away the baby growing inside of me. The baby I wasn't sure how I would feed, or clothe, or...

I shook my head and covered my face. *I have enough on my plate without worrying about things that are the better part of a year away. Stop it, Darby.*

I concentrated on my breath, inhaling in fully, and exhaling, slow and controlled, starting over until my body gave in to the exhaustion. One day at a time. That was the only way to get through this. And I would. I'd gotten through worse.

* * *

The alarm bleated four times before I scrambled for the off button and then looked next to me, waiting for Shawn to either roll over and fall back asleep or fly into a rage. He wasn't there. His bed wasn't beneath me. I touched my stomach with one hand, my forehead with the other, breathing hard. The relief that washed over me was so intense, I cried. He hadn't found us yet. We were still safe.

After the involuntary shuddering stopped, I let the fear and worry fall away with a sigh. Nothing bad was happening to me—the opposite, actually. Just down the hall was my new job. No one knew me or my past. Bean and I had everything ahead of us.

I slowly pushed up from the bed and trudged to the window, pulling it open. My view consisted of the heat and air-conditioning units and the maintenance shed, but beyond that was Pikes Peak. I was far away from Shawn and Fort Hood, the heat, the humidity, the fear. My stomach was still flat under my fingertips, but Bean was there somewhere, growing and at peace. A sudden nausea overwhelmed me. My mouth began to water, and bile rose in my throat. I covered my mouth and ran for the bathroom, crouching in front of the toilet and hugging the porcelain, expelling the small amount of meatloaf and mashed potatoes that hadn't digested. After the last heave, I sat back against the wall, feeling the warm tile on my backside contrast with the cold wall against my back.

Most of the pregnant women on base were barely eighteen. I would've been one of the older wives, certainly the oldest without a child. I'd seen all the symptoms: the morning sickness, the tiredness, the heartburn, the swollen feet. But I was an only child; I had no idea what to do with a baby. The Pikes Peak library was on the same road as the hotel, but at least an hour's walk one-way. I could get a card and check out some pregnancy books. Maybe even find out my due date and how to get prenatal care with no way to pay. My stomach lurched, and I covered my mouth. *Toast first, then a walk to the library.*

I hoped Tilde was right, that Stavros wouldn't mind me getting a piece of toast from the continental breakfast bar. The front desk was unmanned, and when I rounded the divider that separated the lobby from the dining area, I realized why: The hotshots were swarming the food, and poor Ander was the only one on duty.

"Need help?" I asked him.

Ander smiled. "I got it. Are you here for breakfast?"

I nodded. "Tilde said it was okay."

"Of course it's okay. Help yourself."

I couldn't help the grin stretching wide across my face. "Thank you."

"Toast?" Zeke said, handing me a Styrofoam plate with buttered toasted bread.

"How did you know?" I asked.

He shrugged. "Wanna sit with me?"

I followed him to a table, and he placed his plate in front of him, a fork already in his hand, hovering about the mountain of food on his plate. "You can have anything you want. I'm going back, anyway. Did you see they have a waffle maker? I'm in heaven."

"Don't they feed you between fires?" I teased.

He grinned. "Carb loading. We hike miles up into the mountains. We don't eat a lot up there, so I stuff it in when I can. I try to stay under a certain weight, though, so I only eat like this just before I go up."

"To fit into your uniform?"

Zeke burst into laughter. "No. No, because if we take a helo in, there are weight limits. If you're bumping the max, you can't take anything with you. Not a blanket, not playing cards, nothing. They're pretty strict, so I like to stay plenty under, even though it's not hard with all the trekking we do."

I bit into the toast, chewing slowly and hoping it stayed put. I would have to tell Stavros about the baby sometime, but not until I had to, and I didn't want him to hear it from someone else. He didn't seem like the type to fire me so he didn't have to deal with maternity leave, but I didn't know him that well, and couldn't take the chance.

After every bite, the nausea subsided. Zeke chatted about Estes Park and his older sister's upcoming wedding. While he spoke, I wondered when he would go out, and if what Stavros said about some of them not coming back crossed his mind. He had plans and loved ones. It didn't seem right.

"When are you going up?" I asked.

"Usually, it's fourteen on, two off, but this is a political fire. Alpines are second in the rotation. We relieve the current crew every seventy-two hours," he said, chewing.

"For how long?"

"Another seventy-two hours."

"You be careful up there, okay?"

He stopped chewing to smile and then to swallow before he spoke. "I will. At least we're not helitack. They work fourteen on, two off, no matter what. Not as many of them, but they get paid more. Think when I get back we can see that space movie? I've been dying to see it, but the guys think it's a chick flick."

I tripped over my words, my upbringing to be polite sword fighting with my new superpower. "I can't. Thank you, though."

"Oh," Zeke said, embarrassed. "You have a boyfriend. Of course you do. That was stupid."

"No, I'm just not..."

"Oh," he said, a glint of recognition in his eye. "A girlfriend."

"No, I just got out of a relationship," I said, trying to get the words out quick before he interrupted me again.

He nodded slowly, trying to process what that meant. "Well...what if it's just to go? We don't even have to sit together. There's always a seat between when I go with one of the guys."

"That's...weird."

He shrugged. "I know. The only one that doesn't do it is Taylor. He doesn't care if anyone thinks he's on a date with a dude." He took another bite.

"Just as friends?" I asked. He stopped chewing to wait for my answer. "I mean, yeah, if it's just a movie. How much is it?"

Zeke waved me away. "I got it. It's like eight bucks."

I shook my head. "I'd better not. I'm trying to save money."

He chuckled. "I got it, silly."

I pressed my lips together. That would mean I'd owe that Trex guy and now Zeke. "I'd better not."

"You won't go with me over eight bucks?" He seemed disappointed instead of indignant.

I breathed out a laugh. He was right. It was ridiculous. "Okay. But I'm paying you back."

He nodded once. "Deal." He used his thumbnail to pick something out of his teeth quickly before standing for another round. He pointed to the buffet with his plastic fork. "Want anything?"

"Actually," I said, standing, too, "I have to go pick up a few things downtown. Thanks for the toast."

Zeke waved at me with his fork, and I squeezed the leather loop of my wristlet in my palm.

I used a map from the stack we had at the front desk to find my way to the Pikes Peak library. The walk wasn't as long as I'd thought, less than half an hour, and the doors were open by the time I arrived. A tiny, gray-haired woman pushed up her glasses with her free hand as she held open the door for me with the other. I peered around the room, then headed for the Pregnancy and Childbirth section. Even though it was just the librarian and me, the urge to peek over my shoulder became too intense to ignore. In a book with a pink cover, I found a due date wheel. Moving the bottom section to the first day of my last period, the top part showed me an approximate due date. I wasn't even six weeks pregnant. I remembered the night Bean was conceived, with Shawn's hand around my neck, squeezing it so tight I could barely breathe.

My knees felt weak as I stared at the month and day Bean might come into the world. Suddenly, it was real. On February 1, everything would change.

The small stack of books fit into the thrift-store backpack hanging from my shoulders, and I followed the map back to the Colorado Springs Hotel, thinking about who to call to help me find prenatal care, worried Shawn would be able to find me if I signed up for assistance and was logged into the system. I would need to pay cash, and I didn't have anywhere close to the amount I would need.

What am I going to do?

Adoption was the only option, but as the thought entered my mind, an overwhelming sadness came over me. I imagined holding the tiny baby that I'd carried for months, then giving that precious bundle to the nurse and the silent pain burning through my body as I watched my son or daughter being handed over to strangers. It would be selfish to keep Bean just because the alternatives would hurt, but the images made me sob all the way home.

A group of hotshots, dirty and covered in soot, trudged from their interagency trucks to the front doors with me. They looked exhausted but happy, some of them already with room keys in hand, ready to wash the wilderness off and crash into their beds.

Stavros waved to me as I passed, and Tilde had already

replaced Ander, standing behind the front desk with a bright smile on her face.

"Good morning, Darby," she said, her voice sounding like she'd scrubbed the inside of her throat with sandpaper. Her smile faded. "You okay?"

"Morning," I said. "I'm fine, thank you. How are you feeling?"

"Oh, you know. All right. You're out and about early."

"Walked to the library," I said in passing.

Hotshots waited for the elevator, filling the hall with the thick stench of smoke. I could still smell them when the stairwell door opened and Taylor stepped out.

"We've got to quit running into each other like this," he said. He looked happy, his buzz cut and clean-shaven face a contrast from the other hotshots. "You okay?"

"Yeah. Yeah, I'm fine," I said. "Are you going up today?"

He shook his head. "I've got a date with a waitress."

"You're still chasing her?" I asked.

"Still chasing her," he said with a grin.

"Good luck," I called over my shoulder. When I reached my door, I was sure to unlock and close it quickly behind me to try to keep the lingering smoke from seeping into my room.

By the time I reached my bed, I was already tired and wondering how I would make it through an evening behind the check-in desk. A nap was necessary, but I wanted to crack open at least one book before I fell asleep. I wanted to see what Bean looked like, and one of the books I'd borrowed from the library was full of in-color pictures of babies in utero.

I flipped to the first chapter and squinted. Bean, five weeks and four days, looked more like a lizard than a baby. I turned the book to one side and then the other, trying to make out features even though the caption of the picture was *A Face Emerges*.

I stared at the lizard baby until my eyelids grew too heavy to keep open, and just as I drifted off, jerked awake. A mental check scrolled through my mind, that everything in the house was in place, the dishes clean, the laundry folded, ironed, and put away, and dinner was planned for the following night. Just a second later, my muscles relaxed against the mattress. Shawn wouldn't be home to yank me out of bed if something set him off, he wouldn't spit in my face while he turned red and the veins in his neck bulged. The panic I'd felt every night for more than half a year was just a knee-jerk reaction, but as I remembered where I was, and that Shawn was more than eight hundred miles away, the fear subsided, and I drifted away, at peace knowing Bean and I were safely alone in the dark.

chapter six

Trex

The clip snapped shut on the front pocket of my shirt. The picture in the ID seemed pointless, pixelated and grayscale, but it was the bar code that would get me inside the Cheyenne Mountain Complex and from one section to another. Everyone seemed on edge about something. I theorized it was possibly because the Air Force had moved back in not more than a year before. The guards were quiet, and most of the employees and military kept their heads down.

"Is it because General Tallis is coming in?" I asked, keeping my voice low.

Bianca smirked, her short legs taking two steps to my one. "General Tallis is here every day. Everyone is nervous about the new head of security."

"Me?" I asked. I wasn't exactly known as the easygoing one in my unit, but not someone to be feared unless you'd shot at me and were on the wrong side of my rifle.

"You're surprised," Bianca said, more a statement than a question. "It seems your reputation precedes you. You're the man who took down Jabari Tau and his entire entourage."

I looked down and pretended to scratch my nose while taking in the expressions of those we passed. Most were trying not to stare. "It's not what they think."

"Isn't it?"

"I was waiting for my team to come back. That is exactly the kind of shit that happens out there."

Bianca wasn't fazed. "You weren't waiting. You were wounded and sent them ahead to catch up with the militants on their way to massacre the next village. You killed twelve of the most ruthless killers in South Sudan, including their leader. You stopped a coup. Jabari's death created instability and infighting within his militias, and that rippled throughout the region, setting free hundreds of child soldiers."

I breathed out a laugh—from disgust, not pride. Bianca made me sound like a superhero. My knee was blown out by a kid barely big enough to hold the Soviet-made assault rifle that was forced into his hands. The damn thing misfired, crafted two decades before his father raped his mother to create him. I was wounded because I couldn't shoot a kid before he shot me. I was waiting because I commanded my team to go on to search for the rest of the boy's unit while our blood mixed and pooled beneath us. He stared at the ceiling and exhaled for the last time in my arms, and I'd set him down gently when Jabari's men crept inside the first of a line of shacks I'd holed up in.

"The only thing I did was not die," I said, irritated the memory still had the power to catch me off guard. Even when the fighting stopped and I came home, my heart still warred with the images in my mind.

"And he's humble," Bianca said to herself. "If you wonder why the general chose you—"

"Fuck me in the ass," Martinez said, standing from the long, rectangular table he was leaning on when I stepped through the door.

The boy's dark, vacant eyes faded from my mind as Othello Martinez opened both arms wide and took me in for a hug. He slapped my back twice and then squeezed, as happy to see me as I was him. The darkest hour before sunup, some-where on the South Sudanese border, was the last place I'd seen him, his face appearing and reappearing as I blinked in and out of consciousness. Martinez went south after that. Drug cartels were easier to aim at than kids. He hadn't changed much, maybe five more years of squinting against the South American sun evident around his eyes.

I turned to hug Kitsch, Sloan, and then shake Harbinger's hand. He couldn't stand to be touched much; he saved the effort for his kids.

"You were all in the same squad in Sudan?" Bianca asked, even though she already knew the answer. I nodded. We'd survived a night stranded in a rebel-controlled area on the Sudan–South Sudan border, full of bullet holes and half starved, trying to head off a small but particularly blood-thirsty squad mowing down any vulnerable village in their path, and were ambushed by a bunch of kids. Nights like that cemented brotherhoods, and we were exactly the team the general wanted to run his security.

"Looking dapper, T-Rex," Naomi said.

"Nomes," I said, bringing her in for a quick hug. She was hypersensitive about appearing too emotional or weak in front of anyone else—a symptom of being a woman in the military. She slapped my scruffy cheek once and grabbed it before Bianca cleared her throat and checked her watch.

Sloan wrinkled his nose. "Does this place smell like mildew and dirty socks to everyone or is that just me?"

"We should start the tour and meet the general. There will be plenty of time for greetings and opinions on the distinct odor of a man-made cave dwelling later," Bianca said.

I traded glances with my team and gestured for them to follow. Bianca described each section: hallways with men and women in white coats sitting in front of tech I'd never seen, labs, doors thicker than I was tall, airmen with patches on their sleeves that read CMAFE, doors guarded by soldiers in uniforms I didn't recognize. The further we dug in, the staler the air.

The painted walls became steel tunnels. Pipes ran along the curved walls and ceiling, our feet clanged against a metal grid that made up the floor. A low hum churned throughout the corridor, interrupted by the intermittent dripping of water sliding down the already damp rock walls.

"Doesn't feel right," Sloan said.

"Easy," I whispered back.

"What you're feeling is a combination of frequency and vibration experiments and the way it affects the mountain. You're not wrong," a woman said from behind us. We turned to face her, a mess of blond, frizzy hair and square, peach-hued plastic glasses sitting on the tip of her nose. She held her hand out to me. "Dr. Sybil DuPont."

Kitsch sniffed. "Doctor of what?"

"Astrophysics," Dr. DuPont said.

My team traded glances.

"What's an astrophysicist doing here?" Naomi asked.

"It's classified," Bianca said.

I shifted my weight. "I'm the head of security. I have top security clearance."

Dr. DuPont smiled, amused about something. "For the facility, Mr. Trexler. Not government programs."

"What's this?" a man asked, stepping next to Dr. DuPont. He was barely taller than her shoulder, the light glaring off the deep umber skin of his bald head. Tight, white curls clung to the section above his ears, as if his hair had run away scared from the top, clinging to his ears in groups for safety.

"Dr. Angus Philpot," Bianca said, "this is Mr. Trexler, our new head of security, and his team, Harbinger, Sloan, Kitsch, Martinez, and Abrams."

I didn't miss that Bianca said Naomi's name like a dirty word she couldn't wait to set free from her mouth. There was more to it than trust, and I got the feeling it was likely Bianca, not the general, who didn't trust Naomi.

I shook Dr. Philpot's hand, but he seemed to be more interested in Sloan—arguably the lankiest member of our squad. He was six feet two inches of solid lean muscle, but he was still the thinnest of us, no match for Naomi's curves.

"Just Trex," I said, snapping Philpot from his preoccupation.

"Oh. Very well, then," he said. The lenses of Philpot's round, wire-framed glasses were so thick, they accentuated every time his telescope eyes would blink. He was no more than a half-pint, swallowed by his white lab jacket. He was too close to the size of a child, and I knew my team was as skeeved out about it as I was.

"You've got uh…" Sloan said, gesturing to his own tactical vest.

Dr. Philpot looked down.

"Jesus, Angus," Dr. DuPont said, taking a step back.

"Oh, it's uh…it's Sriracha," he said, wiping it with his finger and licking it away.

Dr. DuPont looked revolted. "I hope so. You could wake up with parasites burrowing through your brain tomorrow."

Martinez scanned the hall. "What the hell kind of place is this?"

"Lock that down," Kitsch growled.

"Mostly, it's a scientific facility," Dr. DuPont said. "But if you ask the general, it's a military operation. Upstairs is

NORAD, downstairs is off-limits." She flicked a small, plastic octagon on Naomi's vest. "Keep those on."

Martinez pulled his own octagon a half inch off his vest. "What is it, anyway?"

"A dosimeter," Bianca said.

"A doe what?" Sloan asked.

Dr. DuPont seemed charmed by our ignorance and flicked her own. "Dosimeter. A measuring device for radiation."

Naomi sighed. "That's why this job pays so well."

"Why don't you have one?" Martinez asked Bianca.

"Because I'm rarely beyond the blast doors or labs," Bianca said, matter-of-fact.

"What's downstairs?" I asked.

"It's classified," Bianca said.

"How can we secure the facility if we're not allowed in every section?" I asked.

Bianca seemed bored with our questions, but still expected them. "Those sections have their own security."

"Another security unit? When do I meet them?"

"You won't," Bianca said. "They're deep in Echo and their quarters are there."

"Echo?" Naomi asked.

"The lower corridors," Bianca said, checking her watch. "Let's continue the tour. We have eight and a half minutes before we turn back to meet the general."

"Doctors," I said, nodding before following Bianca farther down the hall.

Harbinger kept close and leaned in when he spoke. "What the fuck is going on here?"

"Not sure yet. But I'm going to find out."

"You'd better," he said, pulling his rifle close.

We were shown corridors Alpha, Bravo, Charlie, and Delta and then taken upstairs to meet Senator Bennett.

"Good morning. What a nice surprise," Bianca said. An expression I hadn't witnessed yet softened her features as she waited for the senator to respond.

"Is it?" he asked, one corner of his mouth turning up.

Naomi shot me a wry smile, and I tried and failed not to roll my eyes. The senator was wearing a gold wedding band, while Bianca's finger was bare.

"Peter," Naomi said, stepping out from behind.

Bennett smiled, looking more relieved than surprised. "Naomi."

Harbinger whispered in my ear again. "What's a junior senator doing here?" Before I could answer, he spoke. "Bennett. As in Speaker of the House Bennett? I'm guessing that's your father?"

Bennett straightened his tie. "You are correct."

It made sense then. Bennett was probably assigned to some needless committee and was overseeing absolutely nothing to claim Congress was on top of defense spending. Mostly he was spending too much time staring at one of my team.

"You know him?" Martinez asked.

Naomi shrugged one shoulder. "We've met."

Bennett couldn't have looked more heartbroken, and Bianca was displeased. She cleared her throat. "Shall we go? We don't want to keep the general waiting."

Naomi couldn't help but look over her shoulder at Bennett before we left the NORAD Operations room for the elevator. No one spoke while we retraced our steps back down corridor Charlie, through the blast doors, and to the administrative offices. Bianca left us in a large conference room alone.

The white walls were blank except for a few cracks and a line of portraits of white men, possibly former generals who had run the Complex in the past, but with no dates or names beneath, it was hard to be sure. The paint seemed to be the original coat, the bookshelves nearly empty, the large rectangular oak table with far fewer chairs than it could accommodate.

"Did they bring us here to die?" Sloan said, looking around.

"It's where Dr. Philpot is going to make you a candlelight dinner," Naomi teased.

"Fuck off, Nomes," Sloan said, but he didn't mean it. He would take a bullet for her, just like any of the rest of us would do for anyone on our team. Just like Abrams did for us.

"How do you know that jackass upstairs?" Martinez asked.

She shrugged without making eye contact. "We met in DC."

"And?" Martinez asked.

"And none of your fucking business," Naomi snapped. "Do I ask about your conquests?"

Sloan snorted. "He was a conquest?"

"You don't ask because I don't remember their names," Martinez said with a smirk.

"Except your dad is militia, and he hates Bennett," I said.

She shot me a death glare. "I'm holding a loaded gun. Shut up, or I'll blow out your other knee."

I frowned, but before I could retort, the general waltzed in with his entourage, including Bianca. She still looked pissed.

Kitsch barked for us to stand at attention.

"At ease," the general said. "You're all discharged or retired, anyway," he said, sitting at the head of the table. "Trexler, have a seat. The rest of the team can wait in your quarters."

My team looked to me for approval, and when I nodded, they headed out without another word. I took a seat next to the general and tried my best not to appear too rigid. He didn't seem worried about it.

"I trust your team have all been situated?" he asked.

"All but me, General Tallis."

"Oh?" He eyed Bianca.

She stepped forward, but I stopped her from answering. "I wanted to find my own place."

The general considered my words and then nodded. He had no smile lines, but the bags under his eyes and the scar on his cheek were familiar. "Bianca has gone over the rules? The tour? Procedure?"

"She has. Ad nauseam," I said.

He chuckled, but the expression looked awkward on his face. He cleared his throat and sat up, interlacing his fingers on top of the table. "Lieutenant Saunders will help you familiarize yourself with the monitoring and alarm systems. I'll let you delegate to your team as you see fit."

An air jockey in dress blues stepped forward, a CMC patch sewn to his sleeve. "Good morning, Trexler. I'm Saunders. I'll be training you on the systems. I'll be meeting you in the control room in fifteen."

I scanned him from shined shoes to hat. "Thanks." My first inclination was to offer him a smartass remark about an echo in the room, but the general's vicinity kept my mouth in check. Saunders already looked annoyed that he didn't get my job.

The general scanned the room. "Leave us," he said to Bianca and the few guards still present.

Everyone behind me turned on their heels and filed out of the room. Once the door closed behind them, the general sat back in his chair. "You probably think you're someone special getting this job."

I arched a brow. "Excuse me, sir?"

"You heard me. We have a security team, handpicked by me, downstairs that can more than handle anything thrown at this facility. An army, a Scud missile, a goddamn nuclear bomb. Scott Trexler and his band of PTSD-ridden misfits aren't going to make one shit ounce of difference."

I sat forward. The general smiled. "You bowin' up to me, son?"

"I'm not your son."

He wasn't fazed. Not a single muscle twitched, and one corner of his mouth turned up as if he knew I was fantasizing about using my sidearm to bitch-slap him. "You're here because the son of the Speaker of the House has a crush on your girl."

"*My* girl, sir?" At first I thought he was talking about my sister Hailey. He was making no fucking sense.

"Naomi Abrams."

"Bullshit."

"Not at all. Senator Bennett's great-uncle is Walter H. Bennett. Not only is he on the House Armed Services Committee, but the Oversight and Investigations Subcommittee. Peter could request an indoor pool and trained seals, and it would happen. Do you happen to know which state Senior Senator Bennett was elected in? New Mexico. Little Miss Militia was the girl next door."

"You expect me to believe one of the highest-security government bunkers in the US hired us *PTSD misfits* as security all for a crush? Why not just hire Naomi?" I asked.

The general chuckled. "I've seen stupider things in government." He stood. "The senator can't justify his claim that the Complex needs an additional specialized security team if he just hires one Marine, now can he? Enjoy your paycheck, walk the halls, stay out of the way, and hope Abrams has a soft spot for the junior senator."

"Pardon the frankness, sir, but you've gotta be fuckin' kidding me."

"If you were allowed downstairs in Deep Echo, you'd know I most certainly am not. The people leading this country are finicky toddlers with limitless resources and power. Be glad you're benefiting instead of the alternative."

"Deep Echo, sir?"

"Good day, Trexler."

"It's just Trex," I said, standing.

The general didn't look up, instead staring at a pit in the table. "You're not to inform your team."

"About Deep Echo? Hard to inform them if I don't know what it is. I assume it's another corridor?"

"About the arrangement."

"What? Then why tell me?"

"So you know your place. We have strict rules here, Trex. You will abide by those rules, or you'll learn quickly the alternative I was just talking about. Stay in unrestricted areas, babysit the lab rats wearing the white coats, and smile at the tourists. If you or any of your men get curious, you're looking at a cell, and not the cushy ones the pussy civilians occupy."

"Tourists?"

"The Complex offers limited tours the last Friday of every month. Your job is classified. You don't work here. Your team doesn't work here. Make up any story you want, but you can't claim or admit association. You'll have certain knowledge of this base and its functions. You keep it to yourself and avoid questions. Understood?"

I nodded once.

"Dismissed," he said, remaining in his less-than-formal position. "Close the door behind you."

I returned to our quarters in a daze. My team stopped

what they were doing to wait for me to explain my confused expression. Sloan stepped out of the bathroom, still drying his hands on a paper towel. Kitsch was sitting on the end of a long, metal bench centered between the lockers that lined the walls, waiting for me to speak, and Naomi was standing next to the lockers with her arms crossed, her cheeks flushed. Our names were already engraved into metal plates on our respective lockers, all except Naomi's.

"What the fuck is this?" Naomi said, pointing to the green boxes. "My quarters are across the hall. I'm the only one in there. There's twenty empty lockers in there."

I shrugged.

"No," Naomi said. "The special treatment is bullshit. And don't tell me it's for safety reasons."

"I wouldn't do that, Nomes."

"Because he wants to live," Martinez teased.

I wanted to tell her all she had to do was mention it to Bennett, and she'd likely be assigned a locker in this room by end of day, with a solid gold nameplate and some shit like surround sound and climate control. "I'll mention it."

She threw her pack on the ground. "So tired of this shit."

"Just use mine for now," Sloan said.

"What did the general have to say?" Harbinger asked.

"He told us to walk the halls, and that Saunders will train us on the system. They run a tight ship. We cross the restricted line, and we're out. Maybe worse."

Martinez frowned, two deep lines forming between his brows. "The fuck?"

I glared at him. Martinez was a medic, but he was also the prankster. He was always doing stupid shit like sending the new guys all over the hospital looking for spare fallopian tubes. "Don't go anywhere you're not authorized to go. This is a top-secret facility. Don't jack around. I mean it."

"You heard him," Kitsch said. "Keep it tight. Move out."

Kitsch rushed the men out into the hall, leaving just Naomi and me. I had a hard time looking at her, knowing the information the general had shared with me, and knowing I couldn't tell her put me in a situation I'd never been in before. Trust was paramount, and lying wasn't in our vocabulary.

"You're acting weird," she said.

"I am?" I asked, putting my boot on the bench to retie it. "How's the hotel?"

I smiled, thinking of Darby. "It's good."

"Uh-oh."

"What?"

"You have that look."

"What look?" I asked, annoyed.

"That goofy dreamy look you get when you're using your fake future wife to get out of a second date."

I stood and pointed at Naomi. "She's not fake. It's a real thing. No point in a second date if it's not her."

Naomi rolled her eyes. "Just admit it. You're a commitment-phobe."

"That's not true. I'm very committed. Just to her."

"There is no her."

"There is. And . . . okay, don't tell the guys, they'll give me shit."

"What are you talking about?"

"This woman who works at the hotel. I have a feeling about her."

Naomi couldn't hide her surprise. "Seriously? You think you've finally found her? This"—she gestured with her hands—"epitome of perfection?"

"I never said she was perfect. I just said she was perfect for me."

Naomi pulled open the heavy metal door that led to the hall. "I hope you're right. Would save us all from hearing you whine about her for the next ten years."

We met the rest of the team in the hall and walked to the control room. Saunders was standing at the entrance with the constipated look that seemed to be a permanent fixture on his face. As expected, the control room was vast, with television monitors, computers, and an enormous screen on the wall. Most of the equipment looked as old as I was and older. My team noticed our surroundings and then faced forward. It made me proud that they weren't gawking like the tourists that had likely been ushered in and out like cattle the Friday before. They were all business, looking like badasses in a room full of flyboys.

"I'm sure you've seen monitors before," Saunders said. "Or maybe all they showed you in the Marines is how to shoot a gun and spit properly?"

Martinez's eye twitched, and I stepped forward to keep my men in line and Saunders from a near-death experience. "I'm sure we can handle it, Saunders. Just train us as usual. We'll try to keep up."

Saunders blew out a laugh and turned. Martinez took a step forward, but Kitsch held him back.

"These monitor the entrance. This section, the exterior north; the south is there, the east, the west. Then you have the interiors: Alpha, Bravo, Charlie, Delta," he said, pointing to each monitor. "This is Doherty, Haskins, and Lev. They run this area—the monitors, the fire, earthquake, radiation, and blast sensors. This entire facility is on enormous springs. They run those, too. So basically, they're the saviors of this place."

"Springs," Naomi said, amused. "Are you serious with that shit?"

Saunders crossed his arms over his middle and leaned toward Naomi. With one of her famous warning glares, he backed off.

They were focused on the fire monitor, toggling between exterior thermals and interior temps.

"Why are you monitoring a fire that's at least an hour west, especially since this place is a rock?" Sloan asked.

"We have systems in place. We just don't want the fire getting too close. Then we have to fight the news crew helos and people sniffing around. Not good with us being a top-secret facility and all."

"Oooh, I feel so special," Martinez said.

"Secure that, Martinez," Kitsch said.

"You got this, or you need me to get out the label maker?" Saunders asked.

"We got it," I said.

"Good, because it's time for chow." Saunders made an invisible swirl in the air with his index finger, signaling us to move out. "Deefac is this way." Martinez and Sloan were both fighting a laugh. Saunders had probably been waiting to do that his entire life, and finally got his chance with Marines who'd seen enemy fire. *Chow hall*, *mess hall*, *cafeteria*, or *dining facility* instead of *DFAC* was sufficient. Saunders was trying way too hard to fit in with the big kids.

"It's not necessarily his fault," I said, keeping my voice low. "We're a tough bunch to impress."

"I'm sure his grammy thinks he's a warrior," Sloan said.

The team worked even harder not to burst into laughter, but even Harbinger was struggling. He finally cleared his throat. "All right, all right. Let's not get fired on our first day."

The food was better than anywhere else we'd been, with a buffet that offered dishes like organic steak and shrimp bowls, to ahi poke, to a Kotlet sandwich—whatever the hell that was.

Sloan had the largest pile of food on his rectangular plate, the blue plastic reminiscent of the fifties, as was the rest of the room. Nothing had been updated in the facility for sixty years. It didn't have to be. It had been built to outlast the fallout from a nuclear bomb—so at least two lifetimes.

No one had a lot to say while they stuffed food in their mouths, accustomed to limited time to fill their bellies before we were yelled out of the room—or bombed out. The feeling wasn't wrong. Bianca was standing at the door with a clipboard, impatiently waiting for us to notice her.

Sloan frowned while he chewed, a small dollop of mayo on the corner of his mouth. "Have y'all gotten the feeling they don't want us here? Or am I just being sensitive?"

"No," Naomi said. "They're not rolling out the welcome mat. Bianca said they were nervous about Trex. I think they're nervous because we're outsiders."

"I've felt more welcome in an Iraqi village than here," Martinez said.

"All right," I said. "Pack it up. Don't prove them right. We've been through worse. Stop feeling it and handle it."

The team stood with renewed confidence. Lunch and a pep talk were all it took to give them a second wind after a long morning of orientation bullshit no soldier should have to endure. Physical, emotional, and mental exhaustion, yes. Hours of droning on about rules, regulations, and tech manuals? No fucking thanks.

At day's end, we stepped out, even the fading sun causing us to squint. I felt naked after carrying a rifle all day, then leaving it behind.

"You'll get used to the brightness after leaving the Complex," Bianca said, unaffected. "Just be glad you're not a resident."

"People live here?" Martinez asked.

I couldn't tell if Bianca was annoyed with the questions or indifferent. "Some of the scientists, and the other security team."

"Okay. Let's call it a day," I said, slapping him on the shoulder.

Gravel crunched beneath our boots as we left Bianca standing alone at the entrance, if we didn't count the half dozen MPs.

I shook hands, fist-bumped, and side-hugged my team good night, and then climbed into my truck, letting out a sigh. We'd done it.

Naomi perched her arm on top of her open car door with a smug smile.

I rolled my eyes. "What?"

"Is she there? The girl? At the hotel?"

"Yes, Nomes, she works there."

"You really think she's the one?" she said with a giggle.

"Don't look at me like that," I grumbled. "I'd expect this from the guys. I thought I'd catch a break from you."

She shrugged. "It's just a little…fantastical for you. You're usually more utilitarian than this."

"Do you really think I think my feelings about this are normal? That I've ever thought everyone else walks around waiting for someone they've never met? I just know what I know."

"Would that be *faith*, T-Rex? Very spiritual for an atheist."

"Faith and religion aren't mutually exclusive. And fuck you."

"Fuck you, too," she said. "And good luck, Trex. I hope

she's the one." She smooched at me and winked, then closed the door behind her, starting the engine.

The drive back to the hotel was long. The sun was already tucked behind the mountain range, a few stars beginning to pop out from a blanket of dark blue. My face contorted as I yawned, and I fidgeted with the volume on the radio. Twin headlights grew closer and passed, the yellow lines slipping under and past my truck, the road noise lulling me to a relaxed state, but instead of analyzing the day, Bennett, Bianca, and the general, I could only think of *her*. Two days ago my mind was full of things like getting to the gym, looking at Zillow for new real estate properties, and my new job. I somehow knew Darby would be beautiful. I didn't know she'd be that beautiful.

I parked the truck in the parking lot and followed a few soot-covered, smelly hotshots returning from their cycle up on the mountain. The double glass doors slid open, blowing their stench right in my face.

Darby was standing by a waiting area with a few chairs and two sofas, a fake plant as tall as her, and a flat-screen. She was smiling at the fireworks exploding on the screen, with her arms crossed over her middle.

Without hesitation, I walked behind her and spoke into her ear. "Hey." I said it like we were old friends, and at the same time I was unsettled by the need to talk to her. Just like all the other desperate jerk-offs in the lobby. I was disappointing myself.

"Oh. Hey. I get paid next Friday."

I stared at her for a moment, wondering why she'd chosen that to say to me.

"For the food," she reminded me.

"Oh. I'd already forgotten." I nodded toward the screen. "Is it firework time already?"

"They're just reporting on the upcoming Independence Day plans around the state... well, the ones we're not having," she grumbled. "That's from last year," she said, gesturing to the television. "Not looking good for us." She bit her thumbnail, and I decided it was almost as cute as her accent. "Almost the whole state has outlawed fireworks this year due to the fires. Everything south of Kremmling, wherever that is."

"North of here," I said. "I can't blame them. It's been pretty dry and this is the most active fire season we've had in a while. Do you have plans for the Fourth?" I stepped back. *Stay out of her personal space, Trex. She doesn't know you. You don't know her. Settle the fuck down.*

She shook her head and turned back to face the television. "I work nights after I'm trained."

"That sucks."

She shrugged.

Just one more minute. I'm not ready for it to be over yet. "Been busy today?"

"Not really. Did you go up on the mountain?" She turned to face me, and I felt like I could breathe for the first time all day, and still strangled by the lie I was about to tell. Twelve hours before, I'd been instructed not to disclose my employer.

"Uh... yeah," I said. It wasn't a lie.

"You're pretty clean. I guess you call the shots from the base or whatever it's called?" She thought I was a hotshot, or possibly a Forestry Department guy, and if I told her otherwise, that would lead to questions.

"Yep." Also not a lie.

A small smile pushed up her cheeks, and it was all over. Stavros had mentioned the effect the new hire had on the other guys, but the other guys hadn't been waiting for her since high school. I'd tried to explain to myself all day why I thought she was my girl, but I couldn't. She was beautiful, yes, but it was more than that. It was the way I felt every time I saw her, was close to her, heard her voice. I was already wrapped around her finger. It was part relief, part terror, part excitement.

"You're full of charm today." Her eyes sparkled when she spoke, and her plush lips were a natural dark pink, lips that I had to tear my eyes away from. She was stunning. The thin skin under her eyes was a light shade of lavender, and I wondered how she was going to work until eleven. She looked exhausted. "Hungry?" I asked.

"Stavros brought us sandwiches earlier."

"Glad to hear that." I looked down, fidgeting with the keys in my hand. A new one hung from the key ring: blank, matte black—the master key to all authorized areas in the Complex. I had a job to do, and I needed to crash and get away from this girl. She couldn't be her, anyway. I didn't do complicated. Darby wasn't just intoxicating…she was toxic. I could all but read every fucked-up thing that had happened to her, like they were scrolling credits in her eyes.

"Well. Good night," I said.

"Night."

I stopped at the stairwell door, looking back to see Darby still standing in the lobby. She'd barely noticed I left. I hated that, too. And I hated that I hated it. I had to find my own place. Fast.

chapter seven

Trex

It took a special kind of douchebag for me to feel hate almost immediately after meeting him, but the dude standing next to me in the elevator bay was ogling who he'd just called "the hot piece of ass behind the counter." His eyes met mine, his brows lifted once, and then he targeted the same space where *she* was standing. I didn't have to turn around to know who he was staring at. He didn't look like a hotshot, but I'd seen him in the lobby. Then I recalled him standing in line to be checked in, his hand on the ass of the woman with whom he'd checked in.

He laughed once, looking down. "I can't walk away from that," he said, turning for the front desk.

I jabbed the elevator button with my thumb, silently scolding myself. *She's not your problem. You don't care. You don't care. Just go to your room. Stop caring. Fuck.* The silver doors slid open, and I stepped inside. I sighed, waiting for the doors to close and to forget about the girl behind the desk. When the doors began to close, I pushed against them and rushed out like someone had thrown a grenade inside.

The ass grabber was leaned over the check-in desk, practically cooing at Darby. She looked repulsed, and I couldn't blame her. The dude still had bedhead from nailing his roommate upstairs. There was a white halo around where his wedding ring should've been, and something told me the woman upstairs wasn't his wife.

I glared at him before speaking. "Hey, babe. Before I forget, did you need me to bring you anything from the room?" I asked, trying to keep the rage out of my voice.

She blinked, and for half a second, I wasn't sure she'd play along. She glanced at the man in front of her, and her face relaxed with a smile. "No, but you don't have to go right now. You can hang out here if you want."

The man stood upright. "Oh. Hey," he said, holding his hand out to shake mine.

I just stared at it, then returned my attention to the girl behind the desk.

"Have a nice night, sir," she said.

The man simply nodded before retreating to the elevators.

"Sorry. I had a feeling he was bugging you."

"He was," she said, looking relaxed. Getting hit on put this girl in her element. "Nothing I couldn't handle."

Nailed it. I liked being able to predict things about her, and not like it was a game. I felt a weird sense of pride.

"I don't doubt that for a second. Still...this way was more efficient." I wasn't sure that was the truth, and she wasn't going to say otherwise. She'd probably had a lifetime of shooting men down. "Well...good night."

"Thank you," she said before I made a full one-eighty. "I didn't mean that I don't appreciate the effort."

I hesitated before speaking again. Even one more word, and..."Did you say you work nights?"

"Until eleven this week. I start nights next week after I'm finished training."

"Training? Looks like you're doing this solo already."

She smiled, her eyes twinkling. The siren-call thing she had going wasn't even on purpose, and that's what threw me off. She radiated effortless seduction and innocence at the same time. I'd never seen anything like it, and I was completely fucking sucked in.

"Tilde wasn't feeling well. She left a little early."

"You're a champ. Stavros better never let you go," I said. She smiled, and I kept talking just to see if I could make it happen again. "I'm at work by six a.m., so next week I'll probably see you on the way out."

"Probably." She didn't twirl her hair, she didn't stare too long into my eyes, she didn't chat me up or give me a once-over. Nothing about her signaled that she was at all attracted to me, and still all I wanted was her attention. Just one more smile. One more word. Whatever she would give me, and it was pissing me off.

"What are you doing for dinner?" I asked, not knowing what else to say.

"Why?"

I shrugged. "I could eat."

She laughed, and it was the best thing I'd ever heard. In fact, the more she spoke, the more I was sure she was her. "Why are you always trying to feed me?"

I couldn't help but laugh with her. She had a point. "I don't know. You look hungry, I guess."

"Um...thanks?" She giggled.

"I just meant...uh..." I looked around. Floundering desperately was something new for me. I usually met women at the bar, a club, or a party. This was worse than enemy territory. Of course, the one worth having would be a challenge. "The lobby cleared out fast."

She looked around, seeming to just notice. "Most of the hotshots either have to be up early to head up the mountain or are exhausted from just coming in from fire camp."

"Fire camp? You sound like one of them," I teased.

"Them?"

"Us."

She watched me for a moment. She knew I was lying. *Fuck. I'm better than this.*

"I've talked to over a hundred in the past two days," she said. She was trying to let my comment slide off, proud that I'd pointed out how fast she'd picked up the lingo. One thing I learned at the Bureau was how to read people, and this girl—despite her efforts—was an open book for someone like me. She wasn't from Colorado. By the sounds of it, she came straight from Texas. She wore the same clothes to work—not the typical uniform—and devoured the food I'd given her. She had come to the Springs in a hurry, with whatever money she had on her at that moment, and whatever clothes she was wearing. As much as I wanted to ask why she was running—or who she was running from—I didn't want to scare her off.

I shoved my hands in my pockets. "So…how's the training going? Getting dropped in during a political fire had to be daunting."

"I've heard that a few times. What's a political fire?"

"One the news covers, so they bring everyone in."

"Oh. I didn't know that's what this is. Is that why you're here?" I opened my mouth to speak, but she continued, "Because you were here before the fire."

I tried to keep my face smooth, but even if I didn't believe in any god, lying to this girl felt like a sin. If I'd taken a job anywhere else, I could have told her. It was painful to say the words. "This area has been at high risk for a while."

"Is that what you do? Scout potential fire sites?"

I rubbed the back of my neck. "It's…complicated."

She arched an eyebrow. "Mysterious."

She carried a long, black remote to the sofas and pointed

it at the television, changing the channel. The local news was still reporting on the fire, and she hugged her middle.

"It's okay," I said, just realizing I'd automatically followed her. "It's still miles out."

"Zeke said he's going up soon. Seems like it's getting worse."

"Eating up a lot of acreage, for sure. He'll be fine. He's been doing this awhile. You know him?"

She shook her head. "He's just been nice to me. We're supposed to watch a movie when he gets back."

"Oh," I said, understanding, and then feeling an overwhelming sense of disappointment.

She turned to me, noting my expression. "No, we're um . . . we're just friends."

I nodded, trying not to look too relieved. She made me feel more on edge than being alone, at night, bleeding to death on the southern border of Sudan, and I loved it.

Her cheeks filled and she blew out air.

"You okay?" I asked.

"Just feeling queasy and shaky all of a sudden."

"Maybe your blood sugar is low. Why don't you sit? I'll get you something out of the vending machine."

She shook her head. "The vending machine is full of junk."

"Okay. Anything in the breakfast room?"

She thought about that. "Good idea. Probably cereal or a banana or something in there."

She started to get up again, but I held up one hand. She didn't look in any condition to protest. "You just relax. I'll find you something."

I jogged across the lobby to the dining area, searching through the cabinets. I found two bowls of cereal, a banana, and hiding behind a door was a full-sized refrigerator full of school cafeteria–sized cartons of milk and small cups of vanilla ice cream. "Score," I said aloud, grabbing four cups and two spoons.

I jogged back. Her eyes widened and she scooted to the edge of her seat. "Oh my god, are you serious?"

I set down the ice cream, the plastic spoons, the milk, the bowls of cereal, and the banana. "Knock yourself out."

"We have ice cream?"

I watched with strange satisfaction as she opened the milk and peeled back the cover on the cereal bowl and combined them, then dug in. She poured more milk into a second bowl and finished that off, too, before peeling the banana. She hummed, and I smiled, my entire body relaxing as I watched her eat. She tossed the peel to the table, prompting me to open two cups of ice cream.

"To continental breakfasts," I said, holding my cup toward hers.

She touched her cup to mine. "To Stavros. I'm going to have to pay him back for all of this."

I scooped out a spoonful of creamy white and put it in my mouth. "I don't eat breakfast. It makes up for this."

She tried to stifle a smile but failed, and then she scooped a bite, closing her eyes and savoring every moment the ice cream was in her mouth.

"You look pretty happy right now."

"I am," she said, leaning back against the soft cushion. "You have no idea."

"Is it a good time to ask about your name?"

She turned her head toward me. "My name?"

"Yeah. Maddox tells me there's a story."

"Oh," she said, brushing the crumbs off her pants. "So you were talking to Taylor about me, huh?"

I would've been embarrassed, but the slightest hint of a smile curved the corners of her mouth. "Yep."

Her gaze found its way to the ceiling, and a million memories seemed to play in her mind. "It's really dumb."

"Nothing dumb about that name." *Darby*. It fit her perfectly. Unique without being silly. Not too feminine but effortlessly beautiful. "Where did your parents come up with that?"

She sighed. "There's a film about a drunk Irish guy and leprechauns that they used to watch all the time. I guess I'm named after him. Sort of."

"Darby O'Gill and the Little People?"

She giggled. "You've heard of it? My brother used to say it was awful."

Used to. Damn it. Her brother is dead. Don't be an agent right now, Trex. Don't analyze everything she says and grill her about what doesn't make sense right now. Just listen.

"That's quite a story. Not as intriguing as I thought, but unique, nevertheless. Sean Connery was in that movie, you know. The special effects are quite convincing."

She covered her laugh, still staring up at the ceiling. She looked exhausted. I glanced at my watch. The other kid, Ander, should be coming in to relieve her within an hour, and that meant our conversation would be over.

"Your turn," she said.

I settled into the sofa. "I'm from Kansas, originally. Goodland. My dad, Scott, is a Baptist preacher. My mom, Susanne, plays the piano and leads the choir. I have a little sister, Hailey. She'll be a senior this year."

Darby looked at me as if I were describing the perfect family, and I should have just let her believe that, but I was already being dishonest with her about my career. Lying to her about anything else felt even more wrong.

"Nope, it's not as great as it sounds."

"Really? Because it sounds pretty great."

"My dad was strict. As in 'Spare the rod, spoil the child.' He'd beat me, then beat my mom for crying over it. He's chilled out over the years, though."

Darby winced. She was empathic to the point that she could feel the belt on my mother's skin. Probably because she had felt it in the past. My heart sped up, the hairs on the back of my neck tingled as the unavoidable vision formed in my mind. "Sorry," I said, through my teeth. I took a breath to try to relax my jaw. "Probably too much info."

"No, it's okay." She looked at me differently, like we were on the same team. Trust flickered in her eyes, but I knew it would take more than a story to win her over. "How old were you when it stopped?" she asked.

"When I got bigger than him. I moved out as soon as I was eighteen…" I nearly said "to join the Marines," but caught myself. Telling her about my military career would only lead into how I became a hotshot or worked with the hotshots. I couldn't tell her what I really did, and she didn't know me well enough to know I wasn't bullshitting. My choices were to lie…or to lie. I figured keeping that part of my life as vague as possible wouldn't hurt. "I moved to San Diego for a bit."

She nodded, as if she were remembering with me. "My mom was tough, too. She kept me in pageants until I was in high school." She breathed out a laugh. "It's hard to believe she was a pageant mom, now. All my old pageant friends wish their mothers would stay out of their lives. I can't seem to get her attention anymore."

I frowned. Who could be stupid enough to ignore Darby? "What about your dad?"

Two tiny lines formed between her brows. Pain. She was hiding pain.

"I'm sorry. You don't have to talk about it."

She looked down. "No...it's...nice to talk about it. I haven't, really." She looked down at her melting ice cream, then put it on the table. "I'd just gotten my license the month before. Five-car pileup. We were second. It was ugly. Dad and my brother Chase were the only fatalities."

"Drunk driver?" I asked.

She turned her head to face me. The color had returned to her face. She was feeling better, but the pain in her eyes was undeniable. "No. It was me," she said. "Dad was angry that I had kept something from him. We argued. My full focus wasn't on the road. Looking back, he wasn't angry at me at all. He was angry he'd gone all that time being friendly to someone who wasn't a friend. I know that's what he'd tell me if he was still here. I miss them both a lot."

I tried not to smile. Smiling would be out of place in that moment, but she was a realist like me. There was plenty to beat ourselves up about, but we were also aware of our faults without playing the victim. I respected that about her more than anything.

She continued, "The car in front of us turned into the other lane, and in the next second..." She breathed out like the air had been knocked out of her. "I hit the semi in front of us. They died instantly. I woke up in the hospital four days later. Instead of pageants, I practiced walking after my legs healed. Once Mama got me on my feet, she moved to Louisiana. She didn't even say good-bye." She paused, her expression changing. "You look mad."

I smoothed my features. "Me? No. No, just hate to hear anyone treated you bad."

Her eyebrows raised once. "Then I won't tell you the rest."

My adrenaline began to pump, the way it did when I felt something bad was on the horizon. I couldn't quite pinpoint it, but the urge to be a hero was getting harder to ignore with every word she spoke. She didn't deserve the life she'd had. No wonder she'd run away.

"You can tell me whatever you want. I'll listen."

She smiled. "I bet you would."

"You seem to know something about me that I don't."

Surprised, she settled against the sofa and leaned forward a bit. The fact that I could point out what she was thinking without her telling me was intriguing to her. "Tell me. What do I think I know?"

"That I'm just talking to you for a result."

"And what result is that?" she asked.

I smiled. "I didn't take you for a game-player."

She blinked. "I'm not."

"Then just say it. We don't have to dance around it for an hour. Whoever is the bluntest wins."

"Challenge accepted. There is no way I'm sleeping with you. Ever. I just got out of a not-great relationship and I have a lot going on."

"Like what?"

She hesitated, but finally decided to be as blunt as we agreed to be. "That's none of your business." She seemed pleased to say the words; relieved, even.

"Fair enough. But I'm not chatting with you as a segue. I'm interested in getting to know you. We both know you're probably the most beautiful woman in three states."

"Just three?" She smiled, and I nearly forgot what I was going to say next.

"I was being conservative. But this isn't a recon mission."

"Recon mission, huh? What did you do before the forestry service?"

"None of your business," I said.

She burst out laughing. I had to agree, being this honest was refreshing, and I liked her even more for enjoying it as much as I did, even though it was so far against her Southern upbringing she would have to concentrate to sustain it.

"Do you still talk to her?" I asked. "Your mom?"

"I called her just before I came here. I was engaged." She looked over to check my reaction. "She wasn't in a position to help me, of course, so I bailed. I came to Colorado Springs in my wedding dress."

"Runaway bride?" I asked. That part of her story I wasn't expecting.

Her brows turned in, forming twin lines between them. "Shawn was mean. Real mean. I had to get out of there."

"Did he hit you?"

She peeked up at me.

I breathed out, trying to let go of the violent rage building inside of me. I wanted to kill a man I'd never met. Wouldn't be the first time, but I didn't want to explain any of that to Darby.

"I'm not stupid, you know. I mean, I believed him at first when he apologized. After a while, the apologies were the only peaceful moments. I just...I didn't care about myself then. I didn't think I deserved better. I caused a lot of hurt for a lot of people."

"You still...you still didn't deserve that, Darby. I swear to god you didn't."

"Don't swear to God," she said, her smooth features wrinkling in disgust.

"I'm sorry. I didn't mean anything by it. It just doesn't mean anything to me. I forget."

"What do you mean?" she said, her attention piqued. "You don't believe in God?"

"There are over three thousand gods in human history. Which one?"

"The only one."

I chuckled. "Who says?"

"Isn't your dad a preacher?"

"Yes."

"Then how can you not believe?"

"Because I've read the Bible, and then I researched how it was put together. After that, I researched the history of Christianity. Then, paganism and the Second Temple. Does it offend you? Because I don't hold it against you that you believe in an invisible man in the sky."

She crossed her arms and faced forward. "I wasn't offended until now."

"Does he talk to you? Do you hear an audible voice?"

"Actually, he does." She turned to face me, a grimace weighing down her features. I knew I was pissing her off, but I just couldn't stop. It was like I was finally able to say everything to my father I'd been wanting to say, and it was flowing out of my mouth like word vomit, all to a woman whose company I was quickly becoming addicted to.

"Oh? I mean, that's cool. I'm just surprised. What does god sound like? Your god. I'm assuming he's the only one to talk to you, because . . . you know . . . he's the only one."

Her lips parted as she sucked in a tiny gasp, but the corners of her mouth were turned up. She wasn't angry, just surprised. Talking to Darby was like taking enemy fire, both terrifying and comforting. I felt vulnerable, and at any moment my whole world could end, but I was also in my element. I was good at navigating the maze that was Darby Cooke, as if I had a choice. Everything about her drew me in; her voice was soft and soothing, her eyes calm, that sweet smile set the rage inside of me at ease. I hadn't felt that kind of peace in a long time. I knew I could push her a little out of her comfort zone and she wouldn't hate me for it. As a matter of fact, she was leaned forward, begging me to egg her on.

"It's more like a feeling than an audible voice," she said.

"So, your conscience? So it's really you, not god, you're talking to. Because, believe it or not, that makes you sound less crazy."

Her cheeks flushed a bright pink. "It's called faith. I wouldn't be here if it weren't for God."

"What did he do?"

Her eyes narrowed. "He kept me safe. He got me here."

"He kept you safe," I deadpanned. "So why did you come to Colorado Springs with just the clothes on your back?"

She faced forward, folding her arms across her middle.

"Unless you got in god's Mazda and he drove you here...sounds like you saved yourself."

"I..." She stopped, thinking about my words. "I did. But he gave me the strength."

"So, you're weak? I don't buy that. Someone who travels alone without a plan or enough money for food is pretty damn brave."

"Or stupid," she grumbled.

"You left because you decided not to marry an abusive boyfriend. Sounds pretty smart to me."

"That's because you don't know about the hundreds of poor choices I made before that moment and can't judge me for them."

"I wouldn't anyway."

She smiled at me. Darby was a heaven I could believe in.

"You're a decent human being, Trex. Even if you are an atheist."

I puffed out a laugh. "I'll take that as a compliment."

"I don't like that you're an atheist—whatever you are—but I can still like you, I guess."

"Well, that's not very Christian-like."

She glared at me. "We all come short of the glory of God."

"That's convenient."

"*Ugh!* Why don't you just leave and let me work?"

She was still smiling. She didn't mean it, and that made my insides do backflips and high fives and fist bumps and chest bumps. Darby made me feel like a boy and a super-hero at the same time. I was decent because to her, I wasn't a monster. If she knew more about me, she might change her mind.

I lifted my wrist. "I'd let you work, but you've been off for half an hour."

"I have?" she asked, reaching for my watch.

My arm in her hand was the best thing I'd felt in a long time, and I let the muscles in my arm relax, letting her hang on as long as she needed. Her skin was so soft and warm. The sudden urge to touch the rest of her came over me.

"I have," she repeated. She looked at me and then at the front desk. Ander was leaned against the wall, tapping away at his phone. Her eyes fell to my lips. "An atheist. I'm so dis-appointed in you, Trex."

"We just have religious differences. I don't really think you're crazy. Maybe a little misled."

She leaned in, still staring at my lips. Her breath was sweet, the ice cream still lingering on the tongue I wanted in my mouth. I couldn't have thought of anything else in that moment if I needed to.

"I have a long, bad history with jerks," she said.

"I can pretend to be one long enough to get your attention."

"You have it."

I swallowed. I'd never met anyone like Darby. She was like crack and Christmas.

She paused a few inches from my face, blinking as if a spell had been broken. "I should probably..." She stood, bending down to pick up the trash from our meal.

"I'll get it," I said. "You should rest." I stood. "You look exhausted."

She looked up at me. "Is that a dig at my looks, or are you trying to take care of me?"

I pretended to think about it. "Definitely the latter."

"I am tired."

"Good night, then." I stared down at her, never needing to kiss someone so bad in my life.

"You want to kiss me, don't you?"

"Have you ever been alone with a man who hasn't?"

She thought about that. "Besides my dad and brother? No."

"Maybe it's best that we don't. Atheists are terrible kissers."

"Oh, really?"

"Tastes like sulfur."

She giggled. "I guess that means I'll taste like clouds and sunshine?"

"I was hoping for ice cream," I said.

My answer stunned her for a moment, and then she touched my chest, pretending to look at the buttons on my shirt as she contemplated what to do next. I leaned into her hand until I could feel the warmth of her skin through my shirt. Guilt shadowed her face. She patted me twice, and I knew our night was over.

"I'm sorry. I'm not...I can't."

"Don't apologize. Really. You have nothing to be sorry for."

She looked disappointed as she waved. "Good night," she said, walking to her room.

After she disappeared from sight, Ander looked over at me. "Ouch."

"Shut up, kid," I said, bending down to pick up the left-over ice cream cups, milk cartons, and plastic wrap.

"Stavros said something bad happened to her."

I frowned, carrying the trash to the garbage can, tossing it in. "Yeah."

"Do you know what it was?"

"No," I lied, protecting her secret and myself. Before I knew her, I'd have wanted to kill anyone for hurting her. Now it would be all I could do not to call in favors and hunt the bastard down.

"Well, whatever it was, he was a soldier or something. My grandma said she's sworn off military, firefighters, cops...so it's not you. I can tell she likes you. It's just that she's not interested in your type anymore."

"Have a good night, Ander."

Ander bobbed his head once, and I could feel his eyes on me as I walked to the stairs. Darby was a mess, I was a mess, and continuing to talk to her was just asking for trouble. I couldn't tell her about my job, and even if I could, she would write me off, anyway.

I didn't think I could hate the man she left behind more, but with that one thought, I wanted him dead.

chapter eight
Darby

I hugged the toilet while my body expelled the crackers I'd eaten before getting out of bed—a trick I'd read in one of the pregnancy books I'd checked out from the library the morning before. Most of the day was spent reading *The Girlfriends' Guide to Pregnancy*, stopping only when it was time to eat and then again when I had to get ready for work.

Talking to Trex had felt so natural, so refreshing that I'd forgotten to eat all night. I would gladly listen to his story all over again. I wasn't sure if it was just to spend more time with him, or because I found him fascinating. After a short sleep and a few more crackers, I was still sick. I'd have to set my alarm for three a.m. to eat, so Bean didn't have to wait so long between snacks. There was a grocery store down the road. I could get a few items to hold me over until payday.

It was maddening, knowing that it took just one particularly handsome, seemingly nice man to forget to take care of myself and Bean. From the moment we met, Trex's light blue eyes watched me like I was the center of his universe. His dark, wavy hair and constant five o'clock shadow was so different from Shawn that it was easy to believe the rest of him would be different, too. I shook the thought from my head. I'd begun this journey making decisions for two.

I'd hoped that leaving Shawn and Texas behind would

turn me into a new person. The self-loathing I felt at that moment for still being the same silly, trusting girl I was before forced the tears welling in my eyes down my cheeks. Was I so emotionally crippled that I'd cling to anyone kind to me? Attention was something I was used to. For a long time, I thought it was something I'd done, some signal I was sending telling men to target me, but a few reruns of *Oprah* finally convinced me of something that should've been obvious: What happened to me as a girl wasn't my fault. Simply smiling at or being nice to a man wasn't an invitation. It was frightening to recognize that I was still desperate for someone to trust. Desperation was a strong tether that kept me bound to Shawn for so long. I couldn't let it push me toward someone else.

I flushed the toilet and pushed off the tile floor, washed my hands, and then squeezed a dollop of mint-green toothpaste onto my brand-new toothbrush. As I scrubbed my teeth in small circles, I turned to the side to see if my belly was pooched out yet. It was flat as ever, maybe even flatter. I wondered if I was losing weight, and amid the hundreds of other worries, wondered if the baby was still okay. Through the Internet on the front-desk computer, I found that Planned Parenthood took Medicaid, but I had to get to the Department of Human Services to apply, and it was at least five miles away. Gauging by my walk time to the library, it would take me at least an hour and a half. Only being able to make one errand per day was frustrating.

Someone knocked on the door, and I froze, wondering if it was Trex. He was supposed to be at work, but I couldn't think of who else it would be. I walked into the entry and held one eye shut to look through the peephole. It was Stavros.

"Yes?" I asked.

"Morning, sunshine. Think you can handle things by yourself today? Tilde switched with Ander today, but she has a respiratory virus or something and Ander has a thing, so I need someone for the three to eleven." The chain jingled and the lock clicked as I opened the door. Stavros gasped. "You look like hell. You sick, too?"

I shook my head. "No," I said quickly. "No, I'm fine."

"Maya can work until three. She's typically the day shifter on weekends and she fills in. She needs the hours, so that's covered, thank goodness."

"I'm not sure how to close out my shift. Tilde was supposed to show me that tonight."

"I can help you. Ander said you'll do fine on the night shift. Said you were still in the lobby at midnight."

"Um…"

"I'll make sure he comes in early to help. We're expecting more hotshots, anyway."

I was relieved he didn't need me to admit that I wasn't ready to close out on my own. "More hotshots?"

He nodded. "Don't worry. You've got this."

I nodded, watching Stavros make his way back down the hall. My stomach lurched, and I ran to the bathroom, falling to my knees and heaving. Nothing came up, and I hadn't closed the lid from the last time I was sick. Bean was determined to remind me I was pregnant. Alone, on the floor, sick and tired, it was easier to feel like I'd traveled to another planet rather than another state. Downtime had mostly consisted of reading and sleeping, but moments like this reminded me I had no one. I wondered if Shawn was looking for me, if Carly was worried, if Mom had even bothered to call. The wives on base had probably created twenty different scenarios for why I left, what happened to me, and where I went.

I flushed the toilet again, closed the lid, washed my hands, and brushed my teeth for a second time. The clock on the nightstand read noon. No wonder Stavros was surprised I'd just woken up, and no wonder I was so sick. I had to feed Bean.

I got dressed and walked down the hall, hoping there was still food left over from breakfast. As soon as I rounded the corner, I smelled it. Greasy, cheesy pizza. The hotshots were hovering around long, rectangular tables covered with one pizza box after another.

"Darby," Zeke called.

"What's all this?" I asked.

"Lunch, compliments of the City of Colorado Springs. Hungry?"

"Starving," I said. "Can I really?"

"Yeah," he said, leading me to the tables. He grabbed a plate and put it in my hands, the Styrofoam feeling flimsy in my hands. "Are you a pepperoni fan? There's one with mushrooms, too...but...gross. We got sausage. We got Hawaiian." I made a face, and he laughed. "Supreme?"

I nodded. "And pepperoni. With mushrooms, please."

Zeke's smile faded, and he loaded my plate like he disapproved of my choice, and then walked me to a table. "Water or soda?"

"Water, but you don't have to..."

Before I could protest, Zeke was already halfway across the room, greeting his crew as they passed. Zeke returned, sitting next to me with a bottle of water. To his chagrin, another hotshot sat next to me, too.

"Who's this?" he asked.

"Darby. Go away," Zeke grumbled.

I took a bite, ignoring their spat. In that moment, the pizza and only the pizza was important.

"Randon Watts," Zeke's friend said, holding out his hand. I didn't take it, instead shoving a big bite in my mouth.

"She's eating, Watts. Leave her alone."

Watts chuckled, watching me with amusement. "Like a champ. Is she training for a pizza-eating contest?"

Zeke turned his attention to me, his eyebrows shooting up. I was one slice down and starting on the second one.

"Are you from here?" Watts asked. He had the hotshot beard, but his dark sideburns and about two inches of the hair above his ears were shaved, all the way to the other ear. The hair on top was longer. He watched me with the familiar spark of desire in his dark eyes, even as I shoved food into my face.

I shook my head, chewing. Mama would have grabbed my face until I spat the food out, forcing me to start over and eat like a lady...even now. But Mama's priority was Frank and his son, and my priority was Bean. It didn't matter if I behaved as a lady, or if she forgave me for taking Dad away from her, or for taking her only son, the light of her life—and mine—my little brother, Chase. My sins before were no longer important, or even if I made things right. Bean was my salvation in more ways than one.

"No," I said, taking another bite. I imagined I looked like someone marooned on a deserted island for a decade, chewing quickly and checking my surroundings like a wild animal.

Watts raised an eyebrow. "Okay, then. I'll just go check in with Chief."

"You do that," Zeke murmured. When Watts left, Zeke turned to me. "I'm sorry about that." He handed me a napkin.

I used it, swallowing the last bite of pizza before I spoke. "Why are you sorry?"

"I know you don't like people bugging you, and it seems

like every time we talk, one of the guys tries to be funny. They're just giving me a hard time."

"Why?"

He shrugged. "Because I'm talking to a pretty girl, I guess. I don't really...date."

"This isn't a date."

"No, I know," he said, fumbling for words that might save him. "It doesn't matter how many times I explain. They enjoy it."

"They enjoy giving you a hard time? Why don't you date?"

"I haven't since...Damn, this is weird."

I turned to face him, wiping my mouth one last time. "Only if you're a serial killer or something."

"What? No. Nothing like that. It's just...my ex...we'd been dating since the eighth grade. We broke up not long after I joined the Alpines a couple of years ago."

"Oh," I said. The part of me that had been trying so hard not to care was failing. The look in Zeke's eyes brought to the surface something I'd buried deep inside. It doesn't matter how someone disappears from your life. Whether it's death or hate or something in between, loss is loss. "And you haven't dated since?"

"Once or twice. Nothing's stuck."

"Well," I said, gathering our empty plates and dirty napkins. "It wasn't you."

"It was the job. It was a lot of things," he said.

"Still not you." I patted him on the shoulder with my free hand before heading toward the trash can.

"We still on for a movie?" he asked.

I paused. "Uh...I work three to eleven until next week. When I start my regular shift, I can."

"What is your regular shift?"

"Nights. Eleven to seven."

"Ouch. Well, I think we go out tomorrow morning. We'll catch one when I get back."

I remembered what Stavros said about some of the men not coming back. I tossed the trash into the bin and returned to Zeke. He stood, and I hugged him. He wrapped his arms around my middle and squeezed me tight. Having another man's arms around me felt strange, and for half a second, an old worry surfaced. Shawn wouldn't see. He had no idea, and he never would. I tightened my grip around Zeke's neck and then released him, looking up into his eyes. "You be careful out there."

"Yes, ma'am," he said, a satisfied grin on his face.

I returned to my room, gathering the few dirty clothes I had, and taking them to the laundry. The large room full of washers and dryers and folding tables was just a few doors down from my room, and the staff eyed me as I took my things to an empty machine.

"Is this okay?" I asked the woman closest to me. She was about Mama's age, with bronzed skin and dark wrinkles around her mouth, the kind smokers get. One of her front teeth was bordered with gold, and her dark, frizzy hair easily escaped from the banana clip in her hair.

"You're the new girl?" she asked, with a thick Mexican accent.

I nodded.

"Go ahead," she said, nodding to the washer in front of me. "Be back in fifteen minutes."

"Thank you," I said, tossing in the clothes and then looking around for detergent.

The woman handed me a pastel pink bottle. "Goes here, like this," she said, pulling out the soap bin. She showed me where to pour the detergent, then she shut the bin and showed me which buttons to push.

"Thank you so much," I said. "What's your name?" I glanced down to her badge. She covered the name, Ann, before speaking. "Sylvia." She pointed to the others. "Juana, Maria, and that's my daughter, Rosa."

"Nice to meet you. All of you. I'm sure we'll see each other again."

"You're the one staying in one hundred?" Sylvia asked.

"I am."

"I can tidy it up for you. If you'd like."

"Oh, that's so nice. I think it's okay for now."

"You sure?"

I nodded. "I'll be right back." I pushed out the door and rushed to my room, using the key before shoving at the door. I couldn't get to the bathroom fast enough. The smell of the detergent made me instantly nauseous. I stood in front of the toilet, trying to calm my stomach, but with uncontrollable force, my stomach heaved, and all the greasy pizza I'd just inhaled projected from my mouth and splashed so hard in the toilet, the water splashed my face.

Once it was over, I sat with my back against the wall, the floor feeling wonderfully cool beneath my backside. As soon as my clothes were finished, I was going to take another nap, try to eat again, and then go to work. All I wanted to do was to lie down and close my eyes and sleep until this part of the pregnancy was over. I touched my stomach and spoke aloud: "Give me a break, Bean. Please? I'm trying my best."

chapter nine

Trex

The sun was barely peeking over the mountains when I pulled next to the first security stop at the Cheyenne Mountain Complex. Gerald, the first-shift security for Gate One, nervously scanned my badge and gestured for me to move on.

The two miles of gravel road that led to the second gate were bordered with a twelve-foot fence topped with spiraled barbed wire and guarded by armed security every two hundred yards. The men and women were dressed in fatigues and carried semiautomatic weapons. It made me wonder if this was a haven for the warworn, or a place for someone with a higher calling to waste their talents.

Like my team, for example.

Karen cleared me for Gate Two. A traffic arm barrier raised, and metal spikes retreated into the ground. I drove my '78 Toyota Land Cruiser past an outer parking lot and administration building to approach the third gate and then the entrance, a short man-made tunnel poking out from the mountain with CHEYENNE MOUNTAIN COMPLEX in white painted metal letters at the top. I drove through, into the darkness, past the warning signs to follow the two-lane and signs that led to the designated parking for our department.

I was the first of the team to arrive, and I parked my truck in the center of five other empty spots.

The engine sputtered and died once I twisted back the key, and I sat alone, thinking about my night with Darby. Even after I turned in, I slept like shit. The thoughts in my head were too loud to sleep. I jumped out and pulled my pack from the back seat.

Once my team arrived, we walked into the Complex together, chatting about our evening. I tried to stay out of the conversation, but Naomi pegged me before I could finish the combination on my locker.

"You're quiet, T-Rex. What's up?"

"Me? Nah."

Martinez turned to look at me. "Spill it."

"I'm just…uh," I sighed. "I'm staying at the hotel for now. Looking for a place. There's all these forestry crews there for the fire. The Maddox twins are two of them."

"The guys you were investigating for the feds?" Naomi asked. "They giving you trouble? Give me two hours. It'll look like a murder-suicide."

"Slow your roll, Nomes. Let's get settled before you start a killing spree. They're good guys. The whole family, really. They've been cool. It's not them."

"Who is it?" Sloan asked. "Because you're vexed."

"Vexed? What the fuck, Sloan?" Martinez said.

"Shut up, man. It's okay to not dumb everything down all the time," Sloan snapped.

"You sayin' you need to dumb it down for me?" Martinez asked, taking a step forward.

"It's a girl," I blurted out.

"A…what?" Naomi asked.

"A woman. She's the new front desk clerk at the hotel. She's like a runaway bride. She bounced right before promising the rest of her life to her scumbag abusive fiancé. But he's military. She's sworn off us all."

"Well, that's just stupid," Naomi said. "Like any large group, you're going to have your heroes and your villains. My husband lived and breathed the Marines, and he was the best man on the planet, next to you."

"That he was," I said, taking a moment to miss my friend. He'd had a wife at home who he loved more than any of us, yet he jumped on that grenade without a second thought. I strived every day to deserve that.

"Hey," Naomi said, touching my cheek. "Get out of there." She slapped me once and then held her hand against the place she'd just assaulted. Naomi did that a lot, only hitting me hard enough to bring me back to the present. She touched my shoulder like Abrams used to do. "It happened. It's the way he wanted it. Come back to the present."

I nodded, turning away from her to put my things in my locker.

"Hey, Nomes. Look at that," Martinez said. He pointed up, seeing a tag with ABRAMS etched perfectly into the metal screwed into the top border of the locker next to his.

"Son of a bitch," Naomi said. She reached up and touched it with a smile. "They actually moved me from the little girls' room. Matt would have hated this—having a locker... a lunch break."

"Damn sure would have. But he would have loved paying off that FJ of yours with his sign-on bonus like you just did. Let's get rolling. Full battle rattle. Rounds in ninety seconds," Kitsch said, slinging the nylon strap of his weapon across his chest, checking his sidearm and sliding it into the holster, as well as touching the Taser and hunting knife in each of their spots to double-check he was locked and loaded. It was overkill for the job, but then again, the Complex was the type of facility that required nothing until you needed everything.

"Trexler, we've got a four ninety-nine on the south side of the Complex two clicks from the wire," someone said through the radio. Sounded like Saunders.

I pinched the small square clipped to my collar. "Copy that." I looked to Kitsch and he nodded.

"All right. Rounds can wait. Let's load up."

Sloan looked lost, and Harbinger sighed. "The Complex has dedicated codes. A four ninety-nine is a potential perimeter breach. Read your manual."

Sloan nodded. "Yes, sir."

We walked quickly to the Charlie corridor, took an elevator one level down, and stepped out into the massive room that served as an equipment hold. We had everything from joint light tactical all-terrains—Jeeps on steroids—to tanks, armored combat earthmovers, and Hercules recovery vehicles. We jogged to our assigned Humvee and I jumped in the driver's seat, with Harbinger copiloting. Naomi and Kitsch were in the back seat, Martinez and Sloan in the back.

I barreled down the dirt road and crossed through the terrain to the site where surveillance caught a blur of three targets, the tires throwing rocks and dust. The smoke from the fire had been a plume the week before, now it was more like a blanket being lifted and spreading in the stratosphere. We stayed alert. Besides the blind hills, there weren't many trees on that side of the mountain, making it easy to spot any unauthorized persons.

"Twelve o'clock," Naomi said.

I slammed on the brakes, pushing a brown cloud around us. When the air cleared, three kids were standing inches from the bumper of the Humvee.

Martinez and Sloan jumped out, barking for the kids to put their hands in the air. Two shaggy-haired boys about fifteen, and a girl. She was blond, reminding me of my little sister. Their faces were smudged, their hair covered in a light blanket of dust.

"Easy, Sloan," I said, stepping out of the driver's side. "Where the hell did they come from?"

Naomi pushed her sunglasses down her nose and looked down. "They came right over the ridge. Good thing, too, or we would have gone for a ride."

I leaned over, noticing the rocks below. "Ouch. It all looks the same out here."

"I'm driving next time," Harbinger said.

"Was that a joke? Are you making jokes now?" I asked, closing one eye against the sun.

Naomi nudged one of the boys' boots with hers. "What are you guys doing here?"

"Th-there's a party. We took a wrong turn, I think," one of the boys said.

"No shit," Sloan said, still on guard. "A party at six a.m.? Nice try."

"It's over, dumbass," the girl said. "We were walking home."

Naomi smiled. "I like her." She grabbed the girl by the back of the collar and yanked her up. "Let's get them back where they belong."

I radioed in. "Gerald, this is Trex, come in."

"Gerald, sir, hear you loud and clear."

"Have the Colorado Springs police meet us at Gate One for pickup of trespassing juveniles. Just have their parents pick them up from the station."

"Copy that, sir."

Martinez grinned. "I think Gerald likes you."

"Shut your pie hole, Martinez. Put the small one in the back."

"And this one?" Sloan asked, jerking up the tall, lanky

one. The poor kid looked like he was about to shit himself, but I had a feeling they wouldn't venture so close to the Complex next time.

"They all go in the back. Check 'em first. Naomi?"

"Got it," she said, bringing the girl to the side.

"Get your hands off me, bitch!" the girl yelled.

We all froze, waiting for Naomi to snap the girl's neck. Or at the very least, slap the shit out of her. It took Naomi a moment to process that someone had the balls to speak to her that way—I was sure it had been years, if ever—and then Naomi burst out laughing. "I have crossed paths with my fourteen-year-old self. Incredible." She searched the girl and pointed to the back of the Humvee. "I'm guessing your mom hasn't spanked you lately, but if you don't get your ass up in that vehicle, I'm going to do it for her... and it will last you a while. Move. Now!"

The girl startled and scrambled into the back with Martinez and her friends.

Sloan gestured for Naomi to go next, then he followed.

I slammed the door and revved the engine.

"You gonna try to fly off the side of the mountain again?" Harbinger asked.

"Suck my dick, John," I said.

Harbinger laughed once, and then his back pressed against the seat as we took off toward Gate One.

"Colorado is good for you, I think. That's a smile and a half in the same morning."

His smile faded, and he grabbed the handle above his seat, bouncing as we rolled across the rocky terrain.

We dropped the kids off at Gate One, and I drove the team back to the warehouse. The elevator closed behind us, and it was strangely quiet on the way up. The elevator dinged just before it opened, and we stepped out into Charlie corridor.

"All right," I said, holding my rifle to my torso. "Kitsch, Sloan, you've got Alpha and Beta. Harbinger, Martinez, you've got Charlie and Delta. Check in with Saunders in surveillance at oh-eight-hundred. Nomes, you're with me in Echo. See you all in the office at ten, we'll reassign and then meet for chow. Keep comms open."

"Yes, sir," everyone said in unison.

We spread out, walking in opposite directions. When the boots of the others fell away and Naomi and I entered Echo, she asked the question I expected. She knew as well as I did her assignment to make rounds with me wasn't random.

"So? The girl..." Naomi said.

"Yeah. I ended up staying up and talking with her. Then when I finally went to my room, I couldn't sleep for shit."

"Why's that?"

"Her ex, man. He put hands on her. She ran away, came here with nothing. She knows no one. No family, really. Her dad and brother were killed in an accident a few years back."

Naomi sighed. "Sounds like a lot of baggage, Trex. Are you actually attracted to her, or are you trying to save her?"

"That's the thing. She is gorgeous. I mean...intoxicatingly beautiful." I stole a glance at Naomi, who had the expression I expected. "And all those fucking hotshots in that hotel want her. She wants nothing to do with any of us, but she's sweet about it, you know? And I don't wanna be that guy."

"So, you think it's just that everyone else wants her?"

"That's the problem. I don't think that's it at all."

Naomi stopped, her brows pulled together. "You really like this chick. How much time have you spent with her?"

I kept walking. "Like, none. It's the stupidest fucking thing ever."

Naomi shrugged. "You can't control chemistry, T-Rex. You can't explain it. Hell, Matt was a cowboy. Quiet. I could have a conversation with an inanimate object as easily as I could with him. He wasn't funny. Wasn't particularly interesting or a show-off. Not my type at all."

"So why did you fall for him?"

She smiled. "Because he was a good man, humble, he didn't play games...and he had a nice ass."

I chuckled. "That's it?"

"That's it. I mean, yeah, it was nice that he knew his way around a rifle and he wasn't intimidated by me at all. We had a few things in common. But he had his moments. Occasionally, he was charming. It really came down to him being interested in me, the way he treated me, and something else I can't explain. Has to be chemistry. Or maybe we were meant to be."

"You were definitely meant to be. I've never seen a man love a woman the way Matt loved you, Nomes."

She looked up. "He's up there somewhere, still loving me, just like I'm down here, still loving him."

I nodded. I wasn't about to argue. If our energies continued in some way, I didn't doubt that Matt was somewhere, still in love with his wife.

"It doesn't have to be anything specific, Trex. You can like her for no reason. You can even like her a lot for no reason. Maybe it's just that you don't know the reason yet."

"Thanks, Nomes. I knew you'd help me figure it out."

We reached a T and turned right. The air changed, prompting Naomi to hold her rifle closer.

"I think it's those experiments they were talking about," I said. "I'd always heard it was a bunch of space and missile nerds here."

"A lot more than missiles going on here."

We stopped at a large door, a red and white striped banner stretching across the middle, along with a half dozen warning signs. I touched my badge to the black square on the wall out of curiosity. It blinked red, and a single, low-toned horn sounded.

We both took a step back, a small screen near the badge reader lit up, revealing a group of armed men, standing—I presumed—on the other side. One of them stepped forward to press a button on a panel on their side, allowing his voice to be heard on ours.

"Back away, Trexler. You're unauthorized for this area."

"Oh. This is Deep Echo? It's uh... not that deep."

"I've experienced deeper," Naomi said with a straight face.

The men on the screen smiled, smug. "You're nowhere near Deep Echo. Turn around."

"I was told I had access to the entire facility with the exception of Deep Echo," I said. I wasn't sure if I should yell or not, but the men on the other side seemed to hear me just fine. I raised my voice, anyway.

"Take it up with the general. Turn around, Trexler. Last warning."

It took everything I had not to ask what they would do if I didn't. Not a single one seemed to have a sense of humor.

"Let's go, Trex. We'll discuss it with Bianca." Naomi tugged on my vest, and I followed her. "What the hell was that?" she asked once we were out of hearing range. "Deep Echo?"

"I don't know. Above my pay grade, apparently."

"Some weird shit going on in this place. A lot weirder than I thought. So. What are you going to do about the girl?"

"Darby?" I asked, jarred by the sudden change of subject.

"Her name is *Darby*?" Naomi asked. I nodded. "That's unique."

"It's a pretty cool story, too."

Naomi smiled. "You did talk. About, like... real shit."

"Yeah," I said with a grin. It faded. "She won't date soldiers. Her ex is military."

"You're not a soldier. You're a Marine."

"C'mon, Naomi. How would you feel if someone got you on a technicality?"

"I'd kick his ass."

"And we can't talk about this job. She thinks I'm in the Forestry Department."

"You didn't correct her?" she asked.

I shook my head. "She'd ask questions that I can't answer, Nomes."

"She's a runaway who left behind an abusive guy, a dead father and brother, Mom's not really in the picture, and she blames all military for the ex's behavior. You'll have to lie by omission just to date her. You still think this is a good idea?"

I thought about it for a second. "She's my girl—the one."

Naomi shook her head. "You're going to lose her."

"What should I do, then? This is my job. I have an entire team depending on me. I can't walk away from it, and I know it sounds crazy, Nomes…but I've said for years I'd know it was her when I met her. It's her."

"I've always thought you were brave. You know that. I'm not sure that's what this is. If you really think she's the girl you've been talking about since I met you, you're risking a lot."

"You'll get it when you meet her."

Naomi turned to me, flattered. "I'm going to meet her? You must really like her. Because you're going to have to do some verbal acrobatics to explain to her who I am."

I frowned. "I didn't think about that."

"Maybe I'm an old fed buddy?"

"She won't date military, cops, firefighters…that probably includes federal agents."

"Oh. You are fucked. You are totally fucked. She's going to want to know about your past at some point. Then, when she finds out—and she will—she'll hate you for not telling her and you'll be heartbroken."

"She might not even like me, Nomes."

"Is she stupid?"

"No," I said, making a face.

"Then she likes you. And she probably already knows something's not right, that there's stuff you're not telling her."

"She definitely does. I'll explain it to her. Somehow... later. I just want her to get to know me first so she knows I'm not what she thinks we are."

"How are you going to explain if you can't tell her about the job?"

"I can't tell her about the Complex. I can tell her I'm a civilian contractor."

"She's still going to lump you in with military. I'm sorry, Trex. I'm just trying to prepare you."

I cringed. "Fuck, you're right. This is going to be bad."

"You should bail now."

I frowned. "I should. But I can't."

"I know," she said, nudging my arm.

chapter ten

Darby

I pushed off the floor. The next steps were becoming all too familiar: flush, faucet, soap, rinse, toothbrush, toothpaste, scrub, spit, rinse. The only thing surprising was that I was hungry again.

Back in Laundry, I pulled my wet clothes and towels from the washer and put them in the dryer. I took a few steps back and sat in a white molded plastic chair that looked like the ones I used to sit in in elementary school.

"You don't look so good," Sylvia said. The others showed their agreement with nodding heads.

"The um ... There was pizza in the lobby today. It didn't sit right with me."

"Pizza," she deadpanned.

Sylvia didn't believe me, and I couldn't blame her. My forehead felt damp, and I was sure I was a lovely shade of green. The dryer began to spin my pants, shirt, and undergarments in a gentle rhythm. Laundry was calming, even though the baby powder/lavender/old-lady smell made me want to hurl.

Sylvia didn't pry. She and her colleagues went back to folding and ironing, speaking in hushed Spanish.

"Senorita?" Rosa said softly, pressing on my shoulder. "Senorita?"

I blinked my eyes, seeing that the clothes in the dryer had settled at the bottom. I roused, looking around. Rosa and I were the only ones still in Laundry.

"I'm sorry. It's almost three. I needed the dryer, so I pulled your clothes."

I sat up straight. "Almost three?"

Rosa simply shrugged and pointed to an empty table. My clothes were folded perfectly, freshly pressed.

"Did you do this?" I asked, taking them off the table. Rosa nodded, and I sighed. "Thank you. Thank you so much! I have to go! I'm late! Sorry!"

Without waiting for Rosa's response, I ripped open the door and rushed down the hall to my room. The clock on the nightstand read fifteen minutes 'til three.

I pulled up my hair and jumped in the shower, rinsing off in record time before jumping out to quickly shimmy my skin with the towel. In two minutes, I'd brushed my teeth and washed my face, and then I ran into the bedroom to get dressed.

"Thank you, Rosa," I said, putting on my lightly starched slacks and shirt. She could've let them sit in the dryer, and I would be going to work in wrinkled clothes. I brushed my hair and put on my black flats and checked that I had my room key before letting the door slam behind me.

Before I reached the lobby, I could hear the low rumble of chatter, even more than the day before. As suspected, the room was full of hotshots, some back from their cycle at the mountain, others readying to head out, some just arriving.

Maya was still working on a line waiting to check in, and I jumped in to help. We didn't speak, we didn't take time for introductions, instead just working to get the guests their key cards so they could put their things away before rejoining their fellow hotshots. Maya's short, dark hair batted at her cheeks every time she moved, her glasses setting on her full, apricot-blushed cheeks. Her makeup made her look more beauty blogger than front desk clerk, and I made a mental note to ask her if my theory was right later.

After an hour of working together, we conquered the line, and Maya sighed. "Holy hell, that was nuts. Thanks for the help."

"Thanks for staying."

She shrugged. "Stavros told me I'd probably need to. I'm Maya," she said, holding out her hand. I took it, surprised by her firm grip.

She turned and bent down, bringing up with her a purse and a clear makeup bag. It was full to the brim with powders, eye shadows, mascaras, foundations, brushes, concealers, highlighters, and everything else I'd ever seen in a Sephora.

"Wow," I said.

"Yeah." She chuckled, unzipping the top. "I don't even use half of it. I've been meaning to get rid of it. Hey…do you wear makeup?"

"I…"—I shook my head—"used to, but can't afford any right now. It's on the list."

She stared at my face. "My God, the things I could do with those cheekbones and eyes. And your brows…" She reached, and I backed away.

"Need work. I know. I sort of had to leave in a hurry."

"Oh, shit. Was it a fire or something?" She looked down at her makeup bag. "If there were a fire, I'd grab this first."

I laughed, but she was serious. She dug into her bag, pulling out items with the seal still on them, and a few sample-sized pieces. "Here. You can't just not have makeup."

"What? I can't take yours."

"I haven't used them. I have a YouTube channel with like

forty thousand followers. Companies send me free shit all the time."

"A YouTube channel?"

She grinned. "Yeah. I tell stories and discuss random topics. Sometimes I do makeup tutorials. It's so lame, but people love to hear about my misery."

"Oh. I'm sorry."

She laughed. "I make up most of it. Whatever, it's for followers, right? Just look up Maya Bee."

"Maya...?"

"Bee," she said, still picking through her bag. "It's short for Berkowitz. No one is going to the trouble of searching Maya Berkowitz on YouTube. That's why there's Miranda Sings, and the goddess of YouTubers, Jenna Marbles. There. You have the basics. And some kickass highlighter. Highlighter should be a basic. And baking powder. It's my jam."

"I don't..."

"It lightens up your under eye, and honey...you need it. Look at my YouTube channel. I do a whole review on it. The foundation might be a half shade off, but if you'd go outside once in a while it would match."

"Thank you," I said, looking down at the pile of makeup on the desk.

"Okay, I'm off. Have a good night."

"You, too," I said, baffled. No one had ever given me anything before. Certainly not a stranger. I wanted to tell her that I did go outside, that I walked everywhere I went, but then I'd have to explain why I looked like death, so I let her walk away.

Maya waved to Stavros, who was shaking something behind the bar for a bleach blonde getting plenty of attention from the hotshots. Stavros looked at me, and jerked his head up, signaling for me to come over. I complied, wondering if he was going to high-five me for triumphing over the line, or scold me for barely making it on time. By his expression, it could have gone either way.

"Here," he said, setting a bottle of water on the table.

I picked it up and looked over the label. "Do you want me to bring this to a room?" I asked.

"No, I want you to drink it. You look a little green. And parched."

"Oh," I said, twisting open the cap. I took a small swig, then several large ones. I hadn't realized how thirsty I was. "Thank you."

Stavros nodded once. "I know you said you felt fine, but I can see that you don't. The guys over here were talking about it. The dark circles, the drooping eyes. You look like Tilde. I'd send you home, but you live here, and I have no one else."

"I'm really okay."

A small smile cracked his hardened expression. "I appreciate you being a trouper. I really do. If we weren't full of alcoholic firefighters, I'd take over for you so you could rest. Just...take it easy. Nothing extra."

"Thanks, Stavros," I said, noting his guilty expression before I made my way back across the lobby with the bottle of water in hand.

"I've got some Pepto pills in my room."

I looked up with a tired smile. It was one of the hotshots I'd heard called Sugar. All I wanted was a nap. "Thanks, I'm okay. The water is helping."

"You got a stomach virus or something?" he asked. He was enormous, a tad bigger than Maddox, but I could tell outside of fire season, he was even more massive. His clean-shaved head made him look more like a Marine than a firefighter. He would be intimidating if it weren't for the kindness in his eyes.

"No, just trying to adjust to the elevation, I think."

He nodded again, peeking over his shoulder, as I reorganized the front desk for the second time since clocking in.

"Everything okay, Sugar?"

"Yes, ma'am. Can I hang out here a minute?"

"Of course. Are the boys bothering you?"

He shook his head. "No, ma'am. I'm going out soon, and my moms is calling. She's a worrier. She cries. A lot. I can't go back to my room because Fish is rooming with me, and he's a good guy, but he loves to give me grief about my moms. She's all alone at home. It's just us. She wants me to live my life, but she . . ."

"Worries."

He nodded.

"You can take all the time you need."

His cell phone rang a quiet tune. "Thank you. Hey, Mom. Yep, still at the hotel. No, not going out today. They're thinking in the morning."

I could hear her fussing from where I stood, and it made sense why he wanted to stand across the room. She was just telling her son how much she loved him, but her voice was shrill, and it made me nervous. I couldn't imagine how it made Sugar feel. I was going to give him his space, but then decided he was standing beside me for a reason. If I walked away, the other guys would likely take my place and listen in.

I pretended to be busy with the computer, trying not to hear Sugar sweetly comfort his mother, reassuring her about his turn on the mountain. His deep voice was cathartic, lulling the nausea I was feeling away, helping my shoulders to relax and my mind to quiet down. I barely noticed Trex approach my desk.

"Hey there," he said, hope in his eyes.

"Hi," I said, trying not to look so happy he was back. I looked at my watch. "Is it that time already?" I felt awkward around him now. Forget the butterflies, cannons were going off in my stomach, and I was sure that couldn't be good for Bean. *Stop it*, I scolded myself.

"Is this guy bothering you?" Trex asked. He was joking, but I still felt a need to defend poor Sugar. "He's talking to his...sister."

Sugar winked at me.

"You're a terrible liar," Trex said with an amused smile.

Sugar plugged his other ear and turned his back to Trex, keeping his voice low. "Yes, Mama, I will. Yes, ma'am." He waited while she prayed loudly over him, sounding like a sermon during an intense revival. "Amen. Thank you, Mama. Love you, too. Bye now." He slipped the phone in his pocket and nodded to me, looking sheepish. "You see now why I take the calls away from the guys."

"Fuck 'em if they can't understand you're a good son," Trex said, matter-of-fact.

Sugar thought about his words and nodded once. "You're right. I shouldn't be ashamed. I'm ashamed that I'm ashamed."

Trex patted Sugar's enormous shoulder. "That sounds exhausting. You need to let all that go, man. Be you unapologetically. Love your mom, be a good son, let the others hear her be comforted by her prayers. It might do them some good."

Sugar nodded. "Thanks, Trex."

Trex nodded once, watched Sugar walk away with a smile on his face, and then turned to me. "Speaking of being exhausted, I'm sorry I kept you up talking for so long."

"I knew better," I said. "I'm a big girl. I know when to say good night."

"I must have been decent company, then."

I tried not to smile. I tried really, *really* hard, but it happened, and it gave everything I was trying not to feel away. That only made me disappointed in myself, how I could run away from one man and not take enough fear and anger with me to keep me from falling right back into something else. Maybe. Whatever this was.

"I mean, I guess," I said, looking down.

Trex's confident smile wavered. "Everything okay?"

I felt my cheeks flush and my hands shake. This seemed like a confrontation, even though it wasn't. The parts of me ingrained to please and make others happy were warring with my need to raise my baby independent of a man—independent in general. "Yes…I'm just…you're really nice."

"Uh-oh."

I breathed out a laugh. "No, it's not that."

He winced. "Is this the *it's not you it's me* speech? Because we haven't even been on a proper date yet—even though last night was pretty great."

That damn smile stretched across my face again. "It was. It was great."

He watched me for a moment, no doubt trying to use his superhuman people-reading skills to decide what I meant instead of what I was saying. "Darby…I don't know what you're running from, but it's not me."

I shook my head. "I'm not running anymore."

"Like I said…you're a terrible liar."

"Maybe I just don't like you."

He took a moment to answer. For the first time, he seemed unsure. "Why not?"

"I don't know," I said, flustered. It hurt me to see his reaction, and that made me panic. "You don't believe in God, for one."

"You don't like me because I don't believe in god? Jesus hung out with the scum of the earth in the Bible. Jewish tax collectors. Do you know how much the Jews hated men like Zacchaeus for collecting taxes from their own people for the Romans? He was a traitor, and he was also one of twelve of Jesus's BFFs."

"And you're manipulative," I snapped.

Trex didn't get mean or defensive like I expected; instead his smile only grew softer, his shoulders more relaxed. He was much better at this than I was, and he knew I was full of shit. "I'm sorry, that wasn't very nice."

"Don't be sorry!" I closed my eyes tight, feeling like it was a losing battle.

"Why? Because it'll be easier to hate me if I'm an asshole? I'm not perfect, but I'm not an asshole. And I like you, even though you're mean as hell and lie a lot."

"I don't *lie* a lot," I said, exasperated. "I just don't know you well enough to tell you the truth."

His expression grew serious. "Fair enough. But you can talk to me. Whatever you have to say would stay between us. I don't want anything bad to happen to you."

"Then stay away from me," I said, grabbing a small notebook and a pen. I quickly headed for the safety of Stavros at the bar. "Hey," I said, out of breath even though I'd only walked across the room.

Stavros turned his back to the men at the bar, working on drying the same glass. "Is Trex bothering you?"

"What? No. No, he's nice."

"Oh," Stavros said.

"Can you tell me the steps for closing out?" I asked, pen at the ready.

"It's been a while since I've done it. I have notes in my office somewhere."

I sighed. "Can you just...*pretend* to give me the notes?"

He leaned in. "All right, what's going on?" He kept his voice low, too quiet for the hotshots sitting at the bar to hear.

"Nothing. Nothing is going on. Trex is just very..."

"Cute?"

I closed my eyes. "Yes, anyone with eyes would agree he's attractive. But..."

"Just tell him you've just gotten out of a relationship and aren't looking for anything."

I peeked up at my boss, grateful to have someone to talk to. "I can't. He'll know I'm not telling the whole truth."

"Are you looking for a relationship?"

I wrinkled my nose. "Of course not, but..."

"But you're clearly not ready yet, so he'll either have to wait until you are, or move on."

I cringed. "I can't say that to him."

Stavros winked at me, then turned toward his customers. "Sure you can."

I pretended to write things down, glancing over my shoulder at Trex. He was staring right at me. He smiled and waved.

I sighed. "Okay. This is happening. I'm doing this," I said, mostly to myself. I walked back to the front desk, keeping my posture erect and shoulders back, trying my best to stir up a little beauty queen confidence as I strode up to Trex. I smiled, pleasant and confident. "You're right. I lied, and I apologize. You're nice. And funny. And interesting..."

"And handsome. Don't forget devastatingly handsome."

"And arrogant."

"*I'm* arrogant? I haven't even asked you on a date yet, and you're breaking up with me."

"No. We're definitely not breaking up." He smiled again. He was beautiful and sweet and...*No. No, Darby. Knock it off.* "You know what I mean. We weren't together to break

up. I do like you, but I have to be honest. I'm not ready
for a relationship of any kind, and I won't be for a long
time. And, by the time I am, I can promise you won't be
interested."

"Is that so?" he said, picking up on the last part.

I cringed. The goal was to not invite more questions, and
I'd just ripped off my skin and exposed everything.

He ignored my comment for the moment. "What about
just a friendship?"

"You just want to be friends?" *Ugh. That smile again.
Stop smiling, Trex.*

"Of course not. I think you're amazing, even when you
look like you're about to puke."

I sighed. His small grin was adorable, and it was chipping
away at my resolve. And the fact that had I not been pregnant, I would have jumped all over this—and him—was just
flat-out embarrassing. "I don't feel that's possible."

"Because you like me."

"I barely know you."

"But enough to like me."

My shoulders fell, and the confidence melted away under
his assured smile. "How about you just give me some space?"

"I can try. We both live in the same building. And you
work here."

I cringed. "You're right. That's not going to work."

"How about I pretend I don't like you for a little while?
Will that help?"

"Yes," I said, excited. I pointed at him. "Yes, that will work.
Thank you."

He leaned over and kissed my cheek, his lips soft and
warm on my skin. "You got it, beautiful."

I closed my eyes and leaned into him slightly just before
he walked away. I stood holding my hand to the still-warm

patch of skin his lips had just touched. The cannons inside my stomach raged on like I hadn't just lost another battle.

Stavros eyed me, his eyes targeting Zeke when he stood to head toward me. Stavros's expression matched my inner monologue.

My head and my heart were at war, fighting over what I should do and what I wanted. It didn't matter, though. Even if I gave in to my feelings, one of two things would happen: Trex would change, because in my experience, that's what men did when they got what they wanted, or I would fall for him and in four to six months, my growing belly would send him running, leaving both of us—or maybe just me—heartbroken.

chapter eleven

Trex

Nine days. It had been nine fucking days since I'd spoken to Darby except for the occasional polite greeting, and it was making me hate everything.

Even though I'd agreed to pretend Darby didn't exist, I still lived for the twenty seconds it took for me to walk from the entrance of the hotel to the elevators. She always stole a glance, and it made my whole day.

Some days, the drive to the hotel took forever, but this time I felt like I'd just left the Complex when I pulled into an empty parking space near the front. A group of hotshots were walking out, dressed in button-downs and jeans—their best clothes to go scouting the local clubs. I wondered if any would happen upon Naomi while they were out. The thought made me chuckle. These guys thought they were badasses until the moment Naomi showed them otherwise.

"What are you smiling about?" Darby asked, standing behind one of the sofas in the waiting area.

I stopped in my tracks. The sliding doors tried to close and then retreated. Darby giggled and pulled me farther into the lobby. She was wearing makeup, a pair of shorts, and a flowy tank top, her hair falling over her shoulders in soft waves.

"Trex?" she asked. I realized then that I hadn't answered her.

"Sorry, you just caught me a little off guard," I said, feeling my bad mood melt away. "Headed out?" After her training ended, she started the 11:00 p.m.–7:00 a.m. shift, Sunday night through Thursday night. She hadn't gone out once since having that schedule.

"I am. I promised Zeke we'd go to a movie when he got back, and…he's back."

"Oh yeah," I said, unable to hide the frown on my face.

She shook her head, suddenly embarrassed. "It's just… it's just a movie. Besides, he's not my type. Firefighters, cops, soldiers…all off the list."

"Yeah," I said, nodding. "Well…have fun."

I left Darby to stand alone in the lobby. Another group of hotshots walked in, carrying brown sacks with big red logos that read *Colorado Springs Meat & Seafood Co.* As they passed, the faint stench of fish filled the air, and moments later, the sound of dry heaving.

Darby was leaned over the closest trash bin, expelling her latest meal. I rushed to her side, holding back her hair while she lurched again.

"Jesus, Darby. Are you okay?"

She heaved again.

I looked around, noting the shocked stares from everyone in the lobby, including Stavros. He jogged over, handed me a clean bar towel, and then turned away, covering his nose. "Is she…is she all right?"

"She was fine a few seconds ago," I said.

Darby stood, and I handed her the towel. She wiped her face, her breath labored. "I am so sorry, Stavros."

He nodded. "Maybe you should…"

"I'm feeling better," she said.

"Darby," Stavros began, looking around. "You should lie down for a bit. I'll send down some crackers and Sprite to your room."

"I'm really fine. It was just the fish those guys brought in. It smelled rotten or something."

I arched an eyebrow. I barely noticed the fish. Darby must have had a nose like a bloodhound if it affected her so violently. "C'mon," I said. "I'll walk you back to your room."

"You can freshen up before the movie," Stavros said.

I looked to Darby before she protested again. "He's politely trying to tell you to get the hell out of his lobby before you throw up again."

"Oh," Darby said, embarrassed. She seemed to just notice everyone was staring. "I'm so sorry. I'll go."

She kept the towel in her hands, covering her nose and mouth with it as we passed the hotshots with the brown sacks of seafood. Once we got to Room 100, she held her card key to the lock and it beeped just before she pressed down on the handle and pushed her way inside.

I ambled around the small entry hall that was adjacent to the bathroom. Darby went straight in, closing the door behind her. The water faucet and the sound of her brushing her teeth were the only noises.

The faucet shut off, and seconds later, she opened the door, looking just as beautiful as she did when I stepped into the lobby.

"You okay?" I asked.

"Yeah," she said with a sigh. "Yeah, I'm fine. The fish just hit me wrong."

"I barely smelled it."

She pointed to her nose. "Must be my superpower, then."

"Darby," I said, taking a step toward her, brushing her

hair out of her face with my fingers. I was terrified to ask my next question. "Are you sick? You can tell me."

She shook her head. "I've been nauseous. It will pass."

A sigh of relief billowed from my lips. Something was going on, and maybe she was sick, but in that moment, the fear was replaced by curiosity. Darby was hiding more than just her past. Something was off.

"Is there something else you want to tell me?" I asked.

She thought about it for a solid ten seconds before shaking her head no.

There was a knock on the door, and Darby pulled it open. Tilde stood there with a smile, a tray of crackers, and a can of Sprite.

"Thank you so much, Tilde. Really."

"Stavros said you upchucked all over the lobby."

"In the trash can," she said, setting down the tray on the dresser. "Please tell him sorry for me."

"You already said sorry," I reminded her.

"Tell him again," she said, smiling at Tilde.

Tilde nodded her head. "You should rest."

"Thank you, I will," Darby said, closing the door behind Tilde.

Darby looked at the alarm clock on the nightstand. "I'm meeting Zeke in the lobby in fifteen minutes."

"You're not still going, are you? You just puked in the lobby trash can."

"I told you..."

"You're fine. I know. Must be more than just a movie if you're not willing to cancel when you're sick."

"I'm not sick."

"Do you have some sort of mutant gag reflex, then?"

"I just can't stand the smell of fish, what's the big deal?"

"I'm worried about you, Darby. I know you're not telling

me something. And that's fine, it's your business, but I'm worried about you."

She smiled. "And I appreciate it. But, I promise you, I'm okay. I don't even need to rest, but I'm going to lie down for a few minutes because I told Tilde I would."

"Can I stay with you until it's time for you to leave?" I asked.

She couldn't hide the touched look on her face. "I mean...yeah."

I gestured for her to lead the way, and then I pulled up a chair next to the bed. She lay on her back, folding her hands over her middle. She stared up at the ceiling for a few seconds, then closed her eyes. Her chest rose and fell as she took a deep, relaxing breath. I would've given anything to crawl beside her and hold her, but I stayed in my chair.

"We're even, you know," she said, her voice soft and calm.

"What do you mean?"

"You have secrets, too."

I froze, not sure how to respond.

"It's okay. It's your business. We're all entitled to have secrets as long as they don't hurt anyone else."

I stayed quiet. She turned on her side, slid her hands between her face and the pillow, and smiled at me.

"God, you're beautiful," I said. I couldn't help it.

Darby didn't seem to mind. "Thank you."

"I'm sure you've been told that thousands of times before."

"Not by you."

I laughed once and looked down. "I'm sorry. I'm supposed to be pretending I don't like you."

"You're doing a horrible job. You think I don't see you staring at me every morning when you leave for work? You think I don't see you stealing glances in the evening?"

"I don't think it's possible not to look at you. Even the women do it."

"Ask my mom. She has it down pat."

"Does she really hold you responsible for their deaths?"

"I can't blame her. I do, too."

"You know that's bullshit, right?"

"I mean, obviously, I didn't kill them. But..."

"No buts. It wasn't your fault, it was an accident, and I'm sorry, but your mom's sort of an asshole for making you think otherwise."

She blew out a laugh, giggling so much she covered her mouth. "Do you always say exactly what you think?"

"When I can."

She looked at the clock. "Well...I should get going." She sat up, and I stood, reaching to help her off the bed.

"What movie are you going to watch?" I asked, trying not to let the jealousy seep out enough that she could see.

Darby thought about it. "You know, I have no idea. I assume Zeke has something picked out."

She made her way toward the door, and I opened it for her, waiting for her to walk through before I closed it behind us.

"Darby," Zeke said, surprised to see me.

"Hi," she said with a smile.

"Trex." Zeke gave me a once-over, then turned his attention to Darby. "I heard you were sick."

"No," she said. I liked the way she didn't give out all the information. She had mastered the art of omission, making me think back on our conversations, to check if I'd missed anything.

"Oh. Well..." He gestured to me.

I slid by him.

"Bye, Trex," she said.

"Have fun at the movies, kids," I said with a wave.

Zeke was clearly confused that I had just come out of Darby's room, knew they were going out together, and seemed to be fine with it. I smiled, happy to keep him in the dark.

Darby began to walk down the hall, and Zeke followed. He glanced back at me one last time before they rounded the corner and were out of sight.

I decided to take the stairwell, feeling my phone buzzed in my pocket before I was halfway to my room. It was Hailey, and I picked up before the second alert.

"Hey, Bells. How's things?"

"Sitting around being bored."

"No plans? It's Friday."

"I got asked out. He wasn't my type."

"Doesn't go to your church, does he?"

"Catholic."

"Hailey. Just because he has a different set of beliefs than you…"

"Dad won't allow it, and you know it."

"Why can't you be like all the other teenagers and do exactly the opposite of what you're told?"

"I like Rob Major, anyway."

"That half-pint from church camp?"

"You haven't been home in a long time, Scottie. He looks a lot different. And his mom is the praise and worship leader at our church now."

"Oh, goody. Making sure you don't date outside of your faith is a surefire way to keep you in the same mindset."

"Scottie…" she warned.

"Sorry. So, why doesn't Rob ask you out?"

"I don't know," she said in a breathy voice. I imagined her lying on her baby-pink bed, her legs crossed and resting against the wall, her blond hair cascading off the side of the mattress and skimming the floor. Rob Major was probably a skinnier version of my dad. I thought about him losing his temper and yelling at my sister, all while spouting scripture for her to submit and obey her husband—or worse, him laying a hand on her. I'd murder him.

"He better be nice to you, Bells. That's all I'm gonna say."

"Rob? He is the sweetest thing. He wouldn't hurt a fly. That's why I like him. He's so different from Daddy in all the right ways."

"That's a relief," I said.

"How about you? Do you have any plans tonight? How's Colorado? Have you found a place yet? When can I visit?"

"You know all of those answers." She sighed, so I went ahead and made her happy. "I don't have plans. Colorado is beautiful. It's almost July and it still gets chilly at night. Have not found a place yet, but I'm not looking too hard, either. You can visit when I find something. You can't come here. It's crawling with firefighters, and they've all been away from their girlfriends and wives for a few months now. Not a good idea."

"Have you met anyone yet?"

"I've met a lot of people."

"You know what I mean."

"I uh…not really."

Hailey sucked in the tiniest gasp, and I heard her shuffle. "You did. You met someone. What does she look like? Where's she from? What does she do?"

"Hold on, Hailey, Jesus."

"Scott Solomon Trexler!"

I cringed. "Don't use my middle name, Bells. You know I hate it."

"And don't you dare take the Lord's name in vain! You might not care about your soul, but I do."

"Sorry."

"So?" she demanded.

"She works here at the hotel."

"Oh?"

"She's..." I sighed. "She's beautiful, Bells. Not just your ordinary beauty, either. Like exotic, modelesque, breathtakingly beautiful. And she has no idea. I've never seen anyone like her in person. She could start the battle of Troy."

"Wow."

"She's from Texas. She has this cute little country drawl, too."

"Why aren't you taking her on a date?"

"She's at the movies with a hotshot named Zeke."

"No! If you like her so much, go steal her!"

I chuckled. "She's not dating Zeke. Her wedding was a few weeks ago."

"She's married?" Hailey wailed.

"No, no...she didn't go through with it. He was mean and she bailed. She's not looking to date anyone."

"Oh," Hailey said, deflated. "I've never heard you talk about someone like this. Not even Laura. You called her breathtaking. You should definitely tell her that."

"No. She needs time, and I'm going to give it to her. She's been through a lot. And..." I started to say I thought she was sick, but decided Hailey didn't need to know everything.

"And?"

"I'm not in a hurry, Bells, you know that."

"I just wish...I want you to be happy, that's all."

"Who says I'm not?"

"Good. I miss you."

"Miss you, too. Make sure Rob lives a long life by warning him about your brother."

She giggled. "He doesn't like me like that. Yet."

"I doubt that. Love you."

"Love you, too! Night!"

I pushed through the door to my room, and immediately fell on my back onto the mattress. With my fingers laced behind my head, I took a deep breath and blew it out as I stared at the ceiling. If Darby was ill, that was something I couldn't save her from. What if she needed treatment and couldn't afford it because she'd run from that cocksucker in Texas? I could make a few calls to California. Val could find out for me in forty-eight hours, but that was if I wanted to seriously violate Darby's privacy. Nope. No matter how badly I wanted to know, that was out of the question. It was her decision to tell me or not. It was just driving me nuts not knowing, even if she was likely perfectly capable of saving herself. I just wanted to help.

I'd just found her. Losing her made a sick feeling swirl in my stomach.

My cell chimed, and I picked it up, reading a text from Naomi.

I'm at a dive bar downtown. Save me, T-Rex.

From boredom? Because it's not that you can't handle yourself.

*Yes. Two drinks in and it's still not fun. And the men here are annoying **af**.*

I sighed, hearing Matt telling me to get off my ass and go to his wife. I tapped out a reply.

K. Be there in 15.

Make it 10.

I jumped off the bed, hopped in the shower for a couple minutes, then rushed around the room to get dressed before grabbing my wallet, keys, and phone and jogging down the stairs and out the door to my truck. The only woman I'd rush like that for besides my sister was Naomi … and now Darby.

Naomi texted me her location, and I tested my luck by driving eighty mph all the way to the destination. The truck skidded to a stop in a small parking lot across the street and halfway down an alley from McCormack's Pub, and I jogged to the entrance, yanking open the door and looking around for Naomi.

She was staring at me with a smile, her fist against her chin, her other hand outstretched, her fist and middle finger the only thing between her and a hotshot I recognized from the hotel lobby. He was smiling, too, trying to hide the embarrassment of a very public rejection. I'd seen him talking to Darby, too. He looked more like an Abercrombie & Fitch model than a wildfire fighter. He was too pretty to like to get dirty, even with his scraggly beard. His hair was gelled and his black button-down was starched.

"Hey," I said, huffing. "This is it? This is why I risked a reckless driving ticket?"

"Is she uh … ?" Watts asked me.

Naomi answered for me. "Of course! I must belong to him because I'm not interested in you."

"Who said you weren't interested in me?" Watts said.

"Me," Naomi said. "Twice."

"Watts," I said, shaking my head. "You don't wanna rock this boat."

"Is she your sister?" he asked.

Naomi and I looked at each other. She was exotic and wild; I was a plain-Jane white boy from Kansas. We couldn't have looked more different.

"Seriously?" I asked.

Watts sat down. "I'm just trying to figure you guys out. Maybe you're adopted, I dunno."

"We work together," I said.

"Trex," she scolded. She didn't want Watts knowing anything about her.

"Didn't you notice the wedding band? She's married, man, beat it."

Watts looked down. "It's on her middle finger."

"Does she look like a conformist?" I asked.

Watts shrugged and stood. "She's fucking beautiful. If she doesn't want guys thinking she's single, maybe wear it on the correct finger."

Naomi glared at him. "Or believe me when you walk up and the first thing I say is *go away*."

"You're right. I apologize," he said. He nodded to me once and then walked away.

"Why *do* you wear it on your middle finger?" I asked.

"I lost weight after Matt died. It doesn't fit on that finger anymore."

"Get it sized?" I suggested.

"No. Matt picked out this ring. It stays the same as he remembers it."

"Must have been hard for you to move here."

She shook her head. "That part was easy. I couldn't look at that apartment one more day. I didn't realize it until I got the letter. Then I couldn't pack fast enough."

"You hanging in there?" I asked.

She crossed her arms over the table and shrugged. "Some days are easier than others."

I nodded. "I was wondering why you were here if you're not in the mood to socialize."

"I'm allowed to go out and not be presumed to want male attention."

"That's not what I meant and you know it."

She took a swig of her beer. "Damn it. I'm sorry, Trex."

"Talk to me."

"His mom's birthday is today. It's weird what bothers me and what doesn't."

I reached across the table and encircled my fingers around her wrist. "You can call me to come over and hang out if you don't want to subject yourself to dive bars. Then you're not alone, and you're not flipping off total strangers."

She glanced over at Watts, who was talking to his buddies but happened to look over at Naomi at the same time. That's when I saw Zeke and then Darby. She was midstep on her way to my table, staring at my hand on Naomi's. She turned on her heels and returned to Zeke, standing with her back to me.

"Shit," I said, standing.

"What?" Naomi asked.

"That's the um... That's her."

"The girl? Darby?"

I nodded.

"You know what she's thinking, go—"

Before Naomi could finish her sentence, I was already on my way over to the small crowd of hotshots gathered with Darby and a few other women I didn't recognize.

"Hey," I said, putting a gentle hand on Darby's back. She turned with one of her pageant smiles painted on her face.

"Hi, Trex."

"Can I..." I glanced at Zeke. "Can I talk to you for a sec? There's someone I want you to meet."

Darby looked past me to Naomi, then back to Zeke.

"I told you, that's his coworker," Watts said.

Darby closed her eyes, unhappy about Watts revealing they'd been talking about Naomi. "Uh, sure. Yeah. Let's go meet... your coworker."

The walk over to Naomi's table had my stomach in knots. I had no idea how to explain Naomi, but I couldn't let Darby think I was out on a date, either.

"Nomes, this is Darby."

Naomi smiled brightly, something I hadn't seen her do since Matt was alive. "It's Naomi, actually. So, you're the famous Darby. Nice to finally meet you."

Oh my fuck, Naomi, you're brilliant.

"Hi," Darby said, holding out her hand to shake Naomi's. Naomi took it, and I could tell she was skipping the typical tight grip she normally used. Men usually looked shocked at the strength Naomi applied, but Darby let go without reaction. "So, you work in the Forestry Department?"

"No," Naomi said, still smiling. "You work at the hotel?"

Darby glanced at me. "Yes."

"You're as beautiful as he said you were. Wow."

"Thank you." She said the words as if she'd heard them a million times—because she had. "So...what do you do?"

"I'm an independent contractor," Naomi said.

"Oh, okay. Well, it was nice to meet you."

"Would you like to join us?" Naomi said before Darby could walk away. "I know Trex would love it."

"I'm here with friends. But thank you. I know Watts would appreciate it if I offered to have you join us."

"We were just here trying to distract me from my dead husband, but thank you."

"Oh. Oh, goodness, I'm so sorry," Darby said, stunned. Her eyebrows shot up.

"Nomes," I said, closing my eyes. "I'm sorry," I said to Darby.

"I can see why you're friends," Darby said with a smile. "You do prefer bluntness."

"Naomi is certainly that," I said. "But that's not it. Her husband, Matt, was a good friend."

"No wonder," Darby said, then seemed to realize she'd said it out loud. "That...that um..."

"We're sitting here together and he had his hand on my arm? Yes. That's why. Trust me, he's talked about you eighty-five percent of the day."

"That's not true," I corrected.

"No?" Darby asked.

"At least ninety," I said.

Darby and I smiled at each other for several seconds, until Naomi cleared her throat.

"I should um...I should probably get..." Darby's expression changed, and she sat down in my chair, placing one palm flat on the table.

"You okay?" I asked, grabbing her arm. The color drained from her face, and she stared at the table.

"Yeah, just dizzy," she said. "I'll be fine."

"You don't look fine," Naomi said. "You look like you're about to—"

Darby leaned over and heaved, the water she expelled splashing on the floor. Naomi and I watched in shock and confusion.

Zeke and Watts rushed over.

"Darby?" Zeke said, taking her arm.

Watts saw the puddle on the floor and held the back of his wrist to his nose.

"Don't be such a pussy. Go get a towel from the bartender," Naomi said.

Watts jogged off, and my mouth opened before my brain could catch up. "What the fuck, Zeke? You bring her to a bar when she's sick?"

"She's sick?" Zeke asked. "I...I didn't know."

"You knew she was puking in the hotel lobby earlier."

Darby heaved again.

"Was it something she ate?" Naomi asked, mostly unaffected.

Zeke shook his head. "She hasn't eaten anything. She hasn't felt great all night."

"So you bring her here instead of taking her home?" I growled, grabbing his shirt.

"Stop. Stop! I'm okay," Darby said, her head still down.

"I...She said she was okay," Zeke said. He clearly felt bad. I didn't need to make him feel worse. I knew Darby was a chronic fibber when it came to admitting her health. I released him and looked to my friend.

"Nomes..." I said.

"Yeah, go..." she said.

Watts brought a towel, and Darby took it.

"I'm so sorry," she said, dabbing her mouth as I helped her to stand upright.

I lifted her into my arms. "C'mon. Let's get you home." I glanced at Zeke, who nodded. He knew I didn't need permission, but it was decent of him not to argue.

Darby held the towel against her mouth and rested her head against my shoulder. Once she did that, my pace picked up, and I barely noticed that I was carrying her. Holding her so close created a strange conflicting feeling between wanting to walk slowly to make it last and running to get her somewhere comfortable. I settled for walking quickly across the street and down the alley, pressing the unlock button on my key fob at fifteen feet out. The lights blinked once, highlighting the alley for a moment before we were bathed in darkness again.

My feet crunched against the dry gravel as I struggled to hold her, keep my balance, and pull open the door.

"I can walk," Darby said.

"We're here," I said, opening the door and setting her in the passenger seat.

"I just waited too long to eat...again. I'll get the hang of it."

"Get the hang of what?" I asked. "Darby, tell me. How sick are you? How serious is it?"

She dabbed her mouth again and looked down. "Please don't tell Stavros. Or anyone. I don't want him to fire me."

I swallowed. "What is it? Cancer?" My stomach sank. I wanted her back in my arms.

"No," she said, shaking her head. "I'm, um..." She winced. "I didn't realize how hard it would be to say it."

It's not cancer. Once that was out of the way, my mind was clear enough for the answer to dawn on me. The puking when she hadn't eaten in a while, the dizziness, her drinking ice water in a bar, the exhaustion, the fact that she'd left her fiancé at the altar—her being so adamant on not starting any kind of relationship. I was a fucking idiot. She had someone else to protect. "Are you pregnant?"

She stared at me for a moment, deciding if she could trust me, then she nodded slowly.

I walked away, interlacing my fingers on my head. "Thank fuck!" I yelled. I grabbed my knees, feeling an overwhelming urge to cry. I wasn't sure if I'd ever felt that way, even as a child. I breathed out and then stood, turning to face Darby.

She watched me, her eyes wary.

I went over to her and wrapped her in my arms, laughing once, rocking back and forth. "I thought you were dying." She didn't hug me back, so I let her go, scanning her eyes for a clue. "I'm sorry. I should've asked before I hugged you. I'm just so goddamn relieved." She watched me like she was waiting for me to burst into flames. "What?"

"Don't you understand?" she asked.

"That you're pregnant?"

She nodded. "I'm pregnant."

"Yeah…but…" I looked down at her stomach, "are you sure it's mine?"

Darby was quiet for a few seconds. She breathed out a laugh, and then she couldn't stop laughing. She covered her mouth, her face morphed from giggles to fear, and she started to cry. "That's the first time I've said it out loud."

"No one else knows? Not even…"

She shook her head, her hands trembling.

"Darby," I said, holding her again. "It's okay." I kissed her hair. "It's going to be okay."

She nodded against my chest, grabbing my shirt in her fists. In that moment, nothing else existed; it was just us and the baby growing inside of her. The urge to keep her safe doubled.

chapter twelve

Darby

My eyes peeled open, and the first thing to come into view was Trex asleep on the chair next to my bed. His arm was outstretched over the top of the chair, his hand holding mine. I sucked in a deep breath and stretched, letting my hand slip from his, but his fingers squeezed around mine.

I looked at him, expecting his eyes to be open, but they weren't. His other hand was pressed against his perfectly relaxed face. I settled against the mattress, letting the back of my head sink into the feather pillow as I stared up at the popcorn ceiling. We didn't talk much on the way home from McCormack's because Trex had to pull over twice, even though I was just dry heaving. He carried me to my room and fetched me crackers and made sure I ate them before asking me if he could sit in the chair while I slept.

I turned, reading the clock. I'd only been asleep for four hours, but I felt rested. When I looked back, Trex was awake.

"Hey," he said, rubbing his face and eyes. He squeezed my hand. "What time is it?"

"A few minutes after five."

He smiled. "This was probably like a long nap for you."

"Yeah," I said, sitting up. "Don't want to mess up my schedule too much. I should probably be back in bed by ten."

"You'll probably be tired again by then, considering."

I raised an eyebrow. "Know a lot about pregnancy, do you?"

"Just the basics, even though I totally missed this."

I frowned. "I need this job, Trex. Stavros is a good man, but he's also a business owner. I need more time to prove to him I'm a good employee, and it will be worth waiting for me to come back to work after..." I looked down at my stomach.

"I won't say anything," he said immediately. "You're safe with me, Darby. I promise." He interlaced his fingers with mine.

I pulled my hand from his and picked at my nails, staring at the jagged edges of my thumbnail. "I like you, but relationships are complicated enough."

He nodded. "You're right, and I don't do complicated."

I swallowed, thankful for the hurt I was feeling. Later, it would have been much worse.

"And I wondered while I watched you sleep, why you being pregnant with someone else's baby changes nothing for me. None of this makes sense, but I can't stop thinking about you."

"I just think it's best if I do this alone. It's not smart to run from one relationship into another. And we don't know each other. Not really."

"So, get to know me. And let me get to know you. This wasn't an accident, us both ending up here."

I arched an eyebrow. "Finding religion, Trexler?"

He shook his head. "No. I found you."

I felt my cheeks blush, and I pointed to them. "See? I don't want to be a blushing, giddy, infatuated little girl."

"You're none of those things, Darby. It could be the easiest thing in the world. Let's just...let's just see."

"I have to have a plan. I can't just wing it anymore."

"Who says we're winging it? I'm very purposefully sitting in this god-awful chair to be as close as you're comfortable with." He grinned, making my heart flutter. I wondered in that moment if not following my heart was allowing Shawn to control me in a different way. *What do I really want?*

I stood. "I'll be right back," I said, making my way to the bathroom. The door closed quietly behind me, and I pressed my palms against it, touching my forehead to the hollow wood. I'd known a lot of men in my life—some good, most bad. But Trex was at that dive bar with the widow of his best friend, and later watched over a sleeping pregnant woman, holding her hand, and not because he was hoping to get laid. I'd seen men look at me with that familiar hunger in their eyes. He was attracted to me, but he wasn't trying to conquer me.

I reached for my toothbrush and turned on the faucet. As I scrubbed my teeth, I reminded myself that I may have put up with Shawn, but that didn't make me stupid. I could still make good decisions, and Trex...he was good, I knew it.

I spit in the sink, rinsed my mouth, and stepped out. "You're still here," I said.

He sat up. "Did you want me to leave?"

I sat on the bed, pushed myself back to the headboard, then held out my hand. He looked down, unsure. "You said you wanted to be as close as I was comfortable with. Come closer."

He stood slowly, looking down at me while he kicked off his boots, and then crawled onto the bed to lie next to me. He looked into my eyes for a few moments before stretching his neck to kiss my cheek. His forehead touched my temple. "I'm so glad you're going to be okay," he whispered, then sighed with relief.

"You really thought I was dying?"

He gently pulled me next to him and buried his face in my neck.

It had been a long time since I'd been comfortable being held that way. It occurred to me it was strange to just lie there, so I rested my hand on his back. Without thinking, I ran my nails up and down, from just above the top of his jeans to the space between his scapulae. A memory resurfaced, a night when I tried my best to keep my body relaxed, hoping Shawn would just pass out and sleep off the tequila and rage, and that he'd do it before something set him off. I stopped and lay my palm flat on the small of Trex's back. It was something Shawn had insisted I do until he fell asleep every night he was home, and I wanted as far away from anything he wanted as I could get.

"Habit?" Trex asked.

"It's going to take me a while."

"Take as long as you need. I'll be right here."

I breathed out a laugh. "Comfy?"

"Like never before. Not sure I'll be able to move the rest of the weekend."

I touched my chin to his hair. I'd let Shawn treat me horribly for so long, I wasn't sure why I was so against letting Trex treat me the way I deserved. I closed my eyes, and let it be easy, silencing the screams inside of me, those fears that were sure something bad was on the horizon. That was the funny thing about fear; you couldn't be sure if it was a warning from the subconscious about the future or the past.

"You know," I said in the darkness. "Some men run when they find out women are pregnant with *their* baby."

He lifted his head. "Do I look like the runnin' kind to you?"

I smiled and shook my head.

His eyes fell to my lips, and warmth began in my chest and traveled all the way to my toes.

"Can I kiss you?" he asked.

I stared at his lips. They looked soft, even though they were surrounded by three-day-old scruff. I remembered the way they felt against my cheek, the way their warmth lingered until he was halfway across the room. "Yes."

His hand slid behind my head, cupping it gently as he pulled me closer. It had been so long since anyone but Shawn had touched me. Alone in a dark room, wrapped in the arms of Scott Trexler, I felt anything but afraid.

I closed my eyes, and then his mouth was on mine. He tried just a small kiss at first, waiting for more permission, so I touched his cheeks with my hands and brought him closer, opening my mouth and hoping he'd feel confident enough to . . .

Trex's tongue slipped inside, tasting me. I had no expectations other than the previous kiss on the cheek, but Trex was blowing anything I could have hoped for out of the water. His mouth moved faster, less gentle, and he positioned himself so that he was leaning over me instead of lying next to me. From hair to toes, my skin began to tingle. I gripped his shirt in my fists and pulled him closer.

He pulled away, then touched his forehead to mine. "Just . . . wait a sec," he said, trying to catch his breath. He returned to my side, bearing most of his weight on his elbow.

I looked up at the ceiling, already knowing what he was going to say next. I was pregnant. That wasn't exactly a turn-on.

"What are you doing tonight?" he asked.

Not what I expected.

"Huh?" I asked, unable to hide my surprise.

He chuckled, and kissed the bare skin just behind my ear.

His lips lingered there for a moment, then he sat up to look me in the eyes. "I want to take you to dinner. I tried this pasta place when I was pretending not to like you. They have gelato. I was thinking the whole time I was there that you might like it."

"You did?" I asked, trying not to melt over the fact that he'd been planning our first date.

"So...dinner? Tonight? With me?"

"Dinner," I said, nodding once. Of course. That's what nice guys did. "Is later okay?"

"Eight?" he asked.

I nodded, and he sat up, pushing himself off the bed. He pointed to the door. "I'm fairly certain I'll do an NFL illegal-level celebration in the hall. So don't watch me leave."

"You're leaving?"

"I'll be back. I'm just going to grab you some breakfast."

"Oh," I said with a grin.

"Don't want to wait until you get sick, right?"

"Right. Let me get you some..."

"Nope. On me."

"I..." I began.

"What?"

"I don't want to owe anyone anything."

He frowned. "You don't owe me shit, Darby."

I pulled my mouth to the side, trying not to smile. "Hmmm."

"I'll be back. Do you like OJ?"

I nodded.

"Can I take this?" he asked, holding up my key card. When I nodded, he grinned. "Please don't move. Breakfast in bed is happening in less than twenty minutes."

"Okay."

"Okay," he said, picking his wallet and phone off the

floor. He patted his pocket to make sure his keys were in his pocket, then he leaned down, his hands sinking into the mattress as he gave me a quick peck on the lips. He hummed in satisfaction, then rushed out the door.

I sank down against the pillows, covering my mouth. *How did this happen? I leave an awful situation, pregnant, and wind up in the arms of the sweetest man I've ever met?* A feeling of dread washed over me. Too good to be true usually meant it was. And even if it wasn't, having something wonderful was that much harder when it was gone.

I covered my eyes with one hand. *Stop it, Darby. Just because it's always happened that way doesn't mean that's the way it will always be.* I tried to enjoy the quiet moment in bed, waiting for a very handsome, very thoughtful man to bring me breakfast in bed. Fear wriggled its way in, even as I identified it and pushed it away. Even as I gave myself some grace and let myself be afraid—because who wouldn't be after a year with Shawn Littlefield? Then I cried. I mourned who I was before Shawn and then remembered I didn't really like her, either. I was glad I had a pregnancy to blame my scattered emotions on. I was an absolute flippin' mess.

The lock clicked and Trex walked in, holding up two white sacks. His wide smile quickly vanished when he saw my face. He set the sacks on the end of the bed and sat next to me, brushing stray strands of hair from my face.

"What happened?"

I shook my head. "Hormones. I hope."

"Tell me."

"This," I said, gesturing to the space between us, "feels like a good thing."

"You're afraid it's not."

I liked that I didn't have to explain everything to Trex. He just needed a tiny clue and could figure it out for himself.

"And I hate that I feel that way. I feel horrible, but I can't stop these thoughts from entering my head."

"It's normal that you'd be worried. So incredibly normal. Every new relationship in most cases is basically one person's hope that a total stranger won't let them down."

He made so much sense. I loved the way he looked at the world.

"And believe me, I know all about being unable to stop your brain from working overtime. PTSD is PTSD, Darby. Doesn't matter where it came from."

I sniffed and looked at him, surprised. It had never occurred to me that's what it was.

"Have you thought about talking to someone?" he asked.

"Even if I did, I can't afford it."

"There's a YWCA here. I can take you there this week, see what services they provide."

"How...*how* do you know all of this? Is that what you do? Are you like a psychologist to the hotshots or something?"

He handed me a tissue from the box on the nightstand. "No. I've just been around death a lot in my line of work."

I dabbed my eyes and nose. "Like your best friend?"

He nodded, but the two lines between his brows deepened. "Darby..."

"Yeah?"

He cleared his throat and shook his head, seeming to change direction. "Time is the only thing that will help you trust that I'm not like him. And all I've got is time."

"You mean until the fire is out."

"No," he said, sliding his fingers between mine. "I'm looking for a house here. I'm staying."

"You are?"

One corner of his mouth turned up. "I am. Let's eat."

He pulled out a Styrofoam box and handed it to me, then opened a bag of plasticware. I popped the lid and it sprung open, revealing a stack of golden-brown pancakes.

"Buttermilk," he said, handing me the fork and knife. "There's an omelet and sausage in the other boxes." He peeled open the lid of a small syrup container, then paused over the top of my pancakes. "A little or a lot?"

"A lot."

"Attagirl," he said, drenching the pancakes with the thick, brown syrup.

I cut into a piece, took a bite, and hummed, smiling and chewing at the same time while Trex carved out a piece of the enormous omelet in the Styrofoam box on his lap.

"Is it a Denver omelet?" I asked. "I smell bell pepper and ham...and...onion?"

He nodded, still chewing. He carved out another piece and offered it to me. I opened my mouth and he shoveled it in, laughing when I hummed even louder.

"Oh my gosh," I said, my mouth full.

"I know, right?" he said around his food. He pulled a foam cup with a lid and straw from a holder and handed it to me. "OJ."

I took a sip, and I watched him eat for a moment. He looked so happy, having a breakfast picnic in my bed. I tried to push all the thoughts about not deserving him or fears that I would get attached and then he would leave from my mind.

"You're thinking," he said, wiping his mouth with a napkin. "Bad thoughts or good?" When I didn't answer, he nodded. "I'm scared, too. This feels really, really good. What if you decide you don't want me around, or that you just don't like me? What if someone better comes along? What if I fall a million feet deep for you and then it's just over?"

"Has that ever happened to you before?"

"My job has made it hard to get too attached. But the traveling is over. I'm planting roots. And damn it if I'm not lucky after all. You happen to be here, too."

"Okay. So, we just go into this scared?"

"Terrified."

I sighed. "Okay, then."

He held up his orange juice to mine. "To staring fear in the face."

"I'll drink to that."

We sipped our juice from our straws, smiling at each other. It was the best breakfast of my life...so far.

chapter thirteen

Trex

Flowers were so cliché, but I brought them anyway. Dinner and a movie were also nothing special, but that was the plan. I'd been out of practice for so long, everything seemed wrong and stupid, but when Darby opened the door and saw the roses in my hand, she covered her smile with both hands and gasped.

Darby wasn't difficult to impress. She didn't need diamonds or travel to luxurious places. She just wanted kindness and consideration, and those I could do, but she deserved more. Her curves filled nearly every inch of the simple navy-blue summer dress she wore, white pinstripes running from the high neckline to the hem just above her knees. I had to stop myself from gasping, too. The different shades of blond stood out more in the braid that cascaded down her left shoulder. No earrings, no necklace, just her golden-brown eyes and pink lipstick.

"Wow," I said. It was all I could say.

She looked down. "Picked it up earlier. It was on sale at TJ Maxx for seven bucks."

I'd never seen someone like her in real life before, and even as she pulled me in for a hug, it was hard to believe being that close to her was real.

"They're beautiful," Darby said, hugging the flowers gently to her chest as she breathed them in.

She spun on her heels and made her way to the bathroom sink. I stepped into her room and peeked in to where she stood. She was filling the basin with water, the bouquet lying on its side, still in the plastic. "Vase. Next time I'll get a vase."

"I can get one from storage later," she said, smiling at the pink petals. She ran her finger down one before taking my hand and pulling me into the hall. She was light, smiling like she had not a care in the world. I hoped I was the reason.

"Excited?" I asked.

"Aren't you?" she asked.

"Nervous excited," I admitted.

She twirled around, hooking her wrists behind my neck. "You don't get nervous."

"You're right. Most people are nervous around me."

"Not me."

"Just another reason to like you."

"Don't be nervous." She tilted her head, closed her eyes, and pecked my lips. "This is the fun part. C'mon," she said, pulling me by the hand across the lobby.

The hotshots stared, some with curiosity, others with envy. Stavros watched us, not an ounce of surprise on his face. The attention made me stand up taller. I needed those guys to know this date was a final decision, not an open invitation, because the reality was that some guys saw a woman's interest in someone else as a reason to be interested. A desirable woman was somehow open season. Or maybe they'd backed off because of Zeke. Either way, I didn't want more of them sniffing around Darby because they'd seen she was open to dating.

The sliding doors opened, blowing hot wind in our faces. Darby didn't seem to mind, but I was already sweating by the time we reached my truck. I opened the door for her and held her hand while she climbed into the passenger seat.

"What?" she said, looking up at me.

"You just look damn good sitting there," I said. "That seat's been waiting for you."

She laughed, sitting back and relaxing. She was beautiful before, but something about seeing her so happy took my breath away.

I sat next to her and reached over the center console to slide my fingers between hers. It took me longer to detail my Land Cruiser than it did to shower and get dressed, but I wanted to make sure the things I could control were perfect. The truck smelled like cleaner and new car scent, and I suddenly wondered if the chemicals would be bad for her or make her sick.

"You okay?" I asked, pulling out of the parking lot.

"Yeah, why?"

"I just realized I detailed the truck today and it smells like—"

"Chemicals and new car smell?"

"Yeah," I said, unhappy. So much for perfection.

"I like it."

"You do? What about the baby?"

"Oh. I didn't think about that." She smiled at me. "Thank you, but I'm sure it's fine."

I cracked my window, just in case, and she squeezed my hand.

We parked in front of Laundry, a place Harbinger said his wife liked. The orange brick was covered by an old Laundromat mural, lending to the name. Inside were low-hanging lights and industrial modern pipes and metal hinges on gray wood. I wasn't a fan of what Hailey called rich-people food, but Darby was grinning from ear to ear.

We approached a silver-haired man standing in front of a computer, and he immediately greeted us. "Good evening, sir. Do you have a reservation?"

"We do. It's under Trex."

"Trex. Yes. We spoke earlier. Right this way."

He led us to a corner table next to the window, and I was proud to beat him to Darby's chair, pulling it out for her. She sat, looking almost giddy, and I took the seat next to her instead of across. The host pulled my place setting over without hesitation, and Darby began looking over the menu.

All but one table and one stool at the bar were full. I hoped it was because the food was good. There weren't exactly guidelines for taking a pregnant woman on a date, but I was sure food was at the top of the list of things to get right.

"The napkins are just like my granny's," Darby said. "Thick and white with red stripes on each end. You're taking me down memory lane and don't even know it."

She couldn't have paid me a bigger compliment. "I like the braid," I said.

She touched it. "It was fast. My hair is not behaving lately. The book says it's the hormones."

"You're beautiful."

She smiled at the menu. "Thank you." She said the words mindlessly, and I had to remind myself that the phrase didn't hold water for her like it did other women. She knew she was beautiful. "I'd like to hear about your granny sometime. And the rest of your childhood."

Her eyes brightened. "My granny? She was the best. She made these cinnamon rolls...oh my gosh. They melted in your mouth. Covered with icing. She never skimped on the icing. Have you been here before?"

"No."

"Look at this food. It's super weird."

The waiter approached, pouring water into our glasses with a metal pitcher. "Good evening. My name is Shawn, I'll be your server tonight. Have you dined with us before?"

Darby and I held each other's gaze while I waited for her reaction. I wasn't sure if that was going to ruin our night or not. A laugh tumbled from her throat, and she covered her mouth. I chuckled, too, and looked up at Shawn. "No, we haven't."

"Our dishes are shareable. Choose three or five. I suggest five for a full meal, but everyone is different. Do you know what you'd like to drink?"

"I'm fine with ice water," Darby said.

"Me, too," I said.

"Very well, I'll give you a few minutes. If you have any questions, let me know." Shawn left us as alone as we could be in a room full of people.

"This is a good test. We'll either have to agree on everything or compromise."

"Easy," I said.

She smirked and then returned her attention to the menu. "What do you think about the beef carpaccio?"

"Let's do it."

"The pow pow shrimp?"

"I'm in."

"The chicharrones and bean dip?"

"Hit me with it."

"The goose?"

"All day."

"Pork cheeks?"

"Pork cheeks?" I said, taking a second look at the menu. It didn't look too bad, but Darby was enjoying my hesitance so much, I went with it. "As in the cheeks of a pig?"

She giggled. "It's cooked! I'm sure it's better than the round!"

"What the hell is the round?"

"The rump of a cow," she said, still giggling. I made a

face, and she burst out laughing. "You don't know about ham, do you?"

"Aw, shit. Is that pig butt? Because I eat one every Thanksgiving."

She held her stomach, leaning over as her body shook with laughter.

Shawn returned, and Darby ordered, looking like a pro as she pointed out each dish.

"All my favorites," Shawn said. "Well done. You're sure I can't get you a nice white wine?"

"I'm…" Darby touched her stomach.

"Oh." His eyes lit up with realization. "Congrats to you both," he said, nodding once before leaving again.

"Sorry," Darby said, her cheeks red. "That's probably weird."

"Not at all."

She hesitated to say her next words. "I'm…not looking for a father for my baby, so you know. I don't need saving. I made a choice to do this on my own, and I'm still comfortable with that choice."

"I know. This situation isn't typical, but that doesn't change how I feel about you. Your independence is one of the reasons I'm attracted to you, and the last thing I want is to think I could take that away from you. You don't need to be saved, anyway, you're having a baby. There are a lot worse things in the world."

She nodded. "Exactly."

I could tell she was trying to decide if she could believe me or not, if I was just telling her what she wanted to hear, and then I watched her make the choice. She grinned and leaned toward me. "This is really nice. Thank you."

I looked at my watch. "The movie is in ninety minutes. Do you want romantic comedy or action?"

"Action."

"Okay, then we're watching *War Gods*."

"Oh, I saw the trailer on the TV in the lobby. It looks really good!"

"Gotta love summer movies."

"I saw on the news they're not allowing fireworks this year." She sighed. "Bummer. But I guess it's good for you guys."

"Yeah," I said. It wasn't a lie. Saunders had said more than once to start watching for kids coming closer to the Complex to set off fireworks. "Maybe I could take you up north? Steamboat Springs has a huge fireworks display. Or we could go even further to Deadwood, South Dakota. Or Mount Rushmore if you're feeling particularly patriotic."

"I have to work," she said, her voice thick with regret.

I shrugged. "Maybe next year." She held my gaze. "I wish I could read your mind sometimes. So much going on behind those eyes of yours."

"Just that you said next year. I wondered if you meant it."

"Yes," I said without hesitation.

"I'll have a baby this time next year. Travel would be complicated."

She was right, I hadn't thought about it. "True. What are we talking? A car seat? Baby bag? Diapers? Wipes? Mobile crib? We got this. My truck is a crew cab, Darby. We could make it work."

"That's a long time from now. A lot could happen between now and then."

"I hope so," I said.

The touched look on her face was the last thread to break before I fell. It was so easy to make her night, her day, her week…Whether she wanted me to be her knight in shining armor or not, she sure made me feel like it.

"You're making it very difficult to stay guarded," she said.

"Good. I thought we weren't doing that, anyway. I thought we were laying it all out on the table. Terrifyingly honest and real."

"Easier said than done."

"But I'm doing it."

"Okay." She blew out a single laugh to cover her fear.

Shawn brought over a round plate covered in thin slices of meat with large, broken pieces of cracker-like bread. He pointed out the cheese, caper relish, and lava salt.

"Thank you," Darby said, nearly salivating over the plate.

"Go for it," I said, gesturing to her silverware.

She used her fork to scrape a piece of meat off the plate, and she placed it on the bread. She took a bite and hummed. "Oh my stars, that's good."

"Yeah?" I said, scraping off a piece of my own. I'd gotten a bigger slice than I'd meant to, but that didn't stop me from heaping it on top of the bread and shoving it all in my mouth. Darby was right. It was amazing. "Holy shit."

Darby nodded, giggled, and forked another piece. We plowed through the beef, the pow pow shrimp Shawn brought to the table on a wood plank, then the bean dip, the goose, and finally the pork cheeks. They came with steamed buns, some sort of orangish sauce, sliced red peppers, ginger…like a make-your-own tiny sandwich. Just touching the buns was so fun it made eating pork cheeks worth it.

At the end, I wasn't full, but satisfied, and Darby looked so happy it was hard not to reach over every few seconds to touch her.

We talked until it was time to pay the bill and leave for the movie, where we cuddled in the scratchy theater chairs until the credits rolled. I thought about shooting for something else cheesy, like parking on a dirt road and lying in the back of my truck to look at the stars, but the smoke from the fire blanketed the sky.

I decided it was best to get her home to let her rest. The circles under her eyes were getting darker as the night wore on.

In front of her door, I kissed her cheek, forcing myself to pull away to tell her good night.

"Good night," she said.

"What are you doing tomorrow? When do you go back to work?"

"I work Sunday through Thursday."

"So, you're free?"

She nodded.

"Wanna do this all over again?" I asked.

Even tired, she couldn't stop the grin from stretching across her face. "I do, but I just got this dress today. I don't really have anything else."

"Wear your wedding dress," I teased.

"I pawned it for work clothes, shoes, a backpack, and cash."

I shrugged. "It's gorgeous on you. Wear it again. Or wear your work clothes. Or your pajamas. I'll take what I can get, as long as I'm with you."

"What if we order in?" she asked.

"Perfect. I'll have pizza and myself here at seven."

She leaned up on the balls of her feet for a second. "Yep. Sounds perfect." She bit her lip, and that was it for me. I had to kiss her.

She willingly leaned into my arms when I wrapped them around her, and giggled against my lips when I leaned her back. Upright again, I kissed her slower, pulling her closer. She might have let me keep her there all night, but I knew she was tired.

"Tomorrow," I said. "And maybe Sunday afternoon?"

"Maybe," she said, opening her door.

She gazed at me until the door was closed, and I folded my hands on top of my head, blowing out a breath. I smiled and then jogged up the stairs to my room two at a time, wondering how in the hell I would be able to sleep and keep my ass upstairs knowing she was so close.

But I would. We had time. Darby didn't protest when I mentioned plans for next year. I fell onto my bed, staring up at the ceiling, thinking about a road trip with a baby. I was excited instead of scared. Curiosity filled my thoughts instead of dread. For a guy who'd never wanted kids before, I couldn't figure out my lack of hesitation. I guess Dad was right about one thing: When you know, you know, and I knew the second I saw Darby Cooke. It was that first-sight nonsense that until that moment I would've said was bullshit. Since that moment, she'd been the center of my universe, and there was so much more to get to know. It was amazing, and terrifying, and so simple yet complicated. However it ended up, I made the choice right then, staring at my ceiling in room 201 of the Colorado Springs Hotel, to hang on until then.

* * *

The noodles swirled around my fork like a boa constrictor, squeezing the metal as I twisted it in my hand. The inevitable thoughts of twisting a knife into the soft flesh of the abdomen of an old enemy flashed in my mind. I closed my eyes tight, replacing the thought with the feel of Darby's long, soft hair in my fingers, gently holding it back while she heaved the contents of her stomach in the toilet for the third time that week.

Darby's nausea was lessening, but sometimes a smell would hit her wrong, and no matter how often she ate, the nausea would hit so hard she had no choice but to find the closest trash can or toilet. That particular morning, just after she got off work, a group of hotshots came in, and the stench on their clothes was different this time. The fire had reached a herd of cattle, and the burnt flesh was too much for Darby's sensitive nose.

"Where are you?" Naomi asked. We asked each other that question often, when we saw one of our team was lost in a thought or memory. Most of the time we were trapped in a nightmare, frozen in a moment of time we wanted anything but to remember. I was slowly beginning to replace my dark memories with thoughts of Darby.

"I was in Sudan. Right now, I'm in the hotel. Darby's bathroom."

My team traded glances. Sloan and Martinez chuckled like boys.

I frowned. "I was holding her hair. She was sick."

"Virus?" Harbinger said. "My kids had that a couple of weeks ago. It's going around."

"No," I said, shaking my head. Naomi looked at me from under her brows, silently asking me if I wanted to open that can, and I instantly regretted answering so quick.

"Food poisoning?" Martinez asked.

I narrowed my eyes at him, and he held up his hands. "I wasn't being a smartass!" he said. "I'm serious! I am a fucking medic, you know."

"I know," I said, focusing on my food again. I'd never lied to my team, and I didn't want to start. They would find out eventually about Darby's pregnancy; no point in making up a story.

"So she was puking and it's not food poisoning or a

virus," Martinez said. "Is she pregnant or something?" He chuckled.

When I didn't answer, Sloan's eyes grew bigger. "T-Rex! You wasted zero time!"

"Mind your business, Sloan," Kitsch warned.

Harbinger cleared his throat, scratched his nose, and looked down. "You know him better than that, Sloan. C'mon."

Sloan's eyebrows shot up. "Dude, is she trying to trap you? You got a level-twelve clinger on your hands?"

I frowned. "No. She didn't say it's mine. She's not like that."

"So, she *is* pregnant?" Martinez asked.

I looked at Naomi, who already had an *I told you so* look on her face. I chunked my fork at my bowl. "Goddamn it, guys. It's none of your business."

"Oh, shit," Sloan said. The table grew silent.

"You sure about this?" Harbinger said. "A single mom isn't something you consider halfheartedly, Trex."

"She's a mom. She's not single," I said.

Naomi raised an eyebrow. "That's why you've been so ambitious looking for a place all of a sudden. It's getting serious, I guess?"

I met everyone's gaze and then blew out a laugh. "I really like her. She's amazing."

"You're sure it's not because she needs saving?" Naomi asked.

I frowned. "I'm sure."

"What's so amazing about her?" Sloan asked.

"She's fucking brave for one thing. She was minutes away from marrying that dick ex of hers. She fucking walked, all alone, with no one's help. You know she showed up in the Springs in her wedding dress? Barely any money, no clothes, no nothing. That takes balls, man. She's funny, sweet, gorgeous . . . we're attracted to each other. Does she need a master's degree? Hours logged in the Peace Corps? What constitutes amazing these days?"

Naomi shrugged. "I'm just glad to hear you say it. And I'm happy for you. I just . . . Are you going to be someone's dad? Is that where this is headed? And don't say *I don't know*. This is definitely something you should know."

"I know!" I barked. I sighed. "I know."

"Should we get cigars?" Sloan asked, looking around. "I'm thinking we should take T-Rex out and celebrate."

"I can't tonight. I have plans," Naomi said quickly.

"With who?" Martinez asked.

"Attention!" Saunders called. We stood as General Tallis walked in, followed closely by Bianca. He looked over the food, and then at us, before approaching the table.

"It's pasta day, sir," Bianca said.

He nodded. "Enjoying the pasta?"

My team traded glances and nodded to the general.

"How has your first month been?"

"Uneventful . . . sir," I said.

"Oh? I heard you found your way to Echo. As we discussed, that is a restricted area."

"We like to be thorough when making rounds, General," I said. "That includes sweeping the entire corridor, up to the blast doors. The security team on the other side has stopped pissing themselves every time they see us coming."

Martinez let out a small chuckle, but the general didn't find humor in my comment. "Abrams."

"Sir?" Naomi said.

"You've officially completed one-sixth of your probation. Congratulations."

"Thank you," she said, unsure. She searched my expression

for a clue, but I kept my face smooth. The general, for whatever reason, was trying to destabilize my team.

Without another word, the general turned and left the room, Bianca in tow. I closed my eyes, waiting for Naomi's wrath.

She grabbed my shirt by the collar. "What the fuck is he talking about, Trex?"

I opened my eyes and looked straight at my friend. Even when your men are right, they still have to know their place. "Turn me loose, Lieutenant. Now."

She let go, surprised at her own reaction. She didn't like losing control any more than she liked being surprised. "Excuse me, sir."

I straightened my shirt. "For the record, I protested. They didn't like your record, Nomes," I explained. "That's all it boils down to. Has nothing to do with you being a woman."

She snarled. "My record is impeccable."

"Your previous record leading one of your father's largest militia companies, and the fact that you joined after Matt's KIA."

"It makes sense, Naomi," Harbinger said. "We all knew your history with the militia would be an issue at every turn. This is just one of them. Just ignore it."

Naomi tossed her tray onto the counter and frowned. "Something ain't right, Trex. I can smell it."

I sighed. Omission now would be too close to a lie. "Nomes, you're safe. They can't fire you."

She narrowed her eyes. "What do you mean?"

I hesitated, then decided to just say it. "We were all brought here for you."

It took her seconds to figure it out. She paled. "Peter."

"The junior senator?" Harbinger asked.

Naomi shoved her hands in her pockets. "I knew he...he

has a thing for me. He always has, but even when I saw him...I didn't think he'd go that far to..." She looked at me. "Tell me he didn't."

"He did."

"Did what?" Martinez asked.

Naomi went from unsure to pissed. "He brought us here? The whole team? It doesn't make sense, Trex. He hasn't even tried to talk to me."

"Wait. What?" Harbinger said. "That punk kid is why we were brought here? Because he has a crush on Naomi?"

"Since we were kids," she said with a sigh. "I met him when his dad was in talks with mine. They're both Arizona congressmen."

"So, what happens when he figures out she doesn't like him?" Martinez asked. "Are we out?"

"He knows," Naomi said.

Six weeks before, I wouldn't have cared, but now I had a reason to stay in Colorado Springs. "If he knows, why did he pull so many strings to get us here?"

"He pulled me from contract work," she said. "He wasn't happy when I was deployed. He warned me that he'd stick me behind a desk."

"Why didn't he?" Harbinger asked.

"I threatened to permanently cripple him, and he knew I meant it," Naomi said, her voice cold. "I'm going to talk to him." She zipped her vest and took a step before I grabbed her arm.

"Hold on. Let's think this through. Do you want to leave?" I looked at Harbinger. "Does your wife? Your kids?"

"The kids weren't thrilled at first, but they're warming up. We went to the Garden of the Gods over the weekend. They loved it."

Naomi frowned. "So...we just let him get away with it."

"We're settled, Nomes," I said. "We had a choice. We're making six figures a year, better pay than we've ever had, and it's a day job. Harbinger can go home to his family every night; we can all have lives now."

"And you falling for a local has nothing to do with this, I'm guessing." Naomi smirked.

"What does it matter? It's done. I see why you're pissed that he set this all up for you, and if he becomes a problem, you bet your ass we'll deal with it."

"I'm more pissed that you knew about it," she said. "We don't keep shit from one another. Ever."

"You're right. I shouldn't have kept it from you. From any of you. That's not how we work. I knew better."

"So, the general knows?" she asked.

"He informed me. And he's not happy about your stalker changing things up in his facility. I assume that's another reason for your probation—to keep Bennett on his toes."

"All right. Break's over, let's get moving," Kitsch said.

I patted Naomi on the shoulder. "Want to fuck with the Echo team again?"

She smiled. "It's the best part of my day."

I gave everyone else assignments, and Naomi followed me to the mouth of Delta corridor. I looked up at the ceiling, the moisture collecting on the pipes and electrical lines, dripping intermittently. If the water didn't hit us, it fell through the metal grid we used as a path down the Delta corridor to Echo. The stench of mildew grew thicker with each step, the further we pushed into Delta toward Echo.

"I have to say it, Trex. You and Darby, it's fast for anyone, but especially fast for you. You never fall so quick for anyone. Not even Laura, and I thought you two would get married," Naomi said.

"Exactly. My hesitation with her was spot-on. She married Brad, remember? No hesitation this time."

Naomi nearly choked. "What? You're already thinking long term? Trex," she protested.

"It's headed that way. I'm not even ashamed to admit it. She's the one, Nomes, I know it. We went on our first date last week. We've spent every evening together since. It would be more if she didn't work eleven at night to seven in the morning."

"Well, well... I guess she likes you, too."

"God, I hope so. This is everything I was missing with Laura."

"I was going to ask why it was different."

"It's just better. Way better."

"Because of the sex?"

"Not there yet."

"What? You're falling for this girl and you haven't bedded her yet? She must have some sort of spell over you."

"No, and I can't explain it. I just can't wait to get back to the hotel to see her. I want to spend every second with her. I make up excuses to visit her at work. She works nights and I have to force myself to go to bed instead of hanging out with her."

"That explains why you've been so tired lately."

"You know, with Val, she had the whole still-married thing, and I didn't want anywhere near that."

"And now you're speeding toward insta-Daddy at a hundred miles per hour and that's A-OK. It must be love."

As crazy as it sounded, I didn't deny it. We approached the blast doors at the end of Echo corridor, and as usual, the yellow lights began to spin, and a single, low alarm sounded. Security on the other side stood in formation, pointing their rifles at the door, even though we could only know that from watching the screen.

"Step away from the doors, Trexler," the officer on duty said through the speaker.

"Did you miss us?" I asked.

"You have ten seconds," he said.

Naomi tried not to smile, but failed. "You look forward to this every day. Admit it."

"Five seconds," he said, unamused.

"Isn't that..." she began.

Dr. DuPont and Dr. Philpot were standing fifty yards behind the security team, in a heated discussion.

"Yeah, but we should move," I said.

We made a wide U-turn, and walked in the other direction, our boots clanging against the metal floor.

"They're so cranky," Naomi said with a chuckle.

"I hope the general never asks us to take their place. I'd hate to be that pissy all the time."

"Or stuck in there," she said, looking over her shoulder. "Do they ever leave?"

"I don't know. For their sake, I hope so. If the doctors are going in and out, they must."

"Boss, come in," Kitsch said over the com.

"Go ahead," I said.

"We've got some weird shit on the south side."

"You're exterior?" I asked, confused.

"Rounds completed. Saw something on the camera. You should come see this, sir."

I met Naomi's gaze. "On our way."

chapter fourteen

Darby

For the first time in weeks, my body didn't fight me with every step, and I didn't feel like at any moment I would throw up whatever happened to be in my stomach at the time. My energy was back, and so was my appetite.

The feeling that an alien had taken over my body was beginning to go away. That, of course, brought on new worries, so I was glad Health Services could push through my assistance and I could make an appointment with Dr. Park right about the time I was beginning to stress about Bean.

I sat in the waiting room, watching updates about the fire scroll across the bottom of the television screen. I'd filled out a dozen forms, stepped on a scale, and peed in a cup, now all there was to do was wait. Not a first-timer at the gynecologist's office, I was used to seeing the mix of very pregnant women, either miserable or obnoxiously happy—there was no in-between—a few toddlers playing with or fighting over toys on the floor, a chatty grandmother, and a small handful of women like me, there for an annual, infertility, or just not showing yet. Most of the husbands looked uncomfortable, but there was always the super-supportive one. And, of course, the one mom-and-daughter duo, trying not to speak to one another while they wait for the teen's first gyno appointment, both very nervous.

A nurse in lilac scrubs stepped out. "Darby," she said. Her full cheeks rounded when she smiled. I stood, looking very much *unpregnant* and single, surrounded by women with skin barely fitting over their perfectly round middles, their noses and ankles puffy, their husbands' hands on the babies they'd helped create.

"Hi, I'm Shannon," the nurse said, closing the door behind us. Her sun-kissed spirals hovered just above her shoulders, her curves filling out her scrubs. She had silver rings on all eight of her fingers, a tiny diamond in the crease of her nose, and a tan that boasted any spare time was spent in the summer Colorado sun. "You'll be in room two, second door on your left."

I stepped into the room, deciding in the moment where to sit. The wax paper pulled over the table for sanitary reasons made a sound that was worse than nails on a chalkboard to me. So I skipped the table and sat in the chair.

"Hi, Darby. It's nice to meet you," Shannon said, standing next to a tablet on a stand. She tapped it a few times and then smiled at me. "The lab confirms it. You're pregnant. Congratulations."

"Thank you."

"Do you remember the first day of your last period?"

"Uh...May sixth."

She tapped the screen a few more times. "Okay, looks like you're due February first."

I grinned and nodded, not knowing what else to say.

"Any questions or concerns?" she asked, slipping a small clip on my finger and a blood pressure cuff over my arm.

"I've been feeling a lot better. The nausea, dizziness, and vomiting let up finally. I just want to make sure everything's all right."

"Was the morning sickness pretty intense?" she asked.

"It wasn't fun."

"I'm so sorry. If you have any issues again, don't hesitate to call. Even if we can't get you in right away, the doctor can prescribe something to help. We got you in today because of cancelations for the holiday...yesterday being the Fourth and all that."

"I appreciate it."

"Did you do anything fun despite the firework ban?"

"Spent the evening with a friend."

"That sounds fun! Everything okay at home? Do you feel unsafe? Stressed? Are you eating properly? I see no drugs or alcohol. You don't smoke..."

She was going down the list of things I'd answered in the paperwork, sometimes talking to herself, sometimes asking me questions. I wasn't sure if she'd peppered in the tough questions with the easy ones to trip me up or if it was typical.

"I feel safe. I'm a little stressed. I just moved here, but I work at the Colorado Springs Hotel, and I live there, too. My boss is great, but he doesn't know I'm pregnant. I'd like to keep it that way for a while. Just trying to get my prenatal care started and figuring out how to pay for everything is a little stressful. I don't have a car, but it's nothing I can't handle."

Shannon blinked. "You moved here alone?"

I nodded.

"From where? Do I hear a Texas accent?"

"Yes, ma'am."

"Where is the father?"

"Back in Texas. He doesn't know, either. I didn't feel safe there."

"But you do now?"

"Yes."

She smiled. "Great! Dr. Park will be in shortly."

Shannon squirted a gel onto a napkin on a silver tray, and then she left me alone. I tapped my nails on the wood arms of the chair I sat in, looking around the room.

"Good afternoon!" Dr. Park said, breezing in. Her blond hair was pulled into a low bun, her glasses sat low on her nose. She sat on a rolling stool, her white lab coat over a pair of light gray slacks and white blouse. "Vitals look good. Labs look good. I hear you've had the barfs. That's no fun. But you're feeling better?"

"Um…yes. The past couple of days have been good."

"Shannon tells me you moved here from Texas, and that maybe you weren't in the best situation before."

"Correct. But I'm good here now."

"No family, though? No emergency contact? And you don't have transportation, correct?"

"No."

"Okay, good to know. We'll need to get a plan together when we're closer to"—she checked the chart—"February. Can I have you sit on the table? Any allergies? Latex?"

"No. None." I climbed up, and she warned me before leaning the seat back.

"We're going to take a look, is that okay? See what we can see?" she said. The way she asked multiple questions at a time made me feel more overwhelmed by the minute. "It's a little early, but we can try it."

"We're going to see the baby?" I asked, surprised.

"Is that okay? Can you lift your shirt for me?"

"Yes, I just wasn't expecting that, I guess."

She tucked a napkin into my jeans and squirted gel onto my stomach. "Just going to squirt a bit here, and…" She dabbed the microphone-looking thing in her hand in the gel, spread around what she'd put on my stomach, and then stopped down by my pelvic bone, pressing down.

"Well, hello there, baby," she said, smiling at the monitor. It was black and white, and not much of anything. She pointed out the sac to me, showing me the tiny grain of rice that was my Bean. My eyes filled with tears as she measured and tapped out data, cooing to Bean like he or she was already here.

She pushed a few buttons, and the room filled with a fast but rhythmic beat.

"Is that...?"

"The heartbeat. Nice and strong." She pulled the probe away and wiped off my stomach with a clean white rag, leaving it for me to finish up. Just like that, Bean was gone.

"Everything okay?" I asked.

"Everything looks wonderful. You've got a few weeks of your first trimester left, then we're on to the fun stuff like feeling the baby move for the first time, showing, maternity clothes. Exciting stuff! Have you started prenatal vitamins? They have some great over-the-counter ones. They might make you start feeling icky again, so just play around with it. Try to take them right before you go to bed, or maybe after a meal...everyone is different. We'll find something that works for you. It's important to find something with folic acid."

I nodded. My brain felt full, and I was beginning to get a headache.

Dr. Park laughed. "I'll have this all on paper for you, no worries. Want a picture?"

"A...?"

"Copy of what's on the screen," she explained.

"Um...yes?"

She pressed a few buttons, and a series of pictures began to spill out from the ultrasound machine. Dr. Park took off her gloves, tossed them in the trash, and stood. "Okay.

You're all set. We'll see you in four weeks." She tore off the photos and handed them to me.

Dr. Park closed the door behind her just as I said thank you. I sat in the room alone, then looked down, wiping the remaining gel carefully off my stomach. The fluorescent light above glinted off the pictures in my hand, catching my attention. What was supposed to be my baby looked like a mess of black and white. I didn't really see anything. I put the pictures in my back pocket, said good-bye to Shannon, and checked out at the front desk with Michelle.

"See you next month!" Michelle said with a bright smile.

The walk home was hot and felt like it took longer than it did to get to Dr. Park's office. The wind was blowing the smoke into town, and my throat felt dry and scratchy. By the time I reached the hotel, I was coughing, and went straight to the bar for a glass of water.

"Darby?" Stavros called. "How are you feeling?"

"Great," I said, clearing my throat.

"Good, because Tilde had to leave early. Maya is covering, but she's already put in forty hours this week. Can you come in early? Like . . . soon?"

"I can," I said.

"You look nice," Zeke said with a smile.

"Thanks," I said, using the gun to pour cold water into a glass. I cleared my throat.

"I know. The smoke is bad today. The winds changed. They were saying that might happen. Glad they were prepared."

"Me, too. When do you go out again?" I took a drink, feeling the cold liquid extinguish the burning sensation in my throat.

"They're saying tomorrow morning."

I frowned. "Well, be careful, okay?"

He smiled. "We always are."

"Where've you been lately? I haven't seen you around."

Zeke smiled. "Doing stuff. Same as you."

"Same as me?" I smirked. "Trex is busier than I thought."

Zeke chuckled. "Not Trex."

"A girl?" I asked. When Zeke didn't offer more, I insisted. "Oh, really? Where did you meet her?"

"Out one night."

"So mysterious," I teased, taking a drink. "Is she nice?"

"She's everything," Zeke said.

"Good. You deserve nothing less."

He got that aw-shucks look I'd fallen for so many times. But Zeke was genuine. I was glad the mystery girl was putting a smile on his face, and I realized Trex had had the same one.

"Thanks," Zeke said. "So, you're feeling better? You look like you feel better."

"I am."

"I still feel bad…about the bar. Trex was right, I shouldn't have taken you there."

Stavros approached, straightening his tie before he began cleaning behind the bar. "Have you eaten?"

"Yes." I chuckled. "Everyone acts like I'll die if I don't eat."

"No, you just puke all over my lobby," he teased. He nodded to Zeke. "What are you kids up to?"

"Just relaxing before dinner," Zeke said. "Hitting the sack early tonight. We were told we'll likely go out tomorrow."

"You don't look so happy about it," Stavros said.

"He just met a mystery girl. I bet leaving her for ten days is bugging him," I said.

"Darby, damn," he said. He tried and failed to look upset.

"Mystery girl. She sounds intriguing," Stavros said.

"Not talking about it," Zeke said.

"You talked about it with Darby, but you can't talk about it with your bartender? That's not right."

"I didn't," Zeke said, pointing, "talk about her to Darby."

"It's true, I don't know much," I said.

"Well, I was wondering," Stavros said.

"What?" Zeke asked.

"You have a new distraction. Explains how you got over it so fast that Darby wasn't interested in a relationship of any kind, and then Trexler came along and she was all for it."

My mouth fell open, and Zeke pulled his ball cap lower on his forehead. "Don't know anything about that."

Stavros was more than pleased with himself, nearly giddy. "I admit it. I'm a drama whore." His smile vanished and he became serious. "But I don't gossip. Gossip isn't true."

I frowned. "I'm going to get ready for work."

"Have a good day, sweetie," Stavros called after me.

"I'm not speaking to you!" I hollered, hurrying to my room.

I pulled the photos from my back pocket and placed them on the nightstand, and then I slowly made my way to the shower, to wash the dried remnants of gel off my stomach and the sweat from the walk home. I wondered what Trex was doing, and if he thought about me during the day, too. We'd spent so much time together that week, it was like we'd been together twice as long. No games, no wondering if he liked me, no wondering what kind of mood he would be in. Trex listened, he had so many great stories, and there was still so much to learn about each other. It was so refreshing it almost made me miss having a cell phone so I could text him during the day. Almost. Freeing myself from my phone was the best decision I'd made in a very long time.

I dressed and played with the makeup Maya had given

to me, pulled my hair into a bun, put on my freshly pressed shirt and pants, and headed down the hall. One day, when I could afford an apartment, I was going to miss the convenience of walking down the hall to work.

I greeted Maya, and she smiled at me. "Wow. You did great."

"I um...used to do pageants. I wore a lot of makeup back then."

"You look like a supermodel," she said. "Don't you just love it?"

"It's fun when you don't have to."

I checked in a line of hotshots, and between breaks I chatted with Zeke, Watts, Sugar, and Kasen and Sweets, hotshots from two other crews. They were buzzing around me, seeming intrigued by the products on my face.

"Hi," a man said in a thick Australian accent. He towered over me, as did the other blond-haired, ocean-eyed man he was with. They were standing with Maddox. "Checkin' in, sweetheart. We should have a room reserved."

"Name?" I asked.

"Liam Walker. Unless it's under this bloke's name."

As I checked the men in, another from the back snapped something just loud enough for me to hear.

"All right, we don't have all day," Maddox said.

"Hi, Taylor," I said. "Everything okay?"

"It's Tyler," he grumbled.

"Pardon?"

He sighed. "I'm Tyler. Yes, we're twins. Yes, we're identical. Yes, the resemblance is uncanny. It's been a long day. Can I please check the fuck in?"

"It's my fault, darl. I made him cranky on the ride over," Liam said.

I typed in Tyler's name, trying to keep a smile on my

face. I was half pissed, half intimidated, and then pissed for feeling intimidated. Tyler wasn't Shawn. He wasn't going to come over the desk at me and squeeze my neck until I thought I might pass out. But still, a man speaking so gruffly to me had me on edge.

"Just one key?" I asked.

"No, two."

His answer gave me pause. "One adult, correct?"

He looked over his shoulder at the dark-haired woman a few feet behind him. "No, she's with me. Ellison Edson."

I tapped the mouse and moved it around. "I have her in a king room, booked by . . . *MountainEar Magazine*."

Tyler glanced over his shoulder at Liam and Jack. They were having a conversation between them, not paying attention. "Just the one room."

"You want me to cancel hers? I'll have to confirm with her."

"No . . . no," he sighed, frustrated. "Fuck it, never mind. Just . . . put hers on my card."

"I can do that." I processed his card, created his key, and set them aside. "Just need you to sign here for yours, and then I'll start hers." By the time he'd finished signing, I was already running his card again. He sighed a second time, and he leaned closer.

I tried not to lean back, so I held my breath and stood still instead.

"Can you make sure she has a nice view?"

"I'm sorry, Mr. Maddox, it's our last room. It's a parking lot view, but it's on the third floor, and—"

"Christ, forget it."

I raised an eyebrow. "Have a better day . . . sir."

Tyler cringed. I could tell he felt bad, but I wasn't going to forgive him until he was sorry. He turned to hand Ellison her room key, and I watched them have a hushed conversation for a few seconds.

"Fuck you," she said, snatching the key card from his hand. She marched to the elevator, and Tyler chased after her. He didn't quite make it before the doors closed, though, and looked relieved when the next one opened seconds after he pushed the button.

Liam stepped forward. "He's really not a bad guy. They're just..."

"Dysfunctional," I said.

"Pretty much."

"Is she going to be okay?" I asked.

"Ellie? Shit yeah. She'll knock him into next week."

"Bloody likely," Jack said, nodding.

I sighed with relief. "Good. That's good. You gentlemen have a nice night."

"I'm gonna have a beer. Want one?" Liam asked.

"I'm...working," I said.

"Damn," Liam said, peering into the meeting room. The Alpines' head guy, Chief, looked unhappy. Liam tapped Jack on the shoulder. "We should see what's going on."

The hotshots in the lobby made a beeline for the meeting room, standing behind Chief as he gave the Forestry Department heads a stern speech. I wondered why Trex wasn't in on the meeting. If Chief was losing his temper, maybe Trex was up on the mountain. That made me nervous. I pulled out a pen and pad, drawing the forest. It wasn't on fire; everyone was safe. That's how I would imagine Trex.

"Hi," Ellison said, standing in front of me.

I smiled, pushing away the notepad.

"That's pretty good," Ellison said.

"Thanks. What can I do for you?"

Ellison placed her credit card on the front desk. "Can I change the card on my room?"

"Sure," I said, sliding the silver rectangle off the desk. I clicked my mouse a few times, swiped the card. "For incidentals, too?"

"Yes. Everything."

"Got it," I said, handing the card back to her once the screen confirmed approval. The receipt printed, and I placed it in front of her. "Just sign here."

There was something about Ellison that just made her likable. She refused to take crap from anyone and seemed like she'd been telling people no and saying what was on her mind since birth. I envied that about her. Her short, razored hair was fuss free, and she wasn't wearing much makeup, but she was stunning. Exotic. Wild. I was none of those things.

"Thanks, Darby."

"No problem, *MountainEar*," I said. It was meant to be a joke, but I realized how lame it was the moment Ellison didn't even attempt to laugh. She left me to sit at the bar in front of Stavros, unconcerned about making me feel better about my socially awkward moment. That was freedom I'd never experienced.

"She's sex on a stick, that one," Jack said, crossing his arms and lifting his chin as if he were proud just to know her. "We've already seen her naked."

"Meeting over?" I asked.

"We're not invited for another fifteen minutes," Liam said, standing with Zeke.

"Nice lipstick," Trex said as he made his way from the elevator bay to the front desk.

I smiled. I'd tried one of the reds Maya had given me. "Hey, handsome. I didn't see you come in."

"Welp," Zeke said, saluting before heading toward the meeting room.

"It's called Fly Girl. You like it?" I asked.

"I like you," he said, leaning his elbows on the desk. "Get called in early?"

I nodded. "You're off early."

"Just stopping by for a second. On my way back. How's your day been?"

"I had an appointment. It went well."

"An appointment? Like with the..."

"Obstetrician," I said quietly.

"Oh." Trex was making a strange expression, a mixture of surprise and disappointment.

"What is that face?"

"I just thought...I don't know, I guess it's stupid to think I'd be invited."

"To my appointment?"

"Well...yeah."

He seemed embarrassed to admit it, but part of me found it endearing. The other part thought about how disastrous that could be. I thought about Trex being in the doctor's office with me, looking like every other couple who waited in the lobby. The bigger my belly grew, the more of a relief that would be, but having to explain to the doctor who he was this soon into my pregnancy wasn't something I was prepared to do.

"Trex—"

"It's okay. You don't have to explain. I get it. It's weird."

"It's a little weird."

"I'm sorry. I don't mean to pressure you."

I laughed. "You're not. I don't feel pressured."

"Good," he said, standing up. "Gotta run back to work for a bit. Are you getting off early?"

"Nope, I'm here until seven a.m. You're not going up on the mountain, right?" I asked.

"Yes, but not anywhere near the fire."

I smiled, relieved. "Good."

His lips formed a hard line. "I wish you weren't at work. I have an uncontrollable urge to kiss you."

I leaned in, stopping just short of his mouth. "Come back soon, then."

He groaned, but smiled as he turned on his heels and breezed through the sliding doors. He looked around before climbing into his truck and backing out, his engine growling as he drove out of the parking lot.

I made my way to Stavros, trying to pretend I didn't already miss Trex.

"Hanging in there?" I asked, leaning on the bar.

"Some of the hotshots don't tip," he grumbled. "And, so far, all of them are straight."

"It's been like this all week," I said, resting my chin in my hand. It was that time of day I wished I could have caffeine. Coffee or a soda would have made the rest of the night more manageable. Ellison leaned away from me and fidgeted. "Are you all right?"

"Who was that guy who just left?" Ellison asked. "The one who talked to you before rushing out the door?"

"Trex?" I asked, feeling an uncontrollable smile stretch across my mouth. I was surprised she didn't already know him, between being a reporter for *MountainEar Magazine*, running with the Alpines, and dating a Maddox boy.

"Yeah," Ellison said, shifting on her bar stool. She readjusted the large black sunglasses on top of her head, making a few strands of dark hair poke out in different directions like a black firecracker.

I wasn't sure how to answer that, and knowing she was a

reporter, I blurted out the first thing I could think of. "He's a firefighter staying here until the fire is out. He's like...some kind of special crew. He's not a hotshot or ground crew. He doesn't really talk about it." It wasn't technically a lie. He didn't talk about it, and he was a special...something. And he was looking for a place. He would be moved out by the time the fire was over. Probably.

"Like fire secret service?" Ellison asked.

I giggled. "Probably. He's about that uptight."

"So, don't you know him?" she asked.

I was beginning to wonder what her interest in Trex was about. "A little."

"Just a little?" Stavros asked with a smirk.

"What about you?" I asked Ellison. I combed through my ponytail with my fingers, hoping Ellison would see it as a sign of me just wanting a casual conversation. I did, but now I was feeling the tiniest bit territorial. Ellison was beautiful and wild and *not* pregnant. She had the respect of the Alpines...she had a lot going for her. If she turned her attention to Trex, I wasn't sure I could compete with that. I felt my eyes water and willed the tears away. The vomiting and dizziness might have gone away, but the mood swings were still obnoxiously present. "I'm guessing you're a reporter from your credit card?"

"Photographer. I'm following the Alpines around."

"Oh. I've met Taylor Maddox and Zeke Lund. They're sweethearts. They've been hanging out with Trex." *Maybe mentioning her boyfriend's twin is a friend will deter her?* I felt like a child, but Trex was finally something good in my life. I had to protect it.

"They have?" Ellison asked, surprised.

"Yeah, been up in his room almost every night since they got here."

"How long has Trex been here?"

Stavros looked suspicious, and I was glad I wasn't the only one who found Ellison's line of questioning... aggressive.

I shrugged. Something told me not to answer any more of her questions. "Two weeks." *Ish.* "He got here before the fire started." *Damn it, Darby, shut up.*

Ellison frowned. "That's weird."

I smiled, trying to play it off. "Maybe it's not the fire secret service. Maybe it's the fire secret psychic."

A family walked into the lobby, looking hot and exhausted. I returned to the front desk to greet them before they got there, grateful for the distraction. I was failing at protecting anything.

"We have a reservation," the father said. "Last name's Snow." The kids were whining and fighting, the mother too tired to intercede. I typed in their name, stopping when I heard Ellison yell across the lobby.

"Maddox!"

Taylor was walking away from her, looking angry. Ellison turned to Stavros, and he smiled at her.

I tried my best to get the Snows checked in as quickly as possible, giving them their cards, and showing them to the elevator bay as a segue to find my way to the bar.

"Everything okay?" I asked.

Stavros put another drink in front of her. "She has vodka now. She's fine."

A sudden collection of walking, shuffling, and rattling grabbed my attention, and I watched the Alpine hotshots walk across the lobby from the elevator bay to the parking lot, outfitted and gear in hand. I waited for Ellison to turn around, but she pounded back her drink. Tyler didn't even turn to look in her direction.

"Wow, he's really pissed," Stavros said. "He didn't even look back."

"Stavros," I scolded. I sat next to Ellie. "He needs to concentrate. I'm sure he's just trying to focus."

"I'm sure," Ellison said, pushing her glass forward. She wasn't turning it in, she was asking for another. "Let's save us all time and make it a double," Ellison said.

"The girl can drink," Stavros said, impressed.

"This is over Maddox?" I asked.

"Actually," Ellie said, taking two big gulps until the clear liquid was gone. She pushed the empty glass toward Stavros. "This is not over Maddox. This is my stand against the patriarchy."

"This will get 'em good," Stavros said, pouring another double.

"I mean, I like him. He's a good guy. But let's be honest. A ball sack would get me a ride to fire camp."

Stavros spit out a laugh and looked at me, thoroughly amused.

"Are you originally from Estes Park?" I asked.

"My family has a house there."

"I knew it," Stavros said. "Ellison Edson. You're related to the Edson Tech people, aren't you?"

"Sort of," she said, taking another gulp.

"Do you drink like this…often?" I asked.

"Not lately. I'm just in a hurry to get drunk before I change my mind." She raked her dark hair back with her fingers before crossing her arms on the bar. She downed the next drink, and then Stavros made her something more…recreational…to sip on for the next hour. He warned that if she didn't sip, she would be cut off. She played the game, talking more than she drank, but the moment her hour was up, she ordered another double.

"It's still bullshit," Ellison said. She was talking more slowly, and I was torn between wishing the liquor would hit her hard and fast so she'd need to pass out, or hoping Stavros would just cut her off and feed her something. Unfortunately, he didn't get many women in the hotel who could drink like Ellison, and he was supremely amused.

"You don't think them grounding you has anything to do with safety?" Stavros asked. "You might be a tad sensitive about this," Stavros said.

"No, Judge Judy, I don't. I've been traveling everywhere the Alpines have been, including the goddamn fire line. A fire is never safe. This is a political fire, and wouldn't it be bad press for the Forestry Department if the daughter of Edson Tech's CEO was crispy fried? That's what this is about, and it's bullshit. And...Tyler didn't even stick up for me."

"He said he did. They all did," I chimed in. She gave me a dirty look, and I could tell the alcohol was already beginning to take effect.

"Clearly, he didn't try hard enough," she grumbled. She took a normal-sized drink, squinting her eyes as she became lost in thought. "Anyone know where the fire boundaries are? I could get behind it and shoot the black...at least end up with something."

"Well, you're drinking," Stavros said, "so that's the first reason that's a bad idea. Second, you could be arrested. Third, it's dangerous."

"That it's dangerous is *third*?" I asked.

"Fourth," he continued.

Ellison was already bored with his list. "I've been drinking since I was eleven. I can outdrink six large Russian men—that's not an analogy, I actually have."

"I believe it," Stavros said, pouring her another.

I shot him a look, hoping he would cut her off soon. She was drinking so fast it was all going to hit her at once.

"Last one for an hour," Stavros said.

Ellison tipped her head back and swallowed the entire double in one gulp. "I haven't eaten today. I'm not going to need you in an hour." She stood and slammed her hand on the counter. She wasn't weaving yet, but I could see in her eyes that her thoughts were cloudy.

"Ellie," I called after her. "Please don't try to go out there. It's not safe."

"Exactly," she said, pulling her sunglasses down over her eyes.

chapter fifteen

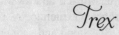

Trex. I need your help." I could hardly believe the words coming through the phone from Tyler Maddox.

"What happened?" I asked, still sitting in my truck in the hotel parking lot. I'd been excited the entire ride home to see Darby, but my phone rang just as I put the truck into Park.

"It's Ellie. She fell off the wagon and hitched a ride out to the base of the mountain. She got lost—"

"What wagon?" I asked.

"Damn it, Trex! She's an alcoholic. She drank after the Alpines left...after *I* left her there...and wandered around on a burning mountain for hours."

"Why?" I asked, incredulous. Ellison sounded like a crazy, complicated mess.

"She's usually our photographer. She follows us around up on the mountain. She couldn't go this time, she was pissed, she went up anyway. We finally found her, they arrested her, she's sitting in a jail cell in county jail."

"That sucks, man. I'm sorry. What do you expect me to do about it?"

"You were FBI, right? Waltz in there and get her out."

"I'm not 007, Tyler. I'm also not a criminal. That's illegal."

"No, I mean, talk them into letting her go."

"Tyler. I can't."

"You fucking can. And you will."

"I don't have time for this—"

"I talked to Darby earlier. She has no idea who you really are, does she? Why? What are you hiding?"

"Tyler—"

"Why haven't you told her you're former FBI? What are you doing now?"

I sighed. "It's classified."

"So, you are lying to her."

"It's complicated."

Tyler waited a beat. "It could get even more complicated if Darby knew you weren't part of the Forestry Department."

"You're pissing me off."

"Just…" He sighed. I could almost see him rubbing his temples, trying to keep his shit together so he could help the woman he loved. "Help her. This is my fault."

"Fine. I'll make a few calls, but I can't promise anything. But in return, you and Ellie have to promise to keep your fucking mouths shut. You have no idea what you'd be getting yourselves into. It's national security, asshole, and if they think you or Ellie know anything about my employment, it's not good for either of you. You're not allowed to know. Do you understand?"

"I understand. Thank you."

I hung up, and let my head fall back to the headrest. I was about to do a lot of illegal shit to keep Darby from hating me, and I wasn't sure I could pull it off. I rushed into the hotel, sneaking past Darby to run upstairs to fetch a suit, and then snuck past her again. It wasn't easy. I had to wait until she was busy with hotel guests, and the lobby was nearly empty except for the few hotshots gathered to shoot the shit. I stopped in the parking lot, staring at my Land Cruiser. No

way was that hunk of beautiful junk going to pass for official
transportation.

"Hey, Stavros," I said, standing behind the biggest hotshot
I could find near the bar. "That's your Audi out front, right?"

"Yeah, isn't she gorgeous? Fancy is black on black on
black on black, and tinted windows."

"So...my truck won't start, and I have a meeting in fifteen. Can I borrow Fancy for an hour?"

Stavros frowned at me.

"Please?"

He reached behind the bar and put down his keys. "You
break her, and I'm billing it to your room."

"Deal," I said, scooping up his key ring and walking
quickly out to the lot.

I drove to the gas station and changed, then slid back behind the driver's seat, breathing hard and straightening my
tie. The summer sun was beating down on Fancy's black
paint, creating an oven effect that the AC was having a hard
time keeping up with.

Baking, with hot air blowing through the vents at me in
a hot suit, I scrolled through my contacts and then tapped
Val's name.

"Well, well, well..." she answered on the sixth ring.
"This is the second favor you've needed in as many months.
What is it this time?"

"I'm actually the one doing the favor this time," I said
with a sigh. I pulled out into the street, hoping some movement would help the AC.

"Do tell," she responded. She didn't sound like the light,
giggly Val I remembered. The emotional attachment was
gone.

"This fire north of the Springs...a photographer was
caught trying to make her way up the mountain to shoot it."

"Is she missing?"

"No. She was caught and arrested. She'd been drinking. She's sitting in county."

"Sounds like she broke the law."

"She did, but she's Tyler Maddox's girlfriend. So it's my favor. In return for one."

"That's a bizarre plot twist. And you've got some fucking balls, you know that?"

"I need you to look up some names for me."

She sighed. "The ASAC—"

"Maddox will clear it. You know he will."

"I don't know it. He'd do it if it were one of his brothers, but a girlfriend…Probably not."

I rubbed my temples with my thumb and middle finger. The Assistant Special Agent in Charge of the San Diego office happened to be Taylor and Tyler's older brother, Thomas. "Tyler is desperate. I'm right here. I can help."

"It's not going to happen, Scottie."

"If he says no, tell him I'll have Tyler call him to ask his big brother for his own fucking favor."

"Don't push him, Trex. You should've done what he asked."

"Goddamn it! I went to Estes Park, questioned Taylor and Tyler. They didn't know anything about that campus fire. I can't help that the ASAC's baby brother broke the law. And I did what Thomas asked, Val. He fucked me over for it."

"You were on your way out, anyway. You hated the job."

I couldn't argue. But Thomas made it easy to leave.

"Trex," Val began again, "listen…If it's Tyler's girlfriend, you're right, he'll probably go for it. You know he'll do anything for family. Even if it's for you. He might even appreciate that you're trying to help."

"I called him an overbearing pussy when I left, Val."

"He doesn't hold grudges. I'll patch you through."

"Wait. Val!" An obnoxiously calming instrumental came over the receiver. "Fuck," I hissed.

"Well, hello to you, too, Trexler," Thomas Maddox said.

I gripped my steering wheel. "Maddox, I don't have much time."

"Val filled me in. Ellison?"

"Yeah, and Tyler is freaking out."

"What's in it for you?"

"None of your fucking business," I said, my voice low.

"I thought you said you didn't have much time?"

I sighed, my knuckles turning white under the pressure as I squeezed the steering wheel tighter. "The girl I'm dating. She's running from a real sick fuck. Fort Hood."

"Well, that's unfortunate."

"Meanwhile, Ellie is sitting in a cell in county and your brother is pissing himself."

He took a moment to think, and then he spoke. "I'll make the call. The story is that Ellie's an asset. You're an agent as far as they know, and you're welcome. You said you needed names?"

"Darby Cooke," I said. "The ex's name is Shawn. He's military at Fort Hood. Didn't sound too high up. Can you see what you have on them?"

"Dixon," Maddox said.

"What? What does that mean?" I asked.

"Val looked her up a while ago. A woman scorned is even better than the best FBI agent. Val liked you, you know."

"Get to the point, Maddox."

"Your girl's real name is Darby Dixon, she's clean, but keep an eye out for her ex, Shawn Littlefield. He's got some interesting shit on his record. I'm surprised he's still on base. He must know someone who's keeping him protected."

My jaws ticked under the skin. "You don't think you could have told me this sooner?"

"It's unauthorized, Trex. You think I'm going to stick my neck out for you?"

The hairs on the back of my neck stood on end. If Thomas had been standing in front of me, I would have thrown a punch. "She's terrified of him. She still has nightmares. I need to keep him away from her."

"I don't owe you shit, Trex."

"Just be a decent fucking human being, Maddox," I growled.

He sighed. "I'll have Sawyer keep an eye on him."

"Sawyer?" I groaned. "What the fuck, Maddox?" Sawyer was Val's husband, and he was not going to be happy about doing any favors for me.

"He's the best, Trex. Do you want him, or not?"

I looked at the ceiling, swearing under my breath. "Fine."

"Good luck, Trexler. Sounds like you need it."

I tapped the End button, slammed the gear into reverse, and tore out of the parking lot toward the county jail.

* * *

A sheriff's deputy with *Duffy* inscribed on his metal name tag was waiting on me when I arrived, eager to show me past the regular, protected check-in desk, through a code-protected door, to a long, white hall where Tyler was sitting in a chair. He was alone, holding his face in his hands. He was so worried that he barely noticed when I approached.

"Mr. Maddox," I said in a firm tone.

Tyler stood up, his face red and blotchy. "Did you, uh . . . ?"

"I'll be transporting you and Miss Edson to a safe location. For now, I'll need you to wait here."

Tyler nodded and sat, catching on quickly that I needed him to stay silent.

"So," Duffy said, going through the paperwork, "you're a fed, huh? What are they? Witness protection? Because you don't see this every day."

"I'm not at liberty to say. As quickly as possible, Deputy. We can't have her in one location too long."

He nodded, hurrying through the papers. "Chuck!" he called. Another deputy, this one was large, square-jawed, and unimpressed with my suit. "Edson is being released into federal custody."

Chuck eyed me for a moment.

"We'll need her immediately, Deputy," I said.

Chuck nodded and then held an ID card against a black box. The lock clicked, the door buzzed, and Chuck disappeared into the back.

"She'll be right out, Agent Trexler. I just need you to sign these forms," Duffy said, sliding a dozen papers toward me.

Within five minutes, the door opened, and Chuck was holding Ellison by the arm. Her hair was a mess, her face smudged with soot and a cut just beneath her eye. She wasn't as smooth as Tyler, looking confused to see me. She opened her mouth, but I stood, took her from Chuck's grasp, and whispered in her ear as he turned from us.

"Don't speak," I warned her.

"We're releasing Miss Edson into your custody, Agent Trexler," Duffy said. "We assume you'll make sure she's not in a restricted area again?"

"She'll be north. Nowhere near the fire," I said.

Ellison stayed quiet while I escorted her down the long

hallway to Tyler. He hadn't moved, in the same position as before. When the door closed behind us, he looked up.

"Oh, thank Christ," he said, standing up and wrapping his arms around Ellison.

It was hard to imagine the feeling of knowing Darby was in a situation from which I was powerless to save her. Fighting a battle we couldn't win didn't happen often for guys like Tyler and me, but no amount of muscle or skill was going to get Ellison out of that jail cell. And no amount of coaxing from me was going to pull Darby out of her shell any faster. She wouldn't trust me until she was ready, and I had no idea when that would be—if ever. Patience, love, and a little luck were the only things that helped in these moments, and my mind and heart were warring over waiting as long as it took and wanting more.

Tyler kissed her temple, then held her away from him. She winced.

"What the fuck were you thinking, Ellison? I mean... what in the actual *fuck*?" he asked.

"Not here," I said, holding open the door to the lobby. We walked through and exited out the front. I opened the back passenger side door of the Audi, and Ellison slid in, followed by Tyler. Once the door shut, Tyler's yelling was muffled, but it blasted me when I opened the driver's side door. I closed it quickly and backed out before Tyler drew attention.

"I'm really, really sorry. That was so stupid. I wasn't thinking," Ellison said.

"That tends to happen when you're drunk," Tyler snapped.

"I'd only had two drinks," Ellison said.

"You're really going to lie to me? After I just pulled a hundred strings to get you out of jail?"

"I'm not... lying," Ellison said, sinking back into her seat.

"Wow. Okay, then," he said, facing forward. His jaw muscles were twitching as he clenched his teeth.

"Technically," I said, "I'm the one who pulled all the strings."

Ellison wasn't happy. "How did you get him to do it?"

"Don't ask how, Ellie. Just say thank you."

"To who? The FBI? I want to know. What's in it for you, Agent Trexler?"

"It's not Agent anymore," I said.

"What?" she asked.

Tyler nodded. "He's serious. He no longer works for the Bureau. Apparently, his boss is a real dick."

I laughed, wishing I could tell him my former boss was his oldest brother.

"How did he pull strings, then?" Ellison asked. She was a smart cookie, I'd give her that.

Tyler sighed. "He just did, Ellie."

"*Why?*" she demanded. "What did you do in return, Tyler?" She also didn't back down. She'd make a good agent.

"It's what you're *not* going to do," I said.

"All of us," Tyler added.

Ellison crossed her arms and glared at me via the rearview mirror. "What are you talking about? What do you mean?"

"Darby," I said simply.

"*Darby?*" Ellison wrinkled her nose. "She thinks you're a hotshot, you know."

My muscles tensed. I hadn't thought that Ellison might have run her mouth to Darby when she was drunk. I might already be too late. "I'm aware. Did you tell her otherwise?"

"No."

My shoulders fell.

"Good," Tyler said. "We need to keep it that way. That was the deal."

"That we let Trex lie to Darby?" she asked. "Who is she?"

"Just a girl," I said, even though the words tasted bitter in my mouth. "But you blow my cover with her, and you're back in that cell."

Ellison sat back, pouting. "You're not going to hurt her, are you?"

I frowned, the thought making my stomach turn. "That's the point, Ellison. Do you agree or not?"

She looked at Tyler. "Do you trust him?"

A part of me liked that she was looking out for Darby, the other part just wanted her to agree.

"He got you out of jail, didn't he?" Tyler said. He was as impatient as I was.

"You're not investigating her?" Ellison asked.

"No."

"Fine," Ellison snapped. "You're a hotshot."

I couldn't help but smile, the feeling of victory tempting me to roll Fancy's windows down and test out her speakers. "Thank you."

chapter sixteen

Darby

The drawing on the scratch paper I'd dug out of the trash can behind the check-in desk was beginning to look somewhat like a burning forest, but I'd made it beautiful. A single rose bloomed in the black clearing the fire had left behind. *Always making the best out of things*, I thought. Not that there was anything wrong with that, but a turd shouldn't be called a rose. Trex was a rose. Unlike Shawn, Trex hadn't shown a different side. He was kind, and thoughtful, and had every intention of sticking around. Once in a while, dark thoughts would creep up, but I shoved them down as many times as I had to. Trex made me happy, and I deserved to be happy. No more *should*s or *shouldn't*s. Those were someone else's rules, anyway. Not mine.

I stopped drawing when Trex walked in just steps behind Ellison and Tyler. Ellison's face was dirty, a bloody cut under one eye. Her spirit had been broken, shame darkening her eyes. Tyler didn't look much better. He was still in his yellow uniform, his white helmet in his dirty hand. He looked helpless and defeated. My first thought was that they'd gotten into a fight, but I knew Tyler better than that. And he'd have had bruises of his own. The shame on Tyler's face was because Ellison had crossed a line, to a place he couldn't follow.

Trex didn't seem to notice.

"Hey," he said.

"Stavros said he overheard the hotshots say Ellie was arrested. Is that true?"

He looked at Tyler and Ellie stepping into the elevator. "I heard that, too. Stavros has you working another double?" he asked, unhappy.

"Tilde is seventy-one, Trex. She hasn't been feeling well a lot lately. I'm worried about her."

"It's not good for the baby for you to be on your feet for so long."

I smiled at him. "I've been feeling really good."

"Wow," he said, looking down at my doodle. "Don't throw that one away. I want to keep it."

"Oh, quit it," I said.

"I'm serious. You're really good."

I gestured to the empty hall in front of the elevators. "Is Ellison okay?"

Trex looked in the direction I was pointing. "I don't know. I'll see what I can find out."

I nodded, watching Trex walk into the room just off the lobby that the higher-ups from the Forestry Department had claimed as headquarters.

Tyler walked past me alone, keeping his eyes to the floor until he left out the sliding doors. He caught a ride with a small group in an interagency vehicle, and the truck peeled out of the parking lot. Ellison trudged toward me a few minutes later, her bag in her hands. The marker fell out of my hands, and I bent down to pick it up and then stood. "Ellie? Are you okay?"

She placed her card key on the upper part of the desk. "Yeah. I have to leave." Her voice sounded like she was on the verge of tears.

"I screwed up. I'm being sent home."

I shook my head. "Screwed up how? Because you were drinking?" I knew exactly what she'd done, but not the details. I was hoping she'd fill in the blanks.

"It's a long story. Trex can explain it to you."

Her answer took me by surprise. I looked to the meeting room. "Well…if you ever come back…be sure to stop by and say hi."

Ellison smiled, looking tired but appreciative. "I will."

An older man in a worn suit waited for her in a car outside. I waved to Ellison, but she'd turned before she saw me.

The meeting room's glass door swept open, and Trex stepped out. He was smiling at me, and that's when I noticed his combat boots. He wore all black from cap to shoes, except his yellow aviators. He was at least six feet two, and walked like he was invincible, like he owned the world because he'd survived it. Soldiers had a certain strut, different from firefighters or policemen, and he'd been practicing for a long time.

"They found her wandering around in a restricted area," he said. "She's in a lot of trouble. What's that look?" Trex asked, his brows pulling together.

"Nothing," I said, looking down. Either way, I didn't want to know.

"Tell me," he said.

I shook my head. "Nothing."

He frowned. "I thought we agreed that we preferred bluntness."

"We also agreed it was okay to have secrets, but not lies."

The two lines between his brows deepened. "What the hell happened in the three minutes since I walked away?"

"Fine. Why are you dressed like a soldier?"

He looked down at his clothes, taken off guard by my question. "What?"

"You walk like one, too. Are you military? Because you know how I feel about—"

"Okay," he said, glancing over his shoulder. "This is a private conversation for another time."

"We've been alone more than once."

He closed his eyes tight and rubbed the back of his neck. "Can this wait? It's been a long day."

I narrowed my eyes. "I guess."

"Thank you," he said. He kissed the corner of my mouth and rushed to the door to the stairwell.

Stavros approached the check-in desk. He'd been waiting for Trex to leave. "I appreciate you working Tilde's shift. Maya is covering the three to eleven tomorrow. I'll get someone hired for nights soon."

"What?" I asked. "But I have third shift."

"Tilde isn't coming back. I'm going to need to move you up. Unless you just like nights, then I'll leave you there."

"Is she okay?"

"She has several appointments the next few weeks. Her doctor had some tests run. It's not good."

"Pneumonia?"

"Lung cancer. Stage four."

I covered my mouth. "Stavros, no."

He patted my shoulder. "She's been smoking a pack and a half a day since she was fourteen. It's not a surprise."

I let my hand fall away from my mouth. "It's still sad. You're still sad. She's your grandma."

"Of course I'm sad." He took a step toward the bar, but then turned to me. "I appreciate you stepping up and covering her shifts. I promise I'll get someone hired soon. Did you want to stay on nights?"

"Yes, that's fine. I don't mind. But I can train your new three-to-eleven hire."

He smiled, but his eyes were tired. "You really are an angel. Okay, I'll keep everyone else where they are, too. Ander on days, and Maya will stay weekends and fill in. Sound good?"

"Yeah. Yes, whatever you need."

"I might be in and out for the foreseeable future. Know any good bartenders?"

"I'll ask around," I said.

Stavros scanned the lobby before fishing his phone from his pocket and making a call.

My shoulders sagged. Tilde had been sick on and off since my first day. I had no idea it was cancer. That made me more resolved to keep things in order for Stavros. I was the oldest lobby employee. Ander and Maya wouldn't be able to run things while he was gone.

Trex didn't come back to the lobby until almost dinnertime. He passed through in his gym clothing, purposefully not making eye contact, and hurried out the door in his gym clothes. An hour later he came back, three half circles of sweat darkening his T-shirt on his chest and underarms, and a stripe going down his back.

"Hey," he said, nervous. He handed me a Styrofoam box and a clear bag with plasticware inside. "I got you meatloaf."

"Thank you," I said, opening the box.

Stavros, walking toward us from the bar, caught my eye.

"Darby, why don't you take a break? I'll cover while you eat," Stavros said.

"But the lobby is full of hotshots, and..." I began.

"I can handle the lobby and the bar for an hour. Go." He jerked his head toward my room.

"An hour?" I asked.

"Yes. Go," he said, shooing me away from the front desk.

"Okay, okay," I said, carrying the white box with me.

I stopped, seeing Trex still standing by the check-in desk. "Are you coming?"

"Am I invited?"

I frowned. "Yes. Why wouldn't you be?"

Trex followed me to my room and waited quietly while I used my card key to get in. I sat on the bed and opened the box, freeing the fork and knife from the bag and digging in. "Oh my God, that's good," I said, closing my eyes.

"I should have left the gym sooner," he said, pacing. "I shouldn't have made you wait so long."

"You're not in charge of feeding me, Trex."

"I care about you. A lot. That means I get to take care of you, and I didn't do a great job tonight."

I carved another piece off the meatloaf, mixing it with the mashed potatoes. "I had a sandwich in the fridge in the back. I planned to eat when I had a free moment. Not as good as this, though. Thank you."

"You need more than a PB&J. We should hit the grocery store this weekend." He looked at his watch. He was stalling and pressed for time at the same time.

"My brother used to do that," I said. "Work out when he was upset. Sometimes he couldn't use his arms after or stand because his body was so exhausted. But... why are you so upset? At me?"

Trex stopped, sat on the bed, and slid his fingers between mine. "No, I'm not upset with you."

"Then what is it?"

"Just trying to figure a few things out."

"How to be with a pregnant girl?"

He chuckled once, the tightness around his eyes disappearing. "No. That part is easy. It's the losing her part I'm trying to avoid."

"Why would you lose me? Is what you have to tell me that bad?" I asked, feeling my appetite disappear.

He stood again, paced again. My eyes followed him, back and forth, while he interlaced his fingers on top of his head and blinked a lot. I'd never seen him so nervous. "It's not what I have to say. It's what I can't say. So I'm going to tell you everything else, and"—he looked at his watch—"I have forty-five minutes to do it. But you should eat while I talk. Deal?"

I nodded.

He was taking deep breaths, walked to the small table and chair in the far corner of the room, to the mouth of the short entrance hall and back.

I took a bite, chewed, and swallowed, barely tasting my food. I took another. "Trex," I prompted. My eyes filled with tears. "Are you married?"

"No." He stopped, but he didn't look at me, instead sitting on the end of the bed, his back to me. "Ander told me you said you wouldn't date military, cops, or firefighters."

"True," I said.

Trex sighed. "I haven't been honest with you, Darby. I wasn't trying to manipulate you. I just needed you to get to know me first, before I told you the truth. Because I can't tell you the whole truth, and I needed you to trust me."

"You get me to trust you by lying to me?"

"I omitted."

"Omission is lying," I said.

He turned, meeting my gaze, gauging my expression, then he looked at the Styrofoam. I took a bite, and he faced the wall again. He was hunched over, his back muscles pressed against his gray T-shirt, the wet line down the center beginning to disappear.

"You're right. I lied to you, and I'm sorry."

"So which are you?" I swallowed. "Military or cop? Because I know you're not a firefighter."

"FBI."

"You're an FBI agent?" I asked, trying to process everything he was saying. "Is that how you got Ellie out of jail?"

He winced. "You caught that, huh?"

"You used your contacts at the FBI to get her out of jail?" He nodded, and I grinned. "That was really cool of you, Trex." I was trying really hard to be mad at him, but no matter how hard I tried, I couldn't. He'd kept things from me, and that wasn't okay, but other than hiding part of his past because he thought he'd lose me, he had proven over and over to me that he was good down to his core.

"I left the Bureau several months ago, traveled to visit friends, and toward the end of my trip, I was offered a new job here in Colorado Springs. So, I moved all my shit from a storage unit in San Diego to a storage unit here, and I've been looking for a place."

"The job you got..."

"Not the Forestry Department, or Department of Agriculture."

"You really can't tell me what you do now?"

He crawled closer to me and sat. "I'm private security. That's all I can say. Eat, Darby. I don't want you getting sick."

"FBI, huh?" I asked, taking a small bite of mashed potatoes. I shrugged one shoulder. "That's kinda impressive. Part of me knew at least part of it. I'm not stupid, you know."

"I know. I've never thought you were."

"You didn't think I was stupid, but you hoped I wouldn't figure it out?"

"I planned to talk to you about this, but we're good together. I don't know about you, but it was instantaneous for me. I didn't want to tell you for you to write me off before I even had a chance."

"Why can't you tell me what you do now?"

"I can't tell anyone. It's part of my contract. I could lose my job, and there are people depending on me."

"So you do have a family?"

"Huh? No. I mean…only the ones I told you about. My parents and my sister, Hailey. My grandparents are gone. I have an aunt and uncle in South Dakota, but I haven't seen them in years. I've never been married. No kids…yet. My team depends on me."

I took another bite and chewed, thinking over what he could tell me. "Have you ever hit a woman?" He paused for a long time, and I could feel the muscles in my shoulders tensing. "Trex?"

"I've shot a few who were shooting at me. I'm not proud of it, but I didn't have a choice."

"You've shot a woman?" He nodded, clearly ashamed and trying to push away the image in his head.

His face darkened. "I've killed a lot of people, Darby. Too many to count."

I touched his hand. "So you were what…? SWAT?"

"Field agent."

I wasn't exactly sure what that was, but I knew Trex wasn't the typical personality I had sworn to avoid.

"Darby?"

I looked up, meeting his gaze. I hadn't realized I'd been staring off until that moment.

"I'm sorry I haven't been completely honest with you."

"I'm kind of glad you weren't. You're right. I would have assumed you were a megalomaniacal jerk and we wouldn't be here right now."

He grinned, relieved. "Any more questions?"

I considered his offer for more answers. "Have you had a girlfriend in the past?"

"Yeah, a few. The only serious one married my best friend."

I had to get my surprise under control. I felt a little mad, even. "Lucky for me, I guess. Why did you break up?"

"She wasn't the one. We both knew it."

"How did you know?"

"Because she wasn't you."

One corner of my mouth turned up. Trex had always been charming, but lately, he never missed an opportunity to make me feel like I was everything to him. "Did you fight?"

"A few times."

"How did you resolve them?"

He laughed once. "Oh. This has turned into an interview, hasn't it?"

"Are you evading the question?"

"Usually with me apologizing."

"For what?"

The small smile on his face disappeared. "For whatever made her mad, which was a lot. I couldn't blame her. It had to be frustrating being with a man who was in love with a woman he'd never met."

Trex watched me, and I took another bite, thinking that's what he was waiting for.

"Is what you're doing now illegal?" I asked. "Are you selling drugs or something?"

"*What?* Hell no, I'm contracted with the government."

I nodded.

"Are we okay?" he asked. "I'm pretty good at reading people, and right now, I have no clue."

"Honestly?"

He nodded again.

"I'm trying to decide if I can trust you."

He held my hand with both of his, kissing my wrists and closing his eyes. "I know. I know it's weird that I can't tell you. And I'm fully aware of how nuts it is for me to ask for forgiveness for lying to you and then ask you to trust me in the same breath. But I've never felt like this about anyone." He met my gaze. "Fear can make people do stupid things, and nothing scares me more than losing you."

I pulled my hands from his grasp and moved the Styrofoam to the nightstand.

"Are you finished?" He swallowed. "Are we finished?"

I sat up on my knees. "How much time do we have?"

Trex blinked and looked down at his watch. "Thirty minutes."

"Good enough," I said, unbuttoning my shirt. I peeled it off, pulled my arms from the sleeves, smiling at the look of disbelief and desire on Trex's face. I tossed it over the chair and then climbed on top of his lap and straddled his legs.

He lifted his chin to look up at me. I took his jaw in my hands and bent down to kiss him, parting my lips to allow his tongue inside. Without pause, he wrapped his arms around me and pulled me closer, working his mouth against mine. The way he kissed me was healing. He took my guilt and shame and hurt and replaced it with confidence and kindness and...

"I love you," he said. *Love.* "I know it sounds crazy," he whispered against my lips, "but I've known for a long time you were out there somewhere. I just had to find you."

There was an awkward silence for a few seconds, that moment when I was supposed to say it back, but I couldn't. I had thought I'd loved Shawn, but that wasn't what it was. Trex deserved for me to be sure. Instead of repeating his sentiments, I kissed him. He didn't seem to mind, his hands left my middle and gripped my thighs, pulling me closer. My lips wandered to his neck, tasting his flesh until I reached his ear. He moaned, and I could feel him bulging against my thigh. I took his face in my hands and kissed him again. We stared at each other for a moment, breathing hard.

"I want you," I whispered against his mouth. "But we have to be careful."

He instantly slowed down, his hands seeming less desperate. "You're right. We should wait until...we know for sure."

He meant we should both get tested for diseases or infections. I was glad he agreed. I couldn't be reckless, not while I was sharing my body with someone else. Not ever again. I pulled on his wrist, looking at his watch. "We still have twenty minutes."

I reached back, my gaze meeting Trex's as I unbuttoned my bra and pushed the straps down until it fell to the mattress between us. I didn't own the sexiest undergarments in the world, but it was impossible to find a sexy full support for a size E bra. During my pregnancy, my double D's had grown out of control.

Trex put one hand on my back, the other behind my neck, and slowly lay me onto the mattress. His lips touched the skin just beneath my collarbone and I sighed. It was a place that was low enough that it wouldn't be seen or touched in any situation other than intimacy, and that made the kiss that much more arousing. Shawn had never paid attention to details like that, and I could tell Trex was relishing the privilege to kiss me in that exact spot.

Trex undressed me one piece of my clothing at a time. We were aware of the minutes ticking away, but he was savoring every second. When I was finally naked and beneath him, he ran his fingers from my collarbone, and made a tender, slow line from between my breasts to my navel, then reached down between my thighs and caressed my tender skin. His fingers moved in small circles, and he bent down to kiss me occasionally, but mostly he took simple enjoyment in my expressions and the way I writhed and trembled under his touch. I moaned, and whimpered, and then cried out. Trex covered my mouth with his while I shivered beneath him.

His fingers slowed, and he settled between my legs, bearing his weight on his elbows. He was still dressed. "Your cheeks are flushed. And your hair is a mess."

"I should probably brush it before I go back to work. And maybe get dressed."

"Definitely get dressed," he said with a wink. "Those hotshots would catch on fire if you walked out there like this."

"And you?"

He squinted one eye, thinking. "I'm not sure if I would burst with pride or die of jealousy."

"You'd be proud of me walkin' around in my birthday suit?" I said with a giggle.

"I'm just proud of you in general. You're tough as nails, you're the most beautiful woman I've ever seen, and you let me do this." With that, he bent down to peck my lips. "I'm a lucky, lucky man, and don't pretend you don't already know it."

I touched his lips with my index finger, then his chin. "I'm the lucky one."

He leaned down to kiss me again, this time slower. His hips rocked into me gently, and he hummed. He sat up quickly and crawled off the bed. "I should leave. Let you get ready. See you later?"

I sat up on my elbows. "Yeah."

He nodded once, walking backward to the door. "Awesome."

The door cracked open just enough for him to slide out, and then he was gone.

I lay back, covering my mouth, my body feeling relaxed, my heart full, hoping Trex was everything he seemed.

chapter seventeen

Trex

Her bare back was exposed, the sheet wrapped around her from the waist down. She lay on her stomach, her left arm bent, her palm down, her thumb touching her perfect nose. The only light was coming from her bathroom, the door cracked just enough for me to avoid tripping over something and waking her. I tried to memorize every freckle, every curve of her body in that position, her eyes closed, the corner of her mouth slightly turned up from a good dream. It was the second night I'd spent in her room, and I wasn't looking forward to returning to sleeping in my room Sunday nights through Thursdays.

Although I'd spent most of our time alone pleasing her, I was determined to wait until we had a chance to get tested before we went any further. I didn't trust my willpower enough to have nothing between us. Our opposite work schedules would help a little, not that I was happy about it.

Darby had Fridays and Saturdays off, but she had to work doubles until Stavros hired someone new for Tilde's three-to-eleven shift. Those were the only two days where she wasn't at work when I was getting off work, sleeping, or leaving for work. I spent dinner and a few late-night hours with her when she wasn't busy. I'd encouraged Stavros more than once to get someone hired as soon as possible.

I slipped out into the hall, walking down the hallway to the lobby.

"Morning," Stavros said from behind the checkout desk. "That's twice in a row you've come from down the hall and not the elevator."

"Mind your business," I said as I passed. "You have one week to get someone hired and get Darby off doubles."

"She won't quit."

"No, but I'll steal her. I think I've found a place."

"Don't you dare!" Stavros called.

"One week!"

I jogged out to the parking lot, in a rush because I'd spent too much time lying awake with Darby, then watching her sleep before I left. It was still dark, the crickets and frogs still wailing. There was nothing I hated more than leaving her alone in that bed. It made it hard to leave for work, to enjoy my job, even though my team made it bearable.

Naomi skidded into her parking spot, Harbinger and Kitsch next. Just before we'd decided to walk in and clock in, Martinez parked, followed by Sloan.

"You're late," I barked to the last two.

"We're not late! We've still got ten minutes!" Sloan said.

"That's late!" Kitsch said.

We reported, and then I gave assignments. I wanted to check the perimeter again. It seemed after the weekend, we always found weird shit near a group of residual boulders near the fence line. The rumors ranged from satanic rituals at the base of the mountain to gang activity. We found dismembered rabbits and fire pits with burn marks that somehow never showed up on the security cameras, but today there was nothing. Harbinger and Kitsch had a bet going, and I'd hoped Harbinger's thought that it was just bored kids would win. Naomi and I went down Echo to bother the Deep Echo security. They'd gotten to where they'd turn on the light and sound the warning horn before we reached the door.

"Don't you wonder what they're guarding down there?" Naomi asked, walking with me toward the chow hall.

"Aliens, probably."

Naomi laughed once, and then her eyes grew wide. "You're serious."

"Completely."

"Wow. I thought I knew you."

We stopped at our lockers before heading to the chow hall. It was Italian day, and Naomi was overly excited about the Make-Your-Own-Pasta-Bowl option. As soon as we pushed through the orange double swinging doors, the smell of oregano, basil, and tomato hit our noses, and we breathed it in. Naomi grinned wider each time she added an ingredient to her pasta.

We sat, waiting for the rest of the team. Martinez and Sloan pushed through the doors, barely acknowledging us before making a beeline to the noodle buffet.

"You've been smiling a lot today," Naomi said. "Don't think I haven't noticed. Things going well with Darby?"

"That's an understatement."

"Oh?"

"I told her I loved her the other night. She hasn't said it back, and I don't even care. She's everything I thought she would be."

Sloan and Martinez sat, followed closely by Harbinger and Kitsch.

"Already? You said the L-word already?" Naomi said in disgust. She wiped her face with her napkin and threw the wadded white paper to the table. "Right after you told her the truth, I hope?"

"Most of the truth," I clarified. "She knows I was a federal agent."

"Wow," Harbinger said. "How did she take it?"

"Amazingly well," I said. "I'm telling you, she's the one."

We were nearly alone in the far corner of the large room, a dozen rows of long tables, and chairs that squeaked against the linoleum floor every time we moved, echoing to remind us we were deep underground. The low hums of the men and women who worked in the kitchen were the only competing noise to our forks scraping against the plates.

"How is she not running away screaming?" Martinez said with a smirk.

"All right, that's enough," Kitsch said.

"I've never seen you like this," Naomi said. "You've been smiling for days."

I shrugged. "I'm in love, what can I say?"

The team traded glances, not sure what to say next. I couldn't blame them. They were used to seeing me brood. Seeing me grinning like an idiot and talking about love must have been jarring.

"How do you know?" Sloan asked.

"Because now that I've found her, I never want to know what it's like to be without her."

"Hey," Martinez said, exchanging pushing me for hooking his arm around my neck. "We're happy for you, man."

"You know, I remember you talking about her a couple of years ago," Kitsch said. "On our last deployment. It's cool that you've finally met her. I know you didn't actually mean Darby, but that you feel like you've met that one person out there for you."

Everyone nodded, and Sloan slapped my shoulder. "Perfect timing, now that we're all settled."

The double doors swung open, and Senator Bennett came in. He loosened his tie, sweat glistening on his forehead. Being underground, we didn't have an air-conditioning unit, but that was because there was no need. We were too deep for the sun to warm the air. "I just heard about what guys walking the perimeter found the other day. Why the hell wasn't I informed?"

I wiped my mouth with a napkin and sat up tall. "Uh, I apologize, sir. You're not in the chain of command, and I—"

"The hell if I'm not. I run this goddamn facility. I should be the first to know if there's a bunch of sacrificed animals found on the property." He glanced at Naomi. Unsettled.

I cleared my throat. "My apologies, sir. Nothing out of the ordinary has happened since. We think it was one of the lab rats or maybe one of the flyboys playing a prank."

"You're sure?" Bennett said.

"What else could it be?" Naomi asked, eyeing Bennett.

"I came here to ask you that question. I want anything else suspicious reported to me immediately." Bennett swiped a napkin off the table and dabbed his brow. He glared at me. "Naomi, bring me a full report in an hour."

"There is no report, sir," I said before Naomi could respond.

"I'm sorry, Trexler. I misheard you. It sounded as if you didn't complete an official report of suspicious activity near a top-secret government facility," Senator Bennett said. "When you're the goddamn head of security!" he yelled.

"The general was very specific," I said.

"Peter, why are you so nervous about this? What's up?" Naomi asked.

"If this gets out, the media will be all over it."

"Over a few dead animals?" Naomi asked.

"There's been an underlying fear in Colorado Springs of the cult activity around this mountain for decades. You know a girl was found murdered not three miles from here fifteen years ago? They're still doing stories about her on the six o'clock news! How the fuck am I supposed to explain the no-fly zone to news helicopters? It's a goddamn PR nightmare." He straightened his tie and then loosened it again. "It's bad enough with the fires. We have to warn off news choppers every day."

"This mountain houses NORAD, sir," I said. "This is a restricted airspace. With all due respect, you don't have to explain shit."

Bennett resituated his tie and walked away. He looked back, pointing me out to Saunders, who was standing at attention by the door. "I like him. Make sure he stays put."

"I'll tell the general, sir."

We all relaxed once the last man had followed Senator Bennett.

"Jesus Christ, that's not normal," Harbinger said. "Surely he's not that uptight about a little conspiracy-theory press."

"He's young and he was put on the committee for this facility because of who his dad is," Naomi said. "He doesn't want to be in the spotlight. Not yet."

Everyone stared at her.

She held up her hands. "It's just a guess."

"Sure," Martinez teased.

Naomi grabbed her fork and stabbed it into the table centimeters from Martinez's hand. He stared at the fork, wide-eyed.

Sloan chuckled. "Haven't you learned yet?"

"We were talking about Trexler's love life, not mine," she said. I frowned. "Aw, c'mon. Did you lose your sense of humor when you moved here?" Naomi said, nudging my arm.

"Did he ever have one?" Martinez asked.

"When do we get to meet her?" Sloan asked.

"Never," I said.

The team complained, quickly shushed by Kitsch.

"I haven't told her I'm a Marine. She can't know. Not yet."

Naomi frowned.

"I'm going to tell her. I just need her to get to know me first so she knows I'm nothing like him."

"Like who?"

"Her ex, Shawn. He was a real bastard. He hurt her. She's said on several occasions she wouldn't date a military guy, and I don't—" Naomi kicked me. "Ow! Fuck!"

"Trex," Naomi snapped. "You continue to keep shit from her and she won't just accept that you can't tell her the details of your job. And if she figures it out, she's a threat to national security."

Martinez pointed to Harbinger. "What do you tell your wife?"

Harbinger shrugged. "Just that I got new orders. She doesn't ask. I'm not missing soccer games or birthdays anymore...that's all she cares about."

Sloan pointed at Harbinger. "See?"

"This is still new, Sloan. I'm not fucking it up to introduce her to you heathens."

"Heathens? Now I'm offended," Kitsch said, unable to keep a straight face.

A group of whitecoats pushed through the doors, Drs. Philpot and DuPont among them. The group eagerly moved toward the noodle buffet. As far as we knew, they'd all just spent the past months in Deep Echo. They looked pale and tired, but excited to venture out.

Dr. Philpot rubbed his hands together while he pointed out ingredients to the cook, and then chatted with another man in a white lab coat twice his size. Philpot had to stand back several steps just to avoid cranking his neck back. One by one, they took their trays and sat at the table behind me.

Naomi was eyeing them, chewing her food at the same time. "What?" she said finally.

I turned to see Dr. DuPont smiling at her.

"Isn't it interesting," Dr. DuPont began, "that there are thirty tables in this cafeteria, and Dr. Cohen—the first of us to get his tray and sit—chose to sit at the table next to yours? Humans inherently fear loneliness. We crave belonging, whether we realize it or not."

"It ain't because we smell good," Sloan said. The team chuckled, but Dr. DuPont's small, creepy smile didn't change.

"You're looking a bit tired, Dr. DuPont. We haven't seen you in a few weeks. Where have you been?" Harbinger asked.

"Deep Echo," Philpot said, chowing down on his bowl of noodles.

"Have you been sleeping down there?" Naomi asked.

"We do when there's a lot of work to be done," Dr. DuPont said.

"Not that it's necessarily voluntary," the tall doctor grumbled.

"Trex, meet Dr. Andrew Cohen. He's our biophysicist."

"Biophysicist?" Martinez asked. "Why the hell does the mountain need a biophysicist? I guess that's classified, too?"

"Yes," Dr. DuPont said.

"Are there some kind of crazy-ass experiments on people happening down there? Aliens?" Martinez asked.

"All classified," Dr. DuPont said.

"Horseshit," Sloan said, gaining Dr. Philpot's attention.

"Be glad you don't know," Dr. Philpot said. "In the mountain, ignorance truly is bliss."

"At least you have the knowledge to make an informed decision whether you want to be working for this outfit or not," Harbinger said, unhappy.

"No, you're wrong," Dr. Cohen said. "Knowledge here takes away decision."

"Well that's just creepy as all hell," Martinez said.

"All right." I stood. "Break's over, let's reconvene in our quarters."

My team followed me out, across and down the hall to our locker room. I sat on the center bench, typing out a message to Darby that would never reach her since she didn't have a phone.

"That's so . . . creepy," Naomi said.

"Mind your business, then," I said.

"Why don't you just get her a phone?" Sloan asked. "Girls like that stuff, don't they?"

"I've asked. She likes not having one. Shawn freaked out if she didn't pick up on the first ring or text back immediately. I can't blame her, but now . . . I have to figure out a way to get her one. I'm looking at a house soon. It'll be easy to wire security cameras and an alarm system. Panic buttons. It's a mile and a half from a police station. If I could get her there, she'd be safe around the clock."

"Not sure about the house, but maybe if she knew all you wanted it for was to write her love notes on the phone, she'd go for it," Naomi teased.

My radio scratched, and Saunders came over the speaker. "Trex, report to the control room with your team immediately."

"Copy that," I said, gesturing for the team to roll out.

Saunders was standing in front of the entrance when we arrived. He escorted us across the room to the exterior monitors. "The fire is within ten miles of the Complex."

"So? The irrigation systems and the Complex fire department can handle it. We can bring all personnel and equipment inside," I said. "We should get started."

"The winds aren't in our favor, and..." He pointed to a section a few miles out from the outer fences. "There's a small group of wildfire fighters who are getting closer to our outer perimeter. They've been instructed to save the Complex. But if the winds change...they're fucked."

"The Alpines are out there today. Did they happen to say it was them?" I asked.

"No, they didn't say," Saunders said.

"We should get out there. Keep eyes out, maybe be ready for a quick evac," Naomi said.

"You're not trained for that," Saunders said.

"Get the satellite on the area," I said, pointing at the monitor. "Now."

"Your objective is to make sure the people in this facility and property are safe. That's your only objective," Saunders said.

"We've all been staying at the same hotel for months. They're all friends, and they're not only civilians, but civil servants," I said, taking a step toward Saunders. "And they're protecting this complex. This falls under my objective."

"With all due respect, Trexler, I disagree."

"I don't give a fuck if you agree or not." I walked past my team. "Let's go."

Harbinger, Kitsch, Naomi, Sloan, and Martinez followed, stopping just outside the metal door of the control room. "Naomi, go upstairs and get us clearance to help."

"What? How?"

I frowned, unhappy about my own plan. "From Bennett."

Her mouth opened, her cheeks flushed. "You want me to owe him a favor? Are you fucking serious? There's gotta be another way."

"This is the quickest way. Go upstairs and don't take no for an answer. Kitsch, take Sloan and bring in the equipment.

Martinez, make sure all personnel are inside. Get on the alarm. Harbinger, you're with me."

"Where are we headed?" Harbinger asked.

"To the warehouse to find a vehicle. If the winds change, we'll need to get those men out fast."

We had just hit the halfway point to the warehouse in Charlie corridor when the alarm sounded. Harbinger and I rushed to a Jeep and hopped in.

One guard jogged over to us. "We've been instructed by the general to lock down, sir. I'm sorry, but—"

"Trex," Naomi barked over the comms. "We've got clearance for evac only. Best I could do."

"Everyone have their objectives locked down?" I asked. "Sound off."

"Personnel inside," Martinez said.

"Last of equipment coming in now," Sloan barked, his voice muffled by the sound of machinery.

"Meet us in the warehouse in five. We're going to be there to evac that crew if needed."

We passed the Complex fire crew on the way to the warehouse. They were spraying down the perimeter with retardant, checking hoses, and making sure all employees were inside. We arrived at the hangar-sized metal door just as the guard was lowering it. The Jeep just barely slid beneath, and I jumped out. "What are you doing? You've still got your fire crew out there."

I pointed to the slowly closing door. "My team has been cleared by Senator Bennett for evac of the hotshots on the mountain."

"I'm sorry, sir, but I don't report to Senator Bennett. This is a direct order from the general," the guard said.

Naomi, Martinez, Sloan, and Kitsch arrived, breathing hard but amped up. We'd been walking the halls too long. We were all ready for more action.

"Are they going to open it again or what?" Martinez asked. His faced darkened as the door pinched off the sunlight.

I shook my head. "The general has the Complex on lock-down."

Naomi nodded to a smaller door. "We can fit the ATVs through there."

I looked to the guards. "Close it behind us?"

The older one pondered, then nodded.

"Load up!" I yelled, jogging to the corner of the ware-house with rows of ATVs.

We each grabbed helmets, chose an ATV, revved the en-gines, and ramped out the smaller door, zooming past the Complex firefighters and the still-open gate they were work-ing out of. We kept our radios on, and fanned out, rolling over the rocky terrain of the Cheyenne Mountain toward the area where we last saw the Alpine crew on the screens in the control room.

"Bark if you see anything," I called across the radio.

We drove for ten minutes, then fifteen, our ATVs kicking up enough dust to rival the smoke. The dark cloud settling in the Rocky Mountain National Forest grew thicker the more distance we created between us and the Complex.

"Flames, one o'clock!" Kitsch said.

We drove past aspens and blue spruces that stood helpless in the crosshairs of the fire. We stopped at a shallow cliff, looking across. The fire was less than two hundred yards away and barreling toward us.

"What the hell?" Sloan said. The smoke was clearing be-fore our eyes. The winds had changed.

"Zeke!" Naomi yelled, scrambling from her ATV. She pulled off her helmet, and fell to her knees, looking below.

I followed her, standing at the edge of the cliff and

looking down. The small group of Alpines that had broken off from the others were standing at the bottom, working against the clock to fashion a hoist for Fish, whose leg was injured. He was propped against the twisted trunk of a large aspen.

"Everyone all right?" I asked, looking down. They were trapped, and one of them was hurt.

Taylor Maddox stood next to his twin brother Tyler and Zeke, looking up at us in confusion.

"What are you doing here?" Zeke asked, his eyes bouncing from Naomi to me, then the rest of our team.

"Does it matter?" she asked, smiling. Dirt lined her face.

Zeke and Taylor glanced back at the approaching flames. "You got a rope?" Taylor asked. "Fish rolled his ankle. We're not going to beat the fire outta here."

"Lucky for you," I said as Harbinger let down a rope. "We've got wheels, too. Is this everyone?"

Tyler nodded. "If you don't have room, just take out who you can. We'll try to bypass."

"Not leaving anyone behind," I said. "Let's get Fish up first. Let's go!" I yelled.

The hotshots sprang into action, tying the rope around Fish's chest. We pulled him up first, and then the rest of the Alpines climbed up one at a time. They were all spent, but used the last of their energy to pull themselves up to where we were. We yelled encouragement to each one as the fire burned closer. The smoke began to surround us just as the last hotshot, Taylor, had nearly reached the halfway point. The fire crawled across the ground and soon the end of the rope was flickering.

"Let's go!" Tyler barked. "Double time!"

Taylor put one hand over the other, but the flame was climbing faster than he was.

"He's not going to make it," Zeke said.

"Move your ass, Maddox!" Tyler yelled.

As the fire climbed the rope and reached Taylor's feet, his brother smacked Zeke and lurched forward, his top half falling over the edge, his legs following. Zeke dove for Tyler's ankles, grabbing them just in time.

"Got him!" Tyler yelled.

The other Alpines joined Zeke and heaved both Maddoxes to the top.

I kicked off the rope, letting it fall to the bottom, watching the fire engulf what was left.

The Alpines were covered in soot, their shoulders sagging from exhaustion.

Taylor looked at me from beneath his dirty brow. "Don't tell Falyn."

I pointed to the patch on my arm that read CHEYENNE MOUNTAIN COMPLEX. "Don't tell Darby."

Taylor climbed on the back of my ATV, Zeke on the back of Naomi's, Fish was with Martinez, Runt and Smitty crawled on with Kitsch, Tyler with Sloan, and Watts and Cat with Harbinger. The smoke was already choking us by the time we pulled away, the heat at my back reminding me to keep my thumb pressed all the way down. Even with Fish's injury, Martinez didn't slow down, swerving around trees and ramping over bumps like the rest of us, hoping to keep ahead of the flames.

Taylor patted the back of my helmet. "Faster!"

I didn't bother explaining that the ATVs were built for checking the perimeter, not outrunning fires. My thumb was pressing on the throttle as far as it would go. The only thing I could do was not slow down.

The Complex fire crew was gone when we arrived at the fence line, and even through the smoke, I could see that the warehouse doors were closed. The ATVs kicked up dirt when we paused, ash falling around us.

"Keep going?" Naomi asked, yelling over the roar of the fire.

I nodded. "Southwest side."

The massive sprinkler system was triggered, steam rising just outside the fence line.

"Go, go, go!" I yelled.

At full speed, driving through the gallons of water flooding the Complex exterior felt like riding a rocket through a storm, and the hotshots all ducked their heads from being pelted with stinging rain.

Soaked, bleeding from sharp branches, saturated with mud, soot, ash, grass, gravel, and leaves, we slowed to a stop near the entrance of the Complex. The parking lot was just a few hundred yards away. A flicker caught my eye, and I turned back, watching the fire twist and devour everything in its path, but heading away from the Complex.

We sat for a moment, in disbelief that we were no longer being chased.

Sloan removed his helmet. "Holy shit. It's like that damn thing has a mind of its own."

"I have to remind myself that it doesn't," Zeke said.

Fish groaned, looking down at his swollen ankle. He was missing a boot, and Smitty's arm was burned.

"Trex to Saunders. Come in, over," I called over the radio, leaning my head toward the mic.

"Saunders," he repeated, his radio clicking off.

"These men need medical attention. Call for a couple of ambulances to meet us at the first security check, and make a call to their HQ to report their guys are safe, over."

"Copy that, over," Saunders said, his side going silent again.

I nodded to my men, and we continued on the ATVs, transporting the dirty, sweaty, exhausted hotshots to the first booth.

Taylor hopped off, checking on Fish before coming back to me and holding out his hand.

I took it, shaking it a few times.

"You saved our asses back there, Trex," Taylor said.

Naomi hugged Zeke, grabbing his cheeks and evaluating the cuts on his face.

Zeke winced. "Did you have to drive through every tree branch between the cliff and the Complex?"

"Yes," she said. "Did you notice we were the first ones back?"

One side of his mouth turned up. "You're so damn competitive."

She winked at him. "You have no idea."

The ambulance took the hotshots away, and we stood at the checkpoint and waited until they were out of sight.

"What the hell was that, Nomes?" Sloan asked.

"None of your damn business," she said, walking to her ATV.

Harbinger slapped my back. "Good call, boss. Felt good to save lives again."

"Oorah," I said, putting on my helmet.

chapter eighteen

Darby

Y ou look nice," I said to Tyler. "But you also look nervous."

"What do you think?" he asked, holding up a small, dark red box.

"May I?" I asked. He nodded. I tipped back the lid, revealing a small white gold band with a single, round solitaire diamond.

He shrugged one shoulder, wrinkling his nose. "Her dad's a billionaire, you know. But she likes simple things, so I thought..."

"She'll love it," I said with a smile.

"Yeah?" he asked, still unsure.

"Absolutely."

He closed the box and looked away, pain in his eyes. "Ellie's been through a lot. She's been gone awhile and we didn't part on good terms, so I'm not sure."

"Do what feels right," I said.

Tyler smiled. "Thanks, Darby."

I nodded, then pushed his shoulder. "Now, go. Go before you're late. You wanna make sure you're standing there when she gets off the plane."

He jogged off, waving once before leaving through the entry doors.

I made my way back to the check-in desk, situating papers and entering the wake-up calls in the system. Trex would be home in four hours. This was the longest part of the day, and I'd be glad when I could wake up, run errands, and see Trex for a few hours before my shift. He was pretty much my life outside of work, even though Maya had asked me to go out with her a few times, but our schedules never seemed to work out.

The phone rang, and I answered. "Colorado Springs Hotel, how can I help you?"

The other side of the line was quiet, but not dead, as if the other person was waiting. "Hello? This is the Colorado Springs Hotel. Can I help you?"

Still nothing, but I could hear movement. A chill went down my back, and the dread I felt in Texas, hearing Shawn's truck pull into the driveway, came over me. I hung up, staring at the receiver. It felt like a lifetime had passed since I'd felt that fear, but it didn't take me long to remember and appreciate that it was gone.

"Hi," a high-pitched voice said from the other side of the desk.

I jumped. "Oh, God!" I touched my chest. "I'm sorry, I didn't see you come in. How can I help you?"

The woman in front of me was four shades darker than her natural shade should have been, her hair bleach blond, and her lips an almost glowing bright pink. "My name is Jojo. I'm the new girl for *MountainEar Magazine*. I'll be replacing Ellie."

"Replacing?" I said, surprised. "Are they letting you go up?"

"Oh no." She looked around the lobby, pleased. "I'll be hanging out here, interviewing the hotshots, getting a few photos of them between shifts. There's a story there, too."

"I see," I said, clicking on the mouse. She had a reservation.

She must have made it in the few hours a day I wasn't at the front desk. Part of me felt defensive of Ellie's place here, and it was hard not to hold that against Jojo. "I'll need an ID and a credit card, please."

Jojo was on her way upstairs, as far away from any hot-shots as I could place her, when Stavros made a quick dash to my desk from the bar. "I just wanted to tell you while you've got a spare minute. I've got great news. I have an interview with a girl this afternoon, and I'm pretty sure she'll be the new hire."

"Yeah?"

"So, prepare to train her for a week, and then you'll be back to your regular shift."

"Thank you," I said, relieved.

"And…this…" He handed me an envelope.

"What's this?"

"A bonus in addition to the overtime, for working your ass off without complaint."

I opened it, seeing a stack of bills. *"What?"*

Stavros walked off without another word, and I thumbed through the twenties. *Five hundred dollars!*

"Thank you!" I called after him, attempting and failing to will back the tears in my eyes. I folded the envelope and shoved it as deep into my pocket as it would go, already making a mental list of things to use the money on. Prenatal appointment, groceries, diapers, savings. There were so many things I could spend it on, it was hard to choose. Life was looking up.

I touched my stomach. "We're doing good, Bean."

After tending the bar and checking out two dozen hot-shots headed home for two days of R&R, Stavros came back with a tall brunette. "Darby, this is Lane. She'll be working the three to eleven."

"Congratulations," I said with a smile. In that moment, Lane, with her long, shiny chestnut hair, her tiny waist, her round backside, full lips, and perfectly proportioned double D's, was my best friend. She would give me more time with Trex, more time to rest and take care of Bean. Even though my best friend was beautiful and one big nervous ball of energy, I couldn't ignore the strange expression on Stavros's face. "What is it?"

"Just…don't look at the television," he said.

I glanced to my right through the fake bamboo plant to see a group of hotshots and Forestry and Agriculture officials gathered in front of the flat-screen. Most were frowning or holding their chins in their hands.

"Is it our guys?" I asked.

Stavros nodded twice. "They're trying to reroute the fire from the Cheyenne Mountain Complex."

"The what?"

"It's a government facility. They're saying it's a risk. The wind isn't in their favor."

I used the desk to steady myself. Zeke, Sugar, Maddox, Dalton…too many to name.

"Can I get you a water?" Lane asked.

"That's a good idea, Lane, thank you," Stavros said.

She jogged across the lobby to the bar, and Stavros came around the desk to grab my arm. "You're not going to go all Southern on me and get the vapors, are you?"

"I'm fine," I said.

"You're white as a sheet, kiddo."

"Do you…do you know if Trex is out there with them?"

"I'm not sure. Does he work with them? He's never said."

I shrugged one shoulder, not sure what else to say.

"He's never told you?" he asked. When I shook my head, he frowned. "That's weird, Darby."

"It's policy."

"Oh," he said, recognition lighting his eyes. "I knew it. He totally fooled me. I bet he really does work for the mountain."

"Which one?"

"The Cheyenne Mountain Complex. It's a top-secret government facility. You can't even drive down that road without getting arrested at gunpoint. It explains why he can't tell you what he does. Maybe he *is* out there."

I wrinkled my nose. "*Trex?* No. He's private security."

"Oh, c'mon. Maybe he's their security. Or he could totally be part of a secret program. Maybe NORAD. They're housed in there. Maybe he's being experimented on. Does he glow at night?"

I nudged him with my elbow and rolled my eyes. "Quit it." Then I paled, pushing my way around him and through the officials to get a good look at the flat-screen. There was only a reporter in the studio with an old picture in a square hovering over her right shoulder.

"Have they shown the hotshots?"

Lloyd, one of the officials, shook his head. "NORAD is in the mountain. It's a no-fly zone."

"Even for helitack?"

"They're waiting on clearance."

"What?" I said, looking around for someone else to weigh in. They were all staring intently at the screen. "Is anyone from the . . . mountain thing helping?"

Lloyd seemed to just notice I was standing there. "They haven't said."

Lane brought me a plastic cup of water. I took a sip and thanked her, watching Stavros smile at her like she'd just won the Nobel Peace Prize.

"Feeling better?" Lane asked.

"Yes. The water is helping," I said, returning to the check-in desk. Stavros and Lane followed, witnessing me drink my water like they were in charge of my intake.

"When is your baby due?" Lane asked.

My mouth fell open, my eyes dancing between her and Stavros. Having no idea she was right, he was offended for me.

"She's tiny, Lane. What would make you say...?" He noticed my expression. "Darby. Are you?" His voice went up an octave.

I sucked in a breath while I thought of what to say. "I was going to tell you," I blurted out.

His nose wrinkled. "All the puking, the exhaustion... you're pregnant?"

I grabbed his arm. "Stavros, I need this job."

The hurt look on his face intensified, and he glared at Lane. "Could you excuse us, please?"

"Of course," Lane said, turning on her heels and making a beeline for the bar.

Stavros turned to me. "Do you honestly believe I'm the sort of person who would fire a pregnant woman? Especially knowing your situation... or what I know of it?"

My shoulders sagged. "You're not. I know that, but I didn't know at first, and I wanted to prove to you that I was worth keeping through a maternity leave. I was going to tell you. It's just been so busy and there wasn't really a good time."

His expression softened. "I think I'm more pissed that I didn't already know." He stood up tall, upset all over again, narrowing his eyes. "And you let me work a pregnant woman half to death with sixteen-hour shifts for weeks. Shame on you."

I sunk back. "It's really okay. I needed the money."

"I'm training Lane. You're off at eleven."

"No! I can do it. Please? I really do need the hours."

Stavros looked down at my stomach, then left me alone for the bar. He bent down, popped up, carried a stool over, and set it down behind my desk. "Use it when you're not with a guest. No cleaning. No lifting *anything*. Or I *will* fire you."

My mouth fell open for the second time, but I snapped it shut and sat on the stool. "Yessir."

Stavros returned to the bar, sending Lane over to me. She didn't look particularly sorry, standing next to me, waiting for me to train her on something.

"You're starting now?" I asked.

"Yes," she said with confidence.

"How . . . how did you know?"

She blinked her long, thick lashes, hiding her warm russet eyes. "My sister is pregnant. She gets dizzy and touches her stomach just like that. But she is super fat, so it's more no-ticeable. She's built like my dad's mom. I'm built like my mom, and she never gained more than eight pounds. You're not there yet. Think you'll get huge? You're Southern, right? I bet you will."

Lane was not my best friend.

"I have no idea. I've lost weight so far." I looked over at the crowd around the television, trying to gauge the situation by their expressions.

"You're not wearing a ring. Who's the baby daddy?" she asked.

I stared at her for a moment. "To check a customer in," I said, looking down at the screen, "you make sure you're on the main screen, then hover the mouse over the check-in button. Click on it, and you'll see a detailed list of reservations that haven't arrived yet. Get their ID. If they have a reservation, you just click on their name like so. See the checked boxes? Everything is non-smoking, but make sure things like pets and the bed preference is correct. We have no suites, so that's not an option. Make sure to put all feeble elderly on the first floor... and... yeah, then click on the box where you input the card, then swipe it. If the card reader isn't working, it's probably because you haven't clicked on the credit card box."

"Got it," she said.

Lane watched me, catching on more slowly than I would've liked. I helped her check in the next four guests, all hotshots returning from R&R. They all went straight over to the flat-screen TV.

"Excuse me," I said to Lane after we finished with the last guest. I squeezed through the crowd and bent down to get the remote, pointing it at the screen and turning up the volume.

A female reporter stood next to a wooded area, haze in the background, a RESTRICTED sign behind her with a United States emblem under the fine print. "The Forestry Department has reported that the Alpine crew just narrowly escaped once they diverted the flames from the Cheyenne Mountain Complex, with the help of the Cheyenne Mountain Fire Department and Complex security."

I exhaled and touched the closest person to me. "Oh, thank God. They're okay."

The entrance doors swept open, and a strong stench of smoke preceded the entire Alpine team. They were all covered in soot, and smiling. The hotshots in the lobby burst into applause and cheering, high-fiving the Alpines as they walked to the bar.

"Okay, okay," Stavros yelled. "Everyone gets a round of drafts on me!"

The entire lobby ignited in cheers, and dozens of hotshots

and officials crowded that side of the room, leaving me alone. I stared at the television screen, waiting for any more news. Something didn't feel right, keeping me from returning to my desk even though I knew Lane was waiting.

The smell of campfire intensified. "Hey," a deep, hoarse voice said just behind me.

I turned around, looking up at Trex. His face was red and sweaty, all but his eyes dusted with soot.

"Thank God," I said, hugging him. I gripped his dirty T-shirt in my fists, pulling him as close as I could.

He chuckled. "Did you miss me?"

"You were at that fire, weren't you?"

Trex hugged me, touching his cheek to the top of my head. "I'm sorry. But I can't give you an answer and you guessing is dangerous. Oh, shit," he said, stepping back. His clothes had streaked my white button-down. He took his thumb and wiped my cheek. Then he held out his hand, letting it fall to his side. "I just made it worse."

"It's okay," I said, looking down at the proof he'd been against me. "You're back early."

"I happened to be close. I helped out. They, uh...we... we had a...thing."

I hated to watch him struggle to tell me what he could without lying. It was admirable, and I appreciated it. "A thing, huh? I'm jealous."

Trex's mouth pulled to the side in a sweet grin.

"Glad everyone's okay," I said.

"I have to hand it to the Aussies. They know their shit. Knew down to the minute how long we had before the fire tur—" Trex looked past me with an expression I'd never seen on his face before.

"Darby," Lane said, leaning forward. She suddenly had the body language of a little girl, a timidity that wasn't present earlier. "I'm sorry to interrupt"—she glanced at Trex for less than a second, then licked her lip—"but there's still a lot I'm not sure on."

"Sure, I'll be there in a sec."

Lane walked away, a bounce in her step. Trex and I watched her turn to give us one last smile over her shoulder.

Trex returned his attention to me, immediately noticing my expression. He swallowed, suddenly uncomfortable. "What?"

I blinked and shook my head. "Nothing."

"Don't tell me she's the new hire," he said, the color leaving his face.

I arched an eyebrow. Jealousy was not an emotion I was familiar with. I'd always been attention's sweet center, and for once, I wanted to be. When the man I'd dreamed about finally arrived, I happened to have someone else's baby growing inside of me, and that put me at a disadvantage when up against someone like Lane—a woman who was above average in beauty, and already had every hotshot in the room scrambling for a reason to talk to her. But if I was honest, it wouldn't have occurred to me to be jealous of her before I was pregnant, just a few short months before.

"What's the problem?" I asked, crossing my arms. "Will she be a distraction?"

"Hell no," he said, his nose wrinkling. He started to reach out for me but looked at his dirty hands and then crossed his arms. "I want Stavros to get someone hired to help you. I'm just surprised Stavros hired her. She used to sit at the bar before you started here. She's not here for the job. She wants to land a hotshot. Trust me, she's not a distraction." The scowl on his face softened. "I get to see you after I get off work, take you out to dinner, and hold you while we watch a movie until your shift starts. The only thing I'm interested in is that you'll be getting some free time soon."

"*Ugh*," I said, my cheeks feeling hot. "I'm sorry. Jealousy is not something I'm used to feeling."

"No, I like it," he said, unable to stop smiling. "I've never seen you jealous before. It's pretty damn cute. And now I know you like me more than you let on."

I pressed my lips together, trying not to smile, and he kissed me quick, making my efforts useless.

"I love you," he said, checking over his shoulder before tilting his head down toward my belly, "and you."

"Stavros knows," I said.

"What?" he said, surprised. "Since when?"

I shrugged. "Half an hour ago. The new hire spilled the beans." I narrowed my eyes at her for the two seconds she wasn't staring at Trex. "Pretty sure she's some kind of clairvoyant demon."

"How in the hell did she know?" he asked. "What did Stavros say? You must still have a job."

"He was pretty mad at me for not telling him. He put a stool behind the desk. I'm supposed to sit when I'm not helping a guest." I looked at Stavros, and he pointed at the floor, signaling for me to sit.

"Good," Trex said, following me to the desk.

"Hi." My new coworker smiled wide and held out her hand. "Lane."

"Trex," he said with a coolness I didn't experience when we first met. He had always been attracted to me. He'd asked me out in the first five minutes. He couldn't be less interested in Lane, and it was nearly impossible to hide my satisfaction. I managed until he grabbed her hand and tried to pull away. Just for a millisecond, she held on.

When Trex got his hand back, he understood my earlier suspicion. Realization twinkled in his eyes just before he winked at me and smiled. "Love you, baby. See you at dinner."

I grabbed his wrist and glanced at his watch. "Just a few hours."

He brought my hand to his lips and kissed my knuckles before releasing me to walk to the elevators.

Both Lane and I watched him walk away with the same expression.

Lane finally sighed and shook her head, looking down at the computer. "He is something."

"Yes, he is."

"Does he know about the baby?"

"Of course he does," I snapped.

She held up her hands. "Just asking. Stavros didn't know, so I wasn't sure. Is he happy about it?"

"Must be," I said, sitting on the stool. "He didn't run when I told him."

"That's going to be one hell of a good-looking baby," Lane said, gazing toward the empty elevator bay. She returned her attention to me. "Where did you meet him?"

It took everything I had not to claw out her wandering eyeballs, so I changed the subject. "Ready to go over checkout?"

Lane smirked. "Sure."

chapter nineteen

Darby

Nope, this one," I said, correcting Lane.

"I was getting there," she said, annoyed.

Lane didn't learn as fast as I had, but she hated being corrected in front of guests. It was a tricky balance to train her correctly and pacify her so she didn't throw a small hissy fit at the desk. It was going to be a long shift. Again. I couldn't wait until Lane was trained, but it had already been twice as long as it had taken for me.

"Thank you," Lane said with the fake smile I'd grown accustomed to. "Enjoy your stay, Mr. Bringham."

Lane turned to me, the smile gone. "Could you just give me a few seconds to figure it out? That's why it's taking me so long to learn."

"I can. I'm sorry," I said, offering a fake smile of my own.

"Right," she said, turning.

I looked over to the sudden activity happening in the meeting room. Some of the hotshots had noticed and were heading in.

"I'll be right back," I said to Lane, making my way over to the bar.

"Looks like a problem," Stavros said, staring at the glass door of the meeting room.

"She sure is," I said.

Stavros jerked his head to face me, confused for half a second before he realized I was talking about Lane.

"She's still being a bitch?"

"Those are your words, not mine," I said.

He returned his attention to the meeting room. "I'm sorry. I thought I'd gotten lucky again. You make beauty, brains, and kindness look easy."

"Aw," I said, nudging his upper arm with my shoulder.

"You should be sitting," he said. I took the closest stool. He frowned at the hotshots as they left the meeting room. "This doesn't look good at all," he said. The hotshots were all immediately making phone calls and heading over to the television. Stavros picked up the remote and turned up the volume. "Channel 7 said earlier the wind picked up and burned three hundred acres just this morning. Embers are flying and creating dozens of new fires up to six miles away. They're evacuating people along the highway, including some of the oldest ranches in the state."

"The Alpines were called out a few hours ago," I said, hearing a break in my voice. Goosebumps formed over my entire body.

The bar cleared, and the lobby was suddenly abuzz with movement. Two lines were formed as people went in and out of the meeting room. Phones began to go off, creating a messy symphony, the bass line a constant hum of chatter.

"Hey," Stavros said, trying to catch the attention of one of the hotshots passing by. "Everyone all right?"

"We've got some guys missing."

"Missing?" I asked, standing. "Which crew?"

"The Alpine crew was split up by the fire. We think the smaller group was separated from the rest when the two fires converged. They only had a few minutes to get clear."

I covered my mouth. Stavros hooked his arm around mine and patted my wrist.

"When will we know something?" I asked.

"We're coordinating search and rescue now," he said, rushing away.

"They're okay," Stavros said, feigning confidence.

As the minutes passed, it felt like a lot of talking and not enough action was happening, but I was sure there was a rescue under way at the mountain that we couldn't see. I returned to the check-in desk to find things to keep me busy, relieved to see Tyler walk in with Ellison. He walked straight into the meeting room with the officials and some of the other crews. I knew then that his brother was one of the Alpines they were searching for.

Ellie made a beeline for the check-in desk.

"Ellie! I was hoping you'd come."

She offered a half smile, digging in her bag. "I'm here. Need a room," she said, handing me her ID and credit card.

"Do me a favor," Ellison said quietly, leaning closer.

"Sure," I said with a smile, still going through the checked boxes, trying to check her in as quickly as I could.

"I'm not going anywhere near Stavros while I'm here."

I looked up to see her expression, trying to decipher what she meant.

"I don't drink anymore."

"Oh. *Oh.* Yeah, last time was…bad."

She nodded. "And it didn't get better after that."

A sparkle caught my eye, and I reached over the desk to grab her hand to get a better look at the ring on her finger. Tyler had done it. He'd asked her, and she'd said yes. "Chicken nuggets, it can't be too bad! Congratulations!"

"Yeah," she said with a smile—a real one, something I hadn't seen from her before.

"Hot damn, that is pretty. And don't worry, I'll let Stavros know you're on the wagon."

"Thank you," Ellison said.

I coded two key cards for her and handed them over, and watched as Ellison looked at the envelope I'd placed the cards in and then looked over her shoulder to check on her fiancé. She readjusted the strap of her camera bag and made her way to the elevators.

A few minutes later, the crews filed out of the meeting room, including Tyler. He was tapping on his phone as he walked out with the others. I hugged my middle, knowing he was probably telling Ellison good-bye. He was going to get his brother.

* * *

As the sun set, the lobby doors swept open and Trex walked through, stopping when he saw Ellison standing close to the couch where she'd been watching the news on the flat-screen. They traded words, and then Stavros brought her a soda.

Trex winked at me, then reached over to slide his finger down my hand from wrist to the tip of my pinky. "My people say they have eyes on the rescue crew." He checked his phone and put it away.

I hooked my arm around Trex's and pulled him a few feet away. "What do you mean 'your people'?"

He answered with apology in his voice. "My team stayed behind so I could keep you guys updated here and they could keep an eye on the situation on the mountain. That's all I can tell you, Darby, I'm sorry."

"I know," I said, shaking my head. "I just…Zeke's still out there."

"I know. Trust me, they're pulling out the big guns."

"You're okay?" I asked.

"Yeah. Yeah, honey, I'm fine. How are you feeling? Have you had dinner?" I thought for a minute, and he frowned.

"With everything happening, I just forgot. I'm just glad you're back. When you didn't show up at the regular time, I got worried."

"I called," Trex said, surprised. He glanced at the front desk. "Lane answered. She said you were busy. I told her to tell you I'd be late."

I turned, seeing Lane smiling at Trex, but that smile vanished the second she realized she was caught. "She must have forgotten to tell me."

He kissed my forehead. "I'm sorry I made you worry, baby. I should've known better than to trust her to tell you."

"It's not your fault," I said, glaring at Lane. I smiled when I returned my gaze to Trex. "Are you staying?"

"Yeah. C'mon, let's get you something to eat."

While we poked through the refrigerator in the back of the breakfast room, the officials called another meeting. The lobby was nearly empty for half an hour, and I sat on the sofa, letting Lane handle the front desk.

"Feeling better?" Trex asked.

"I'm fine. Have you heard anything?"

He looked down. "Sometimes I wish you wouldn't ask me things, Darby. It would make things a lot easier on me."

"I'm sorry. Normally I wouldn't, but Zeke is out there. I have to know," I said.

He laced his fingers between mine. "We haven't heard any radio communication from the smaller group since six. Their last radio call said they were deploying their fire shelters."

I instantly teared up, twitching my nose when it suddenly felt on fire. My throat tightened, and as hard as I tried not to cry, twin streams ran down my cheeks. "Who's in the smaller group?"

The meeting room door opened, and everyone who was crammed in the small space filed out, walking across the room to crowd around the flat-screen.

Trex kept his voice low. "Don't say anything. Only the higher-ups know right now, and it would be extremely difficult for me to explain how I know."

I held my knuckle to my nose and nodded, waiting for his answer. Ellison was standing feet away, and I didn't want her to see me cry.

"Taylor Maddox; the Aussies, Liam and Jack; Jew...and Zeke. Zeke was the farthest out. The others ran to warn him, and then they had to get clear. It's rough terrain, and that slowed them down. Their last communication was..." He swallowed. "It was intense, Darby. I hope they're okay."

I pressed my trembling lips together, nodding. I wiped my face quickly, and we walked closer to the others around the television.

A woman reporter appeared on the flat-screen looking somber. She was standing in front of tall grass and burning trees, holding a microphone in both hands.

"No no no no no," I whispered. "Please Jesus, keep them safe."

Ellison sat next to me on the couch, covering her mouth with her hands.

"Turn that up!" someone called from behind us.

I scrambled for the remote and pressed on the volume until it was at maximum level.

"The last reported communication with the Estes Park crew was at six o'clock this evening right about the time the two main fires converged. They've reportedly deployed their fire shelters."

Ellison stood, looking lost. I grabbed a tissue out of the box on the coffee table and handed it to her. Ellison wiped her cheeks quickly, snapping out of it.

"They're okay," Lloyd said, patting Ellison's arm.

"Ellie!" A woman with an apron around her waist ran into the lobby, looking panicked and wild-eyed. Ellison hugged her. "I just heard," she said, breathing hard. "Any news?"

Ellison shook her head, wiping her nose with the tissue I'd given her. "Nothing. We arrived just after seven. Tyler drove like a maniac. He's out there with the crews looking for them."

The waitress hugged her again.

Trex leaned into my ear. "That's Falyn, Taylor's girl-friend."

Ellison and Falyn sat on the couch, teary-eyed and holding on to each other for support.

As the hours passed, I took care of them to keep my mind busy, even though I got several dirty looks from Trex and Stavros. The hotel was at capacity, and most staying there were waiting in the lobby for news, but as the night wore on, the chatter turned to whispers, and the calls stopped coming. The crowd around the television thinned, but I stayed with Ellison and Falyn on the couch, losing hope with each update from Trex.

Trex put away his phone, dark circles under his eyes.

"Anything?" Ellison asked.

"Just that no bodies have been found," Trex said. When Ellison covered her face in frustration, Trex sat next to her on the arm of the chair. "That's a very good thing, Ellie. That means they found a way out. No bodies mean movement. Movement is life."

"I hope you're right," she said through her hands.

"The helos are up with spotlights, but the smoke is making

it difficult to see." He looked down at me, the skin around his eyes tight. "I'll call them again in ten minutes. I'll let you know the second I hear anything."

He gently took my arm and brought me with him, whispering in my ear. "Tyler's rescue team is on their way back. The smaller group isn't with them. I didn't want to be the one to tell Ellie and Falyn, but…it's not looking good. I'm going to head back to work soon. I'll try to get clearance to do our own search."

I closed my eyes, tears pushing down my cheeks.

"You'll be off soon. You should get some rest."

"I'm fine," I said, turning to the doors as they swept open.

For a second, Falyn was hopeful. For a second, she thought the man walking in was Taylor Maddox, but his twin, Tyler, removed his hard hat, covered head to toe with soot except for twin streaks down his cheeks. Ellison ran to Tyler, throwing her arms around him and crying.

"We didn't find him. I can't find him, Ellie," Tyler choked out.

"No!" Falyn cried.

Tyler walked over to her, pulling her into his arms. He whispered in her ear, and she shook her head, her knees giving way. Tyler held her there, standing sturdy and strong.

Stavros came over holding a tray full of coffee, water, and one milk. "Guess who the milk is for?" I offered a tired smile and took it off the tray. "Go ahead. Get some rest. I'll do the morning audit."

"You're sure?" I asked.

He nodded, taking the tray to the coffee table.

I touched Trex's arm. "You haven't slept. At least try to take a nap before you go. Come with me."

Trex watched Tyler help Falyn to the couch, and then he took my hand, leading me past the check-in desk and down the hall to my room. He didn't talk as he untied his boots and peeled off his shirt and pants. I undressed and slipped a nightshirt over my head, pulling Trex by the hand into my bed. We settled in, holding each other tight. My head fit perfectly under his chin, my lip grazing his collarbone.

I was tired, but my brain wouldn't stop running scenarios, both best and worst. I prayed, I begged God and Jesus and the Holy Ghost to keep them safe. Then I decided to start thanking him for keeping them safe. He would. I believed it. No matter how many frightening thoughts passed through my mind, none of them were of Zeke or the others dead. Hurt, maybe. A few burns, but I imagined them huddling together to ward off the cold, in a cave somewhere, just beyond the reach of the fire. They were walking to fire camp at this moment, dirty, tired, but happy to be alive, all under the Lord's protection.

"Darby?" Trex whispered. "You okay? I worry about all the stress you've been under."

"Zeke is okay, I know it."

He kissed my hair, his warm skin against mine. Even with the AC blowing on high, the parts of our skin that touched were instantly slick with sweat, an acceptable trade for finally being able to be held by him after so many hours from each other. "When is your next doctor's appointment?"

"Next month."

"Would it be weird if I wanted to go?"

I couldn't help but smile. "We'll see. I'm not sure how to explain who you are. They'll assume you're the father."

"So, let them assume. Why does anyone need to know any different?"

I lifted my head. "Because we haven't known each other long enough."

"No one needs to know that, either. And it happens all the

time. My cousin Christopher was the product of a one-night stand. My aunt had him when she was nineteen."

I frowned. "That's what you propose we tell people? That this baby is a product of a one-night stand?"

"I'm not saying we should go out of our way to tell everyone I'm the father. I'm just saying I'm okay to let them assume if they want. That way you don't have to explain."

I laid my head down and sighed. "Maybe." Trex was quiet, prompting me to say more. "I'm just starting to get me back. It's not a simple thing to explain. Shawn took more than I gave him." I touched my stomach. "And now I'm here."

"With me."

"And a baby...I'm a mother." It had just hit me. I was someone's mother. I was a mess. How did God choose this? It didn't make any sense.

"You know now that you're tough enough to do what needs to be done, even if it's hard and terrifying. You're fearless. You walked away from a man who tried to own you instead of loving you. I'm sure the girl you were was great, but I'm in love with this one. The one whose eyes fill with fire a little more each day."

"You make me sound like a superhero."

He hugged me to him. "You're mine. And for the record, I don't care that we met less than sixty days ago. If everything that happened before hadn't happened, and I was the one who'd helped you make that baby the same night I'd met you, I'd be right here, just like this, just as happy to be holding you both as I am right now."

I closed my eyes, hoping he wouldn't notice the tear that had pooled in the corner of my eye, and was now dripping off the tip of my nose. "I'm not fearless. Since the day I walked out of that church, I haven't really had time to do anything but tread water. I haven't had time to really think about anything except how scary it's been and feeling sorry for myself. I've fantasized about starting over, doing things differently. I've wished this baby away, and in a way wished you away, because I would have neither of you if I had left Shawn when I should have. That's not a superhero. That's not brave. It's selfish."

"Why are you so much harder on yourself than you are anyone else? You don't think every woman in your situation has felt the same? It's okay to want things to be a little easier. It's okay to want things to be different. You've been through a lot, Darby."

"I have to be better. I have to make it up to Bean for ever having the thoughts that I did. This baby deserves a mom who makes good decisions, who thinks about things and doesn't just feel them."

"So, what you're saying is you're feeling things," he said, only half joking.

"Yes."

"I call that progress," he said, resting his cheek against my temple. His phone chimed. He glanced at it and sighed. "They found them."

I sat up. "They're okay?"

"They're okay and headed back now."

I collapsed onto his chest. "Thank God."

"Thank the helitack. They spotted them walking back to fire camp. Their comms were damaged."

I sat up and looked into his eyes. "How can you hear that they survived and not think God had anything to do with it?"

He hesitated.

"Say it," I said.

"I don't want this to become a source of contention."

"I want to understand you."

He held his breath as he decided whether to answer. "If they didn't make it, would you have blamed god?"

"Blame him? No."

"Is it god's fault they were separated?"

"Of course not."

"Then why does he get the credit for saving them? If they would have died, you would have prayed for them and their families. It would have all been in god's plan, right?"

"Right," I said immediately.

"I can't worship a god who plans for good men like that to die. Or plans for childhood cancer. Or tsunamis, or pedophiles. That's not a good plan."

"We just don't understand it."

"I do." He touched my stomach. "I plan for this baby to be healthy, and live a long, happy life. Anything he or she needs to know, I'll do my best to teach instead of giving him or her cancer to prove a point. If this baby was sick, and I could heal him or her, I would. If a pedophile was in my house, abusing her, I would stop it. Wouldn't you?"

I twisted my face into disgust. "Of course."

"Then we're already more moral than your god."

I frowned. "Don't *say* that."

He let his head rest against the pillow. "See? I can't win. I explain, and I'm guilty of talking you out of your beliefs. I'm okay with your beliefs. We don't have to talk about mine."

"You don't have any."

"That's not true. I believe in science. I believe in love and equality. Doing no harm but taking no shit. I believe in helping who I can, and not hurting those I can't. I believe in duty, sacrifice, and loyalty."

"Those are all good things," I said.

"I want you to have something you believe in. I don't

think less of you because of it because I want you to feel the same about me and my beliefs."

"Okay," I said, nodding against his chest.

"Okay?" he asked, surprised.

I pressed my lips against his skin, letting them linger for a moment. I laughed once. "As if we didn't have enough working against us...I fall in love with an atheist."

He didn't move. For several seconds, he didn't even breathe. "You love me?"

I sat up, looking him in the eyes. I was too chicken to say anything else, so I simply nodded.

He took my cheeks in his hands and sat up, his mouth on mine. I covered his hands with my own, letting myself feel the emotion he was conveying with his lips. He'd needed the acceptance I'd just shown him for longer than I'd known him, from someone other than me. He didn't say it, but I could feel his relief when he settled back against the mattress and wrapped me in his arms.

"Thank you," he whispered, his body relaxing.

chapter twenty

Trex

Double-sided tape was the perfect solution to fasten the poster-board fireplace Darby had drawn. Once it was up, I crawled back, sitting next to Darby on the floor at the end of her bed. She handed me a mug of hot cocoa.

"It's perfect," she said, touching the barely-there bump poking out from the oversized T-shirt she was using as a nightgown. She touched her belly every time she thought of Bean, which was a lot.

"This looks good on you. You should keep it," I said, referring to the shirt. Just when I thought she couldn't be more beautiful, she started wearing my shirts. Her bare, toned legs poked out of a heather-gray FBI tee that fit nicely over her growing middle.

"Thanks, I think I will. And thanks for grabbing the tape on your way home. And for my art supplies."

"Best boyfriend ever?"

She nodded once, then took a sip from her mug. "You are, actually."

I smiled. Darby was good at holding back and not getting too carried away, but as the temperature cooled, she was warming up to the idea of us. She hadn't yet let me accompany her to a doctor's visit, but she'd at least let me drive her and we'd finally gotten tested at her last appointment. The more patience I showed, the more she trusted me.

The fire outside Colorado Springs had been controlled for nine weeks. The plume that had been a fixture on the summer horizon was gone, the haze in the sky that had veiled the mountains had dissipated. The ash and stench of smoke were gone, too, replaced by a subtle briskness in the air. Darby talked a lot about the leaves changing, snow, and a trip into the mountains, while I held my mug and listened. I savored the few hours we had between the time I got back from work and when she'd have to clock in at ten forty-five. By Friday, I was usually exhausted, but the growing baby gave us both a perfect excuse to catch up on sleep on the weekends.

She sat back, looking up at the ceiling. "So...I have an appointment coming up. Another ultrasound. I can find out if Bean is a girl or a boy. I'm not sure if I want to know. Would you? Want to know?"

"Hell yeah, I wanna know."

She laughed, but her smile vanished. I worried I'd said the wrong thing until she spoke again. "Did you still...you know...wanna go?"

"Do you even have to ask?"

She looked at the pretend fireplace. "You'd have to take off work, so if you can't—"

"I've done it before. You know I don't mind. Just tell me when."

"Tuesday at ten."

"Done."

Her award-winning smile stretched across her face, and she relaxed against my shoulder, taking a deep breath. I hesitated for maybe two seconds before I decided it was time to tell her more good news.

"So," I began, "I found a place."

"Oh yeah?" she said, sitting up again. She blew the steam away from her mug and took another sip, her eyes round with excitement.

"It's a little big, but I'm thinking long run, so just...have an open mind."

"Okay," she said, turning more toward me.

I couldn't help but smile. Her enthusiasm was endearing. "I'll just get the scary shit out of the way first. It's four thousand square feet, five bedrooms, good-sized backyard in a cul-de-sac. Three-car garage."

She nearly spit her cocoa back into the mug. "Five bedrooms?"

"I know, it's bigger than we need, but it's a great neighborhood. It's not far from I-25, so we'd have quick access to Denver, and it has a gourmet kitchen. The house is brand new. The contractor finished it a couple of months ago."

She wasn't going to let the kitchen distract her from what I'd said. "We..."

"Okay." I held up my free hand. "I know it probably feels like pressure, but it's not. I'm just a planner."

"A planner," she repeated. Emotion was absent from her words, so my heart began to thud like an antiaircraft gun hammering away at my rib cage.

Fuck it. "What if...I mean, I'm taking off anyway. Hailey's been asking me to come home. What do you think about, after your appointment, we could head over to Kansas and spend a couple of nights?"

She picked at the handle of her mug. "Um...I think that would be nice, but I can't take off. There's no one to cover my shift."

"Okay, so what about next weekend?"

I could tell by the look on her face she was thinking hard to find an excuse not to. "I think Stavros is going to need me to—"

"Just say it, Darby. Let's talk about whatever you're worried about."

She looked down. "You're really going to make me meet your parents like this? I hesitate to explain this to my doctor, and you want to sit down to dinner with your parents and have this conversation?"

"I think it's a good story."

She narrowed her eyes. "You just want to piss off your dad."

"No," I said, firm. "That's not it. Hailey wants to see me. She asks about you every day. And what does it matter if they find out now or later?"

"It's just..." She shrugged and closed her eyes. "It's embarrassing somehow. I can't imagine your preacher father is going to be happy that your girlfriend is pregnant, and then when we tell him it's another man's baby? You're just asking for an ugly family fight."

"There are worse things than a baby. Like the fact that their son is an atheist, for instance. When they find out you're a god-fearing Christian woman, they won't care if you have six kids. You'll be in like Flynn."

"I don't know," she said, standing. She put her mug on the nightstand. Her baby bump was becoming obvious. "Maybe after the baby comes. Maybe it's not the right time. I don't want to upset anyone. I don't want to get in the way of you having a good visit with Hailey."

She doesn't want to tell me no. "Darby, it's okay. I don't want you to do anything you don't want to. If you don't want to go, we won't go."

"You should go see your sister," she said. I could see the guilt in her eyes. I wanted to say I wouldn't go without her, but I refused to manipulate her that way, even if it was the way I felt.

"Okay. One thing at a time. I'm just happy about the doctor's appointment."

She looked down and ran her hand over the small bowl shape under her shirt. "Lane said I'm going to get fat."

I smiled and walked over to her, wrapping my arms around her. "I hope so. I hope you look like you have triplets in there somewhere."

She giggled, and her head fell back. "No!"

"Yes!" I said, getting on my knees. "I want Bean to have plenty of room to grow. I hope you're big as a house!"

Her stomach bobbed as she laughed, and I kissed it once, then stood.

"You talk about forever like…it just is," she said.

"It *is* just is. I finally found you. I'm not letting you go. Pregnant, fat, skinny, stubborn, separate residences. Even if it takes you five years to get up the nerve to meet my parents. I'm yours."

She cringed. "What are you going to do with all of those rooms?"

I shrugged. "Office. Storage. Guest rooms. Bedrooms. Whatever life throws at us, I guess."

"Us," she repeated, shaking her head and cupping my face. "I've never met anyone like you, Trex."

"And you won't, because no one can love you like I do. I'll make sure it's impossible."

Someone knocked on the door, and I stood up to answer. Ander was standing in the hall, holding a stack of mail.

"Is this both of ours?"

"Yep."

"Thanks," I said.

"Sure," he said, turning.

I picked out mine and handed Darby hers, noticing we had the same unmarked envelope. Darby hardly got any mail, so it was hard to ignore.

"Oh," she said, looking down at the rectangle in her hands.

"I think it's the results."

Darby tore into hers, reading it over and then looking up at me as I did the same. "All clear?" she asked.

I sat down next to her. "All clear."

She set down her mug a few feet away and crawled back, standing on her knees, grinning with a new sparkle in her eye.

"Hi," she said with a smirk.

"Hi."

She reached under the hem of her T-shirt, and with a small tug, her panties were pooled around her knees on the carpet.

I looked down, my dick instantly hard. "Black lace."

"I went for a walk yesterday."

I frowned. "You know I can take you. Or I can catch a ride with Naomi to work and you can have my truck."

She shook her head slowly, moving toward me. "Then it wouldn't be a surprise."

"You've been thinking about this?" I asked, surprised. I'd been trying not to. Limited intimacy with a girl I was madly in love with had been torture—and I knew a thing or two about actual torture.

Darby nodded, planting one knee on the outside of one of my thighs, the other on the other side. Knowing she had no panties on under that T-shirt, hovering above me, drove me crazy, but I was determined to keep my expression smooth.

"No?" she asked.

I laughed once. "It's never, ever no."

She reached down, pulling my belt open, tugging on the button of my jeans until it popped free. She slowly peeled down my zipper and then sat up on her knees just enough to reach inside my boxer briefs. I sat back, unable to move. No one had touched me in a long time, and Darby's hand felt like silk around my cock. I couldn't remember anything feeling better. Her hand moved down my shaft slowly, and I moaned. She leaned down, touching her tongue to the tip of my dick, and I couldn't help but reach for her hair. "Fuuuuck," I said as she fit her wet, warm mouth perfectly around me. "I am so glad I've already told you I love you, because I want to say it right now, and I'm thinking you wouldn't take me seriously."

Darby laughed, the vibration sending chills through my body. Her hand slid up my thigh, slipping under my shirt and reaching up my chest.

"Baby?" I began.

Darby pulled back, creating the tiniest sensation of suction, and I nearly lost it. Right now was not the time to tell her. "I love you. I *love* you. And your mouth is amazing, but you have no panties on, and all I can think about is..." I lifted her in my arms, carrying her to the mattress, slowly lowering her to her back. I kicked off my shoes and pushed my jeans to the floor, watching her take in the sight of me.

"Come here," she said, leaning back on her elbows.

I crawled over to her, hovering just a few inches above, nestling my hips between her thighs. I kissed her once and met her gaze as I touched the tip of my dick to her warm, soft skin. I held my breath for a few seconds as I slowly rocked into her, tensing as I felt her skin envelope and tighten around me. As soon as the bottom of my shaft was touching her, I paused, touching my cheek to hers.

"You okay?" she whispered.

"I don't...want to hurt you."

"You won't," she said, kissing my neck.

She hooked her knees at my hips, and then her ankles

were locked at the small of my back. I fought against an orgasm with every stroke, touching my forehead to hers. She grabbed at me, desperate for me to be closer, to sink myself deeper inside of her. Her expressions were far more intense than they were when my fingers had been between her thighs, making it nearly impossible not to come.

Her body was the beach and mine the ocean. Darby would pull me in, then push me away, over and over until I was overcome, every thought, every sensation, every muscle in my body commanded by her, reacting in ways I couldn't control.

As I tensed, climaxing inside of her, I knew I'd found my salvation, and I was her slave.

* * *

"You okay?" I asked, touching Darby's bobbing knee.

"Yep."

"You don't have to do this, you know."

The nurse walked out with a tablet in her hand. "Darby Cooke."

"Darby Trexler," I whispered as we stood. I'd decided after Maddox told me Darby's real last name weeks before that it didn't matter. It was going to change, anyway.

Darby playfully nudged me with her elbow, and I chuckled, taking her hand in mine. I'd been thinking about the appointment since she'd told me I was invited, wondering if I'd be nervous or scared shitless. To my surprise, it felt natural. More than anything, I was both glad that this could be a thing—me coming with her—and a little bittersweet because I'd missed the previous appointments. For all intents and purposes, I was in love with them both, and that baby was mine. It was hard not to be frustrated that Darby wasn't one hundred percent on board with that notion.

The nurse's eyes lit with curiosity when she realized I was with her patient.

"Hi there," she said, watching us pass by. "Room two."

Darby led me by the hand to the second exam room and I immediately recognized the ultrasound machine. I didn't know how excited I was until that second. I'd seen the fuzzy black-and-white photos of Bean framed in Darby's hotel room, but this was different. I was a part of this moment. I'd get to see Bean in real time.

"I'm Shannon," the nurse said, shaking my hand.

"Trex," I said.

"Is this . . . ?" Shannon began, looking to Darby.

"No," she said.

I sat, trying not to let her answer hurt my feelings. It was technically true, but not for me.

"Trex is my boyfriend."

"Oh," Shannon said with a surprised smile. "Well, nice to meet you, Trex."

"The questions I asked you before, do those answers still apply?" Shannon asked. Vague question. Must have something to do with me.

"Yes," Darby said with a nod.

"Great. Any concerns?"

Darby shook her head. She was still nervous, and Shannon could see it as plainly as I could.

"I can step out a minute," I offered, beginning to stand.

"No!" Darby said, reaching for me and grabbing my arm.

"Okay, honey," I said, returning to my seat. "Calm down a little bit or the blood pressure cuff is going to fly off your arm."

Darby laughed, helping her to relax.

"How long have you two been dating?" Shannon asked, placing the cuff on Darby's arm.

"We met before my first appointment," Darby said, smiling

at me. "I know that's kind of weird, so I've made him wait to come."

"Made *him* wait?" Shannon asked.

"He's pretty convinced this baby is his," Darby said.

"It's not?" I teased.

Shannon's chuckle fell away as she quieted to listen to Darby's heart. Seconds later, the cuff came off and the stethoscope was again resting over her neck. "Blood pressure and heart rate are elevated. Can't imagine why," she said with a wink. "I'm going to check it again before you leave."

Darby nodded, letting her feet swing from the table.

Shannon stood in the doorway, holding the handle in one hand, the tablet in the other. "Dr. Park should be right in."

The door closed, and I scooted forward in my chair, holding Darby's hand. "Thank you."

She smiled. "For what?"

"I know this isn't easy for you, that starting a relationship this way is a little unorthodox. I know you inviting me here is a gesture of trust. I won't let you down, I promise. I'm in this. I'm in love with you, and whoever else comes along."

She squeezed my hand. "I know." I lifted her hand and kissed her fingers. Two weeks before, she'd told me she loved me. I'd said it at least once a day since, and she'd yet to say it back. I'd learned that Darby, for the most part, was more comfortable showing her feelings than saying them. "That's all that matters to me," I said.

"Trex," she began. "I should tell you…"

The door opened, and a woman in slacks, a maroon blouse, and a white lab coat walked in. "Why hello hello," she said, going straight to the sink. She washed her hands and turned to me, holding out her hand. "I'm Dr. Park."

"Trex," I said, taking it. She had a good grip for a woman. Not like Naomi's, but still impressive.

She turned to slide blue gloves over her hands, and then sat on a rolling stool. "So," she said, using her feet to scoot her and the stool to the chair Darby sat on. The doctor was half smiling, half sighing, and staring directly at Darby.

"We met right after I moved here. He's been driving me to appointments."

Dr. Park pointed at me. "But just to be clear...not the father."

"Not technically," I said. "I'm hoping she'll give me the job, though."

Dr. Park looked at me over the thin, rectangular glasses that sat halfway down the bridge of her nose, then at Darby. "He's a charmer, huh?"

Darby nodded. "He's the kindest man I know."

Dr. Park noted that we were holding hands, and she seemed to be okay to continue the appointment. "Good. Very sweet. Okay, let's get you relaxed," she said, pressing a button making Darby's chair turn into a table.

Darby lifted her shirt and pushed down her pants an inch. The top button of her jeans was undone, and I decided in the moment I'd take her to get some more comfortable maternity clothes. The doctor tucked a blue napkin-looking thing into Darby's pants and let it fall over her lap. The gel the doctor squeezed out of a white bottle had just begun to settle when she dabbed the transducer into the gel and began pushing it gently around Darby's baby bump.

Darby looked at the screen, and so did I, waiting.

Dr. Park typed on the ultrasound machine's keyboard, measured a few things, and then paused. "You're sure you want to know the sex?"

"Yes, please," Darby said, nodding.

Dr. Park pointed at the screen. "Can you tell? That would be a hamburger sign. Hamburgers equal girls. You've got a perfectly sized, healthy-hearted girl growing in there. Congratulations."

"A girl?" Darby said, turning to me. The bright grin on her face faded.

"Are you okay?" she asked me.

Dr. Park turned to me, and it was then I noticed the wetness on my eyes. I wiped it away quickly.

"Yeah. Yeah, I'm good." I chuckled. I hadn't cried in so long, it surprised me as much as it did Darby. I watched in awe, Darby's baby girl wiggling, reaching up to touch her face, sucking her thumb, and stretching. Next to Darby, it was the most beautiful thing I'd ever seen.

"Wow," Darby said, reaching to touch the screen. "That's my daughter."

"That's her. Now you just need a name," Dr. Park said. She pulled away the transducer, and the screen was black. A strange sense of loss came over me, and I had to remind myself that the baby wasn't in the monitor but that Darby was carrying her with us everywhere we went.

Darby and Dr. Park went through a short Q&A, Shannon came in for one last check of Darby's blood pressure, and Dr. Park gave her a long printout of pictures before saying good-bye. Shannon left Darby with paperwork, and Darby sat up, wiping the remaining gel off her skin. She was bent over, her hair obscuring my view of her face as she wiped slowly. She sniffed once, and then again, so I bent down.

"You okay?" I asked, combing back her hair.

She looked at me and then down at the photos, her eyes red and wet. "I don't deserve this. I don't deserve any of it."

"Well, that's a load of horseshit," I said, frowning.

"I didn't want this." She touched her stomach. "I accepted it, but I didn't want her, and she deserves to be wanted."

"You don't want her now?" I asked, feeling bile rise in my throat.

"I do," she whimpered.

"Babe," I said, standing and hugging her to my side, "I had no intention of having children, either. It's totally normal for you to feel the way you felt. Unless it's planned, most people feel that way."

She shook her head and sniffed again. I crossed the room to pull a few tissues from a box, handing them to her.

I helped her to her feet, and we walked out hand in hand, but she didn't seem to feel better, even when we were in the truck. Tears were still intermittently falling down her cheeks. I didn't know what to say or do to make it better, so I just held her hand.

"Is this what you were getting ready to tell me before the doc walked in?" I asked. "Are you thinking about adoption? Or...were you...?"

She stared at the wadded tissue in her hand. "I would have given all of this up if I could have gone back and done things different. If I could unmeet Shawn, be someone different, and start over. This isn't easy for me to say to you, but you deserve the truth."

My entire body was tense as I braced for whatever she was about to say.

"Not to say you're not amazing. You are. Who else would fall for a woman who's pregnant with someone else's baby and stick around? But this isn't what I dreamed about when I was a girl. To be scared every day of how I'm going to take care of us...and I know you want to. I know that, but you have to understand that you're not the first person to come along and make me believe your promises are true."

"Darby." I swallowed. This was not the conversation I thought we'd be having after the appointment. It sounded like she was dumping me, and my mind floundered for a way to save myself. I tried to respond in the most rational way I could. I tried to breathe evenly and not to panic. "Just to be clear...I'm hearing you say I'm the only one who really wants this. Who wants us. Is that...what you're saying?"

She blew her nose and shook her head. "No. Not at all. I'm saying I've been scared and unappreciative of this perfect little girl and the man who loves us both. I don't deserve either of you." She covered her face. "I'm a terrible person."

I sighed in relief, letting my head fall back to the headrest while adrenaline absorbed back into my body. When my hands stopped shaking, I reached over, pulling her over the console until she was in my lap.

"Why do you love me so much?" she asked, barely able to look at me. Her shame radiated off her, and all I wanted to do was take it away.

"You know why. This little girl has two people who already love her—a mama who did something most people won't to keep her safe, and a man who is desperate to be her daddy. What I saw at Dr. Park's today? I can't begin to explain to you how it made me feel. I'm not jumping ship, Darby. I love you." I took the pictures from her hand. "And I love her. I'd take a bullet for both of you."

"I know you would," she cried. "Any decent person would be thankful for her and for you. I'm ashamed that, even for a second, I wasn't. I'm a coward. I'm so sorry."

I pulled her closer, kissing her cheek. I'd never been so relieved to be told I was unwanted. I was just glad she didn't feel that way anymore. "You're so hard on yourself. An unexpected pregnancy would scare anyone, and so would letting a new man in her life after what you've been through. Darby, you might have been afraid, but that just makes you brave. You were unsure about me, and that makes you responsible. I'd only change one thing about you."

That got her attention. She looked at me, her mascara wet and flaking under the pool of tears under her eyes.

"I wish you would love yourself as much as I do. This little girl...she needs to see that. You should practice before she gets here."

She leaned her temple against my forehead, sniffing a few times while her body wound down from crying. "You're right. I have to forgive myself for a lot of things."

"You'd forgive someone else."

She thought about that. "You're right. I would...okay. From now on, Bean gets the old me. But better. I guess that means she gets the new me."

I smiled.

"She needs a name," Darby said. She wiped her eyes. "We can't keep calling her Bean."

"I like Bean."

"We...we could think of one on the way to Kansas."

I leaned back to gauge her expression. "Kansas."

"You said you were in this."

"All the way." I used my thumb to gently wipe away the smeared mascara under her eye.

She touched my cheek, her fingers running over the stubble on my jaw and then down my neck until her hand settled on my shoulder. She mulled over whatever she was about to say. I physically ached for her to say she loved me. "Me, too."

She didn't say she loved me, but I was just going to go with it on the hope that she still did. As I held her, I rationalized that she wouldn't have agreed to meet my parents until she was sure her feelings for me were real, and I believed her beyond any creeping doubt when she said she was in this, too. I had to. The alternative was just too fucking painful.

chapter twenty-one
Darby

I tapped out a reply and then handed Trex's phone back to him. Just as he let it lie in his lap, it chimed again. He laughed and handed it back. "Just keep it."

"I'd forgotten how fun it was to have a phone," I said, reading what Zeke had to say. He was still in Colorado Springs. "He met a girl."

"Good," Trex said with a smirk. "I don't have to worry anymore."

"You never had to worry," I said, smiling down at his phone as I typed out a reply. One by one, as the hotshots found out about the pregnancy, they used Trex's phone to check in on me and the baby. Word had spread once Stavros found out. Ander told me too late that his older brother was terrible at keeping secrets. The entire Alpine crew had shared Trex's number and sent texts every day for weeks.

What's her name? I typed out, and pressed Send.

Nope. Not making the mistake of giving you a name. You see what happens when we hear news. It's like a prayer chain.

I laughed out loud.

I'm glad you're happy. Trex is a good guy.

Thank you. I typed. I'm glad you're happy, too.

If you need anything, call me. Trex has my number. Get a damn phone.

Trex's works just fine.

Call me. I can be there in an hour or less if I don't get pulled over.

I will.

As soon as I handed Trex his phone, it rang.

"Trex," he answered.

He got quiet, listening intently and then speaking vaguely about corridors and assignments. He mentioned names like Sloan, Martinez, Harbinger, and Kitsch, and one name I recognized—Naomi.

He hung up and glanced at me, clearly uncomfortable at having to talk about work next to me. "Sorry," he said, clearing his throat. "So, where were we before Zeke started blowing up my phone?"

"Stuck at H." Half an hour outside of Colorado Springs, Trex suggested we go through the alphabet, choosing names we liked best starting with each letter. It took us half the trip to get to H.

"Your turn," Trex said in his deep voice. I decided I liked taking road trips with him. He seemed so serene, and he drove with his wrist at the top of the steering wheel, making his forearms tense when he made any adjustments. His forearms were sexy. Well, all of him was sexy, and now that I'd been with him in that way, that was all I seemed to think about.

"Hannah."

"I like Hannah."

"I," I said.

"Hmmm...that's a tough one. Uh...Isabelle."

"Isabella?" I asked.

"Yep."

"J. Jasmine? Jillian? Justine? Jenny? Juliet?"

"Juliet," he said, certain.

I nodded in agreement. We continued until we got to Z, only passing on a few letters. Z took us half an hour.

"Zara," I said with a smile.

"I like Zara."

"Okay," I said with a sigh. "That's it. Do you remember them all?"

"Adeline, Blake, Charlotte, Dillon, Evangeline, Finn, Grier, Harbor, Isabella, Juliet, Kennedy, Lydia, Madeleine, Nina, Olivia, Pacey, Quinn, Remy, Sunday, Tegan, Umber, Violet, Wren, we skipped X and Y, and Zara. Now you just have to pick one."

I frowned. "I didn't think this through."

"Can I offer my favorites?"

"Please do."

"Maddie, Grier, Quinn, and Wren."

"Maddie?"

"I figured we could call her that. Short for Madeleine. My best friend...his name was Matt. It was Naomi's husband. He died a few years ago."

"We have to do it," I said. "We have to name her Maddie."

"Yeah?"

I smiled at him, bouncing as the truck went over a few bumps in the highway. "Yeah."

"Naomi is going to love that."

"We should ask her permission. Just in case."

He nodded once. "Good call."

"We need middle names, too."

He blanched and I laughed. "What's your middle name?"

"Solomon."

"Scott Solomon Trexler. It sounds nice all put together."

He reached over, putting his hand on my thigh. "What's yours?"

I wrinkled my nose. "It's awful."

He playfully squeezed. "Tell me."

"Rose."

"Darby Rose Cooke. It's absolutely not awful. My mom used to say she named us if it sounded good when she yelled it out the back door," he said with a smile.

"In that case, it's perfect." I let my last sentence hang in the air while I decided whether or not to correct him, and then it took me a solid minute to get up the nerve. "Trex...speaking of names...remember when I said at the doctor's office that I should tell you something?"

"I thought we had that conversation."

"No, it sort of went in a different direction than I'd intended."

"Oh."

"It's something I haven't told you yet. Shawn's brother is a programmer for the government. If Shawn wanted to look for me, Derek could find me the same day he was asked. I've had to stay off-grid as much as possible. That's why living at the hotel makes it so easy. Nothing that required my social security number. Stavros agreed to pay me in cash."

"Okay...?" he prompted.

"My last name isn't Cooke. It's Dixon." He frowned and began to speak, but I cut him off. "I'm sorry I lied to you,"

I blurted out. "It wasn't to purposefully deceive you. I was just afraid—"

"It's okay," he said, his voice raised. When he saw the hurt look on my face, he reached for my hand. "I didn't mean to yell. I just don't want you to apologize. I"—he sighed—"I already knew your real name."

"*What?* How?"

He winced. "I have a friend at the FBI."

"You... what? Did a background check on me?"

"No! I was worried about you, Darby. I realize how it looks, but..."

I pulled my hand away. "You don't know what you've done. Derek probably gets notice every time someone looks up my name! Shawn probably knows where I am!"

"The FBI system is secure..."

"Nothing is secure! You can't be that naïve!" I leaned against the door, pressing the fingertips of my right hand against my forehead. "When? When did you have the FBI look?"

"Remember when I helped Ellie? I put in the request then, but Val had already done a search."

"Who is Val?" I asked, my tone getting higher with each question.

"She's a federal agent. She and I... it's a long story."

"Oh my God. *Oh my God!* So not only is *my* ex looking for me, yours is, too?"

"That's not what it was. Darby, please calm down."

My cheeks burned, and the heat spread to my entire body. I fidgeted with the AC and then sat back again, breathing hard. "That's illegal! When did she do it? And how? You didn't even know my real last name."

"I'm not sure exactly when. It's extremely hard for an untrained person to go off-grid. There is facial recognition used with traffic cameras, business cameras...She knew where you currently lived, so she could have pulled it from anywhere. Darby, I'm so sorry."

I wanted to crawl out of my skin. Shawn could have known where I'd been for a long time. He could be watching me. I had no idea. "You should have told me, Trex. You don't understand..." I sighed.

"Darby, the baby. You have to calm down." He reached for my stomach, but I pushed his hand away.

"Don't touch me."

"Babe," he half pleaded, half scolded me.

I crossed my arms, pulling inside of myself to think like I used to do when I lived with Shawn. "Turn around."

"What?"

"You have to take me back. I have to get my things. I have to move." My eyes filled with tears.

"Darby, stop. Just...think about this for a second. If you truly believe Derek has the same access as the FBI, he could have looked up the cameras at the bus station. It's possible they've known where you are this whole time. If you move, I can't protect you. Besides, if he hasn't come for you by now—"

"There are three scenarios. Either Shawn has stopped looking for me, he knows where I am and doesn't care, or he's waiting."

"Waiting for what?"

My face crumbled. "The right time. I humiliated him when I stood him up at the wedding. He's not going to let that go." I bent over and grabbed my stomach, a sharp pain running around my side, down my back and my legs. "*Ugh*," I grunted.

Trex jerked the wheel to the side of the road and stopped, running around to the passenger side. He unclipped my seat belt and brushed my hair from my face. "Baby? Breathe. Deep breaths."

I did as he instructed, leaning my head back against the headrest and stretching my legs as far as I could. He was right. I couldn't get all worked up, even if I was afraid. Everything I felt affected my daughter. I worked to stay calm, to slow my heartbeat.

"Darby, I would never let anything happen to you," he said. Worry weighted his facial features. Feeling powerless was not something he handled well. "Please don't..." He swallowed. "Please don't leave me."

"What happens if he comes for me when you're at work?" I asked.

He thought for just a few seconds before he answered. "I'll put a call in. We'll keep an eye on him. Make sure he stays in Texas."

I covered my eyes with my hand, my bottom lip quivering. "You don't know him. He doesn't think like a normal person. He's not...he's not afraid of anything, Trex. When he's angry, he's not human."

"Fear is just as powerful, Darby. The *only* thing I'm afraid of is you getting hurt. And I've been through some pretty scary stuff. I'll handle it. I promise." He gently cupped my jaw and pulled my face to the side to meet his gaze. He lowered his chin. "I swear on my life."

I backed away from his hold, hating that I didn't know which scenario would play out: if Shawn was planning to kill me or take me. "I want your promise that you'll protect the baby. No matter what. If I end up one of those women found dead with my baby cut out of me, you'll go get her. You'll make sure she's safe no matter what."

His nose wrinkled. "Darby, Jesus Christ."

"Promise me!" I screamed.

He cupped my cheeks, desperate to keep me calm. "I'll keep you both safe. I promise."

"How?"

"The house. If you move in, I can. I'm installing a state-of-the-art security system. I can be there in less than ten minutes. A police station is four minutes away. The neighbor four houses down is a police officer for that station. He patrols the area several times during his shift. It's the safest place for you." He released my cheeks and turned me to face him, resting his hands on my knees.

I shook my head and laughed once. He wanted me to move in with him after he'd just told me he'd violated my privacy and kept yet something else from me. I had to decide how many more secrets I was comfortable with him keeping, and if that outweighed his ability to protect Bean and me. "I don't know."

"You don't know?" Trex said, mirroring my expression.

"I don't know, Trex. Maybe when you realize there is an actual baby inside of me who will eventually come out, constantly crying and filling diapers with the worst-smelling filth you can imagine, and our lives and relationship will be forever changed, maybe you'll decide you don't want me so badly after all."

"That's insulting," he said. "I can't believe you just said that."

"No one expects for relationships to end when they start. We have to be realistic, because I don't get to bail."

"Neither do I. Is it that you just don't want to move in?"

"I..." I sighed. "You're doing background checks on me without my permission, and possibly alerting my psychotic ex of my whereabouts. You violated my privacy when we weren't living together. I can't imagine how far you'll go when we are. The security system isn't a comfort. I don't want someone watching me all the time. I moved to Colorado Springs to get away from that."

He frowned. "It wasn't a background check, Darby, and that wasn't my intention. I was looking into Shawn, not you."

"No one asked you to do that!" My sudden anger surprised us both. I'd sacrificed so much and tried so hard to stay hidden, and Trex was the one person who made me feel safe. I realized just knowing him had made me vulnerable.

"You're right. I shouldn't have told Val about you. But moving now won't keep you any safer. It would be the opposite. Have you considered that Shawn has stayed away because of me?"

"There's too much I don't know about you. There's too many secrets."

He reached for me. "Honey, I can't help that."

"Some of it you could help. I don't really know you, do I? And you want us to move in together?"

That made him angry. "You know me better than anyone else, Darby. I might have a few things about me that are classified, but you know me."

"I don't even know your birthday!"

"June fourth."

I blinked. "Really? That's the first day I moved to Colorado Springs."

"Happy birthday to me."

"Do you know mine?" I asked.

He nodded. "March twenty-second."

I frowned. "What else do you know about me?"

"That's it. I didn't pry."

"No, because that would be a *total* violation of my privacy. And you want me to move in with you? With cameras? You're insane."

He was angry again. "You'll know where they all are. It'll be just like the hotel but with significantly better security. If you're that against it, sleep in a different bedroom. We'll be roommates."

"That's ridiculous."

"So is me buying a five-bedroom house in the perfect neighborhood and you insisting on living in a shitty apartment."

"No one asked you to buy a five-bedroom house!"

He craned his neck to look at me for a few seconds before glaring down the road instead. The cars were ripping past us down the highway. The wind was blowing the bushes that crowded Trex's boots. We were out in the wide open, but the world was closing in on us. "Do you think I would kick you and the baby out? Do you honestly believe I'd do that, Darby? Trust me, there is a better chance of Stavros going bankrupt and you losing your room in the hotel than that."

"What? What do you mean? Do you know something?"

He sighed, clearly frustrated with having to share new information. "There are few things I don't know about situations I'm in."

"Is Stavros going bankrupt? Will he lose the hotel?"

"He's been helping Tilde with her medical bills because she didn't have insurance. It's sucking him dry. When the hotel was full every night during the fire, it helped him stay afloat every month, but now..."

I covered my mouth. "Why didn't you tell me?"

He lifted his arms and let them slap to his thighs. "I'd hoped once I told you about our house, you'd want to move on your own."

"This isn't about us! I'm going to lose my job. You didn't think to tell me? It's just secret and secret after secret with you. I thought whoever was the most blunt wins? You haven't even been scratching the surface of the truth."

"Stavros doesn't want you to know. He doesn't want anyone to know. He still thinks he can save it."

"Oh my." I swallowed, feeling nauseous. "God. Poor Stavros."

"He'll be filing just after the first of the year. He might be able to wait until spring if he's lucky."

"I don't have time to save for an apartment even if I wanted to stay," I said, thinking aloud.

His jaw ticked beneath the skin. "Is this really about trust? Or do you...do you just not want to move in with me?"

"I can't trust you!" I yelled. Tears welled up in my eyes and poured over my cheeks.

"Fine. Fine! Then let me help you! I'll get you an apartment. Just...don't leave," he said. His tone had turned to begging. "Darby, I worship you. Don't you see that? There is nowhere else I'd rather be than with you. If you go...don't make me leave my men."

"What do you mean?"

"They all moved to the Springs for this job because I asked them to."

"I'm not asking you to follow me."

"Darby..." He shifted his weight, working up to whatever he was about to say. "Do you love me? Tell me. Because I'm in love with you." His voice broke. "And there is nowhere else I'd rather be than where you are."

My throat felt tight and dry, making me swallow. I wiped my wet cheeks. "I love you."

His shoulders sagged, he bowed his head, and he exhaled. "Thank Christ," he said quietly. "I understand you have trust issues, and I've only made them worse. It makes me feel like I'm suffocating just to think about it."

"You're not paying for my apartment."

"That makes no sense. You'd rather move to a strange town, alone, knowing Shawn could be following you?"

"I've done it before!" I yelled.

He clenched his teeth for half a second before speaking, his face red. "You want me to put the deed in your name? I'll fucking do it."

"Don't swear at me."

Trex sighed. He was fighting to calm down, but losing. "I'm sorry. I just don't understand. Why won't you just let me help you, Darby? If we love each other, and we want to be a family, why can't we just let it be?"

I pressed my lips together in a hard line. "Because you lied to me. And because the last time—"

"The last time you moved in with someone he was an abusive asshole."

"Yes."

He shook his head, angrier than I'd ever seen him, his voice low and controlled when he spoke. "I'm not him, Darby. I don't know how else to prove it to you."

As angry as he seemed, and as nervous as I was that in a flash of emotion he might lash out, I reached for him. Deep down, beyond any instincts to protect myself and my unborn child, I knew Trex would never hurt me. Maybe it was all I needed to know. After a second of hesitation, he took my hand. His thumb caressed my skin, but it was different. Even patient men had their limits. We were together, and almost a family. He didn't understand the holdup, and I couldn't seem to explain it to him. "I know. But you still lied."

"I just found out from you today what your real last name is. Give me some grace."

I looked down the road. The noise had been drowned out seconds before, but now the semitrucks muddled my thoughts.

"Stay," he said. "When I'm at work, I'll have a top-of-line security system in place, cameras, an alarm system, panic buttons in every room. I'll make it a fucking fortress. It will be the safest place for you, I swear. It's not just your ex knowing where you are that worries me. You could trip on the stairs, pass out, go into early labor, you don't have a phone...there are a million things that could happen."

"They could happen to anyone."

"But they *don't* have to happen to you." He sighed, frustrated. "We can be roommates. You can live in the master suite on the main floor and I'll live upstairs. You pay a little rent and bills, and we'll sign an agreement. If it ever goes south, I'll move out until you can find another place."

"I don't want to be roommates."

He put his hands on my knees again, then he touched my belly. "I'm sorry I lied to you. I'm sorry for everything that's happened, and that you don't feel safe anymore. Give me a chance to make it up to you. Give me a chance to fix it."

"I'm sorry," I said, wiping my face.

He breathed out like I'd just punched him in the stomach. "So, you're leaving. You're leaving me."

I shook my head slowly and began to cry. "No, I'm sorry I yelled."

He hugged me tight, and I could feel his heart beating through his chest. "*You're* sorry? Jesus, Darby. I don't know what the hell I'm doing. Screwing everything up, I guess." He held me at arm's length. "Does this mean you're staying?"

The desperation in Trex's eyes was unbearable, so I covered my face. I wasn't even sure why I was so upset. I'd been through far worse with Shawn and hadn't shed a tear. Maybe it was the pregnancy, maybe it was because it was our first fight, or maybe it was because I'd just admitted aloud that I couldn't trust him—or anyone—and that made Bean and me very much alone.

"C'mere," he said, hugging me.

I felt so silly for sobbing into his shirt, but I couldn't stop.

"Honey…" he said in a soothing voice, rocking me. "Don't cry."

"It's okay," I said, leaning back to wipe my face. "It's just that"—I sniffed—"you don't deserve to be yelled at like that, and it's the first time you've ever hurt my feelings."

He interlaced his fingers on top of his head, watching me cry with so much guilt and shame he could barely stand to be in his own skin. "I'm so sorry, Darby." He hugged me to him, pressing his cheek against my temple. "I feel like the hugest douchebag right now."

"And I feel like the biggest baby." I looked up at him, and he kissed the tip of my nose.

"Just…hear me out, and I won't mention it again. Regardless if this baby is biologically mine or not, if I kicked you and the baby out of our new house, I'd still be a special kind of asshole. I'm not that guy, Darby. You know I'm not. Just…think about it, okay? That's all I ask."

He let go of me and walked away, toward the endless field next to the highway, his boots crunching against loose gravel. He stared at the horizon, a gentle breeze blowing the sparse trees in the distance. "Are we still headed east?" He turned and waited for my response.

I nodded.

He walked back, made sure I was settled in the seat, and closed the door, walking around to the other side. The silence felt awkward, eating at both of us like a parasite. We passed the WELCOME TO KANSAS sign, then Kanorado. Trex pointed to an enormous water tower and spoke for the first time in almost an hour. "There it is. Goodland,

Kansas. Home of the First Assembly of God and fifteen other churches, population forty-five hundred."

Trex got off on the second exit and then navigated the roads until he stopped at a small white house with a dark red porch on the end of a dead-end road. It had two front doors, and I stared at it for a moment, confused.

"It used to be a duplex. The church bought it and turned it into one house to make a parsonage."

He hopped out, opening the back door to pull out the suitcase I'd borrowed from him and his duffel bag.

"Scottie!" A girl with long, blond hair burst from the screen door on the right and jumped the two steps to run and jump on Trex. He grunted when she ran into him, but she didn't seem to notice, wrapping her arms and legs around him.

He set her on her feet, all smiles. "Hey, squirt," he said, ruffling her hair.

"You made it!" She looked at me, brushing her hair out of her face. "Hi, Darby!"

"Hi," I said, leaning forward and waving. I looked down to unclip my seat belt, and Trex jogged over to open my door and take my hand to help me step out. By the time we walked around the back of his truck, his parents were at the bottom of the stairs. Their smiles immediately faded when they noticed my round belly poking out of my blouse.

"Mom, Dad...this is Darby. Darby, this is my mom, Susanne, and my dad, Scott."

"Nice to meet you," I said, holding out my hand.

Scott's brown suspenders held up his matching slacks, his already ruddy complexion redder just by his son's presence. His jowls moved when he did, his undershirt pressed against his white button-down. He was large, and he was proud. His shirt pressed, his hair gelled into place, he was trying too hard to show his indifference.

Susanne took my hand first, a pained smile on her face. Trex favored his mother. Her reddish-brown curls were loose, just brushing her chin. She reminded me of some of the old photos of my mom, but looking into her eyes was like looking into Trex's. "Likewise. Well, let's get you kids inside."

Scott and Susanne walked in front of us, talking quickly in hushed voices, and Trex followed me, carrying our bags as he walked next to his little sister. Hailey wasn't as quiet as her parents, whispering the million-dollar question to Trex. "Is Darby pregnant?"

"Yep," he said.

"You're going to be a dad?"

"Yep," he said.

"I'm going to be an aunt?"

"Yes, you are," he said, his tone sweeter and warmer than it had been all afternoon.

My shoes echoed against the wood floor when I stepped inside. Trex's childhood home was not the bright, cheerful home I'd imagined. Instead, the curtains were drawn, and the walls were decorated with crosses and religious paintings instead of framed family photos. Plaques and community awards and acknowledgments for Scott were given prime spots so they were seen by visitors as soon as they walked in. I was beginning to understand Trex's aversion to coming home. To the right was the kitchen and dining room, and to the left was a large living room, a piano in the back corner.

Susanne stopped at the mouth of the back hallway. "We, uh, we had you set up in separate bedrooms," Susanne began.

"Doesn't look like that'll be necessary," Scott said.

I smiled. "Separate bedrooms are fine. We're happy to—"

"We'll just take my old room, thanks, Dad," Trex said.

Susanne gestured to the hall. "You know where it is."

Trex nodded for me to follow. He walked to the end of the hall and turned right. "This is it," he said, setting down the suitcases. "We share a hall bathroom with Hailey, which is always fun."

The wood paneling stopped halfway up the wall; frames of Jesus holding a lamb, crosses, and pictures of children being saved by angels hung from the Sheetrock. A few trophies and books were peppered around the room, but it looked mostly like a generic guest room that was never used.

"This is so awkward. They hate me," I said quietly.

He smiled. "They hate me, too. We're meant to be." His smile faded. "About earlier..."

"I'm still sorry."

"Me, too." He hugged me, kissing my cheek. "It'll be fine. They're just shocked right now. Mom especially will get excited before the night is over."

"Until we admit Bean's not yours."

He shook his head. "Don't tell them, Darby. They don't need to know."

I stepped away from him, sitting on the bed. It squeaked loudly. "I can't *lie* about something like that."

"You don't have to lie. They'll assume."

I narrowed my eyes. "You do that a lot."

His shoulders sagged. "I don't want to fight. It'll be fine, you'll see."

I covered my face. "What are we doing? We're going to make your family think this is your baby?"

"She *is* our baby."

I looked up at him. "It's wrong to lie."

His brows pulled together. He looked at me with desperate eyes. "I don't want them to know. I don't want anyone to know."

"It doesn't feel right."

He sighed and then nodded. "Okay. I understand. Do whatever you're comfortable with." He left me alone in his room, and I could hear him talking with his sister in the next room. She did most of the talking, her high-pitched, sweet voice muted through the shared wall.

She was so happy he was home. He was a good big brother, and he cared about her enough to come back to this place, to be around his father and take all the cruelty Pastor Scott would inevitably dish, all to make Hailey happy. He would be a good father. He would be a good husband one day. We had both lied to each other, me to protect myself and him to protect me. It was a tough situation we were both trying to navigate the best we could. What was I so afraid of?

I stood in his old room alone. *Do I love him? Yes. Is he good to me? Yes. Can I trust him? Debatable. Do I believe he loves the little girl growing inside me? Absolutely.* If the worst happened, and Trex and I decided it was over, I knew he'd give me the house before he'd kick us out. My fears were completely irrational. I had to stop punishing him for Shawn's crimes.

chapter twenty-two

Darby

I unpacked my things, thankful we were only staying one night. Trex had returned from Hailey's room, unconcerned about his clothes wrinkling. Or, at least, he wouldn't let me unpack his duffel bag for him. The whole day had been one awful discovery and disagreement after another. I wasn't used to being given a choice. When I lived with my parents, it was always Mom's rules. When I lived with Shawn, there was only what he wanted, expected, and believed. No discussions, no debate, no consideration of my feelings.

Trex waited for me patiently on the bed, quiet and maybe a little sullen.

"Do you think," I began, "the reason today has been so hard is because we're getting to know each other, and it's not working out?"

Trex paled. He looked exhausted and miserable from all the arguing.

"I don't want to fight," I said, holding up my hands. "It's just something that crossed my mind, and I'd appreciate your honesty. This is normally when people figure each other out, if they're compatible with each other. Maybe... maybe we just want different things. Maybe that's why it's been so hard."

"We want the same things. We just want them at different

times. The pregnancy makes me feel everything is on the clock. And now that I know about this other guy...Rick, or Derek, or whatever the hell his name is...it feels that much more urgent. I get it, Darby. I do. You just got a taste of freedom and that's all I've known for sixteen years. You want to be independent, and I'm ready to settle down. We haven't been honest with each other, even if it was for good reason. But that doesn't mean we're not working out. It means forgiveness and compromise."

"Is there a compromise?" I asked.

"What do you mean?"

"Moving in. The truth about the baby. Is a compromise possible?"

He grinned, his eyes still tired. "I love you for asking." He rubbed the back of his neck. "I've screwed up a lot. I can understand the lack of trust. But you gotta know I'm in this. If this ship went down, I'd go down with it."

"And I understand why you did what you did."

"I'm sorry," he said. "I truly am. If I could take it back, I would."

"Me, too. So...okay. Let's do it."

"Let's...do it?" he asked. "You mean you'll move in?" He tried to read me like he always did. "Don't mess with me, Darby. This is important."

"You were right. I'm still afraid. I'm still back in that house, waiting for him to get home, I...It's an excuse. I'm pushing you away, and you're the best thing that's ever happened to me." I looked at him. "And I don't want to lose you."

He stood and held me tight, kissing the top of my head. "I'm not going anywhere."

He cupped my face in his hands, putting his lips on mine in the way only he could, making me feel safe and loved without condition. No one had ever loved me as much as

Trex. I pulled him closer, allowing his tongue to slip into my mouth. He slid his hand beneath my cotton dress, between my thighs, and just as his fingertips slipped under the hem of my panties, Susanne called for us from the living room.

He groaned in frustration. I pressed my forehead against his chest with a smile, and then he led me to the living room, where his parents and Hailey were already sitting.

Hailey put her cell phone away and sat forward, a bright smile on her face. "When are you due?" she asked.

"Hailey Joy," Susanne scolded.

Hailey didn't seem to notice. "I'm going to be an aunt!" She clapped her hands together once.

"February first," Trex said, squeezing my hand.

"So," Susanne said, trying a smile. "Where did you meet?"

I waited for Trex to answer. I wasn't sure what he wanted them to know.

He cleared his throat. "She works at the hotel I'm staying at."

"I thought you bought a house?" Scott said. His words oozed condescension. He wanted so badly to be better than his son.

"We close on it next week."

"Mom says it's nice. And really big. Can I help you decorate the nursery?" Hailey asked.

I hadn't even thought about that. In the back of my mind, I knew a crib would be necessary, but a crib wouldn't fit in the hotel room. Not even a small one. And Bean had a nice big room of her own waiting at Trex's new house. I was suddenly relieved. Trex had fixed it before it was even a problem.

"That would be nice, thank you," I said.

Hailey clapped with excitement. Trex glanced at me, trying not to smile.

"You're in hospitality?" Susanne asked, standing. She fetched a plate of baked goods and brought them over. "Hailey, get the lemonade."

"I work the front desk," I said, taking a small, round oatmeal-and-raisin cookie and a tiny lemon square.

"How long ago did you meet?" Scott asked, looking down at my baby bump.

Trex touched my belly. "At least four and a half months ago."

Hailey giggled. Scott and Susanne weren't amused.

"I don't see a ring," Scott said.

"No, you don't," Trex said.

"You're not getting married?" Hailey asked, surprised.

"Not right now," Trex said.

"Not ready for that kind of commitment, but you're bringing a baby into this world. Makes sense," Scott said.

"Dad," Trex began, already annoyed, "marriage is a piece of paper. There is no stronger bond than a child."

"The Bible says—" Susanne began.

"To submit to one another out of reverence for Christ," I said.

"You're familiar with the Word," Scott said. "Then you're familiar with First Corinthians seven, verse eight and nine."

"Where Paul tells the unmarried and widows to abstain or marry? Yes, I'm familiar."

Scott seemed impressed. That was why Trex wasn't jumping in. He knew they were about to find out their atheist son had impregnated a God-fearing woman. And somehow, that would turn a sinful act into a grandchild to be excited about.

"Which church do you attend in Colorado Springs?" Susanne asked.

"I don't. Up until recently I've been working sixteen-hour days," I said.

"On Sundays?" Scott asked.

"On Sundays, she rests," Trex said. "She's prayed about it, Dad. Even god rested on the seventh day."

Scott narrowed his eyes. "How exactly is this going to work? With you being a Christian and Scottie an atheist."

I shifted in my seat, taking a sip of my lemonade. "We've discussed it."

"Are you okay with your child growing up with atheist influences?" Scott asked.

"Better than her growing up without a father," I said.

Scott nearly snarled. "I'm not sure He would agree. He is the only father we need if we're without a godly influence, and the Bible very plainly says that if anyone causes little ones to stumble in the path to God, it is better to hang a millstone around their neck and be thrown into the sea," Scott said, puffing up with each verse he spewed.

"You're right, that's a serious threat," I said. "I don't think that means a child would be better off without a good father. The Lord isn't going to make her breakfast or take her to soccer practice."

Trex stifled a chuckle.

"Daddy," Hailey said, disappointed. "Stop it. Scottie will be a great dad."

"Scottie," Susanne said in a motherly tone. "It's important for you now more than ever to return to God. You want the best for your child, don't you?"

"Yes, I do. And it's so fortunate for her that she's born right here in the United States where Christianity is the primary religion, and she can worship the one true god."

Susanne frowned. "No need for sarcasm, Scottie. We say this because we love you. It's our duty to witness the truth to those we love."

"I know," Trex said. "But Darby and I have decided to

respect each other's beliefs, and we'll do the same for our daughter."

Hailey held her hands to her mouth. "You're sure it's a girl?"

I smiled and nodded, and Trex dug an ultrasound photo from his back pocket, standing and leaning forward to hand it to Hailey. She stared at it for a moment, and then Susanne leaned to the side, pointing out features.

Susanne smiled, the first real one she'd managed since we arrived. "Oh my. Would you look at that pretty little girl. I think she's going to have your nose, Scottie."

Trex grinned and squeezed my hand. "You think?"

Susanne took the photo from Hailey to show Scott. It took him a full minute to soften up, but when Susanne pointed out Bean's feet, he finally cracked a smile. "She looks like a Trexler," he said.

We sat down to dinner, talking about normal things like Hailey's homecoming date and the weather. Trex talked more about the new house, and he pulled up pictures of it on his cell phone. I tried not to seem too excited or surprised as I scrolled through the pictures. Trex's family assumed I'd seen the house already. Then I ran across several of us together. Mostly selfies, and a few of just me.

"That's a good one," Susanne said. "You should frame that."

"That was our...fourth date."

"Pasta," I said.

He chuckled. "Pregnant girls remember by food."

"She was pregnant by your fourth date?" Scott asked.

"Our first, actually," Trex said without shame.

Scott frowned.

Trex went back to the photos of the house, pausing on one photo, pointing out the plush carpet of the living area.

"Look at all that room to crawl," he said. He scrolled to another pic. "This is the office across the hall from the master suite. Perfect place for a nursery."

I nodded, then looked at him. "It is."

The corners of his mouth curved up. He looked so different than he did an hour before in the car. His face had been heavy with pain, uncertainty, worry. Now he was relieved and happy.

"That was a fine dinner, Susanne. Thank you," Scott said, pushing away from the table. "I have Sunday's sermon to study. It was good to see you, son."

Trex nodded once, staring at the table while his father retreated to wherever he studied for sermons. As soon as Scott was gone, Trex continued the conversation, the air lighter than it had been just moments before.

"Thanks for dinner, Mom. It was great."

Susanne smiled. "Made all your favorites. I'm hoping it will convince you to come home more often."

She stood, gathering the dirty dishes, and the rest of us helped, the plates clattering as we cleared the table within minutes. The kitchen was once again a center of activity, the faucet on full blast, steam rising from the single basin.

Trex took a dish towel from Hailey, but I shooed him out of the kitchen.

"I can help," he said with a chuckle.

"We've got this," Hailey said. "Beat it."

Trex held up his hands. "I guess I'll take a shower."

"Hailey, don't forget your homework, now."

"It's done, Mom."

Susanne nodded, passing me a dish to dry. "I've never had to worry about this one. That one"—she gestured to the hall—"all we've done is worry. How far along did you say you were?"

"Twenty weeks and a few days."

"Halfway mark," Susanne said, scrubbing a pot. "I'm surprised. Trex isn't a kid. I just thought of him as more... street smart, I guess."

"Mom," Hailey warned.

"I know, I know. I don't mean anything by it. I'm glad he's home. He doesn't visit much since he decided, you know, that he doesn't believe in God."

"It must be hard for him," I said, looking down at the plate in my hand. I moved the microfiber rag over its dry surface while waiting for Susanne to hand me the pot she'd been scrubbing. The plate had been dry for a solid minute, but I needed something to do with my hands. "To know he's disappointed you."

"Oh, I don't think that bothers him," Susanne said, smiling out the window over the sink. It was pitch black outside, so I wondered what she found funny. "Sometimes I wonder if he's just doing it to get back at his father."

"For what?" Hailey asked.

"You just never mind," Susanne said. She looked at my bump. "He has a history of doing things he knows would upset his father. Ever since he was little. I mean since he could walk. It's hard for two strong-minded men to be under the same roof."

"Daddy pushes Scottie's buttons, too, Mom."

"I'm not saying Dad's innocent," Susanne said. Her voice sounded tired. "There's a lot of animosity there that I just don't understand. I don't think they do, either."

"He loves you, though," I said. "He was looking forward to coming home."

She finally passed me the pot. "His sister has always been the apple of his eye. He comes home to see her when he can."

It bothered me that she wouldn't admit Trex was abused,

but I decided to leave it alone. Trex hadn't talked much about his parents, and it wasn't my place to try to heal them. What had happened scarred Trex enough to keep him away for months and years at a time, despite his strong love for Hailey, and maybe it was too long ago to heal. I knew exactly what that felt like. Even the thought of trying to fix the pain between my mom and me was exhausting.

"Have you been feeling all right?" Susanne asked.

"The morning sickness was pretty brutal. I've been feeling better and I'm back to one shift at work, so everything feels easier."

"Good. That's good. I know my pregnancy with Hailey was a lot tougher than the first time. Maybe it was because I was so much older, who knows?" She dried her hands on her dish-towel apron. "Thanks for the help. I hope you'll keep us updated. Our first grandbaby and all."

"Yes. Of course," I said, hoping the guilt I felt wasn't all over my face. "Good night."

"C'mon," Hailey said, grabbing my hand and leading me out of the kitchen.

Hailey collapsed in a chair in Trex's bedroom. The shower was running in the bathroom across the hall. I leaned against the headboard of the bed, waiting for Trex to get out of the shower. He had talked about Hailey a lot, and he was right. She lit up the room. She was so innocent and full of life, and even seemed to have influence over her parents Trex had never enjoyed. It was hard to believe they had the same parents.

Hailey yawned. "Trex hasn't come home in a long time. I'm glad he has a reason to now. Maybe I'll get accepted to CSU, and I'll be even closer and can visit a lot. I mean, if that's okay."

"Of course it's okay. You're welcome anytime."

"Really?" she asked, sitting up.

I nodded, surprised at her surprise.

She smiled. "Cool. I didn't think he was ever going to find you, but I'm so glad he did."

"You mean his theory about being in love with me before he met me."

"I don't know," she lilted. "You don't look like a theory to me. He's talked about you since high school. He described you and everything. That's why he's never been serious about any girlfriend, even Laura. He knew he'd find you. We all thought he was delusional or just making an excuse, but...here you are."

"He described me?"

"Yep. More like who you are as a person, but he wasn't wrong."

"That's..."

"Creepy?" Hailey said with a giggle.

"No, it's sort of...comforting. No wonder he's not freaked out by the whole pregnancy and house like I am. He's had time to process it."

She shrugged. "You shouldn't be worried about Scottie. I see how he looks at you. He's a goner."

"I am," he said from the doorway. His hair was still wet, his face shiny clean. He was in a white T-shirt and gray sweatpants, his hands in the pockets and standing in his bare feet. I could smell the combination of his body wash and deodorant, and I filled my lungs with it. Trex had become my favorite smell in the world, my favorite person, my favorite night out. "Shower's open. Still hot water left."

"Thank you," I said, gathering my things.

Trex followed me into the bathroom, showing me how the shower worked. I began to unbutton my blouse and Trex leaned his back against the door, a half grin on his face.

"Thanks for saying that."

"What did I say?" I asked.

"All of it. I'm not sure how quick you meant when you said you're okay with moving in, but I'd still like your help with the nursery."

"You were serious? You're going to make the office into a nursery?"

"Yes," he said, straight-faced. "We'll need a roomful of stuff for her. A crib, diapers, wipes, sheets, toys…"

I shrugged. "Then as soon as the house is ready, I guess."

He smiled. "That's an incentive if I've ever heard one."

"It almost felt too easy to say yes."

"Not everything is too good to be true, Darby."

"I know. You're right. I keep resisting and arguing because it feels so…easy. And easy should be a good sign, not a red flag. Just like you said…we love each other. We should be a family. Bean should live in the home you bought for us—if you still want us to after all the fuss I made today—in a nice neighborhood, and if something happens, if for some crazy reason it doesn't work out…I know you'll be kind."

He laughed once. "If I still want you to," he repeated. He took the few steps to me, wrapping me in his arms, kissing me tenderly. He smelled so good, his hands so warm. I wanted them everywhere, all over me at the same time like a blanket. "I want you to move in with me. I want you to help me pick out furniture, and paint, and dishes, and make this house our home. I want you. And her"—he touched my stomach—"and anyone else who comes along. Ten years ago, the first day we met, four months later, forty years from now…I'll still feel the same. I've never been more sure about anything in my life."

Trex reached down to pinch the bottom hem of my skirt,

and then tugged it down till it was on the floor. He stared at me for a while, his eyes, full of desire, scanning my bare skin.

I touched my rounding belly, feeling I should mention the obvious before he thought it. "Getting big."

The muscles in his arm tensed when he reached behind me to open the shower door to turn the knob. As the water whined through the pipes and began to stream from the nozzle, Trex's fingertips slid over my stretched skin like silk. "I have never seen a woman so beautiful."

He pulled his T-shirt over his head, took off his sweatpants, then he turned us, stopping when his back was to the shower. He slowly walked backward, pulling on my hands to follow until we were both under the steady stream of water just hot enough that it didn't burn. It rained over the top of our heads as he touched his lips to my shoulder and neck, his hands sliding over my curves, his fingers stopping between my thighs like he'd been longing for them to return to that spot since the last time they were there. My breath faltered.

He hooked my knee at his hip and rocked against me, moving his hand to glide his hardness over my tender skin. I reached down, using him to touch myself. He cupped my backside, looking down at where our bodies met. His lips were on mine again, and our tongues danced where our mouths met. He kissed me differently than he had before, a little less careful, as if he finally felt like we belonged to each other and any doubts he'd had were gone. I put my hands on each side of his neck, pulling him closer, letting my fingers slide back through his wet hair. He'd told me so many times that I was his everything, and for the first time, I truly knew he was the one for me. I could feel everything broken inside me getting put back together as I fell more in

love with him within the walls of that shower. I gave myself
to him in more ways than one, because I wanted him to have
me, not because he took what wasn't his.

He turned me away from him, bending me forward
slightly, using one hand to reach around and touch me, the
other to guide himself inside. I pressed my forehead against
the wet shower wall, closing my eyes at the exquisite feeling of his hardness entering me, trying to strangle the moan
building in my throat. He pulled back, and my insides held
him tight, the resistance sending a sharp but pleasurable sensation throughout my body. I wasn't sure if it was pregnancy
or Trex, but everything was more intense with him. He whispered in my ear that I was beautiful, and how much he loved
me, his wet thighs lightly slapping against my backside as
he fell into a slow rhythm.

Trex's fingers slowly slid over my most sensitive skin, in
tune to the way certain motions made me writhe under his
touch. It hadn't taken him long to figure me out, and he ex-
ploited that knowledge in the best way. The fingers of his
free hand dug into my hip, pulling me closer, and I arched
my back just slightly, allowing him to submerge himself. A
low, subdued hum emanated from his throat, and I could feel
my body tighten around his penis even more. He was struggling to stay quiet, gently biting my shoulder. Even from
behind, he made love to me, another first I'd experienced
with Trex. He reached for my jaw, turning me to face him,
sliding his finger into my mouth. I closed my lips, using my
teeth to keep it in place, and tonguing his finger with the
smallest bit of suction. Trex's rhythm slowed, and he held
me close to him, concentrating on his fingers between my
thighs. He kissed my neck, moving inside me in small circles, heightening the sensation. I whimpered, and he covered
my mouth, allowing me to come how I wanted. The orgasm

swept over me like a tsunami, wave after wave, rendering me helpless until it was over.

Once my body relaxed, Trex gripped my hips with both hands, sliding himself into me deep, and then pulling away, his rhythm faster than before. I flattened my palms against the shower wall, jutting out my backside to again give him full access. His fingers tightening around my hips, a strangled moan trapped in his throat. He rocked into me twice more, pausing between, his entire body tense for a few seconds before he hugged me against him, pressing his cheek against mine, breathing hard.

I looked over my shoulder to smile at him, my wet hair plastered against my shoulder. Trex pulled the strands in his way to the side. "It's hard to believe," he said. "For someone like me, who's done what I've done, to get everything I've ever wanted." He turned me around and cupped my face with his hands, brushing specks of water from under my eyes with his thumbs.

"It's hard for me to believe that I'm all you've ever wanted."

He kissed my cheek and slowly turned me around again.

I laughed. "Really?"

He chuckled, reaching for the shampoo. He poured some into his palm, rubbed his hands together, and began to massage it into my hair. "Did you know that I used to have nightmares every night? I'd wake up soaked in sweat. I don't do that on the nights I stay with you. If my mind wanders to things that happened, I just replace them with thoughts of you or our future, or the day I meet Bean."

"I didn't realize the FBI was so intense. I'm glad it's getting easier."

He paused, thinking about his next words. "Not easier. Better. The dreams have haunted me for years, and I automatically default to thoughts of you when they come. I know you deciding to trust me with this wasn't easy. It might even be going against every instinct you've built over the years. I admit I'm feeling impatient because I've been waiting so long for you. I've had over a decade to prepare for this, and I forget it's all new for you. I want this more than anything, and nothing makes me happier than knowing we're buying our first house together. I know this is the best thing for Bean, but..."—he sighed—"I also don't want to pressure you into anything you're not ready for. Either way, we'll make it work. So, you tell me what you want—really—and I'll support you. I'll help you get an apartment, and we can work it in a way that's comfortable to you. That said, if you really do want to move in together, I'm making you a promise right now. I'll spend every second of every day proving to you that I'm not him, or your mom, or anyone else you thought loved you. Even if you're mad at me."

"Even if I yell at you?"

"Even then."

I turned to face him. "I am sorry I yelled."

He kissed my forehead. "Not half as sorry as I am for making you cry. I never want to do that again."

I leaned back, letting the water rinse the suds from my hair, and Trex kissed my neck, stepping closer to me.

I wrapped my arms around him. "I'm beginning to think it's just a turn-on for you to have sex with your parents down the hall."

"I'm not even going to lie. Unauthorized sex is the best."

I giggled against his mouth. "You sound like a soldier."

We went for a quick second round and then dried off, dressed, and returned to his bedroom.

"Hailey," Trex said, surprised. "You're still here."

She arched an eyebrow. "You forgot about me, didn't you? No wonder she's pregnant."

"Hailey!" he half scolded, half laughed at her.

I sat on the bed, feeling sheepish. Trex sat next to me, and I listened to him laugh and reminisce with his little sister, and watched his eyes light up when Hailey asked about baby names. He told her about the game we'd played on the way to Kansas, and she seconded his favorites.

She clapped, her hands in front of her mouth. "I can't believe I'm going to be an aunt. Aunt Hailey. I will be the best aunt! Wait. Am I the only one? Do you have sisters?"

Trex looked to me.

"I have a brother," I said. "Had. I had a brother."

Hailey's smile vanished. "He died?"

I nodded. "We were in a car accident. My dad was in the car, too."

"Is he okay?"

I shook my head.

"That's awful," Hailey said, genuine shock and sadness in her voice. "I'm sorry that happened to you."

"It was a long time ago," I said.

"It doesn't matter. It might not be an open wound, but it leaves a scar," she said.

"Wow, Bells, that's pretty profound," Trex said, impressed.

"Bells?" I asked with a smile.

She rolled her eyes. "Hailey. Hay bale. HayBells. Bells. That was the natural progression, anyway." She rested her cheek on her hand. "Can I babysit?"

"We'll see," Trex said. "I honestly can't imagine leaving her with anyone."

"We'll have to at some point," I said. "I have to go back to work."

He wrinkled his nose. "I make great money. Why would you need to leave her with a stranger so you can go back to work? The hotel is closing, anyway."

I arched an eyebrow.

Hailey stood. "This is why you don't get pregnant early in the relationship. You two clearly have a lot to work out still."

Trex glared at her.

"On that note..."

"Good night," Trex said, not at all sweet or brotherly.

"Night!" Hailey lilted.

Trex looked at me, seeming exhausted again. "We do, don't we? Have a lot to work out."

"I guess that's the trouble with doing this too quick."

"It doesn't matter. Now or over time, we'll have to figure it out, anyway." He looked down. "I'm just now realizing how naïve I was, thinking it would be easy. I'd found you, you happened to be pregnant. No problem, I take care of you and the baby, and we live happily ever after."

"It sounds great in theory."

"It was a fantasy, I guess. I assumed you'd want to stay home with her. I'd come home to you two, and we'd spend the evenings together. But you need a certain amount of space and independence, and I get that."

"Maybe I can find something to do from home. Like sell lipstick or leggings or something."

Trex nodded, reached back to pull his T-shirt over his head, and then crawled into bed, settling into the mattress.

"Why do you look so sad?" I asked, facing him in bed. We were just a few inches from each other, our hands tucked under our faces.

"I want this to be okay."

"The burden of compromise doesn't fall fully on your

shoulders, you know. I didn't know staying home with her was an option. I would love that."

He hooked his arm around me and pulled me closer, resting his chin on top of my head. "You know what I think about? I imagine coming home from work, seeing you and her the moment I walk through the door, our little girl with her fist in her mouth, slobbering everywhere, smiling up at you, and you with spit-up on your shirt, and I need to take out seven trash cans full of disgusting diapers, but I kiss you—and you smell, by the way—and I round up all the trash, put Bean in her bouncy seat so you can take a shower, and start dinner. You come out all shiny and clean, and we cook together and talk about your day—not mine, because it's classified—and then we sit down and eat a cold dinner because Bean threw a tantrum from exactly the time dinner was done until it had just stopped being warm. Then I take a shower, and we put her to bed and we crash on the mattress, way too tired to even make out."

"That sounds kind of terrible," I said.

"No, that sounds like life. An awesome life. A guy I work with, Kitsch, told me that story once. He had two kids, and he said that was one day he thinks about a lot. It was a perfect day. That's what I look forward to."

"It's good to know you have no delusional fantasies about what the reality of all this will be."

"Nope. It's going to suck in the best possible way."

"You said Kitsch *had* kids."

"Yeah," Trex said, pulling me close. "Car accident. His wife, too, while he was out of the country."

"Oh," I said, touching my forehead to Trex's neck. "Poor Kitsch."

"Yeah. He's a good guy."

"Will I ever get to meet any of them, or...?"

He sighed. "It's complicated. Maybe."

"Do they know about me?"

He blew out a laugh. "They're sick of hearing about you, actually."

"Really?" I said, looking up.

He met my gaze. "I've been talking about you since before we met."

I ducked my head, nuzzling his neck, hoping to dream about things that suck, and hoping the days ahead would be exactly as Trex imagined them.

chapter twenty-three

Trex

Turn around, sir," the man on the other side of the blast doors of Deep Echo said through the speaker. He'd stopped getting annoyed a couple of months before and just accepted that we were going to visit them every day. The warning was just procedure. No guns, no posturing.

"Do you ever leave?" Naomi asked the man on the comm. "Do you even know it's Thanksgiving?"

"Turn around and walk, ladies," the soldier said.

Naomi took a step closer. "What's your name, soldier?"

"Logan, ma'am. This is your last warning."

Naomi lifted her fist and gave them the finger. "Happy holidays, assholes."

"Thank you," he said. "Happy holidays to you, too, Naomi."

Naomi and I traded looks and then headed back down Echo corridor to Delta. The Complex was quiet, only a skeleton crew working the control room and security, and a couple dozen essential personnel. Our steps seemed to echo farther than usual against the metal grid that led to Delta, the water dripping from the ceiling louder, the whispers louder.

"Think they'll ever let us back there?" Naomi asked.

"I'm more concerned at this point that those guys will never get out," I said. "No amount of money would make that contract worth it."

"Maybe they know too much, like that lab rat was saying."

"Then I need to mind my fucking business. Tonight's our first night in the new house."

Naomi nudged me with her elbow. "What took you so long?"

"Paint. Furniture just came in. Babyproofing. We agreed to wait until it was ready before we spent our first night there. And since it's Thanksgiving, we thought it would be a good day to move in and make it official."

"Are you all ready? All packed up?"

"My stuff from storage was already delivered. We've been unpacking it. Almost done. I'm already checked out of my room. Darby's things are still at the hotel. She has a couple of boxes, that's it. I'm swinging by to get them before I head home."

"We should go to McCormack's Pub to celebrate." When I made a face, her shoulders sagged. "C'mon. We haven't all been out in forever."

"Maybe."

Naomi smiled, all her teeth showing. "I'll tell the boys."

"I said maybe."

"Maybe means yes. You know it does. You have the most laid-back chick ever. She won't care."

"She has to work tonight, so no, she won't care, but she does want to meet everyone," I said. "We need to plan ahead."

Naomi frowned. "Do you see a problem?"

"Yeah, a big one. When we're all together, we tend to talk shop. She already has an idea. She's sharp as a fucking tack. Misses nothing. It won't take much to confirm her suspicions."

"Well, maybe we'll meet her one at a time, then."

"Not a bad idea," I said.

"How's she feeling?"

I smiled. "She's all belly. When you see her from behind, you don't even know she's pregnant until she turns around, and then it's...whoa. She's been talking about the baby pushing on her lungs and it being harder to breathe."

Naomi shivered. "Weird."

"She's going to start going to the doc's every two weeks soon, then it will be every week."

"Have you named it yet?"

"Her. We've narrowed it down."

"Sorry. Jesus. You sure have become sensitive since you've become someone's dad."

I smiled. "We actually wanted to run something by you."

"Yes, you can name her Naomi."

I laughed. "We went through the alphabet. Naomi didn't make the cut for N, sorry."

"Whaa? Which name beat me out?"

"Nina."

She made a face. "Ick."

"Darby wanted me to ask you if it would be okay if we named her Maddie."

"Sure. I mean, Madison is a little overused if you ask me, but—"

"Madeleine. But she wants to call her Maddie. After Matt."

Naomi stopped. After the initial shock wore off, her eyes glossed over. "That's pretty cool of you guys. Yeah. I mean, yeah, of course." She cleared her throat. "He'd be honored. We're both...we're both honored."

I slapped Naomi's shoulder. "Thanks."

"So, it's official, then? Maddie?"

"Madeleine Rose. I think. I'm still trying to talk her into it."

"Aw, Rose is cute."

"It's Darby's middle name. She hates it."

Naomi laughed. "Of course she does."

We made our way to the headquarters just before lunch. Martinez and Sloan were already there, and Harbinger came in right after us. We had what was essentially an extra-large locker room with a few desks to ourselves, but it seemed extra quiet.

I stared at the door for a full minute and then turned my head toward the comm clipped to my lapel. "Trex actual to Kitsch, check in."

The rest of the team waited, frozen in place.

"Trex actual to Kitsch," I repeated. "Do you copy?"

"It's Thanksgiving," Sloan said.

"I know," I said, staring at the door and waiting for a response on the radio.

"This time of year is rough on him," Sloan said.

"I know," I snapped. "Trex to Kitsch. Do you copy?"

The radio crackled. "Lima Charlie, out," Kitsch responded, signaling he'd heard me loud and clear.

We all sighed and relaxed. "We're headed to chow and it's comfort-food day. Get your ass in here."

"On my way, over," he said. The radio crackled again.

Martinez leaned back, letting his head hit his locker. None of us dared say it aloud, but holidays had us all on edge.

Kitsch was older than me by seven years. He'd married right out of high school, and they had their son, Dylan, right before he left on his first deployment. His daughter, Emily, was conceived the first week he was home. All three were killed instantly sometime during our six-hour firefight six clicks east of Fallujah when they were hit head-on by a sleeping truck driver. Kitsch refused leave to go back for the funerals. He never returned to Quincy after that, wouldn't even step foot in the state of Massachusetts, but he carried a folded photograph he'd printed off his wife's Facebook page all over the world. Karen, Dylan, and Emily had traveled with us to four continents and made it through a war. Kitsch talked about them like they were still alive, at home, waiting on him, and we let him. It wasn't natural for a soldier to out-live his family.

"I invited him over tonight," Naomi said. "I'm cooking if you guys want to stop over," she said to Martinez and Sloan.

"Can I bring a date?" Martinez asked.

"Sure," Naomi said. "Just make sure Kitsch comes."

Martinez nodded once. "Will do."

Lunch was a slice of roasted turkey, mashed potatoes, giblet gravy, cranberry salad, and apple pie with a scoop of vanilla ice cream. We had all sat down by the time Kitsch made it to the table, not mentioning that his face was red and blotchy, his eyes swollen and bloodshot. I noticed the knuck-les on his right hand were skinned and bloody, his napkin soaked with crimson.

"You're not going to flake out on me, are you, Kitsch?" Naomi asked.

"Huh?" he said, snapping out of the hell he was in. "No. I'll be there."

"Good. I'm picking you up. You're my date," Martinez said. Kitsch nodded.

"Everyone be sure to bring liquor. We're going out after and the bar marks up the alcohol on holidays," Naomi said. "And we're going out tonight." Kitsch frowned. Naomi pointed at him. "You're the only one who can two-step." She pointed at his bloody hand. "You're cleaning that shit up, then you're taking me out, fucker."

"Fine," he grumbled.

Martinez smiled. Naomi always knew how to handle Kitsch on his down days.

"I'll be DD," I said.

Naomi grinned. "You're coming?"

I nodded. "Someone has to drive you drunken losers around. I don't want to have to bail you out of jail so you're at work on time. I don't like leaving Darby at home alone on Thanksgiving..."

"Bring her," Sloan said.

I frowned. "I'm not bringing my very pregnant girlfriend to a bar. Besides, she has to be at work by eleven."

"You guys should come by," Naomi said.

"She's been cooking all day."

"So, go after," Harbinger said. "We're stopping by after dinner."

I nodded. "Okay. I'll ask Darby. I'm sure she'll be fine with it. We'll stay until she has to go to work."

Kitsch picked at his lunch, moving it around on his plate but never taking a bite.

"Attention!" Saunders called from the doorway.

We turned to see the general walk in. A few airmen at the other end of the cafeteria stood and saluted. We stopped eating and faced him, waiting to see what all the fuss was about. He walked over to our table. "Trexler, congratulations, your team has the rest of the day off to spend with your families, per Senator Bennett."

"What?" Naomi said, incensed.

"Calm down, Abrams," the general said. "The early release is for all civilian contractors."

Naomi relaxed, putting her elbows on the table and keeping her head down.

"Enjoy your Thanksgiving meal and then collect your things for the weekend."

"The *weekend*?" I asked. "What will you do for Complex security?"

"Deep Echo will take care of it. You go home, they breathe fresh air, it's a win-win. Happy holidays." With that, the general exited, followed by his entourage.

My team traded glances, then we wiped our mouths with our napkins and packed up. Within ten minutes, we were all leaving the parking garage in our various vehicles. I looked at the lavender-wrapped gift with a grape-purple bow sitting in the passenger seat of my truck. I'd had it for a month, waiting for the right time to give it to Darby. Thanksgiving seemed like an appropriate day.

I'd been imagining that drive to the house after work for months—since I'd found the house—pulling up in the driveway, and walking in, and Darby being the first thing I'd see. But I had to pass the turnoff to drive to the hotel. Darby's only two boxes were behind the bar, her room cleaned and empty.

The hotel lobby seemed empty, too, without all the hotshots and forestry officials ambling around with a pint in their hands. I stood at the empty bar, thinking Stavros would show up at any moment. Instead, Lane strolled over, a smile on her face.

"Whatcha doin' here?" she asked. "I thought tonight was your first night in the new house?"

"It is. I'm picking up Darby's boxes. They're supposed to be behind the bar."

Lane leaned over, shamelessly sticking her ass out. I looked away once I realized what she was doing.

"Nope. No boxes. I think Stavros moved them so they wouldn't get wet."

"Damn," I said under my breath.

"I could help you look for them." She lifted her arms and gestured to the lobby. "As you can see, I'm not busy. I'll get a key to her old room and see if Stavros put them there."

"Where is he?" I asked.

She chuckled. "It's Thanksgiving. He hasn't been in all day."

"Okay, well, yeah. We should probably look in her room first."

I followed Lane to the front desk and waited while she coded a card key, and then we walked together down the hall. Lane touched the card to the black box, the lock clicked, and she pushed down on the lever. I flipped on the light, following her into the main area.

"No boxes," she said. "Are they big? Are they small enough to fit under the bed?" She bent down again, and again, I looked away. "Nothing." She sat on the mattress, bouncing. "This is as uncomfortable as I remember. Hard to believe you two lived here for so many months."

"Maybe they're in the back room," I said, pointing behind me.

Lane placed her palms flat on the mattress and leaned back. She wasn't as voluptuous as Darby, but the buttons on her shirt still held on for dear life. "I bet you two used the hell out of this mattress. I remember using the hell out of yours. I was hoping when I took this job that we could, you know, pick up where we left off. I didn't know you were with Darby."

"Speaking of Darby, we should go, Lane. I have to get back. She's waiting on me."

Lane rolled her eyes and stood. I turned for the door and felt Lane's arms slide around my middle. No way was I going out into the hall like that, so instead of reaching for the door, I grabbed her wrists and peeled her off me.

"Lane, knock it off," I said with the same tone I used with my team.

She wasn't intimidated, instead leaning in and tilting her head.

I took a step back, my hands still on her wrists. "What the fuck do you think you're doing?"

She blew out a laugh. "Why are you so angry?"

"Because I'm in love with Darby, and you're trying to hurt her."

"The only thing I'm trying to do is you."

I wrinkled my nose. "I stopped texting you and calling you months before Darby, and then I blocked your number. Why would you think there are any residual feelings? You're delusional."

"Because I see you staring at me, Trex. You can pretend to be the good guy to Darby, but I know better. That can only play out for so long."

"You don't know shit."

"I know you don't fuck her the way you fucked me."

"That's because I don't fuck her. I make love to her. Stay away from me."

She laughed, and I let go of her wrists, reaching behind me for the lever. I opened the door and backed out. Lane followed me, step for step and far too close. When the door closed behind her, I noticed someone standing in my peripheral.

I took another step back, and this time Lane stayed in place.

"Hey, Ander," I said.

"Hey," he replied, his brows pulled together. His eyes danced back and forth from me to Lane and then back to me.

"We were looking for Darby's boxes," I said.

"He was looking *really* hard," Lane said. "Everywhere."

"Shut the fuck up, Lane," I said, disgusted. She was hoping Ander would tell Darby, or at the very least tell Stavros. Everyone knew Stavros couldn't keep a secret.

Ander pointed behind him. "They're in the back, next to

the fridge. Stavros didn't want them getting wet in the bar
area. Darby has books in there."

"Thanks," I said, taking a step, pausing to point at Lane.
"She's a fucking psycho."

"I know," Ander said as I passed him.

I rushed to the back, stacked the boxes, and carried them
out to my truck, putting them in the back seat. I drove fifteen
miles over the speed limit to the house, racing to get home before Darby heard what had happened before I could tell her.

I pulled into the drive, slammed the gear into Park, left
the boxes, grabbed the gift, and jogged into the house.

Darby was standing at the stove, turning quickly when I
walked in, startled. She held her hand to her chest, her eyes
wide. When she recognized me, she relaxed. "Oh, hey."

I closed the door behind me. "I'm sorry. I didn't mean to
scare you."

"I just wasn't expecting you this early. Did you get my
boxes?"

"Yeah. Yeah, they're in the truck." I pointed behind me.

The dark hardwood floors were spotless, the beige carpet
freshly vacuumed, a medley of new smells in the air—wood
stain, paint, upholstery, and whatever amazingness Darby
was cooking. I hadn't thought about that bonus when I fell in
love with a girl from the south. I was standing in my dream
home with my dream girl across the room, about to ruin our
first fucking day because of that idiot at the hotel.

Her eyes glistened more than the chandelier hanging over
the dining table as she waddled toward me, stirring spoon in
hand. She kissed me quick, then waddled back. "Stirring pie
filling! Sorry!"

I followed her into the kitchen, trying not to laugh. Her
shirt was tight, cream and berry horizontal stripes stretching
across Maddie's perfect dome.

"Uh, I need to talk to you about something," I said, setting the gift on the counter.

"What's this?" she asked, picking it up. "For me?"

I nodded, and she tore into it, gasping at its contents. "What did you do?"

"You need a cell phone, Darby. What if you go into labor while I'm at work?"

She picked it up out of the box. "What's my number?"

I tapped on the screen, showing her where to find it.

"It's not in my name, right?" she said, looking at the screen with wide, curious eyes.

"I do know how to keep you safe. I was a federal agent once." She looked up at me, and I winked.

She threw her arms around me, kissing my cheek. Something poked at me, something that wasn't Darby, and I looked down. She put the phone on the counter and held her middle with both hands, giggling.

I got on my knees, palming each side of her belly. "Listen here, missy. You don't kick your dad."

Darby pulled up her shirt, and a small round something protruded from her belly just enough for me to see.

I leaned back, then looked up at Darby. "Holy shit."

"I know. Looks like an alien is inside me. She was rolling around today. Woke me up."

I gently pressed on the knob, and she pushed back. "Maddie Rose, you're grounded," I teased.

"Naomi said it was okay?" Darby asked.

I stood, keeping my fingers on Maddie's elbow, or knee, or whatever part of her was bulging from the rest of Darby's otherwise smooth baby bump. "Naomi said she'd be honored."

The knob disappeared to rise again, this time in a different spot. I laughed. "Is she playing hide and seek?"

"I think so," Darby said, giggling again.

Darby's innie belly button was almost an outie, a dark line now spanning from her belly button to her pelvic bone, and her cheeks were a tiny bit fuller than before, but other than that and her hair growing at least three inches longer and thicker from the prenatal vitamins, there were no differences.

"So," I began.

"Shit!" Darby said, turning to stir the pie filling.

"Baby, I really need to talk to you about something."

"Uh-huh…" she said, stirring.

"When I went to get your boxes…"

"Was Stavros there?"

"No," I said with a sigh, "Lane was."

"Yeah, she asked me to work her shift," she said, making a face.

"Darby…your boxes weren't behind the bar. I went with Lane back to your old room to see if they were in there. She…Jesus Christ…"

Darby stopped stirring and looked at me with an expression that broke my heart. "She what?"

I hesitated. Ruining our official move-in day and our first Thanksgiving was already pissing me off. I had no idea how she would react or if she'd be upset, and the thought of her crying made me lose the will to tell her.

"They were in the back, next to the fridge," I said. "Stavros was afraid they'd get wet by the bar."

Darby arched an eyebrow. "That's it?"

I cringed. If I told her, it would ruin Thanksgiving; if I waited, she could find out from someone else. It was going to suck either way. "Lane came on to me, but *nothing* happened."

Darby's face fell, and she turned to stir again. "Bitch," she grumbled. "What did happen?"

"She coded a card key for your room and took me back there to look. She tried to kiss me. Literally threw herself at me."

She stopped stirring. "Did you kiss her?"

"No," I said, disgusted. Darby stirred again. "I started to leave and she wrapped her arms around me. I peeled her off me and walked out backwards. She followed me, super close. Ander was in the hallway. He saw us walk out. It looked bad, Darby. I admit, it looked really bad, but I swear nothing happened."

She was quiet. So quiet that it scared the shit out of me, but I waited, letting her process what I'd just told her.

"She's gorgeous," she said, quiet. "And not pregnant."

I slipped my arms around her, kissing her neck. "I'm not in love with her. I don't care what she is. And she's not totally unfortunate looking, but she's a psychopath."

Darby breathed out a laugh. "She's something." She shook her head. "Not going to let her ruin today. I'll deal with her later."

"Don't worry about her. She's nothing."

"True."

I squeezed her gently, touching my lips to her cheek. She leaned into my kiss, reminding me of the first time I kissed her in the hotel lobby. It felt like a lifetime had passed since then. Now we had a house together, a baby on the way, and I had everything I'd ever wanted, which was scary as fuck, because when I had nothing, I had nothing to lose.

"How was work?" she asked, still stirring. The pudding had just begun to bubble.

"It's our first night in the new house, and our first Thanksgiving, so say no if you want... but Naomi is having everyone over for post-dinner drinks."

She smiled. "That sounds fun."

"She also wants to go out after. I volunteered to be the DD."

"I have to work," she said, frowning. "How am I going to cross paths with Lane and not slap her? I can't believe she tried to kiss you! What a whore!"

"Babe," I said with a laugh. "Don't get all worked up over her. Not worth it."

"You're worth it," she grumbled.

"Aw. Are you wanting to defend my honor? Because that's kind of badass."

She tried not to smile, but failed.

"I can walk you in, give you a big ole kiss, and reestablish who belongs to who," I said. I held up her phone. "Then I'll blow this up the first ten minutes."

Darby shook her head. "Then she'll think you came in to see her. She's about that delusional."

"No shit," I said.

Darby turned off the stove and the oven, and I opened the door, pulling out the turkey while she set the table. She watched me carve the turkey with the brand-new electric knife I'd bought from Target the week before, and then we brought all the dishes to the table.

"Is it all right if I pray?" Darby asked.

"Of course."

She held both of my hands on the table and closed her eyes. I watched her with a smile.

"Heavenly Father," she began, "please bless this food to the nourishment of our bodies. I thank you for this beautiful new house, for the health of Maddie, and for the many blessings you've brought to my life. Thank you, Lord Jesus, for your sacrifice so that we might have eternal life together with you, and thank you for Trex. I know only you could have blessed me with someone so kind, so loving, and so faithful. In your precious name I pray, amen."

"Amen," I said.

Her eyes popped open, and she smiled. "I almost prayed for Lane. But it's Thanksgiving, and I'm just not thankful for her."

I couldn't help but laugh. Darby was serious, but her trying to be hateful was too damn cute. We talked about her day and her upcoming doctor's appointment, and I tried to enjoy the food instead of inhaling it. It was so damn good. I'd had only a handful of home-cooked meals in over a year, but it was just one more thing Darby was amazing at.

We filled the quietness of the large home around us with our laughter and made the darkness our own with candles. It was the most intimate, wonderful Thanksgiving I'd ever had, and I knew the next year would just be better.

I cleaned the kitchen while Darby got ready for work, and then I drove her to Naomi's townhouse. Several cars were parked in the street, but I didn't recognize all of them. They left a space in the drive for us, but before we even made it to the porch, half the team was outside making a scene.

"They're already drunk," I said.

"Good," Darby said with a smile.

I kept hold of her arm while she carried a pecan pie across the yard. It was dark, it was unfamiliar terrain, and I didn't want her to fall.

"Thank you," Naomi said, taking the pie.

"Well, hello, beautiful," Sloan said, hugging Darby.

"Hayden Sloan," I said. "Meet Darby"—I gestured to her round middle—"and Maddie."

"Darby!" Martinez said, hugging her.

"Othello Martinez," I said.

"Just O," Martinez said, stepping aside. "Or Martinez. Whatever."

I pointed at the rest. "And Terrell Kitsch."

Kitsch just waved.

"John and his family are inside," Naomi said. "Come on in!"

We led the way, and John stood to greet us.

"John and Caroline Harbinger," I said. "Their boys, Henry and Miles."

John shook her hand, Caroline hugged her. It was amusing to watch everyone who went in for a hug bend over to reach her shoulders.

It didn't take me long to figure out who belonged to the car and truck I didn't recognize. Zeke and Watts were sitting at the oval table, a bottle of beer in their hands. Senator Bennett was in the living room, watching the sports news on the earlier football game. Zeke stood, making his way over to Darby. He kissed her cheek, and I felt the blood under my cheeks boil. I glanced at Naomi, and she winked at me, clearly privy to some intel I didn't have.

"Trexler," Zeke said, reaching for my hand. "Congrats on the new house. That's awesome."

"Thanks," I said. I didn't realize I had a hand on Darby's belly until she rested her hand over mine.

"Trex?" Darby said. "I need to sit."

"You okay?" I asked.

"Yeah, just need to rest, I think," she said, rubbing her stomach.

I led her by the hand to the table, pulling out a chair.

"T-Rex! You've turned into a regular gentleman!" Martinez said, slapping my back.

Caroline brought her an ice water.

"Thank you," Darby said.

Zeke whispered something in Naomi's ear and then walked down the hall to the bathroom. Watts tried to hand me a bottle of beer, but I declined. "I'm the designated driver tonight."

"You going out with us?" he asked. He was already a few drinks in, relaxed and happy.

"After I drop Darby off at work, if she's feeling better," I said, looking at her.

"I'm fine," she said.

"You still working nights, Darby?" Watts asked.

"Yep," she said. "What have you been up to?"

"Traveling, mostly. One of the guys has a house in Mexico on the beach. I've been spending a lot of time down there. Is that Laney girl still working afternoons?"

Darby's smile was strained when she looked at me to answer. "Lane? Yep."

"Uh-oh," Naomi said, handing me a glass of water. "What's that about?"

"Thanks. I went there tonight after we were released to get Darby's boxes," I whispered.

"Yeah?"

"Crazy bitch tried to fuck me in Darby's old room."

"What?" Naomi said, trying to keep her voice down. "Does Darby know?"

"Yeah, I told her when I got back. She's pissed, but not at me."

"Makes for an awkward shift transition. Glad you told her. Way to avoid a stupid misunderstanding."

"I almost didn't. I was scared shitless it was going to ruin our first night at the house."

"Well, looky there. You have a reasonable girlfriend. Congratulations." Naomi clicked her beer bottle to my glass, and we both drank.

"Told you she was worth waiting for," I said.

"You still believe that shit? You think she's the one, huh?"

Darby laughed and chatted with Caroline and my team, my past mixing with my future, something I never imagined.

"Without a single doubt," I said, taking another drink. My phone pinged, and I checked it. Val had texted me just four words.

Heads up. He's there.

"Fuck," I said, putting my phone away.

"What?" Naomi asked, instantly on edge.

Kitsch came inside from the porch. "Nomes. You got a flashlight?"

"Just in every room of the house," she teased.

Kitsch wasn't amused. "I need the closest one."

"In the kitchen. Drawer to the left of the dishwasher."

Kitsch went to the kitchen, rummaged around for a second, and returned, rushing past. "It's to the right of the dishwasher," he said.

"Everything all right?" I asked.

Kitsch pushed through the screen door, pointing his flashlight at the ground.

"What is he doing?" Naomi asked.

"Boss," Kitsch called from outside.

Naomi and I made the same face, then I followed Kitsch to the front porch. He stood at the top of the stairs, nodding to the yard. The flashlight highlighted a mound of dead rabbits.

"What the hell?" Naomi said, grabbing the flashlight from Kitsch. She followed the carcasses with the light. She handed it to me, then rushed inside.

"What's going on?" Martinez asked, stopping when he saw the pile.

Naomi returned, a half dozen flashlights in her arms, including a headlamp. Sloan and Harbinger came out, and she handed them to everyone on our team. We each turned on a flashlight and pointed it in the same direction.

"What the actual fuck is going on?" Harbinger asked.

Zeke and Watts came out, talking and laughing, but silenced the moment they recognized what was out in the yard.

"That wasn't there ten minutes ago when we came outside for Watts to smoke," Zeke said. "Is someone...is someone playing a sick joke?"

"It's more than one person. One guy couldn't do all of that in the amount of time he had," Naomi said, shining her headlamp at the carcasses.

"Agreed," Harbinger said.

The screen door opened one more time, and I turned to make sure it wasn't Darby. The senator brought out a bottle of beer, recoiling at the mess in the yard. "Is that...?"

"Yes," I said, glowering.

We peered out over the rabbit carcasses lying in the dead grass, lit up with six heavy-duty flashlights, forming just one word: MINE.

chapter twenty-four

Trex

I went inside Naomi's house with a smile on my face. Caroline and Darby were still talking, but stopped and looked up the moment the screen door slammed behind me. It opened once more when Naomi zipped past to make her way to the kitchen and quietly open the cabinet beneath the sink and then return with a green-and-orange box in her hand, going right back out to the yard.

"Everything all right?" Darby asked.

Caroline stood, leaning over to peer out the windows. "Where's John?"

The others were bent down in the yard, scrambling to pick up the tiny bodies of the rabbits. I didn't want Darby to see them, because she would know immediately, as I did, who had left the message. Naomi was holding up large, black trash bags for the guys to throw them in.

"Trex?" Darby prompted.

"Oh, they're, uh...screwing around. I don't know. How are you feeling?"

"Better," she smiled.

My heart sank. I wasn't being honest again, but I couldn't tell her the truth. She was in third trimester and didn't need the stress of knowing Shawn and his friends had been just outside the door.

"Good. That's good, babe. We should probably..."

"Oh," she said, standing. She shook Caroline's hand. "It was so nice to meet you."

"Likewise," Caroline said. "Let me know if you'd like to come over for lunch."

"I will. Happy Thanksgiving."

I helped her with her coat, and we made our way to the door after Darby said good-bye to Henry and Miles. She looked over her shoulder at them. "They are so well-mannered. I've been grilling poor Caroline all night about tricks of the trade."

"She loves talking about her kids and parenting and stuff. This is probably the best night she's had in a while," I said.

Senator Bennett nodded to Darby as she stepped onto the porch. "Have a good night, Darby."

"Thank you, Senator."

"You can just call me Peter. Happy Thanksgiving, and if I don't see you before then, happy holidays. Good night, Trex."

"Good night, sir," I said, helping Darby down the steps.

The team came around the house as we made our way to the truck. Martinez, Harbinger, Kitsch, and Sloan all hugged her, keeping their bloodied hands away from her clothes. I was thankful it was dark.

"It was really nice to see you again. I'm sure we'll see you again soon," Naomi said, keeping her hands behind her.

"Thanks for doing this. I loved meeting everyone," Darby said in her sweet Southern drawl.

"Come back anytime. It will be nice to see Trex more often again."

I hugged her. "Thanks, Nomes."

"Of course."

When Darby turned, all of their cordial smiles fell away. I reached over to unlock my glove box and then waved to

Naomi. She watched me back out of the drive, a concerned expression weighing down her features. Naomi knew as well as I did we needed a plan.

Darby didn't seem to know anything was up, chatting about meeting Caroline and the kids, and excited to know another mom in town. She was more than thrilled to have met a senator, and I was glad to have the truth to tell her: He'd grown up with Naomi.

"Kitsch…he seemed to be having a rough night. Is that why everyone went outside with him?"

I nodded. "The holidays are really difficult for him. He's been pretty down all day."

"You must worry about him every year."

"I do. I'm glad we're all together this year. It's easier to keep an eye on him. The rest of the year, he pretty successfully pretends they're all still alive, and we let him. But Thanksgiving and Christmas, he just can't."

"That's so sad. He's so nice. Did you know his wife and kids?"

I cleared my throat. "I met them a few times." *Deployment send-offs and returns, and Marine balls, mostly.*

She sat back, rubbing her stomach.

"You okay?" I asked.

She sighed. "Maddie's just trying to find some space. She's running out of room. Not sure how we are both going to make it to February."

"Doc Park said mid-January was good enough for her."

"Let's hope Maddie wants to meet us just as bad as we want to meet her. I can't breathe."

I held her hand. "Sorry, babe. It can't be comfortable."

She peered over at me with a smile on her face. "She's worth it."

I pulled into the parking lot of the hotel, stopping under

the overhang of the entrance. I reached for the keys in the ignition, but Darby stopped me.

"It's okay. Don't even get out to open my door. I don't want her to have the satisfaction of thinking you came in or got out of the truck hoping to see her. You know that's what she'll think."

I shrugged, my hand still on the keys. "Who cares what she thinks. She's crazy."

"I shouldn't. But I do."

I sat back, letting the truck run. "Okay. Have a good night. See you in the morning."

Darby slowly leaned over to kiss me, letting her full lips linger on mine. "See you in eight hours!"

I frowned. "That's a long time."

She laughed as she opened the door and scooted out.

"You sure you don't need help?" I asked.

She stepped down and did a little curtsy. "Tada!"

"I love you," I said with a smile. "Don't forget to text me with your new phone."

"Oh!" she said, looking down at her hand. She held it up. "I forgot! I'll text you. A lot. I'll keep you up all night. You'll throw it away when I get home."

"Don't threaten me with a good time."

She giggled, the sound like chimes cutting through the night air. "Love you."

The door shut, and I watched her walk in and immediately peel off her coat. I wondered if Lane was at all nervous about the confrontation that was about to happen, but probably not. Knowing Lane as I did, I thought she would probably feel justified because, in her narcissistic mind, we'd met first. Lane liked any man who showed her attention, and after the second date, a few wild trysts in my room, she was sure she was in love with me. It was about that time that I knew she was most definitely not the one. Even after I stopped answering her calls and texts, she still stopped by the hotel to see me, more than once going back to someone else's room, hoping it would make me jealous.

I peered around, checking the parking lot for any suspicious activity, and decided to drive around once. I had just parked on the side of the building when my phone rang.

"Trex," I answered.

"Is your girl at work?" Naomi asked.

"Yep. Just dropped her off. I did a sweep of the parking lot."

"Where are you now?"

"Still in the parking lot." Lane walked out of the entrance, her arms folded, her head down. "Lane just came out. Has her tail tucked between her legs like Darby just handed her ass to her on a platter."

"Darby didn't strike me as the jealous type."

"She's not. Just letting Lane know what she pulled earlier wasn't Christian-like."

"I knew I liked her," Naomi said. She breathed out a laugh. "You're not going out tonight, are you?"

"Nope."

"Good thing I stopped drinking an hour ago. Looks like I'm the alternate DD. Have you called Val?"

"I'll call her in the morning. Not much she can do right now. She's probably with family."

Naomi sighed. "This is fucked up, T-Rex. He is clearly a psychopath."

"Darby mentioned that."

"You packin'?"

"Yep," I said. "Glock 19 should put some holes in him, even if he's not human."

"Did Darby say that?"

"She did."

"He's not alone. I wouldn't be surprised if he's armed, too, so eyes peeled."

"Copy that."

"How do you think he found her?"

"Darby said he had a brother in government IT. It could have been anything. But I have a feeling it was when Val ran a check on her."

"What do you mean?" Naomi asked.

"I made the mistake of telling Val about Darby. She ran a check on her. That could have pinged the brother."

"When was that?"

"Not long after we met."

"Apparently he's a patient psycho."

"Takes time to put together a plan," I said, my jaws twitching.

"This is fucked up, Trex. This is next-level shit."

"Being on defense is not my strong suit. I don't like waiting for him to make a move."

"Well, all right," she said. I could hear the smile in her voice. "Call Val in the morning and put us on offense."

"It's going to be a long night," I said, rubbing my eyes with my free hand. I was used to waking up at five a.m.

I blinked a few times, keeping my eyes on the dark lot.

"When we get Kitsch nice and pass-out drunk and I get him in bed, I'll stop by with a coffee."

"Large, please."

"You got it. Call if you need me before."

"All right…"

"Wait. Holy shit. I'm currently overhearing some chick trashing you at the bar. She's gorgeous. What did you do to her?" she asked, laughing.

"Who?"

"She's talking about Darby, too." She paused, listening. "Oh, she works with her."

"Lane," I seethed.

"She's with a few guys. They look like they came here for trouble. I better head in."

"Keep me updated."

"Will do. See you in a few."

Naomi hung up, and I waited. No crickets chirping, no frogs, just the heating units kicking on and the rhythmic noise from the highway. No one came in or out, the windows were dark. The few people on the road for Thanksgiving were in bed, sleeping off their food comas and trying to get a decent night's rest before getting back on the road early the next morning. I wanted to park somewhere else to get a better view of Darby, but because of the risk of being seen, I settled for being able to watch the front door, the only entrance that was open to the exterior at night.

Midnight came and went, then one a.m. blew by. Twenty minutes after the top of the hour, a pair of headlights bounced over the bumpy drive of the hotel. Naomi parked next to me, smiling while holding an enormous cup next to her face. She got out and crawled into the passenger side of my truck, slamming the door.

"Easy, Nomes, fuck."

"Oh, it's fine. Quit being a baby." She handed me the cup. "One giant-sized truck stop coffee."

"Thank you," I said, taking a sip. "Ah, fuck that's good."

"Tired?" she asked.

I nodded. "How long can you stay?"

She shrugged. "I have tomorrow off. As long as you need."

"What do you got?" I asked.

She patted her back. "Vicky didn't want your Glock to be lonely."

I nodded. Vicky was her Glock 26. She also had a Ruger named Chuck Norris and a Beretta named Cecil. Instead of pets, Naomi bought firearms. She cleaned them and named them and treated them like family.

"I also brought Walter."

I wrinkled my nose. "What the hell do you plan on doing with him?"

She reached down and pulled a twelve-inch tactical bowie hunting knife from her boot. It was matte black with a fixed blade and every bit as badass as Naomi. I would expect nothing less.

"There is more than one. I should have more than one weapon," she explained, matter-of-fact.

I laughed.

"So are we taking them down on sight or taking the diplomatic approach?"

"Well, considering the former is illegal, I say we give them fair warning and make sure he doesn't come back."

"Trex. He's hostile and making threats."

"We still have to do this by the book, Nomes. We're not at war anymore."

She looked out her window and snarled. "She's naming that baby after Matt. I'll kill anyone who comes at her with anything but food and baby gifts."

"Thanks for the coffee. And thanks for being a good friend."

Naomi shrugged the shoulder closest to me.

"So what happened with Lane?"

"I was right. The guys who came with her were looking for trouble."

"And?"

"I put one on his back. I could tell once they got close enough they weren't interested. Lane asked where you were. Kitsch thinks they were looking for you."

I frowned, confused. "Big brothers, maybe? Defending her honor?"

She raised one eyebrow. "That one never had any honor. One had his hand on her ass, so not family. The other two were his minions. Did whatever he told them to and looked to him for what to do next. Especially after I took out the big one. And they were all over six one, easy."

"Did Lane ask for me before or after?"

"Before. She came over looking for you. Then they came over. The big one mouthed off."

"Locals?"

She shook her head. "Don't think so. The ringleader was razzing every single one of us. Even the senator. Almost like he was trying to see who would fight him."

"I guess he found out."

"I got between him and Kitsch, then the big one thought he was going to manhandle me, so I put him on his ass."

"I'm sorry I wasn't there."

"No, you're not. You need to be here."

"Yeah," I said, staring at the front door.

My cell phone pinged, and I smiled.

"Wow. Who just made your day?"

"I got Darby a phone today. She just texted me for the first time. She sent a heart."

"Rad," Naomi deadpanned.

How's it going? I typed.

Slow. Quiet. The problem with having a big, amazing home is that I want to be there.

Put in your notice if you want.

You know I can't.

You can. You just don't want to.

I'm going to stick with Stavros until I have this baby or the hotel goes belly up. I owe him that.

He's been good to you, I'll give him that. But you worked doubles for him for a long time too. You don't really owe him shit.

I owe him a lot more than double shifts. He saved me. And if he hadn't given me this job, I wouldn't have met you.

We would have met.

Sorry if I woke you. I'll see you in a few hours.

I would much rather talk to you than sleep.

You should send me all the things you used to write me on your phone at work so I can read them.

I went into my Notes, copied everything, and then pasted it into the text message, pressing Send. I sat back and relaxed for a few seconds before glancing around the parking lot.

"Convo over?" Naomi asked.

"She asked for all of the stuff I wrote to her at work. It's going to take her a while to get through it."

"You two are gross," she teased.

"It's not like I haven't warned you for years." I looked at my watch. Val was in a time zone one hour behind, so it would be after I picked up Darby from work before I could call.

"What about you?" I asked. "What about the senator being there last night?"

"It was just dinner. He couldn't get home. No one should be alone on Thanksgiving. He's the reason we have the weekend off."

"Hoping he could spend it with you, I bet."

She breathed out a laugh. "He did ask to come over tomorrow."

I shrugged. "He doesn't seem too bad of a guy, Naomi."

Her smile faded. "He's not Matt."

"You're never going to find another Matt. Doesn't mean you can't be happy with someone else."

"God, you sound like my sister. I'm okay. I don't want anyone else. I met the love of my life. He's gone. If I can't have him, it's no one. We don't have to be with someone, you know. I'm not alone. I have you, and the guys, and Walter," she said, patting her boot. "I'm as happy as I can be, considering."

"Okay, okay, just thought I'd mention it."

"Well don't," she said, her eyes widening for a second when she spoke the last word.

"Copy that," I said, checking my watch again. "What about Zeke and Watts? What were they doing there?"

"Not being alone," she said, annoyed.

"Just asking."

"Speaking of questions that are no one's business, have you told her everything yet?"

I frowned. "Not everything. Not about the job, obviously."

"What about that little detail about you being a Marine?"

"Not yet."

She raised her brows. "Trexler, what the hell?"

"I know. I know. I've had multiple moments to tell her, but usually we were arguing about me keeping things from her. At this point, I think it's better just to keep it to myself."

"How the fuck are you going to do that? How does she not know? You have a USMC tat on your shoulder."

I shook my head. "It got all fucked up during the surgery. It's a mess. No one can tell what it is."

"She hasn't asked?"

"Yeah. I told her I was a kid when I got it, and that it was a dare, and that it was messed up in an accident, which are all true."

Naomi shifted in the seat. "She is going to be so pissed. You have to tell her, Trex."

"I honestly don't know how. It's too late."

"It's not too late until she finds out someway other than you. Then it'll be too late."

"You're right. I know you're right. Things are so good right now, and with Shawn sniffing around, I just...It's not a good time. I'll wait until after the baby."

She shook her head. "It's a big risk, buddy. She's already said once she can't trust you. She forgave the background check thing because you were trying to protect her."

"It wasn't a background check," I grumbled.

"This is just you lying. She knows you well enough to know you're not like Shawn. That was your original excuse, wasn't it?"

"That's the thing. I feel like she's constantly comparing me to him. Or, at least, she was when this all came up. When she agreed to move in, Nomes...I just want to leave the past where I left it. Things have been really good."

She put her hand on mine. "I hope it works out. I really do. But you gotta tell her. Every day you wait makes it worse."

I nodded. "Can we change the subject now?"

"Sure."

We chatted about everything but potential prospects for Naomi until the sunrise. The job, her house, Zeke, Bennett, the general, the latest news on our buddies still deployed. Naomi stayed another half hour and then hopped down from the passenger seat. She waved before backing out, turning toward home.

I started the truck and pulled under the overhang, waiting for Darby like I did every morning, Monday through Friday mornings. She waved to me from behind the desk and finished closing down her shift. Maya waved to me as she passed in front of my truck, the entrance doors swept open, and a few minutes later they swept open again, making way for my gorgeous girlfriend. She still had not a hair out of place, her red lipstick still just as vibrant as it was when she'd applied it at the house. I hopped out and jogged around to the passenger side, opening the door for Darby and holding her hand while she climbed in.

"Good morning," she said, a bit tired.

"It might be time to get a shorter vehicle," I said.

"Don't you dare. I like this truck."

"Maybe a second one, then." I jogged back to the driver's side, then slid in behind the wheel.

"Trex, I can't afford a car, and you're not buying me one."

"Do you have any idea how much money I make? I can get you a car," I said, pulling the gearshift into Drive. I pulled forward, seeing Darby shake her head from my peripheral.

"No way. Absolutely not. I'll get a car eventually."

As we passed the other side of the hotel, a white sedan caught my eye, four shadows sitting inside. Lane was in the back, the man next to her kissing her neck. She was staring at me, a small smile on her face. The two men in front were facing forward, unfazed about the activity behind them.

I continued to the highway and then turned toward home. The sedan stayed put at the hotel, but I couldn't shake the strange look on Lane's face. Revenge was loud, but the eyes don't lie. There was much more to Lane's smile than hoping for a jealous reaction from me.

"You're quiet," Darby said. "Everything okay?"

"Yeah. Just tired."

"I noticed you had on the same clothes as last night."

"Oh, I have the day off today. Did I tell you that?"

"You do?" she asked, excited. She grabbed my arm with both hands.

"So I just put on the clothes I had last night. But I didn't sleep worth a shit last night. I think I just need you in my bed."

"Are you saying we're going to go to bed together when we get home?"

"That's exactly what I'm saying. I even had this whole cup of coffee and I'm still ready to crash."

"That's not a cup, babe. That's like…a liter of coffee." She squeezed my arm. "But I'm so excited to get into comfy clothes and lay in bed with you!"

I took her hand and kissed her palm, then interlaced my fingers in hers. There were enemies waiting in the wings, and the Lane situation was highly suspicious. I would lie with Darby until she fell asleep, then I had to make that phone call to Val.

Stavros was teetering on a ladder, reaching to put the last few ornaments at the top of the fifteen-foot-tall fake fir tree in the corner of the lobby he'd been putting together off and on throughout the afternoon. I'd come to help him, killing time before Trex got off work.

"Like this?" I asked, turning the small ceramic tree on the desk. "Stavros?"

"Huh? Yes. That looks great, thanks."

I walked over to him and touched his arm. "How's Tilde?"

His tired eyes glossed over. "You should come by the house, Darby. She's not doing well."

"I will. I'll come tonight before my shift."

Stavros nodded.

Lane was not as happy with my décor placement. "It's right in my way," she said, pushing the tree to the edge of the desk.

"Maybe just wait until I'm not here, and then you can try to get what you want," I said. "It wouldn't be the first time you tried that."

Lane's mouth fell open.

Stavros pointed at her before walking to the bar. "Don't act like you didn't deserve that."

I followed him to his corner of the lobby, surrounded by his colleagues Jim Beam, Captain Morgan, and Kim Crawford. He cleaned the counters for the third time that day, even though he'd had few customers.

"Is she in a lot of pain?" I asked.

He simply nodded.

"How is Ander?"

"He's taking it harder than I thought he would. The only time he's not by her side is when he's at work. Maya has already agreed to work his shift after she passes until the funeral."

"That's kind of her." I pulled him into a hug. "I'm sorry."

He hugged me and wiped a bottle top down before waving. "I'm going to head back to the office for a bit. Get some paperwork done. Thanks for all your help today."

"You're welcome," I said, watching him disappear around the corner.

Lane strolled over to me, glancing over her shoulder once to the hallway where Stavros had gone.

"We need to talk," she said.

"No, actually we don't."

She rolled her eyes. "Okay, so I tried to kiss your baby daddy. But I don't think you know the whole story."

"He told me everything, Lane. We've already had this conversation once. Are you sure you want to go there?"

"Did he tell you we've done a helluva lot more than kiss?"

I stared at her for a moment. "You're lying."

"He's been here before, Darby. You think he was celibate before you? We met at Cowboys. He brought me back here"—she looked up—"to that room."

"So? We weren't together then," I snapped.

"There's a lot more that Trex hasn't told you than

about his job. He's all about the secrets. That's just a nice way of saying he can't tell the truth. All he knows how to do is lie, even when it doesn't matter. He just can't seem to tell the full truth. So, yes, I tried to kiss him. There were some unresolved feelings there. But since then, mostly I've found I just feel sorry for you. I dodged the bullet on that one. But you...you're bringing a baby into this world with a man who can look you straight in the eyes and lie to your face like it's nothing. How can you trust anything that comes out of his mouth? Having a man who decides what you get to know and what you don't? Not something I'm interested in, I'll tell you that."

Lane was pleased about the expression on my face. I touched my stomach, pushing at a sore tendon that was stretching as Maddie grew.

"How do you know about his job?" I asked.

"Ask him."

I frowned, seeing Trex's truck pull under the overhang. He jumped out, a smile on his face, happy to see me for a few hours before I had to go back to work. Whether or not to confront him had to be decided in the moment, and it broke my heart. The light in his eyes when he saw me as he walked through the doors was already turning to suspicion. There was no point in trying to hide what I knew. Either he would see through me, or Lane would open her damn mouth.

"Hey," he said, wrapping his arms around me. He kissed my cheek before speaking again. "What's up? Everything all right?" His eyes danced between Lane and me. She had a smug expression, and the last thing I wanted to do was give her the satisfaction of an argument.

"Lane told me about...before," I said.

Trex frowned, and then his gaze floated to Lane. His

shoulders sagged. "What are you doing? I'm in love with this girl."

Lane crossed her arms. "Then why lie?"

"I didn't lie, Lane. It wasn't worth mentioning."

"That's not what you said back then," she snapped.

"I didn't say anything back then. I stopped calling you when I figured out you were insane."

I tried not to smile, instead pressing my lips together. Trex took the look on my face to be anger.

"Baby..." he began.

I patted his chest. "It's okay. Let's go."

I passed him, turning when he didn't follow. Lane and Trex were standing, dumbfounded.

"You already said she wasn't worth mentioning. I agree. Let's go, please."

Trex didn't waste another second, rushing to walk next to me as we made our way to the truck. He helped me in and then jogged to the other side, peeking at me as he started the engine. When he pulled out, he cleared his throat.

"How mad are you?" he asked.

"Furious," I said, turning to face him. "You knew she was going to drop that bomb on me eventually. Why didn't you tell me? I realize she ain't worth mentionin', but you could at least've saved me from the humiliation of finding out from her."

First, he cringed, but as I talked he worked hard not to smile.

"This ain't funny, Scottie!"

My use of his first name wiped the grin off his face. "I know. I know it's not, and I'm very sorry. But when you get mad and Texas comes out of your mouth...it's the cutest thing I've ever heard."

I glared at him.

He reached for my hand, but I crossed my arms over the top of my enormous belly.

"Baby... you're right. I should've told you. There was really no good time to bring up Lane."

"Then maybe not act like you'd never met her?"

"That wasn't what I was trying to do. I was trying to show my indifference. She stalked me for a good five weeks after I tried to let her down easy. It kind of freaked me out that she got a job at the hotel."

I looked out the window, trying not to be flattered. The rest of what she said came to mind. "She said she knew about your job. She said you had a lot of secrets. I don't like her knowing things about you that I don't."

"She doesn't know anything, Darby."

"She knows something."

He sighed. "I can't tell you, Darby. You know that."

He held out his hand again, and this time I took it. He squeezed.

"She said you're not capable of tellin' the truth. She said I couldn't trust you. Just so you know, your job is the only secret you get to keep," I said. When he didn't answer, I craned my neck at him. "Trex."

"Deal," he said quickly, kissing my knuckles.

chapter twenty-six

The fireplace was crackling, two big red stockings with white fur trim and a tiny, sweater-knit cream-colored stocking with red ribbon trim hung from the mantel. I'd ordered them just after we moved in, our names embroidered at the top, even Maddie's. Hers read MADDIE ROSE even though Darby hadn't agreed to the middle name yet. I was already attached to it, and Darby had stopped arguing after I'd hung the stocking.

The room was dim, and Darby was relaxing on the couch with her bare feet in my lap, her belly bouncing as she giggled at the sight of me trying to paint her swollen toes.

"What?" I said, smiling but trying to concentrate. "Hold still! I'm already terrible at this. It's that much harder with your feet shaking every time you laugh at me."

"I can't help it." She took out her phone and snapped a picture.

I looked up. "Really?" I deadpanned.

Darby cackled, and I shook my head, trying again. It didn't bother me in the slightest, but Darby got so much enjoyment from giving me a hard time, I pretended it did. After I finished, I'd put cuticle oil on her toes and rub her feet, and she would lie back and look serene and happy. I loved that part, our quiet nights at home before she went to work. *Life doesn't get better than this.*

Darby's phone rang in her hands. She looked down at the display and then showed me. Unknown Number was listed at the top.

I reached out, gesturing for the phone. Darby reached as far as she could, huffing when she sat back. I slid my thumb across the bottom to answer. "Hello?"

Someone was breathing on the other end of the line. It wasn't a pocket dial. Whoever had called her was waiting.

"Who is this?" I asked.

More breathing. Not the kind you'd expect from a pervert or a bored punk kid. Just waiting. Listening.

"Who is it?" Darby asked.

The breathing stopped, and the call ended. I frowned at the phone. "No one." I'd be calling Val for another favor, even though I owed her ten.

"You, Stavros, Ander, and Maya are the only ones who have my number. And the doctor's office." She smiled at saying the last part.

She was so proud to finally have a number to give them, and they were relieved she had access to a phone. Dr. Park had finally warmed up to me, trusting my intentions. I used my lunch hour to sit with Darby at every appointment, glad that it didn't make a difference to the general. Bianca hadn't even asked about specifics. They only knew that my girl-friend was pregnant.

Darby turned to look at the large clock hung in the kitchen. "This is the only thing I dislike about my job. Hospitality is three hundred sixty-five days a year. It's Christmas Eve, the fire is going, and I have to start getting ready for work soon."

"Have you talked to Stavros yet?"

"I can't," she said, an edge of whining in her voice. "Tilde is still in hospice. She's lasted a month longer than they thought. She's going to go at any time."

"How is she looking?" I asked. Darby visited almost every day.

"Like a skeleton. She sleeps most of the time. It's cruel. Trex? Don't let me...Don't let that happen to me, okay?"

I put her feet gently on the floor and then snuggled up to her. She didn't talk about our future very often, and she had no idea the way it made me feel. Even talking about the frightening end was a comfort, knowing she would let me love her every day of the in-between.

"We're going at the exact same time, in our beds, warm and happy."

"I mean it."

"I won't," I promised. "I'd never let anything bad happen to you."

Darby seemed satisfied with that, and she relaxed against my shoulder. We interlaced our fingers over her belly, laughing when Maddie rolled.

"Should we tell her?" I asked. "I mean...I was thinking, no one knows she's not mine. We could...you could take my last name and that's what would be on the birth certificate. It happens all the time."

Darby was quiet for a long time, and I worried that I'd upset her.

"Unless you...unless you don't want to," I said quickly.

She looked up at me, a tear rolling down her nose. "Did you just ask me to marry you? Because that was terrible."

She smiled, prompting me to breathe out a sigh of relief. "I can do it way better if you want."

"I want," she said.

"Really? You'd marry me?"

She nodded, and I leaned down to touch my lips to hers. I understood then why Kitsch pretended, why Harbinger went through months of therapy to be the best dad to his kids he could be. Family was everything. It was worth dying for, losing your mind over, and facing your greatest fears.

"I won't make you wait long," I said.

"T-minus five-point-five weeks, mister."

"That's not long to pull a wedding together."

"Who needs a wedding?" she said with a tearful smile.

"You're serious, then?" I asked. She nodded, and I kissed her again. "I told you your last name would be Trexler."

Darby hugged me. She held me tight, like we hadn't seen each other in a while. She pulled at me, pressing her cheek against mine. "I'm so happy, Trex. So, so happy. I'm so lucky you think I'm the one you've always loved. I hope I am. I'm going to try my best to be her."

"She's you. No doubt in my mind." Right then. That's when I should have told her. She was in a good mood, she knew we belonged together and that I was not like the other soldier she thought loved her. But it was Christmas Eve, and we were talking about marriage, and the last thing I wanted to do was admit that I had one more secret.

"We should tell her early that you adopted her, and you've loved her from the very beginning. If she ever found out from any way other than us, Trex..."

"You're right." I kissed her hair. "Of course you're right. I get crazy ideas sometimes."

"I like the part about her having your last name. About us having your last name." Her smile turned into a frown.

"Second thoughts?" I asked.

She pressed on the side of her belly, the way she did when Maddie was stretching or growing or her tendons were stretching.

"Wow, your stomach is a perfect ball right now," I said.

"It's hard," she said.

I reached over to touch it and then lifted her shirt, putting my hand against her skin. She was right. Her stomach usually had give except for where Maddie was, but the entire area was a solid rock. "Is this labor?"

"Braxton-Hicks."

I nodded, relieved. "Good. We still have a few things to get yet."

Maddie's nursery was nearly complete, with a rug that looked like a bunch of roses in various shades of pink. The wooden crib was white, the walls white, the rocking chair and ottoman white, on the walls a gold wooden cutout that read MADDIE in script letters, surrounded by paper roses matching the rug. The crib sheet and throw pillow on the chair were the same pink floral material. It looked almost identical to a picture Darby showed me on Pinterest. I made sure she had everything she wanted. We had onesies, sleepers, a few dresses, and a closet full of outfits up to twelve months, socks, a few headbands, diapers, wipes, lotion, baby shampoo, baby fingernail clippers, and a blue plastic bulb that I had no clue what it was for, but Darby was sure we'd need it. The stroller was ready and in the front closet, the car seat already in the back seat of the truck.

The baby bag was packed and ready for the hospital and had been for a week.

"What else do we need?" she asked, stretching to make more room to take a breath.

"I'm sure there's something," I said. "I have this nagging feeling we're forgetting something."

Darby smiled. "You know Maddie won't wait until we're ready."

I leaned down to kiss Darby's bare skin and then covered her up. "I know. I just want to be prepared."

"We're prepared," she said, looking around the house. "It

really is a beautiful home. We have everything we need. I don't know how this happened, but we're really lucky."

"Yes, I am," I said. "So...I need to spring something on you."

She arched an eyebrow.

"My parents have a church thing, but Hailey wants to visit tomorrow. She just told me today, but she hasn't been over since the week we moved in, and I couldn't tell her no."

"Why would you tell her no? It's your sister and it's Christmas."

"Because I hadn't talked to you yet."

"You don't have to talk to me about your sister visiting. I love Hailey. She can come anytime."

I let my head fall back. "I forget how laid-back you are. I don't take it for granted."

"Who would get mad about that?"

I sat up, remembering less blissful times. "Laura. She did not like surprises."

"Well," Darby said, touching her belly. "My whole life is one big surprise." She stood. "I should get ready for work."

"Wait! I have a Christmas Eve present for you." I jogged over to the tree, then came back, sitting next to her. The box was small. "Spoiler alert: It's not an engagement ring."

She pulled on the white ribbon and popped open the lid. "Oh my gosh." She pinched the white gold band and held up the ring to the light. Encircled with tiny diamonds, with just a single amethyst in the center that was the same size as the other stones. "Trex," she said, sliding it on her middle finger.

It fit, and my chest puffed a bit.

Darby's eyes glossed over. "What if she comes early?"

"I worked it out with the jeweler. He'll just switch out the gemstone. Look at the inscription inside."

She took it off and squinted, then covered her mouth with

her free hand. "Madeleine Rose," she read aloud. She put it on again and threw her arms around my neck as best she could over her belly. "I love it."

"I love you," I said, watching her sit back and wipe happy tears from beneath her eyes.

"I just got you a couple things for Christmas. And they're not this special."

"You're here with me, in this house, beautiful and growing my baby. What else could I possibly need?" I asked.

She smiled, wiping her eyes again, then looking down at the ring. "This is not what I had planned for myself. I didn't want it. I had no idea you and Maddie and everything we're building would make me happier than I've ever been... would make me feel at home more than I ever have."

I brushed back the honey strands from her face and cupped her jaw. Her cheeks were a little fuller, rosier than before, and her lips, nose, fingers, and feet were puffier. I'd never seen a woman more beautiful, had never felt the love of a woman so kind, and somehow, I made her happy.

She leaned over to kiss my palm, closed her eyes as her lips lingered against my skin for a bit, and then she worked to push herself off the sofa. "I'm going to find a tent to pull over my body, and then I should head to work. Oh, and don't forget after this appointment, they're every week."

I nodded. "Already asked off."

She bent down to kiss my lips. "Already a good daddy."

She waddled toward the bedroom, and I sat stunned, unable to respond. My eyes filled with tears, and I wiped them quickly, clearing my throat. I never knew how much I'd needed to hear that. My father had been so fucking deplorable, and it wasn't until that moment that I realized I'd needed to be freed from the fear that I'd be the same—a fear I didn't know I had. "Thank you," I said to an empty room.

The white Christmas lights twinkled, casting a warm, white glow against the orange that flickered from the fireplace. The entire living room was bathed in a soft light and I felt damn near euphoric. An engagement ring was on the agenda the second the stores opened after Christmas. I needed to marry that girl.

I sat back and relaxed, hearing Darby hum a lullaby to Maddie as she dressed. Her cell phone buzzed, the lit display catching my eye. It was from Stavros, updating Darby on Tilde.

"Baby," I called, picking up her phone. "Stavros texted you. It's something about Tilde."

"Read it to me, please."

I tapped the message with my finger and opened the text. I spoke loud so Darby could hear me. "Tilde passed away an hour ago surrounded by friends and family. Thank you for spending time with her in her final days. I know she appreciated it. Funeral day and time will be announced soon."

Darby stepped out of the bedroom wearing only a robe and a stunned expression. I stood, holding my hands out to her. "Honey, I'm sorry."

She held me tight, her fists gripping my shirt. I rocked back and forth, paying attention to her every breath and sniffle, waiting for her to let me know how she needed me.

"She's with the Lord now," she said. She let go of my shirt. "It's hard to know you don't believe that."

"Either way, her suffering is over," I said.

Darby nodded and then hugged me again, letting me bear her weight as I rocked her back and forth. "The last time I went to a funeral was Chase and Dad's. It makes me a wreck to think about another one."

"You don't have to go. Stavros would understand. He

might even be glad to have you at work instead, if it's in the morning during Ander's shift."

"No, I should go. Will you go with me?"

"Of course," I said, squeezing her gently. "You know I will."

She nodded and returned to the bedroom, walking more slowly this time, the bounce gone out of her step. Her phone felt cold and heavy in my hand. I looked down at the display, still curious about the unknown caller. Shawn being in the area twice in as many months had me on edge. Val was keeping an eye on him, but she had also found his whereabouts were being hidden. His brother Derek was likely helping him. She was also looking into that, but she wasn't a computer genius and we had to be careful who we asked for help.

Even though we'd been careful, something didn't feel right. I knew it was Shawn on the other end of the line. My thumb hovered over the phone button, and before I could stop myself, I clicked on Recent Calls. I scrolled down, seeing she'd gotten a call from an unknown number twice before.

I opened the garage door, used my key fob to start my truck so it would be warm for Darby, and went into the living room and sat, keeping an eye on the bedroom doorway. I scrolled through my contacts and hit Val's name, then waited.

"Aw," she said. "Did you call me to say Merry Christmas?"

"That, too," I said. "How's it going?"

"It's going. How about you? How's the new house?"

"Really good."

"Oh yeah? That's great. Congratulations. I'm still in the apartment."

"Is your husband still there?" I asked.

"Of course he is. Whoever moves out loses the apartment. That's why the divorce hasn't been finalized yet. He wants the apartment."

"But it was yours. Sawyer moved in with you, right? And if he liked the apartment and living with you so much, he probably shouldn't have fucked Agent Davies."

"Yeah, well...you can't talk sense into an idiot. And if you're wondering, yes, he can hear me."

"So...I was wondering. Any movement?"

"Some. Nothing concerning."

"You still think the brother is interfering?"

"Without a doubt. Sawyer is on it."

"Sawyer?"

"He's our tracker, and he's good. He knows his way around a computer. He's not on Derek's level, but he can see where Shawn's current location has been erased. Derek could be helping him leave base."

"We're at a disadvantage."

"For now," Val said. Her confidence was comforting, but it wasn't enough.

"He's planning something, Val. We can't afford to be two steps behind. She's four weeks out from birth. I'm worried he thinks this baby is mine and he's waiting for her to be separated from me—meaning once she has the baby—to get her back. To take her back. Or if he finds out somehow the baby is his—"

"Trex, she has six extremely dangerous Marines right there at her disposal. You're smart. You may be on defense, but you've got a hell of a team."

"Just do me a favor. Look him up one more time. It'll ring some bells, but I don't think it matters at this point."

"Will do," she said, hanging up.

I put down the phone and sat down on the sofa, rubbing

my hands together. Val was right, but I didn't want to wait until something happened to act. I had to locate Shawn, and…dark thoughts were running through my head, things I'd seen happen to civilians in villages or suspected spies; things I never wanted to think about again.

I'll need rope, and lots of it.

"Trex," Darby said from the bedroom doorway.

I looked up. "Hey, babe. You ready?" I could see that she wasn't. She was lacking pants and her hair was piled on top of her head.

"What are you doing?" she asked, holding her stomach.

I looked around. "I'm just waiting for you to get ready."

"You were on the phone."

"Oh yeah. Just telling some old coworkers Merry Christmas."

She closed her eyes, her lashes pushing tears down her cheek. She turned around and disappeared into the bedroom, closing the door.

I stood and followed her, knocking twice before entering. The room was dark, the only light coming from the bathroom. I went in, seeing her brushing her hair and crying.

"What's wrong?"

"She was right. You can look me in the eyes and lie right to my face?"

"*What?* Who was right?" I asked, confused.

She shook her head, loose, blond curls shaking back and forth. "Will I ever be able to trust you? Can I trust anything you've said up 'til now?"

"Darby, I don't understand…"

"Val. I heard you talking to her. When were you going to tell me? Shawn's been here? You don't get to decide what I know when it concerns my life and my safety!"

I held up my hands. "Okay, just a second, let me explain.

You're nearing the end of your pregnancy. You're experiencing Braxton-Hicks more every day, increasing in frequency and strength. I'm not lying to you, I'm just not telling you things that could upset you. I'm trying to take care of this on my own so you can relax and enjoy the rest of your pregnancy."

She shook her head. "One of these days, Trex... you're going to run out of excuses. You *don't* have the right to keep that from me."

She put on a little makeup and pants, slipped on her shoes, then stood by the door. She held her phone up, tapping on it.

"You ready?" I asked, feeling like a kicked dog.

"I'm getting a cab."

"Darby, I'll take you. It's safer, anyway."

She wiped a tear. "I should have followed my gut and moved."

"Babe," I chided. I slid my arms around her and buried my face in her neck. "I love you. I'm just trying to keep you and Maddie safe."

She turned to me, pointing at me with her phone. "I don't like that it's so easy for you to lie to my face! What else are you not telling me?"

My mouth opened. Before, I didn't tell her about my past because I didn't want to ruin the moment. Now I was afraid she'd leave. I sighed. "Darby, I've told you everything I could. The rest doesn't matter."

"No, but being able to trust you does. Damn you for proving Lane right!"

She yanked open the door and waddled to the truck. I jogged after her, opening the door and helping her into the passenger seat. She put on her seat belt and faced forward. By the time I got behind the wheel, Darby was crying into her hands.

"Baby, I'm sorry. Please don't cry."

"So Shawn's been here? He knows where I am?"

"The important thing is you're protected. He won't come near you."

She wiped her eyes, and the expression I hadn't seen in so long—since the beginning—had returned. She was guarding herself, against the pain, the fear, the stress of what Shawn might do. She crawled back into that hole and stayed there for the remainder of the ride to work. Even the Christmas lights on the houses between our house and the hotel didn't bring her out. Her tears dried; the light in her eyes dimmed until it was completely gone.

I braked under the overhang and put the gear into Park. "Darby..."

"I'm okay," she said, gathering her things.

"We're in this together."

"Actually, I have never felt more alone in my life." As she climbed out of the truck, I turned off the ignition and followed her in.

Maya was just wrapping up, logging out of the computer system and hooking her purse strap over her shoulder. She looked exhausted.

"Where's Lane?" Darby asked.

Maya shrugged. "She didn't show up for her shift. Ander and Stavros are with the family, and you're about to pop. So...I stayed."

"I'm so sorry. She didn't even call?"

Maya shook her head. "I'm sorry, I've gotta crash. I'll see you in the morning."

"Merry Christmas, Maya. Drive safe," Darby said, putting away her personal items, then logging into the computer.

We were alone in the lobby, the only sound the front doors sweeping open and sliding shut as Maya left. The air kicked on, making the ornaments hanging from the ceiling swing back and forth. I stayed silent while Darby set up her workstation.

She was determined not to speak to me, deciding my fate without my input. I chose to let her cool off, to sit across the lobby, maybe win some points by ordering us food too pungent for Darby to ignore, not that I felt like eating. I dialed in some Asian and texted Naomi while I waited.

She was as unsympathetic as I figured she'd be. Naomi had told me to be honest. I thought I could control the situation. I'd led teams out of much harrier situations than this, so I figured this hiccup with Darby brushing me off because I was military would be less complicated. I was completely wrong on all counts.

Once the food finally arrived, it took me eating and the smell to fill the lobby before Darby finally took her share to her desk. She ate in silence, keeping her eyes anywhere but me.

"Darby," I said when she seemed to be finished.

She packed up her food. "Go away."

I retreated to my chair, and I waited. All night I waited, hoping by the time her shift was over she would be more open to hearing my reasoning—or at least listening to me beg. An hour before her shift was up, I decided to try again.

"I know you're angry," I began.

"Angry? I feel betrayed, duped, manipulated...*angry* barely scratches the surface of what I'm feeling." She was shaking as she spoke the words. "You knew exactly how I felt about you having Val poke around in my past."

"I was trying to find out Shawn's whereabouts, Darby."

"How long have you known? When did he start coming to Colorado Springs?"

I shoved my hands in my pockets. "A while. I didn't want to worry you."

"You just completely disregard everything we've talked about, my feelings, my rights...you don't *own* me, Trex. You don't have the right to make those decisions for me."

"No, I don't own you. But I do love you, and that does give me the right to try to take care of you the best way I know how."

She shook her head. "I can't be with someone I can't trust. Please go."

"Darby!" My voice was louder than I'd meant for it to be, the shock coming out as anger. "I'm not leaving. We're going to talk this through."

The doors swept open, and Darby looked up with a pageant smile on her face that quickly morphed into fear. She blinked a few times, letting her gaze fall away from whoever had walked in. I turned to see two men, one that I recognized as the passenger in the white sedan parked at the hotel on Thanksgiving night.

"Merry Christmas," the man said loudly, as if he was addressing a lobby full of people. He was in civilian clothes, but his hair was standard military length. His features were sharp, his chin long but square, and even though he was the shorter of the two, he was a solid six foot one. The light stubble on his jaw crowded his thin lips. I knew immediately who he was when he targeted Darby with his clear blue eyes. His pupils took up most of his irises, his long nose pulled down at the tip just slightly, a slight cleft chin. He looked like Kurt Cobain with a bad haircut.

I stepped closer to Darby. My Glock was in the glove box of my truck, too far away to be of any use.

Darby slowly reached down to the drawer beneath the cashbox, opened it four inches, enough to reach in and tap her nail once against a tiny pistol. I only glanced at it, but from what information I could gather in the second my eyes were drawn to the sound of her nail against metal, it looked like a late sixties model Baby Browning. I had no idea how she'd gotten hold of a weapon that easily cost more than seven hundred dollars, but there it was. Hopefully, if shit went down, it was loaded and ready to go.

"Shawn," Darby said.

There was something on the edge of her voice I'd never heard before, something that excited Shawn. She was still afraid of him, and he fed off it. If I thought demons existed, he was one.

"It's been a long time, bunny."

"Don't call me that," she blurted.

Shawn rested his elbows on the desk and leaned in. She stepped back, and he smiled. "I've missed you. I don't think you realize what it did to me when you left me at the altar. Took me months to even think clearly again." He turned his gaze on me. "I'm Shawn. But you know that."

"Trex," I said, glowering at him.

"Nice to finally meet you, Trex. This," Shawn said, gesturing to Darby, "is my fiancée. Maybe she's mentioned it when you were fucking her."

"Pretty sure you have to be engaged to call her that," I said.

"Oh," Shawn said, his voice smooth, "we're engaged. We never got married, you see, so we're still engaged." He looked at Darby. "We should fix that, bunny."

Darby recoiled.

"Leave," I said.

Shawn cackled, walking away. "These Marines. So goddamn confident!" he said to his buddy. He covered his mouth. "Sorry, bunny. I know you don't appreciate that word." He walked back, returning his elbows to the desk and leaning in, looking straight into my eyes. "I've never liked Marines. Arrogant fucks."

"Is that what you said to Naomi when she put that grunt on his back?" I looked at his friend. "Was that you? How'd that feel?"

Darby looked at me, confusion on her face.

My heart began to thump inside my chest, my breath getting faster to catch up. "Baby..."

Darby stepped back, looking as alone as she felt. Her trembling hands touched her beach ball–sized middle. "I want everyone to leave. You first," she said to Shawn. She reached for the receiver of the hotel's landline phone and held it up for everyone to see. Her voice sounded a bit braver than before, but her eyes stayed on the floor. "Or I'm calling the police."

"What are the police going to do? What have they ever done?" Shawn asked, reaching for her.

She dropped the phone and stepped back, and I put myself between them. Darby was terrified, her entire body was shaking; her breath faltered.

"I'll kill you if you touch her," I said. "That's not a threat. I will fucking slit your throat and shoot you in the face until there's nothing left to identify."

Shawn's smile fell away, and he suddenly looked tired. He pointed at her stomach before he let his outreached arm fall to the desk. "Is it mine?"

It took a moment for Darby to speak. "She's mine."

"She?" Shawn said, his eyes glossing over. "It's a girl?"

Darby nodded.

"Bunny—"

"Get the fuck outta here," I growled. "She's not going home with you. She didn't marry you because you're an abusive piece of shit."

Shawn pointed at me. "Did you know he was a Marine, Darby? Do you know how many people he's killed? Do you know why he and his ex really split up? He wasn't nice to her. You should ask him about it sometime, not that he'd tell you the truth."

"What the fuck are you talking about?" I asked.

"Do you know how his best friend really died?"

"Go fuck yourself," I said.

Shawn pointed at me again. "He's a lyin' ratbag fucker, this one. You don't have to go home with me, but you don't want this guy. He's nothing like you think."

Darby's red, wet eyes pleaded with me to deny it all, but I couldn't deny that I was a Marine, and because of that, she wouldn't believe the rest. Her bottom lip quivered, then she looked at Shawn, reaching again for the phone. She tapped out three numbers. "You have ten seconds."

"Okay," Shawn said, raising his hands.

I could hear the dispatcher on the other end answer. "Nine-one-one, what is your emergency?"

Darby watched Shawn leave, the white sedan peeling out of the parking lot.

The dispatcher repeated herself.

"Um, I'm at the Colorado Springs Hotel. There were a couple of guys here behaving suspiciously, but they left when I called."

Darby vaguely explained the situation, leaving out that Shawn was her ex. When she hung up the phone, she covered her mouth, working to control her breathing.

I reached for her, but she pulled away. "Your turn."

"Darby..."

"I'm leaving," she said, her voice breaking. "I'll get my things later. I'd appreciate it if you weren't there while I do that."

"No. Stop," I begged. I didn't know what else to say. I tried to appear calm, but on the inside, there were alarms, flags, and screaming; panic was about to take over. "Don't believe him, Darby. Don't let him do this to us. What he said wasn't true."

"Which part?" She wasn't yelling. Her voice was quiet, emotionless. I didn't feel truly afraid very often, but in that moment, I was terrified. She was speaking to me and looking at me as if she were a stranger.

"I was a Marine," I began.

"It's too late."

"But I told you the truth about Laura," I blurted out. "Matt died saving the rest of our team. He threw himself on a live grenade. I didn't tell you I was a Marine because everyone at the hotel knew you were adamant about not dating a certain kind of guy."

"It's too late."

"After you told me about Shawn, I was too chickenshit to tell you about my history with the military. I was afraid you wouldn't want to see me again. Even after you were okay with me being a federal agent. Even after you warning me to be honest with you. There were a hundred times I could have told you, and every time I let my fear of losing you talk me out of it."

"It's. Too. Late." She wasn't crying. She began to organize her work space, acting as if I weren't there.

"Baby," I said, walking toward her.

She turned to face me, raising an eyebrow, clearly telling me without words not to come closer.

I swallowed. "We're good together. All that…that's my past, Darby. You're my future. Maddie is my future. We're going to get married. You'll both have my last name. We'll be happy. None of this will matter years from now."

"Because we'll only know what you choose to share?"

"No, because we love each other, we're happy, and our kids are happy."

"You should go," she said, returning to her work.

"You said you were in this."

"I was," she said, finally a glimmer of emotion in her eyes. "All I asked for was honesty. You can't trust me with the truth, and I can't trust you to tell it. I won't settle. I won't. I don't care how nice your house is or how much time I spent on the nursery or how much I love you. Maddie deserves better, and so do I."

"Jesus Christ, Darby, I'm doing my best. You can't just—"

"*You* did this, not me. I begged you to be honest with me! You chose this over and over."

I felt the blood burn under my cheeks. "All I wanted was to protect you. I wanted you to feel safe. I made more than a few mistakes, but it wasn't because I wanted to control what you knew and when you knew it. I did it because I was scared to lose you. That doesn't mean you can't trust me. It means you can count on me to stick around no matter what." I tried to keep my voice calm. "You saw Shawn, emotions are high, you're angry, I get it. But don't tell me like I chose this. This isn't what I want. There's nothing like us, Darby. Two hours ago, we were happy. Our life was amazing. I want to be wherever you are. I belong where you are. Both of you. I'm yours. Yours and hers."

"Please leave."

Her words knocked the air out of me. "Shawn is here in the Springs, Darby. I can't leave you here alone."

She thought about that for a moment. "Doesn't look like I have much choice."

"What if I . . . What if I wait in the truck outside? Just to make sure. I won't bother you."

Her lips pressed together in a hard line, and I could see she wasn't going to let her anger get in the way of common sense. "Fine."

"You really want me to be gone when you come home?"

She looked me straight in the eyes. "Yes."

"Okay, I'll . . . I'll send Naomi over to pick you up and keep an eye out. At least until we know Shawn has left town."

"That's probably a good idea."

My shoulders sagged. "Where are you . . . Where are you going to go?"

She didn't answer, and before falling into a bottomless pit of despair, I grasped at anger. "Let's be clear. I don't want to do this. I don't want to walk away from either one of you. You're pushing me away."

She tapped the keyboard, and I was sure it was just her nails on the keys.

"Darby."

"Trex, just go!" she said, closing her eyes tight.

"Hailey . . . Hailey's coming today," I said, feeling tears burn my eyes. "I need you home. It's Christmas, for fuck's sake."

"Don't swear at me." Her voice was so small. Her lashes pushed mascara-stained tears down her cheeks. She covered her mouth.

My phone began to sing Hailey's ringtone. If it had been anyone else, I would have silenced it, but I knew she'd been planning to be on the road before sunrise and could be close if not already in town. I was afraid she was at the house and I wasn't there.

I cleared my voice before answering. "Hailey?"

"Trex?" she cried. "Trex!"

My whole world stopped. "Are you crying? What's going on?"

"He hit me!"

"*What?*"

"I was just in an accident! The guy at the intersection! He hit my car and I can't get out!"

"Where are you? Never mind, I can pinpoint your location. Sit tight. I'm coming."

"Hurry!"

"I'm coming!" I lowered my phone. "It's Hailey. She's been in an accident. I have to . . . I have to go."

"Is she okay?" Darby asked. It was the first time she didn't look like she hated me since Shawn left.

"I don't know. I'm sorry, I have to go."

"Go," she said.

I met her gaze. That one word was her good-bye. As badly as I wanted to stay, I had to go to my baby sister. Walking away from her was the hardest thing I'd ever done, but I turned and ran to my truck, seconds later peeling out of the parking lot.

chapter twenty-seven

Darby

Y ou look worse than me," Maya said, dragging in holding a large coffee.

"Thanks," I said, putting on my coat.

"Have you been crying?"

I rubbed my aching belly. I'd been suffering through Braxton-Hicks my entire shift. "No."

The printer was vomiting paper from the nightly audit, and I'd just logged out of the system. I'd already booked my old room and coded a key card. I didn't bother to tell Maya that I'd be back. At least that way I wouldn't have to talk about it until then.

I waited for Naomi, and when she didn't show, I called a cab. I assumed she was probably with Trex and his sister. Trex's expression when he left played over and over in my mind. I talked myself in and out of moving out at least two dozen times during the night. My head and heart were still warring when I took a few empty boxes from the bar and walked out to meet the taxi. Winter blew its breath in my face the moment the doors opened. I put my hand on the door handle of the cab, when I heard a familiar voice say my name—the one I hate the most.

"Hi there, bunny. What are the boxes for?"

I stood across from Shawn, the air around me suddenly too thin to breathe.

He walked around the back, taking the boxes from my hand and handing them to one of two men standing just a few feet away. "Going somewhere?"

"Just...bringing those home."

"No, you're not."

My eyes filled with tears, and I reached for the handle again. Shawn covered my hand with his, wrapping his free hand around my middle, burying his face in my neck.

"That's not your home, bunny. Your home is with me." He inhaled through his nose. "God, I've missed you."

"Let me go," I said. I was practically panting, but I couldn't help it. Being in Shawn's arms again was a nightmare I'd had many times since I got on the bus to Colorado Springs, and now I was living it again.

His fingers dug into my middle. "Come home with me, Darby. You leaving, everything I've been through since you left...it doesn't matter anymore. We have a baby now. We're going to be a family."

I closed my eyes tight. "She's...she's not yours."

He grabbed my hair and yanked my head back, and I cried out. "Fuck you, you fucking whore!" he growled.

The cab driver climbed out, nervous but determined not to stand by. "What are you doing?" he said in a thick accent. "You let her go!"

Shawn let go of my hair and grabbed my arm, pulling me with him.

"Hey!" the cab driver yelled. "I call the cops!"

The headlights of a white car lit up. Shawn opened the back door on the passenger side and shoved me into the seat. He pushed me over and sat down, slamming the door.

"Shawn," the driver said, "this isn't what we talked about, man."

"Drive, you pussy, or I'll put my fist through the back of your head."

The driver slammed into reverse and stomped on the gas. I hit my forehead on the back of his seat, and then again on the window when he pulled forward and turned at the same time.

"Wh-where are we going?" I said. When he didn't answer, I screamed, "Where are you taking me?"

"Shut up, you stupid bitch!" he screamed in my face. He sat back, hitting his forehead with the heel of his hand several times. He coughed a few times, then held my hand. "I'm sorry. I'm sorry, I'm just trying to think. Terry, go by her house."

"You want to take her home?" the man in the passenger seat said. He was the biggest of the three, probably the one Naomi had put on his back at the bar Thanksgiving night.

"Drive by," he said.

I worried Trex was there with Hailey. I had no idea what Shawn was planning. "Don't hurt them. I'll go with you."

Shawn combed my hair from my face with his fingers. "You're coming with me either way. We're not stopping, bunny. Just driving by." He smiled at me as if he hadn't just kidnapped and manhandled me, like we were on an early Christmas drive.

I leaned away from him, trying to think of a way out of the car. If I jumped, I could hurt Maddie. There was nothing I could do until the car stopped. As Terry slowed at the next intersection, I put my hand on the handle.

Shawn held a knife to my stomach. "Don't do that."

I looked down. "Shawn…"

"I will put a hole right through you if you don't sit in that fucking seat like a good girl. You hear me?"

I nodded quickly, hot tears streaming down my cheeks. Within ten minutes, we were driving into my neighborhood, passing the police station and our many neighbors. The sun was above the mountains, burning off the night clouds. The driveways were either empty or full of vehicles, everyone somewhere for the holiday. I sighed when I saw that Trex's truck wasn't in the drive.

Shawn reached over me, rolled down the window, and grabbed my phone.

"What are you doing?" I said, watching him toss my phone into the yard. "Why did you do that?" I cried.

He rolled up the window. "Let's go home, Terry."

Terry nodded, and I covered my face and cried.

"Did you fight with that poor bastard after I left? Were you pissed that he didn't tell you about his time in the Marines?" Shawn asked.

I couldn't answer. All I could do was cry into my hands. I did exactly what Shawn wanted. I told Trex I was leaving him, he was going to see the phone he'd bought me in the yard and think I'd decided not to take anything with me. It wouldn't be the first time.

I held my stomach with both hands. It was hard as a rock again, tightening so much that it began to hurt—really hurt—for the first time. It wasn't just aches and pains. I moaned, knowing it was probably too late, but I needed to calm down. I was going into labor. I breathed in through my nose and then breathed out, slow and controlled. The second time, Terry mentioned it to Shawn.

"She better not give birth in this car," Terry said. "Not going to have that blood on my hands, too. You took it too far, Shawn. We're all going down for what you did."

"You said she wanted to come home," the man in the passenger seat said.

Shawn frowned. "Fuck you, Todd. She does. Don't you?" he said, looking at me and nodding toward the front seat.

I nodded. "What happened to his forehead?" I asked, staring at the bloody bandage taped to his hairline.

"T-boned a teenager."

I closed my eyes. "Hailey?"

"We needed a distraction. I thought *I* was persistent. Jesus Christ. That leech was never going to leave the hotel. When Derek said the sister was on her way into town, we took the opportunity that was presented to us." He squeezed my hand, noticing the ring on my middle finger. "What the fuck is this?"

"A Christmas present," I said. "Is she okay?"

"From him?" Shawn said, the anger in his eyes returning.

I shook my head. "A coworker."

Shawn laughed. "Wasn't Lane, fucking whore."

My bottom lip quivered. "Where is she? She didn't show up for work."

Shawn looked at the window, seeming nervous. The other men were quiet, too.

"Did you hurt her?" I asked.

"She was all for trying to fuck your guy. She was all for trying to piss you off and planting seeds to make you question him. She just wanted him," Shawn said, spitting on the floor.

"C'mon, man!" Terry said.

"You fucking women. You make us think you want us until you get what you want. Nobody uses me."

I kept my head down. "What did you do?"

"Taught her a lesson."

"You were right. That was a nice piece of ass," Todd said, laughing at his window.

"Is she okay?" I asked.

"Probably not," Shawn said with a chuckle. "But you don't worry about her. I don't care about that slut. I've got you back. That's all that matters. We're going to get rid of that," he said, pointing at my stomach, "and then we can get on with our lives."

"I lied," I said. "She's yours, Shawn. Do the math. I'm almost thirty-six weeks. I just have four weeks to go. Count the months. She's yours. When she gets here, you'll see. She's ours."

"Whoa," Terry said. "Congrats, man."

He snarled. "You lied before. How do I know you're not lying now?"

"Just...wait until I have her. You can see for yourself. She'll look like you and me. She won't look like Trex. She's your daughter."

Shawn looked down at my stomach, then put away his knife. "She's mine?"

I nodded. I reached for his hands and flattened his palms against Maddie's perfect dome. Tears streamed down my cheeks, and I tightened my throat to keep from sobbing while Shawn fawned over my stomach, talking to Maddie with a soft voice I'd never heard from him.

He looked up at me, annoyed. "Why'd you lie to me?"

"I...was ashamed for leaving. I'm sorry I hurt you. I was just nervous, and I did something stupid. Then I was too ashamed to come back. I'll...I'll make it up to you."

Shawn scanned my face, trying to decide if he wanted to believe me or not.

"Damn right you will."

When the corners of his mouth curved up, I knew I'd bought Maddie and me a little more time.

chapter twenty-eight

Trex

Hailey walked slowly, but with my help she made it from the truck to the front door. Five vehicles pulled into the drive and parked at the curb in front of the house. Naomi was waiting at the door for me and the rest of my team to bring my little sister inside.

I tried not to rush my little sister, but Darby hadn't returned any of my texts or answered my calls, and I was desperate to know if she'd really moved out. I'd sent Naomi to the hotel and then the house, but she'd reported no sign of Darby. It was noon, and there was no indication she'd ever come home. The thought of Darby leaving me was bad enough. Her leaving town pregnant and empty-handed had me near panic.

"Trex," Kitsch said. I turned to see him holding Darby's cell phone. "It was in the yard."

My stomach sank. "It doesn't make any sense. I've scrolled through the security feed. She hasn't been here."

Sloan carefully lifted Hailey in his arms, pushing the door open with his shoulder. "Go," he said, nodding toward the house. "Maybe you missed something."

For the first time all morning, I allowed myself to hope. I pushed through the door, immediately calling for Darby. I checked the bedroom, the bathroom, the nursery; all of Darby and Maddie's things remained. Darby's toothbrush was still in the holder by the sink. Maddie's pink floral dress Darby had picked out and bought herself still hung in the closet.

"Darby?" I called, my heart racing.

"She's not here?" Hailey asked, disappointed.

Naomi brought a glass of water into the living room from the kitchen, popping open Hailey's pill bottle and giving my sister her meds. Naomi turned over her wrist and checked her watch. "You worry about yourself. You're lucky all you got was some bruised ribs and a concussion. If the cops don't find the bastard who hit you, I will."

"Your parents on their way?" Harbinger asked.

I nodded. Hailey had been T-boned at the intersection a few blocks from my house. She couldn't tell us much about the person who'd hit her except it was a guy with dark eyes and that he'd fled the scene on foot.

"It doesn't make sense for Darby to leave with nothing," I said, scanning the living room.

"It wouldn't be the first time," Naomi said.

"Not to come back here, though, when she knows I'm not here to bother her. Not even to get her own things? Not even the things she bought for Maddie?"

Darby's phone rang, and Kitsch tossed it to me. "Hello?"

"Trex?" Stavros said, surprised.

"Have you seen Darby today? Have you heard from her?" I asked.

He hesitated. "No."

"Stavros, this is important. My sister was in an accident. I just got home. She's not here." I cleared my throat, struggling to say the words. "We got in an argument this morning. The last thing she said to me was that she was taking her things back to the hotel."

"To the hotel? What the hell did you do to her, Trex?"

"I…it's a long story. She left her cell phone. I just want to make sure she's okay."

"Call the hotel. Maya would have seen her this morning. Let me know when you find her."

"Will do. Thanks." I hung up, found the number for the hotel, and called the front desk direct.

"Colorado Springs Hotel," Maya answered.

"Maya, hey, it's Trex. Is Darby there?"

"Not since this morning. She got some boxes and took a cab home. She was really upset."

I bowed my head, putting my hand on top of my head. I could barely keep it together long enough to speak. "Yeah, we had a rough morning."

"No, she was, like, yelling at the cab driver."

"She what?" I asked. "That doesn't sound like her. What was she saying?"

"I don't know. I just heard it. By the time I got out there, the cab was gone."

"She hasn't been back?" I asked.

"No."

"Could you ask her to call me when you see her? I'm worried."

"Sure."

"Thanks," I said, hanging up. I threw her phone across the room, hearing it shatter into pieces against the wall. "Goddamn it!" I screamed.

My throat tightened, my nose burned, and then the tears came. I bowed my head and gripped the counter until my palms turned white, struggling to keep it together while I counted to ten. My team had seen me lose control before. That was a side of me I never wanted Hailey to see. My vision blurred. I felt like throwing up, curling into a ball, knocking myself out, anything to get away from the pain.

"Trex," Harbinger began. His voice was calm and level, talking me down from the ledge we'd all been on more than once, a ledge from where only our fellow soldiers knew the way down.

I turned around, glaring at the pieces on the floor, and looked away, already regretting it. My face fell as recognition hit. "No. Please, fuck, no…" I said, scrambling to fish my phone out of my pocket. I scrolled through the front door camera and driveway cameras between seven a.m. and eight thirty, this time looking for more than just Darby approaching the front door. It was then that I saw it. Her phone was tossed into the yard from a passing vehicle. I could barely make out a sliver of a possible white sedan when it passed.

I looked up at my team. "He has her. We have to go. Now."

"Who? Shawn?" Naomi asked. "Let's take one step at a time. We don't know anything yet."

"We're wasting time," I said, rushing into my bedroom, putting my phone to my ear, silently begging Val to pick up. When she did, I barely let her get out the first syllable of hello.

"I need you to find someone for me," I said.

"Another fav—"

"Shawn has Darby! For the love of Christ, Val, skip the fucking snark and just find her!"

The other side of the line was quiet for too long, but just as I began to ask if Val was still there, I heard nails clicking against a keyboard. "Fill me in."

"Shawn showed up at the hotel. A hotel employee reported hearing Darby yell at a cab driver, which makes no sense."

"Checking security footage…" she said.

"My sister was hit and I had to leave Darby alone at the hotel. I sent Naomi to the hotel but by the time she got there around seven thirty, Darby was already gone. She wasn't at the house."

"Cab left without her. She's with someone else, but it's almost off-camera, hold on..."

More clicking.

"The car that hit your sister was stolen," she said.

I sighed. "They fucking baited me."

"Following a white sedan from your intersection just after seven thirty a.m. It left town...hold on, bringing up highway cams..." She sighed. "White sedan is on its way back to Texas. Four passengers. One female fitting Darby's description."

I packed a duffel with clothes and firearms, stepping into the living room. My team and Hailey stared at me, waiting for me to tell them what would happen next. "That was Val on the phone," I said. "He has her. I'm going to Texas."

"Not alone you're not." Naomi glanced over her shoulder at Hailey.

"I'll stay," Harbinger said.

Naomi nodded. "Oorah. Load up, boys."

Naomi sat shotgun, with Martinez, Sloan, and Kitsch in the back seat. I drove ninety miles per hour down I-25 south, having Naomi check and double-check every white sedan and truck stop we passed. Val kept us updated. They were five hours ahead until Val caught Shawn on a gas station camera in Amarillo, Texas. The white sedan didn't leave its parking spot for several hours, and by the time she saw them leave, we were only an hour behind.

"There's a motel next door. It's possible they napped and ate before the second leg of the drive," Val said over the speaker. "It's definitely Darby. She's very pregnant. I don't see a credit card being used at any of the area locations. They must be paying in cash."

"Is Darby okay? Was she in the same motel room with Shawn? Where were the other two?"

"Unknown," Val said. "She's walking. That's a good sign."

I frowned, my knuckles turning white under the pressure as I squeezed the steering wheel.

"What about Derek? Is it possible he's fucking with you?" Naomi asked.

"Nope," Val answered.

"How do you know?" Naomi asked.

"Because he was arrested three weeks ago and charged with willful communication of classified intelligence to an unauthorized person under the 1917 Espionage Act. However, we do have information that he called in favors, and then made a call to Shawn on Hailey's whereabouts."

"Damn," Sloan said.

"That explains why Shawn made his move," Naomi said. "His brother isn't around to cover his tracks or bail him out. The last thing Derek could do for his brother was to help him create a diversion."

"With no help, he's desperate and has likely decided he has nothing to lose," I said, driving faster.

I drove until dark, and then Kitsch got behind the wheel. Naomi sat between us, and despite Val having eyes on every camera between Amarillo and Fort Hood, I still checked every white four-door from the passenger seat. We didn't talk much, except to form a half-assed plan for when we came upon the car. The objective was to get Darby away from Shawn and his thugs before they knew we were there.

"Christ," I said, "she's probably terrified."

"And stressed. Martinez, I hope you're ready for this," Naomi said.

"Always ready," he said. He lifted his medical case by the handle.

The white sedan stopped in Lubbock for another hour, and again just half an hour later. We were twenty minutes behind them when they left George's, a restaurant in Tahoka, Texas.

Just north of Justiceburg, I saw a pair of taillights. Finally, the white sedan came into view. "That's them!"

"Okay, take it easy," Naomi said. "Stay back, Kitsch. We've gotta play this smart."

The sedan slowed from seventy to sixty-five, then fifty-five, then pulled over into an RV park.

"Pass it," I said. "We'll go in on foot."

Kitsch passed the dirt drive, and I turned around in my seat, watching their car bounce over the uneven terrain. Kitsch turned off the headlights and yanked the steering wheel to the left, crossing the oncoming lane and bouncing the truck into a field, parking one klick south of Shawn's location.

"You think they spotted us?" Naomi asked, tying her boots in double knots, securing her hair at the nape of her neck, and taking off her jacket. "The moon is full. It's like we're sneaking around in broad daylight."

"Not sure," I said. "Be ready for anything."

I checked my Glock, took it off the safety, and took point, directing Sloan and Martinez to the outer line while the rest of us moved forward in a wedge formation. *Just like the old days.*

Fifteen yards from the tree line that surrounded the clearing, I could see Darby through the branches. She was sitting on her knees, her pants wet from the mud beneath her. The back doors of the sedan were wide open, the dim light from the cab of the car highlighting the sheen of sweat on her face.

Darby grabbed her stomach, leaned forward, and groaned. I rushed forward, but Naomi grabbed my sleeve and shook her head.

Darby put her hands flat on the ground, panting as she looked forward in fear. "You've gotta...you've gotta get me to a hospital," she pleaded.

"Shut up!" Shawn growled. "I'm thinking."

"We don't have time!" Darby cried.

My jaws ticked, and I squeezed the handle of my gun.

Naomi motioned with her hand for me to be patient.

We took cover behind trees surrounding the RV park. Only the white sedan and two campers were present. I could hear Shawn and the other two talking to one another in distressed tones.

I could only see the top of Darby's hair. She was crouching next to the car. "Fuck," I said, leaning my head back against the tree. "She's close," I whispered.

"Complicates things," Naomi said, her voice barely above a whisper. "Could also work in our favor."

The others were waiting in the wings for an order.

Darby cried out again.

I leaned up, trying to get a better visual. I looked over at Martinez. He signaled he could see her and pointed at his watch. We were running out of time.

"Please!" Darby screamed.

"Shut her up!" the tall one said.

"Oh, I'm going to do more than put him on his ass this time," Naomi whispered.

I gave the signal to move, and as one unit, we moved in.

Darby noticed us first. She was holding her stomach, soaked in sweat. She began to half laugh, half cry. "You came," she said, tears streaming down her face.

"I'm here, baby," I said.

Shawn turned around, took one look at me, and reached for Darby. I squeezed the trigger of my Glock, and the sleeve of Shawn's jacket frayed. He cried out, grabbing his forearm, but I'd only grazed the fabric, a bullet hole appearing in the car behind him. Shawn checked himself over and then held out his arms to the side. The tall one ran, but Naomi put three bullets in the ground around his feet until he stopped.

"Is Hailey okay?" Darby asked.

"She's going to be fine. Let's get you home."

She offered a tired smile. "Can we stop by the hospital first?" Her expression changed, and she doubled over. "It was him," she grunted, lifting a shaking hand to point at the tall one. "Todd. He hit Hailey as a distraction."

I looked at him. "You hit my sister's car?"

He looked caught at first, looking to Shawn for direction. When Shawn didn't say anything, Todd's expression turned defiant. "Yeah, I fucking hit her." He pulled a pistol from the back of his pants, cocked it, and raised it just halfway before I squeezed the trigger of my Glock. Todd fell to his knees, a stunned look on his face and blood spilling from his chest.

I lowered my chin, staring down Shawn. "Now we all have a reason to get to the hospital."

Shawn's other friend lunged at Darby, grabbing a fistful of her hair and yanking her back toward the car.

Darby cried out, reaching for her hair.

"Get . . . get back!" he said.

"I'll cut off that fucking hand if you don't let her go right now," I said, yelling the last part.

"Let her go, Terry," Shawn said, still holding his hands out.

"Get back!" Terry said again. He let go of her hair, but produced a gun from behind him, pressing the barrel against Darby's neck.

"You're outnumbered," Naomi said. "Leave the girl. Get in the car and leave. Now."

Terry and Shawn traded glances. Todd was wheezing.

"Let her go, and I'll tend to your friend," Martinez said.

"His chest cavity is filling with blood. He's closer to suffocating every time he takes a breath."

"Nobody fucking move!" Shawn yelled.

Darby's face morphed as pain took over her body. She cried out, startling Terry. Sloan squeezed his trigger, and Terry jerked back, a bullet slicing through his heart. He fell against the car, a crimson smear left behind as he slumped to the ground.

I signaled for Darby to crawl to me, keeping my sights on Shawn.

"Darby! Don't you do it," Shawn growled.

Darby froze. She was nearly panting, but she closed her eyes tight and then continued. I walked a few steps toward her, keeping my gun on Shawn, and helped her to her feet, hugging her to me.

"You okay?" I asked, kissing her temple.

She looked up at me, tears in her eyes but a relieved smile on her face. "I'm better now," she said, breathing hard.

I held her to my side, letting her put all her weight on me.

"Get your hands off her!" Shawn yelled. "She's mine!"

"Martinez," I barked. Martinez broke formation to attend to Darby, setting her on the ground and checking her over.

"Put that gun down, pussy," Shawn said.

"You wanna go?" I asked. "You wanna find out what it's like to fight someone who hits back?"

"Trex, don't," Darby said through her teeth. "He's got…" She groaned, doubling over.

"Put the gun down. Just you and me, jarhead."

"Trex," Darby warned. "He's…" She grunted and then yelled through the pain.

I put my Glock on the ground and walked toward Shawn. "This is going to hurt like hell, but just remember…I warned you." I threw the first punch with every bit of pent-up rage

I'd had for him since I'd met Darby. My fist connected with Shawn's jaw. Blood burst from his mouth as his head was knocked to the side, but he righted himself, then looked at me and smiled with dark red teeth.

I didn't notice it at first, the subtle stinging in my side, until Darby cried out.

"You won't have her either," he said, pulling the knife out slowly and then jabbing it in again and twisting.

He was knocked backward with a bullet to the shoulder, and as he came at me again, his head jerked to the side. Naomi held Vicky in front of her, the barest whiff of smoke rising from the barrel. Shawn fell to the ground with a thud, and I stumbled back, the sting growing to searing pain.

I fell next to Darby. It was quiet for a moment, the ringing in my ears the only sound, and then suddenly all there was was noise.

Martinez ripped my shirt and scrambled for his pack.

"Trex?" Darby said. Sweat beaded on her forehead. Her hair was soaked. She looked exhausted.

"Sit back," Kitsch said, helping me lie back against his pack.

"It's just a flesh wound," I said, feeling warm blood pour out of my side.

Martinez frowned. "It's more than a flesh wound, jackass. What the hell was that?"

"Always the hero," Naomi said, unhappy.

"Just patch me up. Let's get Darby to the hospital."

"Trex?" Darby said, reaching for me.

I took her hand and kissed it. "I'm okay, baby. I've survived worse than this. Let's get you to the hospital so we can meet our little girl."

"Let's get you both there," Kitsch said, watching Martinez work with a frown.

Martinez carried Darby, and Sloan hopped in the truck

bed to make room. I crawled in the back seat with Darby and
Martinez. Kitsch drove, and Naomi took shotgun.

"You hanging in there?" I said, wiping back the wet hair
that was plastered to Darby's cheeks.

"I've been better," she said through clenched teeth. "How
about you?"

I shook my head and snarled my lip. "Doesn't even hurt."

She breathed out a laugh, then leaned forward, a string of
curse words streaming from her mouth.

I raised my brows and looked up at Martinez.

"They're just a couple minutes apart," Martinez said.
"Darby, can you do me a favor? Reach down, see if you can
feel her head."

"*What?*" Darby said.

"It's forty minutes to the closest hospital," Martinez said.

"That's at normal speeds," Kitsch said. "I'll have us there
in twenty."

"Darby," Martinez said, his voice cool and calm. "Reach
down and feel if she's crowning."

Darby pushed against the floor with her feet and reached
down into the black slacks she'd put on for work the night
before. She shook her head. "Close, but not yet." She looked
at me and smiled. "I can feel her."

I kissed her forehead. "Hold tight, baby. We're almost
there."

"Fifteen minutes out," Sloan said.

Darby took a few breaths and then leaned against my
shoulder, closing her eyes. She was exhausted. I'd lost so
much blood, I wasn't too far behind.

"Stay awake, Trex," Martinez said, slapping my cheek a
few times.

"I'm not going anywhere," I said. "I've got a dinner date
with a couple of pretty girls."

"I'm sorry," Darby said, taking shallow breaths.

I shook my head and began to speak, but Martinez cut me off.

"Darby, you're going to hyperventilate if you don't get your breathing under control," Martinez said.

"In through your nose," I said, taking one with her even though it hurt like a bitch to take a deep breath. "And out," I said, exhaling for five seconds. "Again...good, that's good."

Darby cried out, clenching her teeth and leaning over, her usually smooth, honey-blond hair tangled, soaked with sweat at the roots. "Trex," she said, her voice strangled. "Help me." She began to cry. "Please help me."

I held her hand and squeezed. "Kitsch!"

"Six minutes!" he yelled back.

I could feel the truck surge forward, and then I heard a subtle pop and then a gush, like someone had poured out a pitcher of water onto the floor.

"Water broke," Martinez called. "Darby, let's get your slacks off. We might be delivering in the truck."

"No," Darby whimpered. "I can't, I..."

"Darby?" I said, keeping my voice calm. "We're all here for you. Martinez is a medic. It's going to be okay."

Darby looked at me from under her brow, then nodded. She lifted up, and Martinez helped her out of her slacks, then her underwear. Naomi turned around, placing her jacket over Darby's legs. As Darby leaned against me, Martinez took a quick look, then his eyes darted straight to me.

"Try not to push and we can make it to the hospital. Relax your body between contractions, and as much as you can during."

The truck bounced as we entered the drive of the Cogdell Memorial Hospital, and Kitsch blew past the business office, down a strip of road, parking under an overhang. Everyone jumped but me, and then my door was yanked open. Naomi helped me out, and Martinez carried Darby into the emergency room entrance.

"We need medical!" Martinez yelled.

A small group of nurses ran outside, and I listened to Martinez explain Darby's and my statuses. Darby was seated in a wheelchair.

"Wait," she said. She pointed to me. "He's the father. I need him with me."

The nurses traded looks, and one rushed to get another chair. I reached for Darby's hand, and she took it.

"What's your names?" the nurse behind Darby asked as they pushed us through double doors.

"Scott Trexler," I said. "She's Darby."

The blonde pointed to herself. "I'm Deirdre. This is Leslie," she said, nodding to the smiling brunette.

"I'm a Trexler to-be," Darby said.

I squeezed her hand. "Yeah, you are," I said with a smile.

They wheeled us into Exam Room Two, helped Darby into a gown, and into the bed.

"First baby?" the nurse asked.

"Yes," Darby said.

"First stab wound?" she asked me.

"No, actually," I said.

All the women in the room traded glances, including Darby.

"He's a Marine," Darby explained.

The nurses nodded with understanding, continuing to work.

Deirdre cut my shirt off, using the tear Martinez started as a guide. "Oh my goodness," she said, lifting the bandage. "Your friend has medical experience, I'm guessin'?"

I nodded. She had the same accent as Darby and it made me smile. "Yeah, I'm fine."

"Those are pretty ugly. You've lost a lot of blood." She looked at Leslie. "We should put him in Exam Three."

"I'm gonna hang out here until I see my daughter brought into the world, and then you can take me where you need to take me."

"Trex," Darby said.

"I've been dreaming about this moment for months. I'm not missing it." I held my hand against the bandage. "I've been far worse off than this."

Leslie hesitated. "The doctor ain't gonna like this."

"I think she'll be more interested in the story," Deirdre said. "I know I am."

Darby held her breath, then cried out. Leslie checked her for less than a second. "She's crowning."

Both nurses went into action, setting up the stirrups and a side table. I struggled to wheel myself closer.

"I'll help," Leslie said, pulling me backward so I was sitting at Darby's side.

I grabbed her hand and kissed her knuckles. "You're going to do great, honey."

"Well, hello," a woman in blue scrubs and a white lab coat said as she entered the room. She stood at the sink for quite a while washing her hands before putting on gloves and then sitting on a stool, scooting it forward until she was sitting between Darby's legs. "I'm Dr. Barnes. Looks like I'm going to be delivering your baby in a few minutes." She scanned me, looking over her rectangular glasses. "Should be a good story at birthday parties."

Deirdre stood on one side of Darby, Leslie on the other, and when it was time to push, they picked up Darby's feet and pushed her knees toward her stomach, their palms against the soles of her feet. When it was time to rest, they returned Darby's legs to the stirrups. I held my breath with each push, counting with the nurses. In the thirty or so seconds Darby could rest, she would turn and smile at me.

"I love you," she said. "I don't know what I was thinking. I wasn't thinking. I was just ma—"

She yelled and pushed, and Deirdre and Leslie grabbed her feet again, counting to ten.

"You're doing so good," Leslie said.

"So good," Deirdre said, nodding. She looked at me. "Stop holding your breath, or you won't be conscious when the baby is born."

"Yes, ma'am," I said, taking a deep breath and blowing it out.

Six pushes, and Maddie's little face popped out. Six more pushes, and the rest of her little body slid out all at once like a pea from a pod. Dr. Barnes put Maddie on Darby's stomach while Deirdre rubbed Maddie's tiny body with a receiving blanket.

I waited for her first cry. It seemed to take an eternity, but finally, Maddie took a big breath and the most beautiful sound I'd ever heard filled the room.

Darby laughed and cried, and I did, too. This tiny, slimy, pink baby girl with dark, wet curls plastered to her head was trembling and screaming on Darby's belly, and I felt honored to be a witness to it.

Darby looked up at me with a bright smile, the hours of pain she'd just endured instantly forgotten. I pecked her lips twice, then smiled as I watched the nurses work.

"She's a little early," Deirdre said.

"Is she okay?" Darby asked.

"Right as rain," Deirdre said with a smile.

"Are we cutting the cord?" Dr. Barnes asked.

I looked to Darby for the okay, and once she nodded, I took the scissors from the doctor and snipped between the two clamps like she directed. "Holy shit," I said. "That just happened."

"Indeed," the doctor said. "Good job, Dad."

I breathed out a laugh, feeling tears burn my eyes. I was a father. I was Maddie's father.

Deirdre clamped the cord and wrapped Maddie in another receiving blanket before placing her gently in Darby's arms.

"Oh my gracious," Darby said to Maddie, touching her tiny nose and then her miniature fingers. "You're here."

"Christmas baby," Leslie said, perching her wrists on her hips.

"Look what you did," I said, touching Darby's cheek, watching her coo and whisper sweet nothings to Maddie. "Definitely going to have to change out that birthstone," I said with a smile.

Darby looked up at me, her smile turning to worry. "You look pale. Dr. Barnes, you should take a look at Trex's wounds."

I blinked, suddenly feeling tired.

"I feel kind of weird, actually."

"Trex?" Leslie said. Her voice sounded like it was underwater.

"Trex?" Darby said. "What's happening? Oh my God! Help him!"

"*Trex?*" Leslie said at my side. She grabbed my wrist, taking my pulse. I wanted to talk, to tell them I was okay, but nothing worked.

"Let's get him to Exam Three! Now!" Dr. Barnes yelled.

chapter twenty-nine

Darby

When my eyes peeled open, I instinctually reached over to Trex's side of the bed. It only took a second to remember he wasn't there. I clutched his pillow and pulled it to my chest, hugging it to me, breathing him in. His was my very favorite smell, now tied with the way Maddie's hair smelled after a bath.

I could hear her cooing through the baby monitor, the crib mattress crackling under her as she moved. I let go of the pillow and sat up, letting my feet hang over the side. Maddie loved getting up before the sun, just like Trex. Even though her birth had been surrounded by death, she was still a bright light in the darkness; despite losing Lane, and even Shawn, and...I closed my eyes, refusing to think about the rest.

I slipped my feet into my house shoes and swiped my robe off the end corner of the bed, wrapping it around me as I made my way across the hall to the nursery. The house was nearly silent, seeming even bigger than it did before. Now that Shawn and his friends weren't a worry, I was even more free. No one could ever hurt me or Maddie again.

I pushed on the wooden door of her nursery, the dim light from the kitchen pouring in. Maddie's crib was empty.

"Good morning, Mommy," Trex said softly, holding Maddie against his chest. He was rocking her, gently petting the little bit of blond hair on her head. She was so tiny and relaxed in his arms, her inch-long fingers wrapped around one of Trex's.

I leaned against the door jamb, crossing my arms. "Having fun without me, I see," I whispered.

Maddie shifted, turning her head toward my voice.

"We were trying to let you sleep in. Bad dreams again?"

I shook my head. "Since the senator helped make sure there were no charges filed against any of you, they've been less frequent. It's my boobs. They've become alarm clocks."

"Good about the dreams. Not sure about the boobs."

Maddie whimpered.

"Uh-oh. Someone wants breakfast," Trex said.

Trex stood, and I held out my arms. We switched places, and I lay Maddie across my lap, lifting my shirt and effortlessly latching her on to my breast. Trex handed me a pillow, helping me to situate it under the baby while she suckled. He handed me two burp cloths, and I put one over my shoulder, the other under my nursing bra to keep from making a mess on the other side. We were already a well-oiled machine.

He bent down to kiss me. "How about breakfast for you?"

I sighed. "Anything. I wake up feeling starved nowadays."

"Eggs and bacon coming right up." His socks scooted across the carpet, and then he stepped out into the hall. His footsteps were barely audible, but I could hear him rummaging around in the kitchen as quietly as he could.

I looked down, meeting Maddie's gaze. She was all me: my eyes, my chin, my bone structure. I wished I had my baby photos so I could show Trex just how much she favored me, but he didn't need convincing. "Good morning, my love," I cooed, pushing back on my feet to rock us back and forth.

Trex had taken two weeks off work for paternity leave, but everyone was off work for New Year's Day, and we were expecting all of our friends over for a visit. Trex's entire team was coming, and so were Hailey and Trex's parents, Stavros and Ander, the Alpine hotshots, and a few from other crews that I'd gotten to know from Black Mesa and the Craig crew. J.D., Carly, and their girls were also on their way. I hadn't seen Carly since she dropped me off at the Killeen, Texas, bus station. I was eager to hug her and thank her. If it weren't for Carly, I wouldn't be in this room with my daughter, my boyfriend cooking for me down the hall. It was more likely that I wouldn't be in this world at all.

I'd thought about how to explain all of this to Maddie someday, to be honest in the most gentle way possible, but I just had to hope it would come to me. There was no easy way to say that Trex wasn't her real father and that Shawn had hurt me in ways I could never admit. That he had been killed trying to kill Trex after he'd murdered a young woman whose only crime was to try to use Shawn to make her ex-lover jealous.

"They finally put it in the paper. Lane's obituary," I said.

"I saw," Trex said, his face somber. "She was a mess, but she didn't deserve that."

I shook my head. "I know what she felt. I know the pain, everything he put her through. I can't stop thinking about it. And Stavros and Ander struggling without Tilde..."

"And you struggling without Tilde."

I nodded. We talked so freely now, about everything. With everything that had happened, I had to. "How did you do it? Go on like normal after you know what you know and you've seen what you've seen?"

"It's a new normal. It takes time. Sometimes it takes counseling, and that's okay."

I looked down at Maddie, knowing I owed it to her to heal. "That's a good idea."

"We can go together if you want."

I weighed the pros and cons of omitting the truth and letting my little girl go the rest of her life without that burden. Trex's idea weeks before to keep the truth from Maddie didn't seem so bad. No one alive but Trex and me knew that Maddie wasn't biologically his. No one ever had to know.

When Maddie finished nursing, I held her against my chest, patting and rubbing her back until she let out the tiniest burp, and then I lay her back down in her crib. She fussed for just a few seconds before falling back asleep.

"Trex?" I said, joining him in the kitchen, baby monitor in hand.

"Yeah, baby?" he said, concentrating on not dumping the eggs as he transferred them from the skillet to our plates.

"I was thinking...I've been practically running the hotel, anyway. I don't want it to close. We made so many good memories there."

"What are you thinking?"

"I thought...maybe...we might consider getting into the hospitality business."

He didn't hesitate. "You would be good at it. And I bet Stavros would make you a helluva deal."

I smiled. "Yeah?"

He nodded without hesitation. "Yeah. You loved it there."

"Maybe I will." I hesitated.

"Is there something else?"

"What you said before, about adopting Maddie?"

"Yeah?" he said, using the tongs to pick up the bacon and set them on our plates. He turned off the burners and then turned around, a plate in each hand.

"I've been thinking how we're going to explain all of this to her. You should adopt her, and that's it. She's yours. She's always been yours."

"What do you mean?" he asked, his brows pulling together.

"I think you're right. Omitting the truth to protect someone you love isn't the worst thing in the world. I can't think of a single reason why we should burden Maddie with the truth about Shawn. I think we should bury it and never talk about it again."

"So...never tell her..."

"You're her dad. I'm her mom. That's the truth."

"You're sure?"

I nodded. "You in?"

Trex put the plates on the table and wrapped his arms around me. He kissed me gently, letting his lips linger there for a while before answering. "For life."

I sat down at the dining table next to Trex, holding his hand while I said a quick prayer, and then dug into his famous scrambled eggs. I hummed in satisfaction.

Trex sighed. "Whew, do I miss that sound."

I giggled. "Four and a half more weeks."

He winced. "Totally understandable, and yet, total torture."

"We have a lot to do today," I said. "I'm cleaning, you're getting refreshments, and—"

"Taking down the Christmas lights off the house and putting away the decorations. Also, celebrating the first New Year's Day that I'm not hung over."

I smiled, resting my chin on the heel of my hand. "I remember the first time I saw you, how obnoxiously persistent you were in your kindness, how, without ever being asked or expecting anything in return, you took care of me, watched out for me, showed me what love should look like before I knew I loved you. Even when I wasn't sure, dragged my feet, acted stubborn...you loved me anyway." I gestured to the house. "You bought all of this for us on the hope I'd want it, too." I shook my head. "How? How did I get so lucky?"

He smiled, taking my hand and kissing my palm. "No, I'm definitely the lucky one."

"I've done nothing but fight you every step of the way."

"It was worth it," he said, chewing the bite of bacon he'd just put into his mouth. He looked around the room. "You're my home. This is our home. Maddie makes it complete. Believe me, I've spent a lifetime of not being good for anyone. If I'm good, it's because of you. If I'm kind, it's because you make me want to be."

I touched his cheek, letting my fingers run over the stubble on his jaw. "I am so in love with you."

He sighed, pure contentment on his face. In the next moment, his eyes lit up. "Shit. I was going to do this later when everyone got here." He stood, walking over to the Christmas tree, and plucking a box from the branches in the back. "I can't not do it now. It's too perfect of a moment."

He sat the box in front of me, and my eyes immediately teared up.

"Spoiler alert," he said.

"It's not what I think?" I said, opening the lid. It was my ring, the amethyst replaced with Maddie's December birthstone, a deep blue tanzanite. On the right was Trex's June stone, and mine on the left.

"Moonstone for mine, because I'm manly and pearl just won't do. And yours is aquamarine. It turns out certain months like March have a few options. Yours could have also been a bloodstone but I liked the way the aquamarine looked with the others. Hope that's okay."

The rest of the stones on each side were tiny diamonds. "It's beautiful," I said, wiping my cheek.

"And while I was there..." He held up a second ring between us.

The band was gold, the diamond attached was oval with a dozen tiny diamonds bordering it and lining the sides of the band.

I covered my mouth with one hand, staring at the

perfection pinched between his fingers, my eyes instantly blurred with tears.

"First things first," he said, getting on one knee. "This isn't how I planned. But when you say you love me like that, all plans go out the window. Darby…" He sighed and grinned. "I've been saying for years that you were somewhere in my future. The first time I set eyes on you, I realized love at first sight existed. The night we spent hours talking in the lobby of the hotel, our first date, the first time we spent the night together, the first time I went with you to a doctor's appointment, the first time you told me you loved me, the first time you saw the house in person…they all tie for being the best days of my life…so far. And all of those combined don't compare to the moment I saw you hold Maddie the first time. You and that little girl," he said, stopping a moment to clear his throat, "you've given me something I've never had before. And it would be my extreme privilege and honor if you would be my wife. Darby Rose Dixon, will you marry me?"

I wiped the tears away and nodded, my shoulders shaking as I cried. Trex, as always, waited patiently. It all made sense. I'd been lost for him to find. As soon as I could form a coherent word, I spoke. "Yes."

Trex slid the ring over my finger and then sat up on his knees to hug me. He buried his face in my neck, his cheeks as wet as mine. "I love you," he whispered.

"We love you," I said, knowing Maddie was fine with me speaking for her while she slept.

From that moment on, we would have perfect days, the ones that sucked, the hard ones, the ones that left us lying in bed next to each other, exhausted but holding hands. The kind of perfection where, in those mundane and sometimes chaotic moments, we found the acceptance and happiness we'd both been searching for.

acknowledgments

Thank you to Tyler Vanover for teaching me everything I know about hotshots.

To Andrew Thomure for teaching me everything I know about the FBI.

To Christie Kersnick for teaching me everything I know about the Marines. You, my friend, were a badass then, and everything you've overcome since makes you a badass now!

Also a big thanks to Robert Madson for answering late-night questions about rank, military slang, and filling in the blanks.

about the author

Jamie McGuire was born in Tulsa, Oklahoma. She attended Northern Oklahoma College, the University of Central Oklahoma, and Autry Technology Center, where she graduated with a degree in radiography.

Jamie paved the way for the New Adult genre with the international bestseller *Beautiful Disaster*. Her follow-up novel, *Walking Disaster*, debuted at #1 on the *New York Times*, *USA Today*, and *Wall Street Journal* bestseller lists. *Beautiful Oblivion*, book one of the Maddox Brothers series, also topped the *New York Times* bestseller list, debuting at #1.

Jamie lives in Tulsa, Oklahoma, with her three children.

You can learn more at:
   JamieMcGuire.com
   Twitter @JamieMcGuire
   Instagram @theJamieMcGuire
   Facebook.com/JamieMcGuireBooks

Fall in love with these charming contemporary romances!

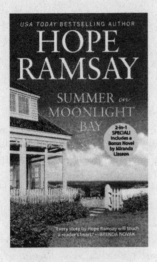

SUMMER ON MOONLIGHT BAY
by Hope Ramsay

Veterinarian Noah Cuthbert had no intention of ever moving back to the small town of Magnolia Harbor. But when his sister calls with the opportunity to run the local animal clinic as well as give her a break from caring for their ailing mom, he packs his bags and heads home. But once he meets the clinic's beautiful new manager, he questions whether his summer plans might become more permanent. Includes a bonus novel by Miranda Liasson!

WISH YOU WERE MINE
by Tara Sivec

When Everett Southerland left town five years ago, Cameron James thought it was the worst day of her life. She was wrong: It was the day he came back and told her the truth about his feelings that devastated her. Now she's having a hard time believing him, until he proves to her how much he cares. But with so many secrets between them, will they ever find the future that was always destined to be theirs?

ALL I WANT FOR CHRISTMAS IS YOU
by Miranda Liasson

Just when Kaitlyn Barnes vows to get over her longtime crush on Rafe Langdon, they share a sizzling evening that delivers an epic holiday surprise: Kaitlyn is pregnant. While their off-the-charts chemistry can still melt snow, Rafe must decide if he'll keep running from love forever—or if he'll make this Christmas the one where he becomes the man Kaitlyn wants…and the one she deserves. Includes a bonus novel by Annie Rains!

SNOWFALL ON CEDAR TRAIL
by Annie Rains

Determined to give her son a good holiday season, single mom Halona Locklear signs him up for Sweetwater Springs' Mentor Match program. Little does she know that her son's mentor would be the handsome chief of police, who might know secrets about her past that she is determined to keep buried. Includes a bonus novel by Miranda Liasson!

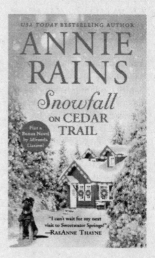

Follow @ReadForeverPub on Twitter and join the conversation using #ReadForver.

IT STARTED WITH CHRISTMAS
by Jenny Hale

Holly McAdams loves spending the holidays at her family's cozy cabin, but she soon discovers that the gorgeous and wealthy Joseph Barnes has been renting the cabin, and it looks like he'll be staying for the holidays. Throw in Holly's charming ex, and she's got the recipe for one complicated Christmas. With unexpected guests and secrets aplenty, will Holly be able to find herself and the love she's always dreamed of this Christmas?

CHRISTMAS IN HARMONY HARBOR
by Debbie Mason

Evangeline Christmas will do anything to save her year-round Christmas store, Holiday House, including facing off against high-powered real-estate developer Caine Elliot, who's using his money and influence to push through his competing property next door. When her last desperate attempt to stop him fails, she gambles everything on a proposition she prays the handsome, blue-eyed player can't refuse. Includes a bonus novella!

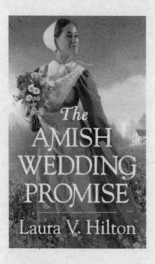

THE AMISH WEDDING PROMISE
by Laura V. Hilton

After a storm crashes through town, Grace Lantz is forced to postpone her wedding. All hands are needed for cleanup, but Grace doesn't know where to start—should she console her special needs sister or find her missing groom? Sparks fly when the handsome Zeke Bontrager comes to aid the community and offers to help the overwhelmed Grace in any way he can. But when her groom is found, Grace must decide if the wedding will go on…or if she'll take a chance on Zeke.

MERMAID INN
by Jenny Holiday

When Eve Abbott inherits her aunt's inn, she remembers the heartbreaking last summer she spent there, and she has no interest in returning. Unfortunately, Eve must run the inn for two years before she can sell. Town sheriff Sawyer Collins can't deny all the old feelings that come rushing back when he sees Eve. Getting her out of Matchmaker Bay when they were younger was something he did for her own good. But losing her again? He doesn't think he can survive that twice. Includes a bonus novella by Alison Bliss!

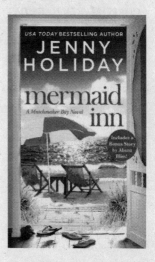